PENGUIN BOOKS
Among Thieves

John Clarkson is the author of five previous novels, including *And Justice for One*. He spent many years in the New York advertising industry as a copywriter, running his own agency, and as a private consultant. He lives in Brooklyn, New York.

Among Thieves

JOHN CLARKSON

PENGUIN BOOKS

PENGUIN BOOKS

UK | USA | Canada | Ireland | Australia
India | New Zealand | South Africa

Penguin Books is part of the Penguin Random House group of companies
whose addresses can be found at global.penguinrandomhouse.com.

First published in the United States of America by St Martin's Press, 2015
First published in Great Britain in Penguin Books 2015

001

Typeset by Palimpsest Book Production Ltd, Falkirk, Stirlingshire
Printed in Great Britain by Clays Ltd, St Ives plc

A CIP catalogue record for this book is available from the British Library

ISBN: 978–1–405–92096–4

www.greenpenguin.co.uk

Penguin Random House is committed to a
sustainable future for our business, our readers
and our planet. This book is made from Forest
Stewardship Council® certified paper.

For my Friends

I

Tuesday morning started out damn near perfect. Right up until Demarco Jones told James Beck, 'Manny wants to kill somebody.'

Demarco hadn't told Beck right away. He'd been waiting for the right moment, as if there were right moments for that sort of news.

Beck was at his usual spot: sitting just past the turn of an old oak bar in a hundred-year-old-saloon that occupied the first floor of a ramshackle building Beck owned in Red Hook, Brooklyn. The bar ran nearly the entire length of the room, curving to meet a solid plaster wall coated in a century of paint, currently a pale green that Beck didn't particularly like, but felt he should leave unchanged. It was a bright, cold February morning, the sun streaming in through the bar's plate glass window, warming Beck's broad back as he made his way through the front section of *The New York Times* and his second cup of coffee.

Demarco stood in his usual spot behind the bar, leaning against the back cabinets. Relaxed. Watching Beck. Waiting.

Demarco Jones could watch someone without them hardly noticing, which was surprising, because when people saw Demarco they usually looked twice. He was six four, wide shouldered, muscular, around ten percent body fat, skin about the color of Beck's strong coffee. He was handsome, but tough looking, especially with his shaved head. He wore a dark blue Nike tracksuit over a black T-shirt.

But Beck noticed. He could feel Demarco waiting for him to look up from his morning paper, even though Demarco didn't give Beck any indication of anything. He just stood there, his long muscular arms crossed, waiting for Beck to put his perfectly fine Tuesday morning on hold.

Beck lifted his eyes from his paper, stared straight ahead for about four seconds, turned to Demarco and said, 'What?'

Demarco turned and gazed calmly at Beck.

Beck waited.

Demarco said, 'Manny wants to talk to you.'

'Manny.'

'Yeah.'

'About what?'

'Manny wants to kill somebody. Figures he should talk to you first.'

Beck knew that if Manny Guzman had said the word *kill*, it was not metaphorical.

And if Emmanuel 'Manny' Guzman, former lord of a Dominican street gang, former shot-caller of several prison gangs including the most feared Latin gang in Dannemora wanted somebody dead, that person's last breath on Earth wasn't far away.

Beck took another sip of his coffee. Now it tasted sour.

He slid off the bar stool, standing there in a pair of worn gray jeans, sturdy black tie shoes, a maroon plaid flannel shirt. Winter clothes. He folded the paper. He stared at the front section of the *Times* and thought about the juxtaposition of a newspaper not even a day old resting on top of a bar more than a hundred years old.

Although property records showed that the old brick building which housed Beck's bar was owned by a limited-liability real estate partnership, it would take a great deal of work to uncover James Beck as the managing partner and owner of 24.75% general shares, and a 1% manager share.

A dense thicket of legal filings designed by Beck's bulldog lawyer Phineas P. Dunleavy stood between Beck and public knowledge of his ownership. Dunleavy was a thorough man, the same man who had taken up Beck's cause while Beck was serving ten to twenty-five years for first-degree manslaughter. Dunleavy had pursued justice for Beck, had burned through Beck's last dollar, but had restored that dollar many times over by winning a settlement for wrongful conviction that netted James Beck $2.1 million, a large part of which Beck used to buy the old bar and the three-story building that housed it, and a small part of which he used to make sure nobody knew about it.

The other partners were a very select group of three men: Manny Guzman, Demarco Jones, and Ciro Baldassare.

The only patrons Beck allowed into his waterfront hangout were members of his network, and a few misfits from the neighborhood he tolerated because they either interested him or because they needed something he felt like giving them ...

Like the twenty-pound sealed bags of ground meat scraps and bones he gave to a wild-haired Greek woman who collected the free mash of protein for the wild neighborhood dogs she fed. Beck liked her spirit, and every once in a while he needed a good way to get rid of ground meat and bones.

Or the shots of Jameson Demarco doled out to Arnold, an aging alcoholic who checked into Beck's bar much like he would to a hospital emergency room. Beck allowed him to sit and sip his Jameson if he remained quiet and didn't smell too bad.

There were others who stepped into Beck's bar, but not many. If they were people Beck didn't like or know, they were quickly told they had entered a private bar not open to the public.

When told this by Demarco Jones, very, very few did anything other than apologize and leave.

But this morning, something else had entered Beck's enclave. Something that had set Manny Guzman on a dangerous path.

Emmanuel Manny Guzman kept the old Red Hook place clean to the core. No grime. No stink of beer. Barely a hint of dust anywhere. And windows polished to a gleam every other week. Even the glass and frames holding faded photos of ship hands and dock scenes were shined to a gleam. Even the insides of drawers were clean all the way to the back.

And everything in working order: the plumbing, the light fixtures, everything.

There was no slippage with Manny Guzman. If Manny wanted something done, it was done.

Shit, Beck thought. He turned and headed back to the bar kitchen where he knew Guzman would be sitting, waiting for him.

But before he had gone three steps, something hard cracked into the plate glass window that fronted Conover Street. It was a brutal, disturbing sound that made Beck turn back and curse.

'Christ, now what?'

He strode quickly to the front of the bar and saw a crack that ran diagonally from the left lower corner of the window to almost the middle.

Demarco joined Beck at the window. The bottom third was painted black so that passersby couldn't see in, but they were both tall enough to see a beat up van parked outside across the street. Four black gangbangers in various sizes stood around one huge, heavily muscled thug who yelled, 'James Beck, come out here before I come in after you.'

Beck grabbed a leather shearling jacket from the coat peg near the front door. He looked at Demarco and nodded. Demarco moved fast in the opposite direction, toward the back of the barroom.

Beck, seething, walked out his front door and stood on the sidewalk across from the rock thrower, breathing deeply, giving himself time to burn off the flight-or-fight hormones coursing through him, forcing the rational part of his brain to start working.

Four of them flanked the big man, two on each side. He dwarfed all of them, standing a few steps out near the middle of the street, wearing a black leather hoodie, unzipped to reveal a torso bulging with muscle under a tight white T-shirt. He had on thick, dark denim pants and heavy Timberland boots.

Beck figured the muscles had been built in a prison iron pile. The clothes seemed to be just-out-of-the-joint new.

What the fuck is this, he wondered. He remained on his side of the street. He didn't see any guns or other weapons brandished, but that didn't mean they weren't there.

The big man's hands were balled into fearsomely large fists. He wore no rings, no jewelry, no watch. It reminded Beck of being called out for a prison yard fight. It seemed absurd. Absurd, but dangerous.

Beck took a couple of steps forward and stopped at the curb, watching and waiting.

'I'm here to tell you what's what, Beck.'

Beck had never seen this guy before. Maybe he recognized one or two of the others from the neighborhood. But not Mr Muscles. He said nothing.

'Them little punks you pay over in the projects to give you a heads-up? They don't do that anymore. I'm back. This is my hood. Now you pay me and my people. And the price has gone up, motherfucker.'

Beck waited a beat, 'When are you going to fix my window, asshole?'

The big man reared back. 'You know who the fuck I am?'

'No.'

'I'm Willie Reese. You want to live here, you pay me.'

'Willie Reese.' Beck shook his head. 'The name doesn't ring any bells. Does your mother know you're out here breaking windows?'

That ignited the spark. Just about the way Beck had wanted it to. Willie Reese puffed up and, ready to enforce his demands, let his anger take over.

Beck had reached an alert state of calm. The trick now was to survive the first seconds.

Reese rushed at Beck in long steps, arms coming up into a fighting position, fists balled into clubs, coming at him fast.

Beck turned to his right and ran. Faster. Faster than he looked like he could.

Beck's sudden move confused Reese. He lunged at Beck, took a wild swing and missed, his Timberlands slipping on the cold, slick cobblestone street. Within three seconds, Beck was ten yards away from Reese and running easily. Reese got his footing and took off after him.

The others hooted and jeered and stepped out into the street yelling at Beck about being a punk-ass coward, cursing him, shouting about how bad he was going to get his ass kicked. Beck ignored them, but Willie Reese listened to his crew and believed them. Beck just kept running, but not as fast now. He slowed down so Reese wouldn't give up. Or do something really stupid like pull out a gun and shoot at him.

But Reese surprised him and closed the gap more quickly than Beck expected.

Shit, Beck thought. He sprinted toward a beat-up Volvo station wagon parked to his right, managed to get a foot on the front bumper, and vaulted up onto the hood just as Reese came close enough to lunge at him, grabbing for his foot. Beck pulled his foot away and kept right on going, jumping onto the roof of the Volvo.

Reese splayed across the hood, having just missed catching the bottom of Beck's jeans. Beck kept going, jumped off the car, landed on the street, slipping a bit on the slick cobblestones.

By the time Reese picked himself off the hood, Beck

had circled wide around him and was running back toward the bar, about five yards out in front of Reese, but this time at half-speed, conserving his wind, staying just far enough in front to taunt Reese into catching up to him.

Beck also slowed down because Reese's gang had come into the street to block his path. They figured they'd keep him trapped, so their man could get to him.

Reese saw it, too. Beck had nowhere to go. He slowed down, slipping a little on the uneven street, trying to get his footing and catch his breath. He'd been raging, burning energy, but now he had this guy. Time to get it together.

Behind Beck, Reese's gang hooted and yelled for blood. In front of him, the big man closed on him slowly.

And then, before any of them realized how it happened, everything changed.

Just as Reese was about to reach Beck, he stopped backpedaling and lunged forward, slapping aside Reese's huge outstretched arm with his left hand, and stabbing two stiff fingers into Reese's left eye. The pain and force of the hit stopped Reese so suddenly that his feet nearly went out from under him.

Back near the bar, Demarco Jones appeared out of nowhere. He stood behind the four gangbangers who were watching their man closing in on Beck. Demarco held a Benelli M3 shotgun firmly pressed into his shoulder, aimed right at the group of four standing near the beat-up van.

At the same time, Emmanuel Guzman, dressed in his usual dark-blue work clothes and stained apron, emerged from between two buildings north of the van aiming a second shotgun at the group. It was a beautiful old

Winchester 12 gauge, its dark grain walnut stock gleaming in the bright winter sun.

At first, neither Demarco nor Manny said a word. The chilling *chu-chunks* of the shotguns being pumped stopped all the bravado and yelling. The shotguns were one thing. The men holding them were the main thing.

Demarco said, 'Hands.'

All four of them, heads swiveling back and forth at the men in front and behind them, raised their hands.

Guzman continued to advance until he had the long barrel of his Winchester pressed into the forehead of the nearest gangbanger.

Manny Guzman was shorter, stockier than the young black man, but implacable. He just kept walking forward, pressing the muzzle of the Winchester into the soft skin of the young man's forehead, pushing him toward the van.

'Leave. Now. Or I kill you.'

All four of them tumbled and pushed their way into the battered van, three of them falling through the sliding side door and one jumping into the driver's seat. He started the engine and accelerated down the street, swerving and sliding on the slick cobblestones.

Now that the four behind him were taken care of, Beck circled to Reese's left, his blind side. Reese had his left hand clamped over his suddenly throbbing blind left eye, giving Beck an opening to slide forward and twist a fast, hard right into the left side of Reese's nose. The septum broke with a sharp crack.

One moment Reese was thinking about taking apart James Beck. The next he was half blind with a screamingly painful broken nose.

Beck stepped back, figuring that should do it. But he was wrong. Taking out an eye and breaking a nose weren't disabling blows, just horribly painful. And pain wasn't going to stop Willie Reese.

He lashed a roundhouse left at Beck, more to knock him away than to knock him out. Beck leaned back from the fist, but not far enough. The fist only grazed the right side of his head, but the power and speed behind the wild punch still were enough to make everything go black for a moment.

Beck didn't hesitate. He leaned right back in toward Reese and fired a fast right fist around the hand protecting Reese's left eye, landing a solid blow to Reese's left temple. Hitting Reese's big head with such force nearly broke two of Beck's knuckles. It was a knockout punch, but it only staggered Reese. Beck followed it with a left elbow to the face, a right to the side of the neck, and a left aimed at Reese's throat.

Reese somehow slap-blocked the last punch and lunged forward quickly enough to grab Beck's coat, rear back, and snap a vicious head butt at Beck's face.

Beck barely jerked out of the way in time. Reese's huge forehead banged into Beck's left collarbone. It felt like being hit with a bowling ball.

Reese tried to throw Beck to the ground, but Beck grabbed Reese's massive forearms, widened his stance, twisted back against Reese, and levered his own head butt directly into Reese's already broken nose.

This time the pain was too intense even for Willie Reese.

Beck heard him gasp and growl in agony. Reese couldn't

move, but he held onto Beck's coat, so Beck pounded six hard fast lefts and rights into Reese's liver, floating ribs, and sternum, twisting, aiming, grunting with exertion as he landed each blow. Reese could do nothing but hang onto Beck, who couldn't believe that Reese was still standing.

Finally, Reese hurled Beck away from him. Beck's feet left the ground and he went down hard onto his back. Reese tried to step toward Beck so he could kick him or stomp him, but his legs wobbled under him as he staggered forward.

Beck rolled sideways and scrambled to his feet, quickly backing away from Reese, who managed to stay on his feet, blood streaming from his nose, left eye beginning to swell, huffing and puffing for air, two cracked ribs splinting pain with every breath.

They both knew it wasn't over. Beck would have to step in to finish Reese off. And if Reese managed to get his hands on Beck, he might find a way to grab Beck's throat so he could crush his windpipe. Or smash Beck's head into the ground. Or manage one hard blow that would knock Beck out.

Beck shook out his arms, staying back, breathing deeply. Getting ready.

He said to Reese, 'You that hard up for my business?'

Reese spat out a mouthful of blood and turned his head sideways to look at Beck out of his good eye.

'Ain't about that anymore.'

'What's it about?' asked Beck.

'You and me,' said Reese.

'Yeah, well, I don't want to have anything to do with you, man. You're a fucking handful.'

Reese looked over at Demarco and Manny, watching, cradling the shotguns.

'Maybe you should have your boys shoot me. You don't want me comin' back for you.'

'Maybe. But there is an alternative.'

'What's that?'

'You working for me, like you said.'

'What?'

As soon as he heard that answer from Reese, Beck knew he wasn't a complete maniac. And that meant there might be a way out of this without one of them dying.

Beck continued to keep his distance and said, 'Hey, like you said, I hired Shorty and his little gang to give me the heads-up on anything coming this way through the projects, but he didn't do it, did he? He didn't have the balls to tell me you were coming.'

'Nah, he didn't.'

'So what do you want more? A job or a chance to keep beating on me? Which I guarantee you isn't going to work anyway, 'cuz they will shoot you down if it gets out of hand.'

Reese looked at Demarco and Manny with their shotguns. He spit out more blood.

Beck said, 'Fuck it. Your guys are gone. Tell them you beat a job out of me. I don't give a shit. Think it over. It's too damn cold to stand out here discussing it.'

Beck turned his back on Willie Reese and headed toward his bar. He told Demarco and Manny, 'Don't shoot him if he wants to come in.'

2

Beck walked behind the bar, flipped open the lid on the ice maker, and shoved both hands into the pile of frozen cubes.

Manny headed for the bar kitchen. Demarco took a seat at the table farthest from the front door. He placed the Benelli on top of the table and sat facing the door.

About the time Beck could no longer feel his hands, the front door opened and Willie Reese leaned into the bar. Demarco didn't pick up his shotgun, so Reese stepped inside.

From behind the bar Beck said, 'So?'

Reese stood near the front door looking at Beck. His left eye was killing him. His nose continued to bleed. His muscle T-shirt was more red than white. The bruises on his ribs and body thrummed with pain.

He said, 'You asked me do I want the job.'

'Do you?'

'Yeah. I do.'

'Well, you fucking failed the first part of the interview.' Beck motioned with his head toward a table near the door, one of three set up against the wall opposite the bar. 'Have a seat, and let's see how you do on the second part. I'll be back in a minute.'

Reese sat two tables away from Demarco, whose right hand now rested on the Benelli's trigger guard. Demarco stared back at Reese without expression. Beck dug out his cell phone and made a call as he headed back toward the bar kitchen.

Beck found Manny at his two-chair wooden table in the old first-floor kitchen where Manny spent much of his time. The shotgun was back in its rack, but Manny's white kitchen apron didn't cover the bulge of the Charter Arms Bulldog revolver that he always carried in his right front pants pocket. It was a small inexpensive gun, but at .44 caliber it had tremendous stopping power. With only a four-inch barrel it was the kind of gun that had to be used up close, which was fine with Guzman.

Manny sat with a cup of the same coffee Beck had been drinking, except Manny brewed his version with twice as many grounds. This morning, however, Manny also sipped from a shot of dark, one-hundred-proof rum. Manny took a sip of the sweet liquor, followed by the coffee. He sat motionless, the air around him pulsing with murderous rage.

'Not a good way to start the day,' said Beck as he took the seat opposite Manny.

Manny made a face. 'I was ready to kill somebody even before those *coños* showed up. That punk don't know how close he came to losing the top of his head.'

'Actually, I have a feeling he does know.'

'Yeah, well, I can see not shooting 'em, but they come up on us like that and don't even get a beating? I don't know.'

'One of 'em did. The others ... maybe their time will come.'

'I don't like that they thought they could do that. Like they don't know who we are.'

Beck answered, 'They do now.'

Manny replied with a half grunt.

They both sat quietly for a few more moments. Manny took another sip of his rum and chased it with the strong coffee. Then a deep breath. And a long exhale.

Beck waited for more of the tension to ebb out of Manny. He shifted in the hard wooden chair. He asked, 'Those guys have anything to do with your . . . ?'

'No. I don't know what the fuck any of that was about.'

'About being stupid, I guess.'

Manny moved his head a fraction, not saying anything. And then, 'Stupid is a good way to get killed.'

Beck nodded. 'Yeah. Well, I'll look into it. So what about the thing D told me? What should I know about it?' Beck leaned forward. 'Is it something to do with us?'

'No. It's my thing. It's family. My family.'

This surprised Beck. After so many years in the gangs and in prison, as far as he knew, Manny Guzman's family had either died or abandoned him long ago. He wondered if there was an ex-wife or a child. Beck knew a great deal about Manny, but he hadn't heard much about any of his family members.

'I see,' said Beck.

Manny swallowed, not coffee or rum, just moving his mouth and swallowing as a way to relieve tension. Beck waited for the rest, not pushing it. Manny sat shrouded in stoic silence.

It reminded Beck of when he'd first met him at Dannemora Prison in upstate New York. Manny's reputation had preceded him, but even if Beck had never heard anything about him, one look at Manny Guzman sitting in the yard at Dannemora, surrounded by his clique, was all Beck needed to know that this was a dangerous man. The kind of man they'd built Dannemora to house.

Located just south of the Canadian border, Dannemora was a cold, desolate place so isolated and remote that even if someone managed to escape, it wouldn't do them much good. There was literally no place to go outside the walls of the prison. The main street of Clinton ran right alongside the prison's main wall, but didn't lead anywhere. Either side of the wall, you were still hundreds of cold, bitter miles from anywhere.

Even though Dannemora had been designed to isolate and demoralize hard men, Beck knew that for some men, men like Manny Guzman, the place actually made doing time easier.

For them, the best way to do time was to never think about the outside. If you thought about the outside, it could drive you into despair. You did your time on the inside. In the here and now. Moment to moment, according to a routine. Inside. The outside couldn't exist in the mind of a long-term convict. And Dannemora was perfect for that. Inside that prison, you were nowhere but prison. Which made Beck even more surprised to hear about this family member Manny had stayed connected to.

For Manny there were three categories of people: those who were with him, against him, and undetermined, which corresponded to alive, dead, and irrelevant.

But now, in the with-him category, was a family member Beck didn't know anything about.

'There's only one,' said Manny.

'Uh, huh,' said Beck.

Again, he waited for more information, watching Manny, feeling his mood. Waiting for the thick-bodied, dark-skinned man with dense graying hair and mustache to say more.

In the quiet kitchen, just the two of them, Beck didn't press. He folded his arms, sat back in the chair, and took notice of the wear and tear and isolation of Manny's OG life. The scar embedded in his right eyebrow, deep crow's feet around his dark eyes, the blue ink of prison tattoos peeking out from his white shirt at neck and wrists. But mostly Beck looked at Manny's eyes for the presence of this new person. He couldn't see a thing.

Beck sniffed. Cleared his throat. Twisted around on the hard wooden chair. Then just came out with it. 'Okay, Manny, who is it? What's going on?'

Instead of answering Beck, Manny asked, 'You okay? That guy hurt you?'

'Little bit here and there.' Beck flexed his fingers. 'I was lucky. My hands are going to hurt. Guy's head is like concrete. His skull must be five-inches thick.'

'You gotta hit a guy like that with a bat, not your hands.'

'I'll remember next time.'

Manny nodded and finally answered Beck's question.

'I got a cousin. She's a lot younger than me. My grandparents had a lot of kids. This is on my mother's side. Don't know shit about my father's side. So Olivia, that's her name, she's the daughter of my mother's youngest sister. My aunt Ruth. Her name is Olivia Sanchez.'

'Okay. A cousin.'

'She's a civilian. Good lady.' Manny waived a hand dismissively. 'All the rest, long gone. I don't blame them. But this Olivia kid, she didn't go that way. She stuck by me. More like a little sister than a cousin. And believe me, I didn't give her any reason to. Back in the day, I didn't give a fuck about anybody. Family, friends, nobody. You know how that works.'

Beck nodded.

'But this Olivia, I don't know, no matter what anybody told her, she didn't give up the connection.'

Manny paused. Beck watched him thinking about it, remembering this part of his past.

'Olivia, you know, in the midst of all the shit around my family, she kept herself together. Stayed in school. Got regular jobs. As soon as she was like, seventeen, eighteen, she'd come to see me. And she wrote me. The whole time I was in that last bit, she wrote me. Visited me twice a year. Christmas and my birthday. Even during those three years I was in Dannemora.'

'That's a long trip.'

'Over three hundred miles she'd come. Christmastime and my birthday.'

'From the city?'

'Yeah. I don't even know how many hours it took. She borrowed a car or something. I don't know. December and August.'

Manny leaned forward and sipped his rum and coffee, grimacing. 'Truth? I didn't like it. I didn't want to see her.

18

You know, getting those connections to the outside, that's not so good for you.'

Beck nodded.

Manny cocked his head, 'But what was I gonna do? She was a kid. She even made sure to send me ten bucks every once in a while for canteen. Can you imagine that? A kid like that giving me money.'

Beck smiled at the notion that Manny Guzman, who ran more drugs and gambling in Dannemora than almost anybody, would need an occasional ten bucks from a seventeen-year-old-girl.

'You must love her.'

Manny blinked. 'I do.'

Beck nodded, feeling Manny's emotion. He could see where this was going. This was going someplace that wouldn't fit. Someplace that might not be easy to deal with.

'She worked in a financial place. A brokerage or something. I don't know what she did there, you know. But with the executives. In charge of something important. Helping run things. Like that. She worked hard. Smart. Good-looking woman.'

'Okay.'

'So, some asshole up there, he likes throwing his weight around. He and Olivia, they don't get along.'

'Who? What do you know about him?'

'I don't know much but a name. Alan Crane. I don't know what Wall Street fucks do. I don't know what this guy does. But he's high up in the company. From Olivia, I get that he was in charge of a bunch of money, and he was cutting corners or doing some risky shit.'

'And?'

'James, this isn't a little grab-ass or something. This guy had a beef with Olivia.'

'Yeah. Okay. I understand. So what happened?'

Manny held up his left hand, his shirt cuff pulled back enough to reveal a bit of the rough prison tattoos on his forearm. He looked Beck in the eye and folded his first two fingers down to his thumb, leaving his little finger and ring finger extended. Beck watched as the lethal anger rose in him.

'So this fucking coward comes in yelling shit at her, and pounds his fist down on her hand.' Manny pointed to the little finger and ring finger of his left hand. 'He breaks two of her fingers.'

Beck squinted, feeling the waves of anger coming off Manny.

'What?'

'You heard me.'

'He breaks her fingers?'

'Yeah. And threatens her, tells her she's fired.'

'Threatens her how?'

'She won't say exactly.'

'Where'd this happen?'

'In her office. Late. She works late. Around seven.'

'And what's she do, this guy breaks her hand?'

'She gets the fuck out. Goes to a hospital. Calls the cops while she's sitting in the emergency room. Of course, by the time she gets her fingers fixed, they still don't show, so the next day she goes to the precinct near where she works. Files a complaint. Big fucking deal. Then, she goes to . . . what do you call it, the personnel people in her office?'

'Human Resources.'

'Yeah. Tells those fucks what happened. Tells her boss what happened.'

Beck saw it now. He started filling in the rest so Manny wouldn't have to go through a recitation that would rile him up even more.

'Okay, let me guess. The guy denies he did anything. Says she's crazy. Says she's lying. Out to get him. Says he has no idea how she broke her fingers. Cops say they have no evidence. He says, she says. No witnesses. She left the premises where it happened, blah, blah, blah.'

'Pretty much. But worse.'

'How?'

'The guy says she's . . . what do you call it? Slandered him? Defamed him? He sues her for a bunch of shit. Everybody at the company goes on his side. They fire her. Now she's got no job. No health insurance. No references. And she can't get a new job. She's got nothing but her two broken fingers and a little bit of savings that ain't going to last long.'

Beck nodded. 'So she comes to you.'

Manny sneered. 'You think the cops and the higher-ups are going to help her?'

'When did she finally talk to you?'

'Two days ago.'

Beck noted how long Manny had sat with it.

'How long since this happened?'

'Couple of weeks.'

'Okay,' said Beck. 'What should we do?'

'James, I appreciate the *we*, but ain't no *we* here. This is my thing. I just wanted to let you know about it.'

'So what are you going to do?'

'I'm going to break every bone in the motherfucker's hand. And then I'm going to break every bone in his other hand, and his arms and his face until I get tired of breaking bones. And then I'm going to kill him.'

Beck nodded. 'Then what?'

'Then I send word to her boss that he better turn the fucking clock back.'

Beck pursed his lips like he was considering Manny's plan.

'Don't worry, James. This thing won't be anywhere near us. Not a hundred miles anywhere near us.'

Beck nodded. 'Yeah, yeah, I know. But you think that plan's going to work for Olivia?'

Manny didn't respond.

Beck leaned across the table. 'Let's step back a second. This situation with your cousin, I get it. She's family. But there's another family.' Beck tapped the kitchen table with his index finger. 'This one. You, me, Demarco, Ciro. It's all connected.'

Beck raised a hand before Manny could protest.

'Hear me out. I'm not saying you can't do something about this. I'm saying you can't do it without me. Without us.'

'No, you guys can't be involved. I have to take care of this on my own.'

Beck shook his head. 'Doesn't work that way. You're involved, we're involved.'

Manny didn't want to agree. Wouldn't agree. But he couldn't disagree. Beck had trapped him. He couldn't answer, so he didn't.

'Just think it through with me for a second, Manny. What does your cousin want? Say we break all this guy's fingers, and his toes and face and arms and legs. You cut off his head and drop it on the boss's desk. But you can't put any of that shit in your cousin's life. You said it yourself, she's a civilian.' Beck continued. 'This guy disappears after she makes all these complaints? She's going to be the first one they look at.'

Manny started to speak, but Beck kept talking.

'All right, so she stands up. Takes the heat, doubtful, but say she does. How long before they connect her to you? Then it all falls apart. They'll arrest you. You'll beat it. But they'll never grant you bail. You'll sit in jail for maybe two years waiting for trial. Her reputation is dead. She'll never work in that industry.'

Manny finished his shot of rum. Glared. Asked quietly, 'So what the fuck should I do?'

'What does she want?'

'She doesn't say. She's scared. She lost her job. She wants this asshole out of her life. She wants everything back the way it was, man. But she don't know what that means. Or she don't want to think about what that means.'

'I understand.'

'Yeah, so do I. But what do you want to do? What should we do?' For the first time in the conversation, Manny's voice rose. 'These fucking assholes don't get a pass just because they work in a big office and have some fucking money.'

Beck's voice hardened. 'Nobody gets a pass. Not for what they did. But not now. Not until we figure this out.'

'So what do we do now?'

'Take care of your cousin.'

'How?'

'I can't tell you until I talk to her,' said Beck. 'Let me hear from her what happened. Let me understand more about all this. Let me hear what she wants. Then we'll take it from there.'

Manny shook his head. 'I don't know. I don't like this.'

'I know you don't. But this has got to be done right. First, we help put her life back together.'

'How?'

'I don't know. I've got to figure it out.'

Manny took in what Beck said.

'Let me talk to her.'

Manny squinted, struggled with it, nodding his head imperceptibly over and over. Finally, he said, 'Okay.'

That was it. He had deferred to Beck. At some level, they both knew that was going to happen. But now it was agreed.

Beck sat back. The wood chair creaked under his weight.

He changed the subject. 'So, thanks for this morning. You got out there and around those guys fast.'

'Bullshit. Not nearly as fast as I used to be. I got downstairs and through the basement, but that fucking hatch door to the street had so much ice and shit on it I could hardly get it open. And the fucking snow and mess between the buildings, shit. Next time I just go out the front door.'

'Nah. You did the right thing. You never want them to see you coming, Manny. Even if it takes a little longer.'

Manny looked at Beck. The corner of his mouth lifted, conceding Beck's point.

'Yeah,' he said. 'I suppose.'

3

A tall, lanky man named Brandon Wright had just finished gently prying open Willie Reese's nearly swollen-shut eye and examining it with a pen flashlight.

Wright looked more like a cowboy than a doctor. He wore blue jeans, a flannel shirt, tan leather ankle boots. He had thick brown hair flecked with gray he didn't bother combing. And he had big, sturdy hands.

Wright worked with the calm, focused attention of a highly trained doctor who had spent seventeen years as an emergency room physician.

Wright was a man of many interests: Eastern religions, quantum physics, French cuisine, art history. Right now, Willie Reese and his injuries interested him, and he took his time tending to them.

James Beck sat at the bar, watching the doctor work on the large, muscular man who clearly had a very high tolerance for pain. Wright had already completed the excruciating maneuver required to position Reese's broken septum. Watching it made Beck cringe. Reese barely uttered a sound.

The doctor stepped back and just looked at Reese for a moment, his lips pursed, running through a silent analysis. Once he confirmed to himself he had done everything he could, he turned to Beck and started checking out his complaints, which were mostly about his collarbone and sore hands.

Wright manipulated Beck's left arm with a hand resting on his collarbone. He briefly looked at Beck's hand and scuffed knuckles.

Beck started to speak, but Brandon cut him off. 'I don't need the details.'

He turned back to Willie Reese.

'You, sir, need to understand your injuries. Forgetting the contusions and all, I'm figuring probably two cracked ribs. That large elastic bandage I wrapped you with might help. I suspect you'll take it off so you can breathe better, but . . .' Wright waggled a hand . . . 'It's probably not so bad if you do. Might mean less chance you end up with pneumonia.'

Reese looked at the doctor with an expression that said he might be either thinking about punching him, or simply didn't understand him.

The doctor rephrased his comments.

'Keep the bandage on if you want, take it off if you want.'

Reese nodded once.

'Your nose is frankly a mess. How many times have you broken it?'

Reese shrugged.

'Well, now the septum is broken, and the cartilage split up all to hell. And you've got lacerations in both nostrils. I've set it somewhat straight, but you really need to see a surgeon who can open the hood and properly repair that mess. Reset the whole thing, pack your nose, and give it six weeks to heal in place.' Brandon began writing on a prescription pad. 'See this doctor. He won't charge you much. Ice the hell out of it. Take ibuprofen, but nothing else.'

Wright waited for any questions. Reese had none.

'Your eye is the worst problem. Potentially. I'm writing down the name of an ophthalmologist. He'll take cash. Do not avoid seeing him. You already have a subconjunctival hemorrhage, which is normally not a big deal, but you also have a deep scratch, perhaps some corneal damage, which raises the chance of infection. So don't tough this out. You could lose the eye. And don't screw around in an emergency room. They don't have the equipment. Okay?'

Reese didn't answer, but again nodded.

Wright turned to Beck. 'You, soak your hands in ice water. Take ibuprofen. Your collarbone isn't broken. For once you've avoided stitches, concussion, open wounds, and so on.'

'Thanks, Brandon. Anything we can get you?'

'No, thank you. Emmanuel already offered me food. Demarco offered me coffee. You, of course, offered me a warm welcome, so I'm all set and I'll be on my way.' He picked up his doctor bag, but before he turned to go he said, 'All banter aside, is this the beginning of . . . ?'

Beck interrupted. 'No. It's just a strange, unavoidable unpleasantness in a world where people act without thinking. On assumptions that are dangerous, but mostly just annoying. But who knows? It could be the beginning of a beautiful friendship.'

The doctor looked back and forth between the two men, said nothing, and walked out the front door.

Beck turned to Reese. Flexed his hands, feeling the swelling and stiffness already setting in. He was already anticipating the morning pain. It would make his workout that much more difficult.

'So,' said Beck, 'Want to answer a few questions?'

Reese shrugged.

'Yes or no. And a yes better goddamn well mean yes.'

'Okay. Yeah. Why not?'

Willie Reese filled the entire space on his side of the table. Sitting down with his leather hoodie off, his muscles bulging against his tight-fitting, bloody T-shirt, he looked even more formidable than he had out on the street. But he didn't sound so tough, forcing his words through his swollen, broken nose.

'When did you get back in the neighborhood?'

''Bout a week ago.'

'How long were you away for?'

'Five year bit. Did three.'

'Where?'

'Ossining.'

Beck nodded. 'They didn't bother transferring you out.'

'Nah. I'd already done almost a year at Rikers.'

'So, you grew up in this neighborhood?'

Reese nodded.

'Now you're out, you have to get back to work.'

'Yeah.'

'What gave you the idea that I would be an easy place to start?'

Reese shrugged.

'Seriously, I want to know.'

'Shorty Wayne makin' money off you, shit, I figure that'd be a easy place to start.'

'You didn't think it through.'

Willie Reese answered with another shrug. He didn't usually have to think about anything much past the end of his fist.

Beck leaned forward, 'You have no idea who I am, do you?'

'I got some now.'

'Yeah? Like what?'

'You smart. You not afraid to bang it with someone like me, but you sneaky. Didn't put yourself in too much danger. Wore me down first. Got in some quick shots, and backed off. You got a crew with shotguns. You the kind of guy gets left alone. Or killed. Nuthin' in between. That's about all I need to know.'

Beck shook his head. 'No man, no, that's not all you need to know. I mean, that's part of it. You're mostly right, but you shouldn't stop there. You gotta face the fact that you got banged up, might even lose an eye over this. Plus, you risked your guys. One or all of them could have easily gotten splattered all over the street. So now you're just going to walk away?'

'You said something about workin' for you.'

'Okay. But first I have to clear up one thing.'

'What's that?'

'If I say no, if I say get the fuck out of here, do I have to worry about you coming back at me?'

Reese looked at Beck. Then at Demarco watching him, the Benelli under his right hand.

'Shit. You think I'm a fool?'

'How so?'

'If I was comin' back at you, I wouldn't tell you. But I ain't. You didn't do anything to me I wouldn't have done.

'Cept have that doctor look at me. I don't know no doctors.'

Beck looked at Reese, deciding whether or not he was telling the truth. He decided he was.

'Okay.'

Reese focused his one good eye on Beck. 'So what you wanna do? You wanna do business?'

'Maybe. Probably. Look, I don't need your crew for protection. You can see that. I just need some eyes on my backside. Any cops heading this way, any people I might want to know about – they have to drive through the projects to get over here. I like to know if that's happening. Not a big deal. Not worth a fortune, but worth something. You're not going to get rich off me.'

'How much you pay Shorty and them guys?'

Beck shook his head. 'You mean you actually don't know?'

'I didn't care. Was going to charge you my price.'

'Okay. It's a thousand bucks a month. And before you tell me that's chump change or some dumb-ass remark, add on the value of me deciding not to be your enemy.'

Willie Reese didn't respond.

Beck looked at his watch.

'Okay. Take it or leave it. But if you take it, first you get my front window fixed. That doesn't mean you give me money or the name of somebody. You get it fixed. Fast. Just the way it was. Painted black on the bottom third. Like it never happened. Do that, and you're hired. And I won't charge you the cost of having my personal physician make a house call and fix you up. Deal?'

'At a thousand bucks a month.'

31

'Yeah.'

'Deal.'

'All right,' said Beck. 'And one other thing.'

'What?'

'I'm counting on you kicking the shit out of Shorty Wayne for letting you come in here without warning me.'

Willie Reese finally managed a half smile. He stood up. 'You a interesting motherfucker, Beck.' Then he turned and walked out of the bar without another word.

As soon as Willie Reese left, Demarco picked up the shotgun and stood up from his table, walked around the bar, and stashed the Benelli in its usual place under the bar top.

Beck said to Demarco, 'Nice work this morning.'

Demarco made a small sound of acknowledgment. He walked out from the other side of the bar, still watching the front door, just in case, sat on the stool next to Beck, and asked, 'You think we'll ever see him again?'

'Maybe,' said Beck, 'There might be something in him that could get him out of the slide.' Beck paused. 'That window is going to be very hard for him to take care of. He doesn't have a lot of money. He doesn't know how to go about getting it done. Doesn't want to. It's absolutely not in his nature to clean up after his shit. But I wouldn't count him out yet. He took in everything that I said. That's fairly unusual for a guy like that.'

'Taking a beating maybe got his attention.'

'Nah, not even half a beating. He could have gone on a lot longer. He'd have gotten me eventually. We'd have had to kill him to stop him.'

Demarco made a face that showed he wasn't necessarily agreeing.

Beck said, 'Guy like that, what do you think it took for him not to jump up and start warring all over again?'

'Not with me sitting there with a shotgun on the table.'

'I suppose. But it still seemed possible, didn't it? The whole time he was sitting there. Right up until the end.'

Demarco considered it. 'Maybe he thought I wouldn't pull with the doctor in here.'

'Maybe. Anyhow, he's not completely the usual. It'll be interesting to see. Keep your eye on the front window.'

Beck stood up and headed behind the bar. 'I gotta get some more ice on my hands, then we have to head out and see about this thing with Manny.'

'What's it about?'

'Trouble. I just don't know how much yet.'

4

Demarco went out the kitchen side door which led out to Imlay Street. They kept a customized 2003 Mercury Marauder in a converted stable about a half-block from Beck's bar. It was a beast of a car with a 4.6-liter super-charged engine, but it was almost always mistaken for a Grand Marquis, or a Ford Crown Victoria. Or even a Lincoln Town Car, which was one reason Beck liked the car.

While Demarco headed for the garage, James pulled a gun storage box from a cabinet behind the bar. He opened the lid and picked up a Browning Hi-Power 9-mm automatic, dark metal with wood grips. A classic firearm. Solid. Crisp trigger action. Hefty, but beautifully balanced. He didn't have to check the magazine or chamber, but he did it anyhow before he slipped the gun under his belt behind his right hip.

Beck heard the rumble of the Marauder outside the bar. He smiled at the sound of the modified exhaust, the low growl that went perfectly with a car that was black from the body to the bumpers. Even the grill and tire rims were black.

Beck turned and lifted his leather shearling coat off the hook next to the front door. He paused, holding the heavy coat in his hand, then pulled the Browning out from under his belt. He put the heavy pistol back into the gun box, and instead pulled out a six-inch leather Bucheimer sap which he slid into his back pocket. He figured visiting Manny's cousin didn't require much firepower.

Beck slipped into his coat, not bothering to button up. The Mercury sat right in front of the bar, its exhaust pluming against the cold February air.

'Where to?' asked Demarco.

'Head through the tunnel and up the West Side Highway. She lives up in Riverdale.'

Demarco slipped the Mercury into gear and drove like he moved . . . effortlessly.

They sat silently while the throaty engine accelerated them toward the Brooklyn Battery Tunnel.

After a few minutes, Beck broke the silence.

'So you didn't stay upstate with Elliot?'

'No. We came in last night. He had to substitute for somebody's class this morning.'

Beck nodded. 'Good weekend?'

Demarco shrugged. 'We went to a dinner party on Saturday.'

'I would imagine gay couples are in demand at dinner parties up there in the shire. Especially a mixed couple like you and Elliot.'

'You looking for an invite?'

'Why not? I got a car. I know how to buy a bottle of wine.'

Demarco smiled at the idea of Beck attending a dinner party in the country.

'I had to come in anyhow. Remember that woman, Maxine Barnes?'

'The one with the restaurant in the theater district?'

'Yeah. She's opening a club midtown on the West side. Wants me to set up security for it.'

Beck nodded. 'Good. You've done enough of it.'

They drove in silence for a while, and then Demarco asked, 'You gonna check with Walter about that guy Reese?'

Beck shook his head. 'Not yet. Walter has enough to do following about a thousand parolees. Let's see how the window thing goes.'

'What do we have in the pipeline now, two guys?'

'Yep. Packy Johnson up at Eastern, and the Irish kid Dermott Ryan has a parole hearing in about six months at Coxsackie.' Beck changed the subject. 'So did Manny tell you about his cousin?'

'No. Didn't know he had any family. Closest thing I thought he had are those cronies he fishes with down on the piers. Did you know about her?'

'No. Nothing.'

'She knows you're coming?'

'Yeah.'

'Manny is pretty riled up.'

'Yes.'

'What's it going to take?'

'Don't know yet.'

They lapsed back into silence, until Demarco guided the Mercury onto the Henry Hudson Parkway.

Beck asked. 'How old you figure Manny is, closing in on sixty?'

'Nah, he's what, fiftysomething, I think. He looks older because he's been at the hard life longer. Takes its toll.'

'He says the cousin is a lot younger.'

Demarco didn't comment.

When they drove over the Henry Hudson Bridge into Riverdale, Beck said, 'Take the Palisade Avenue exit.'

Within a few minutes they pulled up parallel to a small complex of Tudor-style apartments that looked like a cluster of small Mediterranean villas overlooking the Hudson River. Beyond the buildings, the winter water of the Hudson River looked gray, and even a blue sky and bright sun couldn't make the Palisades across the river anything but dull brown.

Beck popped open the door of the Mercury and stepped out. He made his way along connecting walkways, under stone arches, and up freestanding stairways until he found Olivia Sanchez's apartment on the second-floor level.

He tapped the knocker against the sturdy wooden door and waited. He heard someone on the other side of the door and assumed Olivia Sanchez was checking him out through the peephole.

'Who is it?'

Beck answered loud enough to be heard through the thick door. 'James Beck. Your cousin Manny called to say I'd be coming to see you.'

Beck heard a dead bolt lock turn and then a sucking swish as the heavy door sealed against the river winds pulled open.

Beck hadn't bothered to picture Manny's cousin, but if he'd tried he wouldn't have come close to the woman who stood in front of him with a slight smile, her hand extended.

'Hello, I'm Olivia.'

Beck gripped her hand lightly and felt a firm grip in return.

She nodded. He stared. She waited, accustomed to the effect she had on men.

She was about five six. She had strong, but feminine features, an elegant nose, beautifully shaped full lips, large eyes, and a nearly fantasy figure: long-limbed and thin with a model's wide shoulders, but with full breasts and shapely hips. She wore little if any makeup. She didn't need it. Her smooth skin had a natural glow, the tone somewhere between olive and gold.

She took her hand from Beck's and stepped aside to let him enter. He walked past her into a long, narrow, comfortably furnished living room, but Beck didn't notice the room much. He turned back toward Olivia so he could look at her again. She wore jeans and a deep maroon turtleneck cashmere sweater.

'Can I take your coat?' she asked.

'Sure.'

He passed the heavy coat to Olivia. When she turned to put the coat in the closet, he saw that her thick shiny black hair was pulled back into a pony tail that reached just past her shoulders.

When she reached for a hanger a bit awkwardly, he noticed the cast on her left hand, encasing her little finger and ring finger. The plaster extended past her left wrist.

She closed the closet and turned to lead him into the living room. She moved easily, without any affectation, but it seemed like an extra life force animated her body.

Beck forced himself to stop staring at her and take in the room. Dark wood floors, crown molding, furniture in greens and beige, with prewar plaster walls painted in various delicate shades of green. It all served to make the room seem warm, comfortable, and inviting.

She led Beck to a couch flanking a wood-burning fireplace, where embers glowed and occasional flames licked the remains of a small log. She placed a piece of split hardwood onto the embers, and took a seat opposite him in a comfortable leather chair backlit by the late afternoon light coming through leaded windowpanes behind her.

A private, quiet retreat perched above the blustery Hudson River. Beck wondered how many men would have given how much to be alone in this apartment with a woman that looked like Olivia Sanchez. For Beck, however, it made things slightly uncomfortable and off-balance.

'Can I get you something to drink? Coffee?'

Beck remembered he hadn't finished his morning coffee. He checked his watch. Nearly four in the afternoon.

'No, thanks.'

She sat back in the chair, waiting for Beck to start the conversation.

'This is a very interesting apartment. Quite a location.'

'Yes. People love this place. They built these apartments in nineteen twenty-six. It's like nothing else. I love the river. I can walk to the train station in ten minutes. Twenty-two minutes to Grand Central.'

'How long have you been here?'

'Four years. I don't own. I rent from the owner, but someday I'll buy one of these places for myself. When the opportunity comes up. And if I can get the money.'

'It's a co-op?'

'Condo. They don't limit the amount of time an owner can rent out. Just the number of units.'

Beck nodded. 'How'd you decide on this place?'

'Oh, kind of putting all my needs together. When I first moved here, my mother was living in Mott Haven, so I could just cut across the Bronx to visit. But she's gone now. Mainly it's the proximity to Manhattan. Like they say, location, location, location. And you, Mr Beck, where did you grow up?'

'Manhattan. Hell's Kitchen. They call it Clinton now. My father worked on printing presses. There were a lot of them on the west side in those days.' Okay, Beck thought, that should do it for the polite part. 'So, Manny tells me you've been having some trouble.'

'Some trouble?' She emphasized the word *some*. 'It's the worst trouble I've ever had in my life. How much did he tell you? I mean, he told me you'd be coming, and . . .'

'And what?'

'And he said I could trust you.'

Beck nodded.

'Manny never says much, but he did tell me you helped him with his parole. And after he got out. And that you do that for a lot of men coming out of prison.'

'No. Not a lot of men.'

'Well, Manny told me that you're smart and you can help me. I'm glad you're here.'

Beck nodded again, but didn't comment. He noted that Olivia spoke slowly, precisely as if she wanted to make sure she'd banished her Spanish accent. Beck thought he could pick up a trace of it. Maybe it was just a Bronx accent.

'So, what's going on? It's better if I hear it directly from you.'

'Right. Manny wasn't very interested in the details anyhow. I'm sort of worried I brought him into this.'

'Why?'

'Well, you know Manny. He's pretty black and white.'

Beck thought that was a euphemistic way of putting it. 'Yes. He is black or white.' For or against. Dead or alive. 'You're right to be worried about getting Manny involved.' Beck nodded toward her cast. 'His first impulse is to kill the man who did that to you.'

Olivia's brows furrowed. 'That's not at all what I want.'

'Good. But what do you want?'

Olivia looked at Beck for a few moments, maybe trying to decide if he was giving her a hard time or not. Or maybe thinking about her answer.

'Okay,' she said, repeating Beck's question as if asking herself. 'What do I want?' She paused, as if she needed a moment to think it through. 'I got hurt and threatened by somebody who's stronger and more powerful than me. So I reached out to somebody who I think is strong and powerful, too. In his own way. And now I've got you involved. And you don't look like a pushover either. So what do I want? I want help. But now you've got me worried about what Manny might do. I mean, that would just make everything worse, right?'

'Yes. It would. What exactly happened to you?'

She paused. Gathering her thoughts. 'I work for an investment firm. One of the top traders there, a partner who runs a hedge fund for the firm, heard something about me that he didn't like.'

41

'Alan Crane?'

'Yes. Alan Crane. Manny told you his name?'

'Yes.'

'A couple of weeks ago, he walks into my cubicle about seven-thirty. There's a lot of meetings during the day, and a lot of times I stay to get work done. Anyhow, he starts yelling and screaming at me, and carrying on.'

'About what?'

'About me interfering with his business. Sticking my nose in where it doesn't belong. Stuff like that.'

'Okay.'

'He was out of control. He just kept at it, getting more and more wound up.'

'Did you say anything to him?'

'No. I never had a chance. I thought he was going to hit me. And then, without warning, he slammed his fist down on my hand.' She grimaced at the memory of it. 'It was completely shocking. I was stunned. I couldn't believe it. He kept yelling at me. Threatened to kill me.'

'He threatened to kill you?'

'Yes.'

'How exactly did he threaten you?'

Olivia imitated Alan Crane. 'You get in my fucking way, you fuck with my business I'll fucking kill you. I'll have you wiped off the earth. You won't even be a shit stain on the ground when I'm done with you. You'll be gone. Disappeared. Dead.' Screaming them. She returned to her normal voice. 'A string of disgusting threats like that.'

Beck frowned.

'A hedge fund guy?'

'Yes.'

'Threatening to kill you.'

'Yes. I mean, I don't know if he was serious. He was crazy. Out of control.'

'When he smashed his fist down on you, was that intentional? Did he mean to do it? Did he aim, or was he just banging his fist on your desk and your hand was in the way?'

Olivia shook her head slightly, thinking back. 'It didn't seem like an accident.' She looked away, recalling the moment. 'I don't know. I was typing on my computer, facing away from the opening to my cubicle. I turned toward him. One hand on my desk, the other on the arm of my chair. Then the yelling and screaming while he was leaning over me and wham. Maybe he wasn't aiming. I don't know. All I know is it hurt so much, I was so shocked – I just couldn't believe it happened. But it did.'

'You were sitting.'

'Yes.'

'He was standing over you?'

'Yes. But more like leaning over me. His face down in front of mine. Well, yeah, I guess he wasn't really looking at my hand. He was pounding on my desk, yelling at me, and . . .' – Olivia made a hammer fist motion with her right hand – '. . . he slammed his fist down. Does it matter if he was aiming?'

'Everything matters.'

She thought about it, then shook her head. 'I don't know. It all happened so fast.'

'All right. I understand. So, now – why did he do that? You said it was about you interfering with his business. What the hell could you have done that would make him

43

do that to you – show up out of nowhere, smash your hand, threaten to kill you?'

Olivia leaned toward Beck, as if she had prepared for the question and was ready to give her answer. 'Okay, how much do you know about small dealer brokers? About hedge funds?'

'Some. Not much.'

'Well, I'm sure more than Manny knows. Anyhow, Summit is a small company. Started by a man named Frederick Milstein. He opened the place with family money and investments from a few clients about twenty years ago.

'He kept Summit private from day one. Never got acquired, never merged. At his peak he had maybe fifty people working for the company. Financial advisors, traders, support staff. The place ran pretty clean for a long time. Maybe a little trading stuff back and forth inside the firm among the top guys for their better clients, fees and commissions not exactly transparent, but nothing really off the charts.'

Beck wasn't exactly sure why she was telling him all this, but he nodded and said, 'Go on.'

'Anyhow, over these last few years it's been harder and harder for smaller companies to stay profitable. Regulatory costs are crushing them. Competition is insane. Everything's tougher. Clients are less patient.'

'Uh huh.'

'So more and more small firms are setting up internal trading groups to try and generate profits. That's where it gets sticky. They set up hedge funds to get the leeway they need. Black box backroom stuff.' Olivia waggled her hand.

'Some are legit quants thinking they have a system to rule the markets. Some of it's flash trading, but that's way too expensive for an outfit like Summit to set up. Others, not so legit. I'm licensed as a broker and financial advisor, but I don't really run money. I don't trade. I mostly monitor other money managers. And administrate. Part of the risk and compliance group.'

'So you know what's going on.'

'Yes. Although someone at Crane's level, he doesn't really report to anyone but Milstein. We're supposed to monitor every trade, but if they want to intentionally keep stuff from the risk group, we can't really stop them. But I've been with the company for eight years, and I'm close to Milstein. I know who does what, who earns what. Everybody talks to me. So, I pick up stuff.'

'Like what?'

'Like trades that are moving outside the risk parameters.'

'Whose trades? Crane's?'

'Yes.'

'Anybody else?'

'No. Mostly just the money Crane was running.'

'And Milstein knows about it?'

'Yes. I mean, Milstein makes sure the right firewalls are in place. But he lets Crane run his operation. He knows if something blows up really big, it can take us all down, but he needs the profits Crane generates.'

'And how likely is Crane to blow up?'

'Over the long run, it's pretty much inevitable. But short term? Who knows? If he's lucky, it could go on for quite some time.'

'What's he doing?'

Olivia shook her head. 'It's not just one thing. It's a series of things. A lot of it connected to short selling. Do you know what short selling is?'

'It's something you do when you think a stock is going down in value.'

'Right.'

Beck said, 'You borrow shares of a stock, own it at a given price. If the stock goes down, you decide at what point you will pay for it, plus the cost of borrowing. The difference in price is your profit. If the stocks go up, you lose. You have to cover the difference. But I admit, the mechanics of it are a little murky to me.'

'I'm impressed. What about naked short selling?'

'Not as clear on that. Isn't it illegal?'

'It's not completely illegal. You can do it in foreign markets and in the United States if you follow SEC regulations, but those regulations pretty much eliminate the advantages, so the guys who do it often skirt the legalities. It amounts to short selling, but never actually taking ownership of the stock. Never delivering it back.'

'I'm not going to bother asking how you do that. But what's the point? You save borrowing costs?'

'For starters. But the main advantage is the leverage. If you don't plan on delivering the stocks anytime soon, if ever, you can leverage the whole thing by buying up tons of shares. Some guys ratchet up the leverage with options. Crane's been known to do that, too.

'Anyhow, you don't take true ownership. Of course, eventually you have to complete the transaction. You can delay delivery for some time, but not forever. If you cover the short, you get creamed, but traders who don't care about the rules' – Olivia raised her good hand and made a quote sign as she said the word – "*buy*", huge amounts of stock because they don't tie up capital to cover it. And then they do all sorts of shady stuff to ensure the stock price goes lower.'

'Wait, you're telling me they can ensure that a stock goes down?'

'Not really. But they can sometimes influence a stock price more than you think. Don't get me wrong, it's hugely risky. But guys like Crane, they do anything they can to stack the deck. They systematically attack companies in ways to drive down the price of the stock. Naked shorting on a massive level to pull down the price. Poisoning the well with lies and rumors. Any kind of deception they can come up with. Bribes, threats. Collusion with law firms to wage class action suits. Manipulating the media. It can get really bad.'

Beck thought about that for a moment and began to see what he might be dealing with now.

'Bad how?'

'Traders that reckless, guys who go all the way out on a limb, they lose perspective. I'm sure I don't know everything he's doing. There's tons of dirty stuff that could be going on.'

'And how do you know all this?'

'I've been around for a long time. I worked at other financial services companies. I know how things work. There's always some group, some people who go too far. In terms of Summit, I know all the gossip, the rumors. People talk to me.'

Looking at her, seeing how agitated she was, Beck decided she was telling the truth.

'So are you saying that you tried to do something about all the shit Crane was doing? That's what he meant by interfering with his business?'

'Yes. But don't get the wrong idea. I'm not stupid. I didn't threaten to blow any whistles. I mean, one thing I know is that it's impossible to stop these guys. Or at least impossible for me. Maybe some big FBI SEC investigation could do something, but I wouldn't depend on that. No way.'

'So what did you do exactly?'

Olivia sat back in her chair, crossed her long legs, and then her arms. It wasn't her intention, but crossing her arms emphasized the fullness of her breasts. Beck actually looked down to stop from being distracted.

'It really wasn't all that much. A couple of days before Crane attacked me, I saw Milstein sitting at his desk, looking older, more worn out than I'd ever seen him. I guess I felt sorry for him. That's a stupid mistake, I know, but I walked in and asked him how things were going.'

'What'd he say?'

'He said, there'd been better days. I asked him if I could do anything. He said no. And then, I just said, "You know, there's not a lot that's wrong with this place. Most people are doing the right thing. Maybe you should do something about the ones keeping you up at night."'

'Meaning Crane.'

'Yes.'

'And he knew who you meant?'

'Of course.'

'And what did he say?'

'He just said, "I wish it was that easy.'"

'Meaning?'

Olivia shrugged. 'Meaning he needs the profits Crane is generating, even though it causes him a lot of worry.'

Beck thought about it for a moment. It didn't seem like much, but if Crane was unstable, maybe the threat of having his operation shut down would have been enough to push him over the edge.

'But why would Milstein tell Crane what you said?'

'I'm not sure he did. He might have said something to one of the other partners. I don't even know if it was that. Look, it's my job to assess risk, monitor positions. I haven't been totally quiet about Crane, but it's not like I got up on a table and yelled, This has got to stop.'

'But you think it was you going to Milstein that set him off?'

'Yes.'

'Anything else?'

'What do you mean?'

'Anything else that might have set him off?'

'Of course. Guys like Crane are way off the risk charts. They're under huge pressure. Things can blow up any minute. Maybe a big position went south. Who knows?'

'How much money is this guy playing with?'

'I don't know his exact positions, but I'd say well over a hundred million. That's not the leveraged money. That's the principal.'

'How much is well over a hundred?'

'Call it a hundred fifty.'

'And how much of that goes in his pocket?'

'Not just his, all the partners.'

'How much?'

'It's the usual setup. Two and twenty.'

'What's that?'

'Two percent management fee. Twenty percent of the profits.'

Beck calculated two percent of 150 million, frowning at how big the number was.

'Yeah,' said Olivia, 'three million in management fees, minus expenses. And if there are profits, then the numbers go up very fast.'

'How much is fast?'

'Crane is swinging for the fences, so thirty percent easy. Fifty would be more like it. Twenty percent of seventy-five million? Say fifteen million or so. For as many years as they can run it. Fifteen million in pure profit, since the fees are more than enough to cover expenses.'

'Spread around to how many?'

'Not many. That much money goes a long way in a firm the size of Summit.'

Beck thought about what people would do with that much money at stake. Breaking a couple of fingers by accident and screaming threats didn't seem so hard to believe now.

'So after the blowup, what happened?'

'He sort of used up all his anger and then walked out of my cubicle.'

'Did he say anything about your hand?'

'No. It was like he couldn't have cared less. I doubt he even realized he broke two of my fingers.'

'So then what did you do?'

'I put on my coat, picked up my purse, got to an elevator as fast as I could. Went downstairs to the guy at the main security desk, but it was after normal work hours and there was just this young guy there. I didn't bother with him. What was he going to do? My hand hurt so much I felt like I was going to pass out. I went out, hailed a cab, and went to the hospital.'

'Didn't shut down your computer, turn out the lights . . . ?'

'No. Just got the hell out of there.'

'And then what?'

'The closest emergency room is Lenox Hill. I got lucky. There was a hand surgeon available. He set my fingers. Told me I might get away with no surgery. I went back a week later, and he said everything was good.'

'Did you tell them what happened?'

'Yes. I told the triage nurse. She said she'd report it. Told me to just worry about my hand. I don't know what she did or when, but by the time everything was done, the police hadn't shown up. There was no way I was going to sit around waiting for them. So I left. The next day, I called the precinct. I went in and filed a complaint.

'Of course, Crane denied everything. Filed a counter complaint and is suing me for false whatever, and I got fired. I talked to an assistant DA. Basically, he said I had no witness, so no case.'

Olivia looked down at her lap, perhaps to hide her expression.

She looked up. 'I never set foot in that office again. Barred. I'm not sure if I'm actually fired or suspended until all the legal stuff is resolved, but I don't have the money to fight it. And Crane put out the word that I should be banned from working at any other firm. Filed complaints with FINRA and the SEC. I tried everything, believe me. I tried multiple times to get a hold of Milstein.'

'Did he ever contact you?'

'No.'

'So nobody helped you, you're screwed, and Crane is still just fine.'

She stared at Beck. He had put it so bluntly and succinctly that she turned away, her face lit by the guttering fire. He wasn't sure what she didn't want him to see: anger, fear, tears. Whatever it was, he didn't press her.

Beck shifted his gaze to the view out her windows. A red tone had seeped into the winter sky. Beck had missed the sunset, but imagined how stunning sunsets would look from Olivia Sanchez's window.

Neither of them said anything for a few moments.

Finally, Beck said, 'I'm sorry about what happened to you.'

She turned back to face him. 'So am I.'

Beck paused, exhaled, said, 'So you called Manny.'

'Yes.'

'What did you ask Manny to do?'

'To help me.'

'How?'

'I didn't ask him to do anything specifically. I just told him about this guy who was ruining my life. I told him I couldn't afford defending myself against his lawsuits. That I needed to stop him from blacklisting me. That I needed to get back to work.'

Beck pressed. 'How did you think Manny could accomplish all that?'

She looked at Beck, defiance coming into her voice, as she finally admitted it. 'You know how. I wanted him to threaten Crane. To confront him and scare the shit out of him. I wanted Manny to do what I couldn't.'

'You wanted Manny to do to Crane what he did to you.'

Beck's comment confused her. Then angered her. But she didn't shrink from the answer.

'Yes. Yes, I wanted him to threaten to kill Crane if he kept trying to hurt me. Okay. I admit it.'

Beck nodded. He let what she'd said sink in for a moment.

'This threat of Crane's to kill you, did you believe him?'

'At the time, it terrified me.'

'You actually believed some Wall Street hedge fund guy would kill you?'

'I don't know. It sounded real.'

Beck nodded. 'What about Manny? Do you think Manny is capable of killing someone?'

Olivia cleared her throat. She didn't want to say it, but finally she answered, 'I think it's a matter of record.'

Beck shifted around on the couch. Looked at the fire. At the red sky darkening. At Olivia Sanchez. Then he asked, 'Whose money is it?'

'What do you mean?'

'The money Crane is investing. Who is the client?'

Olivia looked down. Then directly at Beck, but this time she didn't say anything.

Beck said, 'Shit. That's what you're not telling me.'

'I can't tell you what I don't know for sure.'

'Are you saying you don't know? You, the person in charge of monitoring risk?'

Olivia's expression tightened. She looked away. Stared at the fire. Finally, she said, 'I don't know all the details. The money belongs to a Russian named Leonid or Leonard Markov. There may be some other money in Crane's hedge fund, but it's mostly Markov's. There's a lot of privacy issues involved. Client's identities and who owns what are kept confidential. But like I said, I hear things. What I hear is, Markov's an arms dealer. He supposedly has all kinds of connections to the government. The US government. Maybe other governments. I don't know. Now, it might not be just Markov. Crane has a reputation of dealing with shady types. I know that he swaggers around like he has friends that . . .'

'That what?'

Olivia didn't back down. She looked straight at Beck, 'That could or would kill people.'

So there it was. Beck grimaced. 'Christ.'

'But I don't know if that's true, or just a bullshit macho image Crane likes to project.'

'Uh-huh.'

'What was I supposed to do? Just let that bastard threaten me; let them take away my job and slink away?'

Beck didn't answer.

'Look, Crane is full of shit. You're right. He's no gangster. No tough guy. He's walking around like a big man because he knows some unscrupulous people. I just figured he'd fold in two seconds if he saw a real tough guy.'

Beck made sure to speak very calmly. 'Olivia, a real

tough guy, a man like your cousin, doesn't go around threatening people. It doesn't happen that way.'

Olivia started to explain more. 'I didn't, I mean, I didn't tell him to . . .'

Beck raised a hand. He had the picture now. 'All right, all right. Take it easy. I'm not out to make you feel any worse than you do now.'

'Well, you are. I thought you would understand.'

'That's the problem. I do understand. Now I get it.'

'Get what?'

'Why Crane went off like that. You say he's running money for unscrupulous people. Maybe a guy with connections to who knows? He's taking big risks. If he gets shut down, and loses a ton of money, what's going to happen to him?'

'I don't know.'

'Maybe what he said would happen to you.'

Olivia looked down, shaking her head, 'Dear God.' She paused. 'So what do I do? Is there anything you can do? Or do I just forget about it? When this mess blows over, I'll just start again. I really can't fight this. I mean, you don't think Crane is actually going to make good on his threat, do you?'

'Crane isn't your problem now. At least not your main problem.'

Olivia looked confused. 'Who is?'

'Manny Guzman. You don't just put him back in a box. Something has to be done about this.'

'What do you mean?'

'Manny is not going to let this slide.'

'Even if I ask him to?'

'It's too late for that.'

'You can't tell him.'

'No,' said Beck. 'And I can't not tell him what's going on here.'

Olivia stood up and turned to the window, the red winter light making her skin seem to glow deep bronze. She turned back to Beck.

'This is a nightmare.'

'All right, take it easy. Let's go back to what you want. You want Crane off your back. You want to be able to earn a living, someplace. Not Summit. That's a dead end, but you want to get back to where you were.'

'Yes. And I don't want Manny involved. Or hurt. Or . . . anything.'

'Yeah, okay. Well let's take it one step at a time.'

'Meaning?'

'For starters, we don't talk about this anymore.'

'What? What do you mean? Why?'

'Why do you think?'

Beck watched her consider the question. He watched her deep brown eyes flecked with gold move up and down as she processed everything.

'I think you mean the less I know the better.'

'Yes. The more I say to you about it, the more you know, the worse it could be for you. You get that, right?'

'I suppose, but I'm not sure where that leaves me.'

She suddenly moved over to the fire, picked up an iron poker, and stabbed at the charred log, sending sparks up the flue, taking her frustration out on the husk of burning wood.

She turned to Beck, 'Are you going to help me?'

'Yes.'

'Thank you. Is there anything I should do?'

'First, don't call Manny. There can't be any record of contact between you and him.'

'For how long?'

'Until I tell you.'

'Okay.'

'If we need to talk, I'll find a way to contact you. Next, and think about this before you answer, you have to assure me that no matter what happens, no matter who asks you, the police, the DA's office, whoever – you will swear to them that you never talked to Manny Guzman about any of this. On the outside chance they go after your phone records and find out you contacted him, you never said anything to him about Summit or Crane or any of it.'

'Yes, of course.'

'You answered that too quickly, Olivia.'

'I don't care. It's true. It's nobody's business who I talk to or what I said.'

Beck made a face. 'Of course it is. The chances of this getting messy are very high. Do you understand? Can you stand up to cops grilling you about it? Pressing you?'

'Yes. If it means just keeping my mouth shut, yes. I'm not all that good at outright lying, but I can refuse anybody.'

I'll bet you can, Beck thought.

'Okay. And the same goes with regard to me. Anybody asks about me, you tell them nothing. Not, you don't know me. Not, you do know me. Nothing. If they arrest you, you tell them to talk to your lawyer.'

'Arrest me?'

'If . . . If . . . On the unlikely chance that happens, you tell them nothing except you want to talk to your lawyer.'

'I don't have a lawyer.'

'Well you will if it comes to that.'

'Christ, what are we talking about here?'

'We're talking about you and Manny Guzman. He is a known criminal. He still has years left on his parole. Anything he gets involved in, the assumption is going to be that a crime has been committed or soon will be. There's none of this innocent-until-proven-guilty shit with convicted felons. Once you're a felon in America, it's the opposite. That's how it works. So the first rule is, you don't tell anybody anything about this. Especially law enforcement. Not one fucking word, except your name and address and get me my lawyer. Got that?'

'Yes.'

'Ever. Name and address and get me my lawyer.'

She raised her voice. 'Okay.'

Beck could see he was unnerving her, but he didn't care. He didn't care how beautiful she was, or how unfairly she had been treated, she had to know what she was getting into.

He stood up from the couch, facing Olivia standing in front of the fire. Whether it was the glow of the fire against the fading twilight, or the intensity of her vulnerability and distress, Beck knew he had to force a distance between them.

'Okay. That's enough for now.'

She could see that Beck was about to leave. 'What are you going to do?'

Beck hesitated, then said, 'I'm going to try to get you

what you want. And then I'm going to try to somehow convince Manny getting you what you want should end this.'

'All right,' was about all Olivia could muster.

'If I need your help, more information, whatever, I'm assuming you're prepared to see this through.'

'Of course.'

'Where can I find Milstein?'

'Why?'

The question annoyed Beck. He ignored it. 'Where can I find him? What's he look like?'

Olivia walked to a desk in the far corner of the living room. She picked up her laptop and brought it over, sat back down, set the computer on her knees, and logged in to the Summit website. She clicked through to the page featuring Milstein's bio.

She turned the laptop around so Beck could see the screen.

'The picture is about five years old. He's a bit grayer, but that's him. He's a small man. Skinny. Always wears a suit and tie. A little hunched over. Not exactly the nicest guy in the world.'

Beck leaned toward her and took in the picture of Milstein.

'Summit is at Fifty-seventh and Lex?'

'Yes. The twenty-seventh and eighth floors. Milstein works on twenty-eight. Crane, too. But at separate ends of the floor.'

'How late does Milstein work?'

'Until six. Pretty much on the dot.'

'What about Crane?'

'It varies. He's one of those guys where things revolve around his schedule. He has a place in Miami, and he lives in a loft in Tribeca. Both residences are hooked in with the Summit computer system. He works from home quite a bit.'

'Where does Milstein live?'

'Seventy-ninth and Park. He has his driver pick him up and take him home, even though it's only a fifteen-minute walk. Always the same driver. A big guy. Ex-cop.'

Beck reacted immediately. 'An ex-cop?'

'Yes. I guess he's sort of a bodyguard, too.'

'Why would Milstein need a bodyguard?'

'I don't think he does. He's mostly a driver, but Milstein thinks it's cool to keep a big guy with a gun around who people will assume is a bodyguard. Like a status symbol or something.'

Beck frowned. Armed ex-cops didn't exactly fit in with a Wall Street type.

'All right, let's leave it at that for now. If I need to, I'll be in touch. If we get lucky, you won't hear from me until this is over.'

'Right.'

Olivia stepped toward Beck and took hold of his forearm. He could smell her soap, or shampoo. Something fresh. Something that fit her exactly.

'Thank you,' she said.

She was holding his arm firmly. The contact unnerved him, which surprised Beck. The closeness of her, the touch, she had crossed the normal barrier that separated them.

Beck gave in to the desire to touch her back. He placed

his hand on top of her hand, almost as if he were going to remove it. Her skin was incredibly smooth and warm. It seemed as if he could actually feel the sheen of it.

'Okay,' he said.

She let go of his forearm; he let her hand fall away from his immediately.

She turned away from Beck, leading him back to her front door. He took his coat from her, nodded once, and walked out the door, wanting to get outside quickly, to get away from Olivia Sanchez.

In a moment, he was making his way through the Escher-like maze of staircases and arches and walkways that connected the condo's units. He checked his watch. He'd been there nearly an hour.

He spotted the black Mercury parked at the fire hydrant about thirty feet down the block. He slid into the passenger seat. Settled back and exhaled.

Demarco looked at him and raised an eyebrow. 'What?'

Beck shook his head. 'Christ.'

'Christ what?'

'Christ sake this isn't what I expected.'

'How so?'

Beck grimaced, scratched the back of his neck, ran his hand back and forth over the top of his head.

'That bad?'

'Yeah. Maybe. I don't know. Not good.'

'Why?'

'It sounds like there might be some nasty players behind this.'

'Like who?'

'Like a fucking Russian arms dealer for starters.'

61

Demarco frowned. 'How'd that happen?'

'Money, man. A lot of fucking money.'

'So now what?'

'I gotta get a handle on this fast. Have to try and make things right for Manny's cousin, at least right enough so Manny will back off for now. And do it fast before too many snakes crawl out from under rocks.' Beck's voice faded out, lost in his thoughts. 'And not leave any trail.' Beck shook his head, stared out the windshield. 'Shit.'

Demarco didn't bother asking Beck what he was wrestling with. He just repeated, 'So now what?'

Beck looked at his watch. Almost five o'clock. There was time.

'Fifty-seventh and Lex.'

5

Traveling against the rush hour traffic, Demarco and Beck reached Milstein's office building on the northwest corner of Fifty-seventh and Lexington Avenue at five minutes to six.

Unlike most of the buildings up and down Fifty-seventh Street, the south-facing side of the structure was scooped out in a gentle arc, leaving a large area for an open plaza.

Demarco parked on the south side of Fifty-seventh facing east, in a no-standing zone.

At exactly 6 p.m. a black Lincoln Town Car pulled up and slid to the far end of the bus stop just in front of Milstein's office building on the north side of Fifty-seventh. The Lincoln was a late model, cleaned and buffed to a high shine. There was no car service number displayed in the window. The driver filled most of the front seat. His head nearly touched the roof.

Beck jumped out of the Mercury Marauder, crossed Fifty-seventh, and blended in with the flow of pedestrians. He walked across the plaza and stepped through a revolving door into an opulent lobby that was surprisingly compact, about seventy-five feet wide from east to west, but only fifteen feet deep.

There was a small security desk just past the revolving door. Straight ahead six elevators emptied into a central corridor.

There were no turnstiles or security guards other than two men who sat behind the desk off to the right. A few people waved keycards at an electronic pad set into the west wall on their way out.

Beck stepped to his left, away from the security desk, out of the flow of people leaving the building. He watched carefully for a short man amidst the groups of people getting off the various elevators.

Beck checked his watch. Three minutes after six. And here he came, head down, slightly bent over, just as Olivia had described him. He was hatless – making it easier to spot his nearly white hair.

He wore a dark overcoat, tie and suit. Dress shoes.

Beck stepped in front of him before Milstein reached the revolving door, calling his name so that he would look up.

'Mr Milstein.'

Milstein stopped, squinted up at Beck. 'Who are you?'

'I'm a friend of Olivia Sanchez. I'd like to speak to you about her.'

Milstein continued staring at Beck. 'Are you a process server?' Before Beck could answer, Milstein answered for him. 'No, or you'd have already served me. I don't know you and I'm not interested in talking to you about Olivia Sanchez, or anything else.'

Milstein tried to step around Beck to get into the revolving door, but Beck blocked his path, saying, 'It would be better if you talked to me.'

Even though Beck was much bigger than Milstein, the smaller man tried to shove Beck aside. He snarled, 'Get out of my way.' Beck hardly moved, but Milstein quickly stepped around Beck and ducked into one of the revolving door sections. Despite his size Beck was just as quick as Milstein. As Milstein began to push the revolving door, Beck slipped into the section behind him, grabbed the door bar, and pulled back hard.

Milstein banged into the glass. Furious, he pushed hard to get out, but found himself trapped. He turned and yelled an obscenity at Beck. Beck shoved the revolving door forward, smacking Milstein with the heavy slab of glass, sending Milstein sprawling out onto the plaza. Beck followed quickly and lifted Milstein up by his right arm, pulling the smaller man nearly off his feet. He spun and pinned Milstein against the wall next to the revolving door.

He'd done it so swiftly that it almost looked as if Beck had helped a fallen man back to his feet. But the flurry of motion caught the eye of Milstein's driver. When he saw Milstein fall, he quickly got out of the car to see what was going on with his boss.

Beck pinned Milstein firmly against the wall with his forearm and elbow.

'I asked you nicely, now I'm telling you. I'm going to talk to you about Olivia Sanchez. It won't take much time. I suggest you answer my questions. It'll be much easier than the alternative.'

Milstein ignored Beck, looking past him. Beck guessed that Milstein's bodyguard was heading his way, because the smaller man threatened him, 'Take your goddamn hands off me or I'll have you arrested. My driver is an ex-cop and he's . . .'

Beck cut him off, 'If you're smart, you'll tell him to get back in the car.'

Instead, Milstein yelled over Beck's shoulder, 'Walter. Walter, get over here and get this son of a bitch off me.'

Beck turned, let go of Milstein and stepped forward a few paces to meet the bodyguard, a big man, pear-shaped, wide-hipped, with long arms and plenty of bulk. Beck figured him to be close to six foot six, at least two hundred fifty pounds. He came straight at Beck.

Beck pointed at him and said, 'If you touch me I'll put you down. If you pull your gun, I'll kill you.'

For a moment the threats confused the big man, but quickly angered him enough so that he came at Beck with surprising speed, rearing back, his right fist aimed at Beck's face.

Beck didn't duck or even blink. He leaned to his right and let the punch move past his cheek, then pivoted, grabbed the big man's right wrist with his right hand, and punched him hard on the back of his arm just above the elbow, hitting a bundle of nerves that paralyzed the bodyguard's arm and caused sharp, intense pain.

Beck turned the paralyzed arm at the wrist, shoved at the back of the man's shoulder and swept the bodyguard's right leg out from under him. The ex-cop went down hard onto his left knee.

Beck kept his grip on the arm and could have twisted the man's shoulder out of the socket, but instead he kept the arm levered high, leaned close, and spoke into the bodyguard's ear.

'You're lucky you still have an arm you can use. I should have you arrested for assault and end your fucking career, but you're just doing your job for this asshole, so we'll let this one go. Don't make this mistake again. Don't ever come at me again, you understand?'

Walter nodded, wincing against the pain.

'I'm going to let you stand up now. Don't do anything stupid.'

Beck dropped the arm. Walter grabbed his shoulder, remaining down on one knee, not moving, waiting for the pain to subside.

Beck straightened up and turned to Milstein, who hadn't moved from the wall. 'Take care of your man here. Next time I see you, I suggest you talk to me.'

Beck had kept his voice down. A small crowd had gathered around Beck and Walter, but nobody seemed to know what to do, if anything. Whatever happened seemed to be over. The big man was slowly rising to his feet, holding his shoulder.

Beck drifted away to his right, stepping to the ramp that slanted down onto Lexington Avenue.

He blended in with the sidewalk pedestrians and disappeared, heading uptown, out of sight to anyone in front of the building.

Demarco had watched carefully from his parking spot across the street, never for a moment worried that Beck would need his help with the bodyguard. As soon as Beck headed uptown on foot, he pulled out onto Fifty-seventh, immediately turning right, heading downtown with the one-way traffic on Lexington. He took the first right going west and accelerated toward Park Avenue. By the time he had gone one block on Park, he spotted Beck coming his way. Beck slipped into the Mercury.

'That was fun.'

'Big bastard, wasn't he?' said Demarco.

'Yeah. It helps when you surprise them. Of course, I knew if it went wrong you'd be right there to jump in.'

''Cept I don't like leaving the car in a no-standing spot, so, you know.'

'In other words, the car is more important.'

Demarco tipped his head, shrugged, and asked, 'Now what?'

'Now we escalate. That little cocksucker Milstein is an asshole.'

'I'm sorry to hear that.'

'What? That he's an asshole, or that we have to take this to the next step?'

'Just a figure of speech.'

'Uh-huh. You hungry?'

'Yes, as a matter of fact. We seem to have skipped lunch.'

'Let's see, where's a decent place to eat in this shit neighborhood? Hey, there's a burger place over on Sixtieth or somewhere. You want a burger?'

Demarco made a face.

'Come on.'

'If you insist, James.'

'See if you can find a parking spot somewhere.'

As Demarco began his search in the crowded neighborhood, Beck pulled out his cell phone and punched a speed-dial number. When the phone answered, he said, 'Ciro. It's me.'

Demarco listened to Beck's side of the conversation, which ended with Beck giving Ciro Baldassare instructions on where to meet them.

'Ciro?'

Beck turned to Demarco. 'Hey, man, I don't want to wrestle with that big son of a bitch again.'

Demarco pursed his lips. 'Pulling out the heavy artillery already?'

'He's actually in the city. One of his customers is in over his head on his football bets.'

'God help him.'

'I don't think it'll be too bad. It's a young guy. His father owns a restaurant downtown. Ciro just had a talk with Daddy about his boy's gambling debt.'

'Does Daddy still have a restaurant?'

Beck smiled. 'You know what Ciro once told me is the hardest part of running his gambling operation?'

'What?'

'Moving all the money around. All that cash. Picking up the cash from the losers and bringing it to the winners. It's mostly a messenger service with guys tough enough to walk around with thousands and thousands in green.'

'With Ciro behind it all so nobody gets any ideas about who that cash belongs to.'

'Exactly.'

Just then Demarco spotted a space in front of a Park Avenue apartment building as a cab pulled away. Demarco deftly parallel parked the Mercury in one move, despite the fact that there was a brass plaque atop a stanchion set in front of the building entrance announcing NO PARKING.

Beck reached out his window and moved the stanchion out of the way so he could open his door. A doorman was already rushing out to tell Demarco Jones and James Beck they couldn't park there. Every spot on the block was filled except for the space in front of the white-glove Park Avenue building.

Beck stood waiting for the doorman. Demarco walked around the front of the Mercury and leaned back on its shiny front fender. The doorman started to say something, saw who he was talking to, stopped, then said, 'There's elderly people in this building. In wheelchairs. You're blocking the entrance.'

Beck reached out and lifted the lapel of the man's uniform coat so he could see the name sewn onto the pocket.

'Is that right, Peter?'

'Yes.'

'Who made that nice sign for you?'

'I don't know.'

'Is that real brass?'

'Yes. I think so. Listen, you can't . . .'

'You think having a brass sign makes it true?'

'You can't park there.'

'Yes I can. Peter.'

'You're blocking the entrance.'

Beck raised a hand. 'Take your bullshit and your little sign and go back in your building. You get an old rich person in a wheelchair wants to come in, you hustle your ass out here and roll 'em to the corner, where there's no curb; roll 'em up nice and easy, and haul them in. And make goddamn sure nobody bumps into my car getting in or out of a cab. Or a fucking limo. Or a delivery truck. Or anything. You got it? Peter.'

The doorman didn't say anything.

'When's your shift over?'

'Midnight.'

'Good. I'll be back before then. Keep an eye on things.'

As they walked away Beck said to Demarco, 'More assholes.'

6

Instead of letting Walter Pearce drop him off at the front entrance to his building, Frederick Milstein rode with him into the underground garage where they kept the car.

Even though he couldn't have cared less, Milstein asked, 'You sure you're okay, Walter?'

'I'm all right. My arm and shoulder will be sore in the morning, but only because that guy held back. He knew what he was doing. Never been hit like that on the back of my arm. Still stings. What's somebody like that doing around you Mr Milstein? Who the hell was he?'

Milstein lied without hesitation. 'I have no idea, but I intend to find out.'

They stepped out of the car. Walter handed the key to the parking attendant and they walked through the garage to the building's service entrance.

'You need to know who he is. And we need to be prepared.'

'What does that mean?'

'That means at least me and another man, both of us armed. I wouldn't take any chances, Mr Milstein. I heard him say he was intending to talk to you.'

'All right, all right, I'll look into it. Are you okay for the walk tonight?'

'Yes, sir. I'm going to get some dinner. I'll meet you in the lobby at the usual time.'

Walter turned and headed back out to the long driveway that opened onto Eightieth Street. Milstein walked through the storage and laundry areas to the building's lobby and waited for the elevator, his mouth moving involuntarily, propelled by anger and confusion and a fear he didn't want to admit feeling. Whoever that man was, Milstein was shocked at how easily he'd handled Walter.

The elevator door opened. One of the amiable doormen greeted Milstein with a respectful 'Good evening, sir.'

Milstein stepped onto the elevator, grimacing, shoving his gloves into his pockets. When the elevator man saw Milstein's face he pressed fourteen, looked forward, and didn't say another word.

Milstein's wife had gone out to dinner with a friend. The housekeeper appeared from out of the kitchen the moment she heard Milstein enter the apartment.

She already had her coat on. Her way of telling Milstein he was later than usual and she wasn't going to spend one more second on the job.

'Your dinner is in the microwave, Mr M. Just turn it on for two minutes and you're all set. Mrs Milstein said she'd be home around ten. I left a red wine out for you.'

Milstein hated that 'Mr M' title. Where the fuck did she get the idea she could call him that? He didn't bother to look at her or answer her as he dropped his coat on the chair in the foyer and walked into the living room.

He headed straight for the phone on the ornate, leather-covered desk that occupied the corner of the room. The only light in the room was from the streetlights outside, another annoyance. Lazy bitch couldn't even turn on a fucking light for him.

He snapped on the desk lamp, revealing overstuffed couches in a gold brocade fabric, oil paintings of Hudson Valley landscapes, plush carpeting, and porcelain figurines resting on every end table, on bookshelves, as well as on the fireplace mantel.

It was his wife's idea of sophisticated Upper East Side decorating. Milstein never really noticed it much one way or the other, but tonight the room felt stifling, almost claustrophobic. He had to stop and catch his breath. He realized how much being roughed up had shaken him. No one had ever done anything like that to him. And that useless goddamn Walter. A big fucking waste of money, and now he wanted to bring in another bodyguard. Perfect. Can't do the job I'm paying you for so now I have to pay for another asshole, while I'm still paying you.

He picked up his home phone and dialed Alan Crane's number. Crane hadn't appeared in the office for two days. Not surprising with all the mess he'd created. The phone rang until the outgoing voice mail message came on.

'Call me,' said Milstein as he hung up with a curse. Goddamn Crane never answered his phone.

He stood for a moment in his opulent Park Avenue living room, trying to decide something. Finally, he reached into his desk and fished around for a cheap cell phone he kept there for just an occasion like this. There were three like it in the drawer. His instructions were to use the phones once and throw them away.

He checked the battery. Half full. That would be

enough. He pushed the speed dial for a preprogrammed number and waited until the call connected and started to ring. Milstein listened to the phone ring at the other end. And continue to ring.

'Fuck.'

7

Leonid Markov heard his phone vibrating on the side table.

About two hours earlier, he had carefully ingested a combination of Adderall, Viagra, GBH (Gamma-Hydroxybutyric), and DOB (4-bromo-2,5-dimethoxyam phetamine) along with slightly less than a half-pint of Stolichnaya vodka.

A precise amount of each ingredient had been consumed in a precise sequence in preparation for the sex session Markov had planned, ending with the Adderall crushed into a fine powder, placed in a small piece of toilet paper, and swallowed with water.

He knew it was impossible to achieve the exact effect he wanted, but Markov nearly always succeeded in bringing himself to a point where he was teetering between sensory overload and mental chaos.

Leonid Markov simply and always wanted more. Drugs were part of getting more. More sensations, more intensity, more phantasmagoria.

It also made him feel superior to be able to maintain control over the overwhelming sensations brought on by the dangerous combination of chemicals that coursed through his system.

When his phone began vibrating, Markov was naked, on his back, his flabby, 255-pound body splayed on top of a sturdy masseuse table, knees bent, his thick legs tented wide, his heels on the edge of the table while a black transsexual stood at the foot of the table, penetrating him anally with long steady strokes as she squeezed and stroked his erect penis.

For a moment, Markov thought the buzzing sound of the cell phone had something to do with his own moaning and grinding of teeth under the Adderall rush.

But he rallied enough to focus and realized the electronic noise came from the cell phone skittering around on the glass-topped side table next to the king-size bed.

Markov was working on the second orgasm of three he had planned, so he held up one hand, indicating that the prostitute should stop. Calls to his cell phone could not be ignored. They invariably involved money, and of all the things Leonid Markov wanted more of, money was at the very top of his list.

He reached over, picked up the phone. 'Who?'

'Milstein.'

Markov grunted, 'Call me in five hours.'

Without waiting for a response, he pushed the END button and dropped the phone on the hotel room carpet, turning his attention back to the transsexual.

Markov focused on the black she-male who called herself Natalie. She was beginning to look more masculine, but at the same time less human, more animatronic. Her abdominal muscles flexed and pulsed, looking like a set of dark, three-dimensional metallic plates. The shaved stubble of her pubic hair seemed to flex on the surface of her smooth abdominal skin, reminding Markov of tiny nail heads or rivets. The black wig she wore swayed as if it were made of plastic strands that had been covered in a resin that made each strand heavy and somehow dangerous. Markov suddenly felt that if she bent over and any part of the wig touched him, it would slice through him, cutting back and forth through layers of skin and yellow fat and making him bleed.

Markov avoided looking at her face, which had twisted into something like a mask made of twitching, flat, shining pieces of dark stone. He wanted to focus on her breasts, to turn his attention to something erotic, but he couldn't stop his eyes from blinking and suddenly watering. Everything began to turn blurry. Her breathing sounded like the hissing spurts that would come out of a steam radiator. Or maybe it was his breathing. Or was it really the hissing of the radiator in the hotel room he had rented in midtown Manhattan?

Milstein checked his watch. He knew calling Markov back and venting his anger in a voice mail would be stupid and dangerous. Five hours. That would mean at about eleven-thirty.

He thought about trying Alan Crane again, but he already knew Crane would ignore him.

No, the hell with Crane, he thought. I'm going straight to Markov. He'd call Markov after he walked the dog.

What the hell was that goddamn Sanchez woman trying to pull? Who was that thug she'd sent?

Milstein slipped the small cell phone into his pocket. He would take it apart and throw away the pieces as he walked the dog.

Milstein took a few steps and sat down on the couch

facing his marble fireplace. Now that he was home, now that there was nothing else he could do, Milstein suddenly felt weak and a bit shaky. A drink. He needed a drink.

Milstein walked into his kitchen, turning lights on as he moved toward the back of the apartment. He pulled a bottle of Lagavulin from the kitchen cabinet where he kept his liquor. He pushed glassware around in the kitchen cabinet, looking for a rocks glass, settling for a water glass. Fuck it.

He poured himself two fingers, tipped the glass back, letting the hot, medicinal whiskey fill his mouth and burn into his stomach. He took a deep breath. Returned to his living room.

The dog had decided to join him. The fucking thing is always hanging out in the kitchen with the housekeeper, thought Milstein. She ought to take the damn thing home someday and keep him.

The dog was a large, overfed Airedale named Tam. Another of his wife's ideas. Not that she did anything to walk it or take care of it. She treated it like another piece of furniture. Cared for by somebody else.

While Milstein had been in the kitchen, Tam had curled up in his oversized Tartan plaid dog bed. Milstein's wife had picked out the fabric with her decorator at a ridiculously inflated price. After much discussion, the dog's bed had been placed under the large window facing Seventy-ninth Street, as if the dog and his bed were a design feature.

When Milstein entered the room, the dog lifted his head, stared at Milstein, waiting for an outburst that would send him scurrying out of the room.

Milstein ignored the dog, took another swallow of the expensive Scotch.

Take it easy, Milstein told himself. Again, his thoughts turned to Olivia Sanchez. Why am I surprised? A woman that good-looking could get plenty of men to help her. But that guy? Not her type. Way too rough. Too blue collar. But then again, maybe not. Maybe exactly her type. He wasn't badly dressed. The coat looked expensive. He spoke well. Goddammit, who the fuck was he?

Milstein took another swig of the Scotch. All right, don't let it rattle you, he told himself. You've got plenty of resources if this gets out of hand. Plenty of people who can handle someone like that. Walter already seems to be figuring out how to deal with him. Too bad that thug didn't go after Crane. He's the one who started this mess.

No, thought Milstein. Sanchez would have made it clear to whoever he was that he should go to the top. Although the guy did seem smart enough to figure that out for himself.

Milstein drained his glass and headed back to the kitchen. He looked at an indecipherable lump of food under plastic wrap inside the microwave.

'I'll be goddamned if I eat that crap.'

He went back to the front hallway, got his coat, and set out to have a sit-down dinner and another Scotch. And think about exactly what he was going to tell Leonard Markov.

8

Even though Ciro Baldassare filled a good portion of the Mercury Marauder's backseat, a passing pedestrian would be unlikely to notice him because he never moved. If Ciro did catch someone's attention, they tended to look away quickly. He was that kind of guy.

Demarco Jones had parked the Mercury in the empty curbside space between the two ends of the half-circle driveway that led to and from the entrance of Milstein's Park Avenue apartment building. Next to him in the passenger seat, Beck rummaged around in the glove box and pulled out a fake NYPD detective badge on a chain. He slipped the chain over his head and tucked the badge under his shirt.

He told Demarco and Ciro, 'Sit tight. Let me see if I can arrange a visit with Mr Milstein.'

The doorman stepped out to greet Beck before he had walked halfway along the driveway. He was a short, slight man, red-haired, boyish. A wide smile dominated his face. His doorman's hat tilted back on his head, he seemed happy to see Beck even though he had never seen Beck in his life.

'Hello,' said the doorman. 'Can I help you?'

Beck didn't smile back. 'Yeah, I want to ask you a few questions.' Beck pulled his detective badge out from under his shirt and held it up for a brief inspection, then let the badge remain on display hanging from his neck. 'My name is Logan. I'm a detective with the nineteenth precinct.'

'Oh, okay,' said the doorman, still smiling. He saluted Beck. 'What can I do for you?'

'What's your name?'

'Owen.'

'Owen. So Owen, we got a report earlier tonight, a complaint from uh . . .' Beck pulled a scrap of paper out of his back pocket. It was the receipt from their dinner. He checked it. '. . . somebody named Frederick Milstein. We were hoping to talk to him tonight.'

'Oh, Mr Milstein just went out.'

'Really?'

'Yep.'

'You know where?'

Still smiling, Owen answered, 'No. I think he went out to eat.'

'Any idea when he'll be back?'

'Well, I'm pretty sure he'll be back by around ten.'

'Oh yeah, why's that?'

'That's when he walks the dog,' said Owen, still smiling.

'He walks his dog around ten?'

'Yes, sir. Most of our people have dog walkers. But Simpson on twelve and Milstein on fourteen, they take their dogs out for the night walk. Milstein likes to have a cigar at night, so that's why he does it.' Owen smiled and laughed. 'I don't think he likes the dog all that much. But his wife won't let him smoke in the house, so the night walk works out for him.'

'Where does he go?'

'Straight from here into the park, then over to Dog Hill.'

'Dog Hill? Where's that?'

'Just a little south of the Seventy-ninth Street entrance.'

'He doesn't mind walking around in the park at night?'

Owen laughed and said, 'Oh, it's not a problem. The dog is huge, and he goes with his driver. Big guy. Ex-cop.'

'I see. That sounds pretty good.' Beck shoved his badge back under his shirt. 'All right, don't bother telling him I was here. Don't make him wonder about it. We'll follow up tomorrow. My shift is going off.'

'Sure,' said Owen, still smiling, as if smiling were part of his job.

Beck looked Owen in the eye and pointed back and forth with his index finger. 'Just between us for now. Got it?'

For once Owen's smile vanished. 'Got it.'

Beck walked back along the driveway and climbed into the Mercury, checked his watch.

'What's the plan?' asked Ciro from the backseat.

'Oh, something for everybody. D gets to be the big scary black man. You get to be the guy with the gun. But you have to promise not to shoot or hit anyone unless I say so.'

'Promise,' said Ciro, 'unless someone deserves it. Who do you get to be?'

'I haven't quite decided yet. Let's find a parking spot around here somewhere. We got a little time to kill while I figure this out.'

9

At ten-fifteen, Beck slipped into the passenger seat of the Mercury parked on Fifth Avenue just past Seventy-eighth Street, Demarco at the wheel, Ciro sitting motionless in the backseat.

Beck used the palm of his hand like he was about to diagram a touch-football play.

'So, the asshole is sitting on a bench, right about here, opposite an open field. He let his hound off the leash to go take a shit somewhere while he smokes a cigar. The bodyguard is sitting on a bench on the other side of the pathway facing him.'

Beck quickly explained his plan.

Milstein sat hunched against the cold February night, puffing on a Montecristo Double Corona, watching the dark open space in front of him, completely uninterested in anything his dog might be doing.

They weren't far into the park, but other than the ambient light from Fifth Avenue, the only illumination came from decorative street lamps spaced along the park pathway that meandered from the Seventy-ninth Street entrance to where Milstein sat, just at the edge of a pool of light facing Dog Hill.

He and Walter heard someone approaching from the north. Both men turned in the direction of the sound.

Walter slipped his police-issue Glock 17 out of his hip holster, laying the semiautomatic pistol on top of his thigh, ready just in case.

The figure came into view. A tall black man wearing a hooded sweatshirt that covered much of his face. He came toward them slowly, giving them the feeling that he was checking them out as much as they were him.

Shit, thought Milstein, this is all I need. But the sight of Walter watching the black man every step of the way with his gun at the ready made Milstein almost giddy.

The hooded man came nearly parallel to them. He seemed to be looking mostly at Milstein, who straightened up, ready to get up and break away if the man made any move toward him. But the menacing black man just kept walking, hands stuffed in the pockets of his sweatshirt. Walter's head swiveled to keep his eyes on the intruder as he passed them by.

Milstein watched, too, as Demarco Jones continued walking slowly south. Neither of them saw where Ciro Baldassare came from. He'd been standing in the dark, out in the field behind Walter. All he had to do was step out and take a seat next to the big bodyguard while Walter had his head turned watching Demarco Jones walk off around the bend on the park pathway.

Walter never even heard Ciro sit next to him, but when he turned from watching Demarco, Ciro's Smith & Wesson .45 automatic was an inch from his face. The gun looked huge.

'Don't move, fella,' said Ciro. 'Not even a twitch.'

Ciro deftly slipped the Glock out of Walter's hand, slid down the bench a bit, rested his right arm on the back of the bench, and pointed the muzzle of the Smith & Wesson at Walter's face.

Milstein hadn't seen where Ciro had come from either, but he saw him now, pointing a very large gun at Walter, saying nothing, not moving, completely calm as if this was something he did all the time.

And then the last piece of Beck's plan fell into place as he stepped out from the darkness behind Milstein, and sat down next to the small man.

Milstein reared back. 'Jeezus Christ, you again.'

'Yes, me again,' said Beck. 'And trust me, Mr Milstein, you do not want to see me a third time, so let's finish our conversation. How about we take a little walk?'

Milstein looked over at Walter and then back at Beck.

'I know,' said Beck. 'How the fuck did this just happen? Don't worry about it. You'll both be all right if neither of you does anything stupid. Come on.'

Beck grabbed a handful of Milstein's coat and lifted him to his feet. Any thought of resisting vanished when he realized whoever this was, he had enough strength to lift him with one arm.

Beck pointed down the path toward the model boat basin, and released Milstein with a slight push in that direction. They arrived at a bench around a bend where the bodyguard couldn't see them or hear them. Beck indicated that Milstein should sit. He settled in next to him, close enough to make Milstein uncomfortable.

'So,' said Beck. 'Olivia Sanchez.'

Milstein puffed on his cigar, grimaced, annoyed, shot back, 'What about her? What is it with you and Olivia Sanchez?'

There was a pause before Beck reacted. Just about two seconds before he backhanded the cigar out of Milstein's mouth and grabbed Milstein by the side of his neck. Beck pressed his right thumb into Milstein's throat.

He spoke very quietly, very intensely. 'Are you fucking crazy? You think you can use that tone with me? You want to end up in that boat basin with your throat crushed?'

Beck squeezed Milstein's windpipe. He stood up off the bench and faced Milstein. Milstein grabbed Beck's wrist and forearm with both hands, trying to pull Beck's hand off his neck and throat. It only made Beck squeeze harder.

Just as blackness was about to envelope Milstein, Beck released him. He stood in front of Milstein, waiting for him to come around.

As Milstein's head cleared, Beck leaned closer and said to him, 'I don't know what it is with assholes like you. You think because you have some money nobody will fuck with you? Or is it because you're such a little shit you think somebody would be embarrassed to beat the hell out of you? Have you lost all sense of reality?'

Milstein rasped air into his lungs.

Beck slapped his cheek, gently, more to focus his attention. 'Answer me.'

'No. No, I haven't lost sense of reality.'

Beck spoke quietly now. 'So you understand if you don't answer my questions, you won't leave this park alive. Nor will your pathetic bodyguard. Do you understand?'

'Yes.'

Beck sat down next to Milstein and asked quietly, 'I hope you don't have any doubts about what I just said?'

Milstein paused. 'No.' But as he answered he was thinking furiously about what to do.

'Good,' said Beck. 'Let's start again. Olivia Sanchez.'

Milstein cleared his throat, thinking before he said anything. 'I'm listening.'

'Tell me what you're going to do about this idiot who works for you breaking her fingers, tossing her out of a job, and blackballing her from any other employment.'

Milstein cleared his throat again, hesitating. Beck asked, 'Well?'

'That's not . . .'

Beck interrupted him. 'You're not going to tell me that's not what happened are you?'

'All I can tell you is that's her side of it. There's another side.'

'Which is?'

Milstein spoke very carefully. 'She has made claims against one of my partners, Alan Crane. Crane has his own side of the story. He says he confronted her. She got hysterical. She attacked him. He grabbed her hand and twisted it away so she couldn't hit him.

'He says he can't believe he broke her fingers. But the point is, Crane says he was defending himself. She's trying to bring charges against him. He's already talked to the police. He says she's lying. She says he's lying. So now it's with the lawyers. His lawyers. And the firm's lawyers, who are very clear about this. They've told me to have no further contact with her.'

'What about with Crane?'

'What do you mean?'

'Have your lawyers told you not to have any contact with him?'

'No. But we've all been instructed not to discuss the case.'

'That's your answer?'

Milstein looked quickly at Beck, who sat next to him, staring straight ahead.

He didn't know what to say, so he continued to look at Beck. They sat far from one of the park lamp lights, but the sky was cloudless and the moon bright enough to cast shadows from the trees around them and illuminate Beck's rough features.

Beck breathed in the cold night air, calming himself, keeping his anger in check. He inhaled the rather pleasant scent of the cigar still burning on the ground near the bench where it had landed.

Milstein finally said, 'I don't understand the question.'

'You'll talk to Crane, but you won't talk to Olivia Sanchez.'

'Yes.'

'Why? They both work for you. Why Crane and not her?'

'Well . . .'

'We both know why. Crane makes more money for you.'

'That's not the only reason. She's the one making accusations.'

'Crane is the one waging lawsuits.'

'Look,' said Milstein, 'I've known Alan Crane for years. He's not the calmest person. He's under a lot of pressure. He admits he confronted her. He admits he gave her hell;

he admits it got out of hand. But he says she attacked him. Tried to slap him and hit him. I've never had any reason to believe Alan would do something like attack a woman. So what am I supposed to do? Olivia has her story. Crane has his.'

'I see,' said Beck. 'But she ends up in an emergency room with two broken fingers. And the asshole who did it gets her fired and blackballed. How's that figure?'

Milstein grimaced, looked away from Beck at the empty model boat pond in front of him.

'I understand what you are saying. Either way, I repeat, what am I supposed to do about it?'

Beck turned to Milstein and stared at him. Milstein started to speak, but Beck interrupted him. 'You asked me a question.' Milstein started to speak again, but Beck held up a hand. 'Now I'm going to give you the answer. Listen very carefully.'

Milstein closed his mouth.

'Here's what you're supposed to do. First, you pay her a severance of two months current salary for every year she worked. How long did she work for you?'

'What?'

Beck turned to Milstein and just stared at him again until he answered.

'I don't know how long she's worked for us. I can't remember.'

'Eleven years. That's twenty-two months.'

'She never worked eleven years.'

'I thought you didn't know.'

'I know it wasn't eleven years.'

'All right, nine. Eighteen months salary.'

Milstein grimaced. How had this thug outwitted him? They both knew she worked for him for a little more than seven years.

'Plus all her hospital bills. And if that fucking asshole Crane even thinks about suing her, it's on you. Lawyers' fees, court costs, whatever.'

Milstein stared straight ahead, not saying a word. How the fuck did this guy think he would go for this nonsense? But if he didn't play along, how the hell was he going to get out of the park in one piece?

Beck pushed. 'Agreed?'

After a short pause, Milstein said, 'Yes.'

'Then there's pain and suffering. She has very nice hands, Mr Milstein. One of them is disfigured now. There's arthritis looming in her future. Fingers are never the same after a break like that. Physical therapy can only do so much.'

Milstein tensed. How far was this maniac going to push this?

'I'll be reasonable,' Beck said. 'Two hundred thousand.'

'What!?'

Beck didn't hesitate. 'Two hundred and fifty thousand.'

'Hold it, hold it, whoever you are, I can't agree to . . .'

'Three hundred thousand. Keep fucking talking and it will be a million, or I swear I will break your neck and throw you in that boat pond. And I will shoot that lummox who's supposed to guard you so there's no witness.'

Milstein forced himself to shut up.

Beck repeated, 'Three hundred thousand for her pain.'

Milstein couldn't speak. He forced himself to nod.

'How much did she make last year. Including bonus. Don't lie about it. You know I'll verify it.'

Milstein grimaced. 'Her salary is one-hundred eighty thousand. And a fifty thousand bonus if memory serves me right.'

'That's nineteen and change a month. So make it twenty even, times eighteen months that's three hundred sixty thousand. Plus the three hundred pain and suffering. Six hundred and sixty thousand. Christ, that's nothing for a firm like yours. Make it in one payment. After you get done writing that check, you are going to pick up a phone and start calling people until you get her a new job. An equivalent job. This shit about Crane blackballing her is over. Now.'

Milstein didn't say a word.

'And remember what I said about Crane trying to sue her.'

Milstein nodded again.

Beck forced him to speak.

'Agreed?'

'Yes.'

'Get this done. Fast. End it now, before it gets too far out of hand. There are people upset about this you do not want coming after you, Mr Milstein. Trust me, they will kill you. And Alan Crane. Do not for one second think you can walk out of here and renege on this deal. You messenger a check to her tomorrow, or I fucking guarantee you, you will suffer much more than broken fingers. Do you understand?'

It was at that moment that Frederick Milstein realized he might actually have to come up with over six hundred thousand dollars to end this problem.

Beck sensed he was thinking it through, realizing that this was not a ridiculous price to pay. But Milstein hesitated. Beck was not sure why.

Finally, Milstein said, 'All right. I'll figure out the money. It might take me more than one day to pull together that amount. But if it does, I'll wire the money to her day after tomorrow. That's as soon as a check in that amount would clear.'

Beck considered Milstein's answer. 'I'll give you one day.'

'And I'll make some phone calls. It shouldn't be too difficult to get Olivia placed. It just might take some time.'

'How much time?'

'A couple of weeks or so.'

'Don't let it be any longer than that.'

'All right. But there's just so much I can do.'

'What does that mean?'

'I can't guarantee what Alan Crane will do. I can't sit here and tell you I can control him. I can't make sure he'll stand down and drop this.'

Beck turned to Milstein. 'Why not?'

'I just can't. I'd be lying to you if I said I could.'

Beck turned to Milstein. 'No, you wouldn't want to lie to me, would you?'

'No. I wouldn't.'

'Tell me where I can find him.'

'What are you going to say to him?'

'Stop asking me questions.'

'You might want to hear his side of the story.'

'Yeah. And I might not. Where do I find this prick who hits women? Tomorrow. At noon. Where will he be?'

Milstein recited an address on Hubert Street in Tribeca and a cell phone number. Beck wrote the information on the back of his receipt from the burger place he and Ciro and Demarco had eaten dinner.

'Make sure he doesn't duck me.'

'I'll tell him you're coming.' Milstein paused a moment and then politely said, 'Can I ask you something?'

'What?'

'What are you going to do to Alan Crane?'

'I don't know,' said Beck.

'Well, all I'll say is that he's important to my firm.'

'I don't care,' said Beck.

'But if he convinces you he didn't do what he's been accused of, don't you think he should be . . . ?'

Beck interrupted Milstein. 'Where's your dog?'

Milstein turned to Beck, surprised at the question. He motioned with his head back up the path where they had come from. 'He's over on Dog Hill. I let him off the leash this time of night.'

'How big a dog is he?'

'Big. Over a hundred pounds.'

'Who picks up his shit? Dog that size must drop at least a couple of pounds every time he squats.'

Milstein frowned. 'Nobody walks out there in the winter.'

'That's your answer?'

Milstein remained silent.

'You know, assholes like you and Crane actually think that because it's in the dark and no one sees it, you can do whatever you want. Dump your dog shit wherever you want. Fuck around with your in-house

94

hedge fund. Scream and yell at a woman and break her fingers.'

Milstein stared straight ahead, trying not to move, trying not to shiver in the cold night air.

'Is it dawning on you, Mr Milstein, that this particular case is different?'

After a few moments, Milstein answered, 'Yes.'

'You figure money will settle this?'

'It's what I have.'

'No, there's lots more you have. Lot's more.'

Milstein spoke slowly. 'You don't need to threaten me any further.'

'Threaten you? That time has long past, Mr Milstein.'

Milstein had no response to that.

'Tell Mr Crane I'm coming at noon to see him. Tell him this is the right thing to do. Tell him to make sure and be at the address you gave me. You know what happens to people who try to avoid talking to me, right?'

'Who should I say is coming to talk to him?'

'Tell him Mr Smith and tell him why.'

Beck stood up and turned toward Milstein, who remained seated. 'Have you got a cell phone?'

'Yes.' Milstein rummaged around in the pocket of his down coat and pulled out an iPhone.

'Just the one?'

'Yes.'

Beck took the phone from him and put it in his pocket. 'Let's go see how your driver is doing.'

They started walking back to the first bench.

'I didn't hear any gunshots, so he should be available if you want to cry on his shoulder.'

When they arrived back where Milstein had been sitting, Beck pointed to the bench. Milstein sat. He walked over to Ciro and Walter. He asked the bodyguard, 'Got a phone?'

He handed Beck an old clamshell-style phone.

'So, your name is Walter, right? That's what your boss over there called you.'

'Yes. Walter. Walter Pearce.'

'Well, Walter, I'll tell you what. You've been cooperative this time. Not throwing punches at people. I'm going to walk back over to Seventy-ninth. Tell your asshole boss to get his dog, take a few minutes, then you two can go home. If I don't hear any yelling or bullshit, I'll put your gun and phones in the trash basket near the exit on Fifth. Okay?'

Pearce nodded.

Ciro handed Walter's Glock to Beck. Beck pointed the gun at Walter as Ciro stood up and joined Beck on the path. Both men turned together and walked into the darkness beyond the lamp light. As they walked, Beck took out the magazine from the Glock and made sure there was no bullet in the chamber.

By the time they were out of sight, they heard Milstein yelling for his dog. Two minutes later, Beck dumped the cell phones and Walter's empty gun into the park's wire wastebasket.

Two minutes after that, they were back in the Mercury heading for Red Hook.

10

Neither Milstein nor Walter Pearce said a word as they walked out of Central Park. Walter lumbered along next to Milstein, silent, expressionless. Twice now he had been rendered useless. Once was bad enough. The fact that it happened again after he should have been on the alert, made Walter even more worried.

He ignored the seething Milstein and tried to sort out the questions running through his mind. How had they found out about Milstein's nightly dog walk? How had the leader pulled together a crew so quickly? Who was he working for? Who had the juice or the connections to send someone like that after Milstein? He knew there had been some trouble between one of Milstein's female employees and his man Crane. But would some woman corporate type be able to pull together people like that? No way. So then who was behind this?

Walter couldn't get rid of the image of that man pointing the big Smith & Wesson at him. He knew without any doubt that whoever he was, he would have pulled the trigger without hesitation. The barrel of that gun never wavered. He didn't say or do anything after the first threat. He displayed absolutely no nervousness. None.

Walter had been so worried he might make a wrong move that he finally had to turn away and look down at the ground.

And the indignity of losing his gun so easily. Walter didn't know which was worse: losing the gun, or the pity they'd shown him by giving it back.

The whole thing had happened so fast. The time between the two incidents was only a matter of hours. Things moved so much more slowly when he was a cop. A case could take days, weeks. Worse, Walter was accustomed to failing without suffering too many consequences. Nothing much happened if you failed to solve a crime. But not with this situation.

Part of him wanted to get as far away from Milstein as possible, as fast as he could. Part of him wanted to redeem himself. Had to redeem himself.

Walter had been smart enough to plan a life after the NYPD. He'd seen so many cops talk big about cutting loose from all the bureaucratic bullshit. Crow about how they'd go work for a private security outfit or go out on their own. And then months later, Walter would see them sitting in a cop bar, drunker than ever, getting fatter and angrier than ever, heading toward a future of wet-brain irrelevance.

So Walter had made efforts to stay in the game. He'd arranged the job with Milstein even before he drew his last check from the NYPD. He'd refused to be unemployed. To be irrelevant. But it wasn't supposed to involve hard men and a gun in his face.

As they approached Madison Avenue, Milstein broke the silence.

'I'm beginning to wonder what the hell I pay you for.'

This was his chance, thought Pearce. Tell him you agree. Cut loose from this prick. Nothing good will come of this. But then what?

'I understand your frustration. But I still think without me it would have been worse. And not to excuse anything, but I don't see anyone else who could have done much; one guy against three of them.'

'Three?'

'That first one walking past us had to be with them. To distract me. Us. While we were watching him, the other two slipped into position.'

'He left. So it was two, not three. And only one with you.'

'The third guy was out of sight, but I guarantee he wasn't gone. Look, Mr Milstein, I don't want to argue with you. If you don't want me around on this, fine. But I'll tell you, this is serious. This is not just one man. He has a crew. And they are good at what they do.'

Milstein frowned as he listened to Walter. 'What do you suggest?'

'What did he say to you?'

Milstein thought carefully before he answered. The light changed on Madison. They headed across, a cold wind suddenly gusting into them as they reached the middle of the avenue.

'I think he's going to turn his attention elsewhere for now.'

Walter responded, 'I'm not sure I know what that means. There must have been more than that. You don't have to tell me, of course.'

'It's complicated. But we came to an agreement.'

'So you think it's possible he's done bothering you?'

'Perhaps. But I definitely want to know who that man is. Do you have any way of finding out?'

Walter saw a chance to earn back some of the status he had lost. 'Absolutely. And I intend to find out as soon as I can.'

'How? How soon can you find out?'

'I can start with the one who had the gun on me. He had a neck tattoo that I could just make out under the collar of his coat.'

'What was it?'

'The number thirteen. Tattoos are very good leads for identifying someone. Hopefully, I find him, he'll lead me to the other one.'

'That's the one I want to know about.'

'You should know about both of them. But you realize I'm going to have to work through a contact on the police force. Unless you want to bring this to the police now. Which might be smart.'

Milstein had no intention of calling in the police.

'Look, I don't see the point of bringing in the police. You can find out who those men are quicker than they can, can't you?'

'Yes. Mostly because we don't have to get anybody up to speed on this if I do it. I'm going to start right after I leave you. Best way is to go into the NYPD databases at the Real Time Crime Center. I might be able to make something happen tonight. If not, first thing tomorrow.'

Milstein quickly thought through the issues. The fact that he might know who that man was before noon changed things. Gave him options with Markov, and perhaps leverage with Crane. But Pearce couldn't know anything about that.

'Okay, do it as fast as you can. Call and leave me a

message on my cell if I don't pick up. Whenever you have something. I don't care what time. By mid-morning, latest. Don't worry about driving me tomorrow. Just keep on this until you find out who those men are.'

They had reached the front of Milstein's building.

'Okay. Good night,' said Milstein abruptly as he turned off the sidewalk and headed for his lobby.

Walter continued east.

Halfway to the lobby door, Milstein unhooked the dog. Owen, the smiling red-haired doorman opened the door and Tam romped into the lobby. Milstein followed hunched over, softly rubbing the front of his neck where Beck had squeezed his windpipe. He checked his watch. Time to call Markov back. This was going to be a much different phone call than five hours ago.

II

Milstein's wife had arrived home while he was out walking the dog. She generally kept her distance from him when he returned because she disliked the smell of cigar smoke that lingered on his clothes and his breath.

Milstein heard her in the bathroom down the hall near their bedroom. The dog hurried on into the bedroom, clearly preferring the company of Milstein's wife.

He checked his watch and continued into the living room, pulled out another disposable cell phone from the desk drawer, and hit the speed dial. He sat down in the plush upholstered chair near the window overlooking Seventy-ninth Street, still wearing his down coat, keeping it on to dispel the chill that seemed to have seeped into his bones.

Leonid Markov answered on the second ring, 'Yes?'

'Leonard, it's Frederick. We have a problem.'

Markov was riding in a 1989 S-Class Mercedes, driven by his regular driver, Vitaly. It was nearing midnight, but Markov was wide awake, heading toward an apartment building he owned in the Brighton Beach area of Brooklyn.

He had cleaned himself, showering and soaping in the hotel bathroom, soaking under a hot shower for nearly a half hour, still enjoying the effects of the drugs and alcohol. He used every last towel, even the hand towels and washcloths; left everything wherever it fell; dressed in one of his custom-made Hong Kong suits, and walked out of the hotel room, leaving it a mess. Not even bothering to check out.

He had rented the room with a stolen credit card, bought from a website run by underground hackers working somewhere in Ukraine. Even though he wasn't going to be paying for the room, beyond the fifty dollars he spent on the credit card, Markov had still booked the room through an online discount service, and only after having compared prices, entered low bids, and haggled for an upgrade when he arrived at the hotel.

Markov responded to Milstein, 'A problem? Why does nobody call me with solutions instead of problems? You are using the right phone?'

'Yes.'

'What's the problem, and why is it my problem?'

'Leonard, I said *we* have a problem. Not you.'

'Tell me what that means, and don't bullshit me. Is it about my money?'

'No. I mean, indirectly, of course everything is connected, but your money is safe and there are no unexpected losses or anything.'

'What is the problem?'

'Alan Crane got rough with one of my employees . . .'

Markov interrupted. 'Who? What do you mean rough?'

'A woman named Olivia Sanchez.'

'What is she to me?'

'Nothing. At least nothing much. She's on the firm's oversight committee. So, she did watch over your holdings. To a certain extent.'

'Did?'

'She's no longer with us.'

'So what's the goddamn problem? Was Alan fucking her? Why did he get rough with her? Why should I give a shit?'

'I doubt he was fucking her. Maybe he was, everyone else around the place wanted to, but I doubt it. He got rough with her because she was making noise about some of his methods.'

Markov watched the dark waters of the East River flow past on his left as the car moved downtown on the FDR. He realized that he had to listen to this. He had to concentrate. His internal alarms were going off. Someone was trying to prevent the man who was supposed to make him money from doing what he wanted to do. This could cost him.

'Okay, Freddy, tell me exactly what's going on. Exactly.'

'This woman, Olivia Sanchez, she was . . . part of her job was to make sure all the firm's investments are . . .' – Milstein paused, thinking of exactly how he wanted to put it – '. . . are within the regulatory parameters.'

'What? What does that word mean, *parameters*? Tell me without bullshit terms.'

'Her job was to make sure anyone trading or investing for the firm wasn't doing anything illegal. Or at least anything that would attract too much attention from the regulators. And as you know, sometimes Alan's methods push the line a bit. Sometimes more than a little bit.'

'What did she do?'

'Nothing crazy. Just poking her nose in. Maybe looking to make a name for herself. Use her job to get some leverage. It's what people do. But Alan heard about it and went overboard. Way overboard.'

'Overboard? What's overboard? You're supposed to watch that fucking guy.'

Milstein told it in one burst of words. 'She claims he got rough with her and broke two fingers on her hand while he was yelling and pounding on her desk.'

Markov barked, 'What?'

Milstein repeated everything he'd said more slowly.

'He does that to a woman? Idiot.'

'Alan says it's not true. Says she started hitting him, and he fended her off. Says he can't believe that would break her fingers. Says it's bullshit. Either way, she tried to make a lot of trouble for us. Went to the police. Filed complaints. So we had to push back. We countersued. Lodged our own complaints. Came down on her very hard. Got rid of her.'

'So if you got rid of her why are you calling me?'

'Somehow she's managed to get some strong-arm types to confront me and demand compensation.'

'What do you mean strong arm?'

'Tough guys. With guns.'

'What the hell are you talking about, Freddy?'

'Three men surrounded me and my bodyguard in the park tonight. One man held a gun on my guard. The other one roughed me up. He told me if I didn't pay off this woman, he would kill me. And Alan.'

Markov did not respond for a moment. And then he said, 'You believed him?'

'Yes.'

'How much did he ask for?'

'Six hundred thousand.'

Markov spoke slowly and carefully. 'You think the six hundred thousand makes this all go away?'

'I don't know. Actually, the way he came up with the number was fairly logical.'

Markov said, 'Who are these men with guns? How does this woman know them?'

'I'm looking into that. I'll know more in the morning.'

'How?'

'My bodyguard is an ex-police detective. He says he can identify them with police records. As for the woman, clearly there might be something in her background I wasn't aware of.'

'Like what?'

'She's Hispanic. I think originally from the Bronx or East Harlem, I don't know. It appears that she might know people who are not all that legitimate. From her past, I suppose. She seems to have turned to them for help.'

'I think it is time to say good-bye to you, and Summit. Why should I have my investments anywhere around men with guns demanding money?'

'I completely understand, Leonard. You can certainly go someplace else. But I'm afraid that won't solve much. Your man Alan caused this. You can walk away from my firm, but unfortunately, as long as you are connected to Alan, I'm afraid you're connected to this problem. I'm trying to protect your investments, Leonard. We have to stop these men one way or another.'

'Then I walk away from both of you.'

'Unfortunately, that would cost you a great deal of money. I hope you understand that nobody can unwind your investments like Alan can. He's the only one who knows how everything is set up. What the time frames are. Look, Leonard, maybe we can buy our way out of this. Not you. Me. The firm. Pay off this woman and be done with this. Let me find out more about who these people are. If worse comes to worst, I have connections to the police. They can help us.'

Markov immediately broke in. 'Be careful about calling in the police.'

'Of course. But why don't we take this step by step. I'll find out more about these men threatening us. You talk to Alan. Tell him if this deal seems like it will work, he should accept it. And drop his lawsuits against this woman. If it comes to it, maybe you can exert pressure on these people to take the money and back off.'

Markov's driver was just exiting from the Brooklyn Bridge heading south on the BQE. The remaining effect of the Adderall had helped to keep Markov focused as he listened. He checked his sense of what Milstein had told him. There was a great deal he didn't know or understand, but he knew whatever was going on, he had to protect his money.

'Three men?'

'Yes.'

'With guns?'

'I only saw one with a gun.'

'One guy who comes to you with the deal?'

'Yes.'

'He didn't beat on you or break anything?'

'No. But he did enough to make me believe he could do worse.'

'He sounded calm?'

'Yes.'

'Professional?'

'Yes.'

'And you don't know how this woman knows this kind of person?'

'No. He seems to have appeared from nowhere. But she's the kind of woman who could get a lot of men to try to help her.'

'Why?'

'She's very attractive.'

Markov grunted. 'All right,' he said abruptly. 'How can I find this guy?'

'I told him that I can come up with the money, but that I couldn't guarantee Alan would back off from suing the woman or blackballing her. He asked me where he could find Alan.'

'You tell him where Alan lives?'

'I'm sure he already knew. Olivia Sanchez obviously told him where I live. He told me to tell Alan to be there tomorrow at noon.'

Markov nodded his head. Milstein was clever. Already setting this up.

'Okay. Noon. Let Alan know. Tell him I will be there at eleven thirty. Now go get rid of that phone.'

Without another word, Markov disconnected the call.

Milstein took the silent cell phone from his ear.

He stared at the phone, his mind spinning off in several directions at once. He kept flashing back to the park. He thought about getting a gun permit. About Walter Pearce's ability to find out who those men were. About Markov's ability to stop the men Olivia Sanchez had set against them. He tried to calculate the odds that Markov would leave the firm, and how much it would cost him.

Milstein took a long, deep breath. He closed his eyes, forcing himself to stop thinking. He told himself he had worked out a plan with Markov. Stick to it. Take it step by step. Stay calm.

Suddenly, he felt exhausted. He had been fending everything off until he'd finished the call. Now the tension, the fear, the worry seemed to smother him.

Well, he thought as he pushed himself out of the sitting chair, there is nothing more to do tonight. Except get rid of this fucking phone. He pried opened the back of the cell phone with his fingernail, dug out the SIM chip, went out to the hallway outside his apartment.

He tried to twist the SIM chip and break it as he walked toward the garbage chute at the end of his hall. He couldn't. He couldn't break it. He just opened the garbage chute and tossed the phone and the chip into the disposal, holding the door open, listening as the pieces fell fourteen floors to somewhere.

12

'So maybe you cut off this *coño's* head and put it on the other motherfucker's desk, and both of them get the message,' said Manny.

Beck pictured a severed head on Milstein's desk at Summit Investing, and tried to imagine the effect.

'I suppose that would get everybody's attention. Not sure Olivia would be all that comfortable with it.'

Manny and Beck sat on couches facing each other on the second floor of Beck's Red Hook building. Beck had returned from Central Park a little past midnight.

'She don't have to know the details,' said Manny.

Manny Guzman sat back on the comfortable couch and took another swig of his favorite Mexican beer.

The second floor where they sat was much different from the bar downstairs. Except for shoring up the floor and some rewiring, the first floor had been left as it was when Beck bought the building. But he'd gutted the two floors above the bar down to the bare walls and rafters, then built everything out to his exact specifications.

The second floor was now an open loft space. At the west end were three large comfortable couches surrounding a six-by-five-foot coffee table made of petrified wood, hard as iron, hundreds of years old.

Manny's couch faced the bare brick north wall where a low mahogany credenza had been placed. On top of the credenza sat a fifty-five-inch LCD TV, with a cable box, Blu-Ray DVD player, DVR, speakers, and a few other pieces of equipment Beck didn't really understand or care much about.

An eighteen-by-twenty-foot Oriental rug with blue and cream colors defined the seating area at the west end of the floor. Dark red velvet drapes covered a long set of double-paned windows at that end of the loft, lending warmth and privacy.

The rest of the space contained a large kitchen, a dining area with a rectangular oak table that could seat fourteen, and finally at the east end of the open space an office area where Beck's custom-made desk sat holding his computer, printer, phones, and two monitors. Behind the desk, papers, books, and files were stored in floor-to-ceiling shelves.

Manny asked, 'You really think this guy is going to come up with that amount of money?'

'Yes.'

Manny made a face. 'If you say so.'

'I'm pretty sure Milstein gets it.'

'But not the other guy?'

'Probably not. Not yet.'

'Which is why you want to go see him.'

'Partly.'

'What's the other part?'

'When was the last time you talked to Olivia?' Beck asked.

'Yesterday. After we talked, I told her you was coming up to see her.'

'You should have warned me.'

''Bout what?'

'Her looks.'

'Easy, amigo, that's my cousin.'

Beck smiled. 'A cousin ain't that close.'

'She is. Maybe the closest I'll ever get to a daughter.'

'I know, I know. I get it.'

Manny took another sip of his Negra Modelo dark beer.

Beck lifted a rocks glass holding three fingers of Jameson, took a long sip and chased it with the same beer. Beck set his drink on the table and leaned forward. 'Manny, the point I'm trying to make – her effect on men is another reason I want to see Crane.'

'What do you mean?'

'Guy does violence like that to a woman like Olivia, it's crazy. I want to know what kind of crazy I'm dealing with.'

'What do you mean? You think she had something going with this guy Crane?'

Beck shook his head. 'Not exactly. I got the feeling she was very careful about how she deals with men in her professional life. But maybe Crane had some shit in his head about her. Maybe this started with more than just her getting into his business. I won't know until I see him.'

Manny nodded, thinking it over. 'So you think this is something about Olivia rejecting this guy?'

Beck could see Manny's anger rising, but he didn't downplay it.

'Maybe. Maybe it's part of it. Maybe not. Either way, I don't want this asshole to think he can continue having anything to do with your cousin. No lawsuits. No blackballing. Nothing. And if he's got some bullshit fantasy about her in his head, it stops. He stops even thinking about her. Not even in his dreams.'

Manny nodded, agreeing. He was silent for a few moments, and then he asked, 'How's some Wall Street fuck get the stones to do any of this shit?'

'It's a good question. I asked Olivia.'

'What did she say?'

'She said the guy's a bit crazy to begin with. Wired up tight because there's a lot of money at stake. Enough to make him reckless. Also, turns out he runs money for some arms dealer. Olivia doesn't know much about him other than he's got connections and isn't exactly legit. She thinks Crane is riding on his coattails. Tough guy by association.'

'An arms dealer? What the fuck is that? What's that mean? Who is this guy? What's he got going for him?'

'I don't know. And frankly, I'd rather not turn over that rock. Let Crane and Milstein worry about their client. My guess is they'll keep their mouths shut about this and pay the money to make this problem go away. Milstein gets it. Now I just want to make sure Mr Crane understands he shouldn't make the mistake of wearing someone else's balls, or try to get in the way of this severance deal for Olivia.'

Manny nodded. 'It's either that, or just fucking kill him now and be done with it.'

Beck shook his head. 'No. Killing him now isn't the right move. Too much chance it will rebound onto Olivia.'

'I bet she'd stand up.'

'Maybe. But what's the point? We get rid of one problem and create an even worse problem for her. Your cousin is a civilian. What she wants is her life back. She gets associated with a murder, no one on Wall Street will come within a mile of her. Plus, we'll have cops and investigators and parole assholes crawling all over you. It's almost certain you'd go back inside until we beat it.'

'Comes to that, I can deal with it.'

'It's not an option.'

Manny made a face, and said, 'Okay. We'll go talk to this prick. Take care of it.'

'Not we. Not yet. Me.'

'You already told me he might be hooked up with some people.'

Beck shrugged. 'I'll make sure Crane gets the message to unhook himself.'

'Then bring Ciro with you.'

'Come on, Manny, Crane is no hard guy. His boss has already gotten a taste of Ciro. Probably already told Crane to stop fucking around. Let me seal the deal and be done with this.'

Manny finished his beer and set the bottle on the coffee table. He stared at Beck with his baleful eyes and said, 'James, I know you always figure shit out five, six different ways, three, four steps ahead. So much I don't even bother trying to track it. But just make sure this motherfucker don't cause Olivia any more problems. Because if he does, he will be chopped up into little pieces and be so fucking gone there won't be nothing left. Not a fucking cry, or a word, or a whisper. Nothing.'

'I know, Manny.'

Guzman shook his head. 'He should already be dead.' He pointed a finger at Beck. 'And don't make any mistake,

James. These high-and-mighty assholes with more money than they can count, they think they have all the power. They look at us like cockroaches. Fucking ignorant ex-cons. They think they can snap their fingers and the system comes down on us and we're gone. Garbage taken out. Like we're nothing. You think you can change that?'

'No. But so what. I only have to convince two assholes this is in their best interests. Olivia gets paid. Puts her life back together, and when the time is right, we do what we have to do. Or not. That's all I'm saying.'

Manny nodded imperceptibly, frowning his agreement.

'You usually don't have trouble being patient, Manny.'

Manny shifted on the couch. 'This feels different.'

'You want something to do, call Olivia.'

'Why?'

'I have to run this deal past her, obviously. I can't see her not taking it. But she should hear it from me, with you in the room. So she knows you agree.'

'All right.'

'Plus, I'm going to brace this Crane asshole at noon. Maybe she can tell me something more about him. The more I know when I walk in there, the better.'

'Okay.'

Beck paused. 'And as long as she's here, talk to her about this arms dealer. How it works. Where he makes his money. His operation. Maybe we get Alex to do some research on him.'

Manny tipped his head and squinted an eye at Beck.

Beck said, 'What?'

Beck watched the wheels turn in Manny's head. He was happy the old con was seeing it now.

Beck nodded, acknowledging that Manny had figured it out. He said, 'I don't like doing something for nothing. I will if I have to, because this involves one of yours, Manny, but . . . you know.'

Manny smiled. 'Okay, James, you keep thinking. Just don't get too cute with this. You know where I'm headed. Down the line, like you say, but that's where this is going.'

13

Milstein lay wide awake next to his softly snoring wife. But it wasn't her snoring that had awakened him. A dream or a half-awake memory of his cigar being slapped out of his mouth jerked him awake.

He laid immobile in his bed, his heart pounding so hard he had trouble breathing. When the beating subsided, he rolled over halfway to look at the glowing digits of his clock radio. 3:14 a.m.

Milstein kept seeing the face of the man who called himself Mr Smith, feeling the hand around the back of his neck and the thumb on his throat, remembering the strength that nearly lifted him off the bench. Milstein wasn't a big man, but he still weighed 155 pounds. How many men could lift that much one-handed? Whoever the man was, he didn't look that big, but clearly he was strong. And he had a cocky invulnerability about him. Who the hell was that son of a bitch?

Milstein tried to get back to sleep. He might have dozed off a bit, but deep sleep evaded him. He finally sat up and swung his feet onto the floor. The clock read 4:32 a.m. He ran a hand through his thinning gray hair. His right hip ached. His bladder was full.

He stood up in his undershirt and boxers. The bedroom was cold. He picked up the cell phone from the night table. He stepped into his slippers, lifted his robe up off the floor and shuffled off to the bathroom.

This was going to be a grind, getting through a day without enough sleep.

Just as he was about to empty enough of his bladder to feel comfortable, his cell phone began vibrating in the pocket of his robe.

'Fuck.' He pulled out the phone. Walter Pearce's number displayed on the caller ID.

'Hang on,' he said.

Walter Pearce filled one side of a small booth in a twenty-four-hour diner located on Trinity Place in downtown Manhattan, his phone held to his left ear.

The diner was within walking distance of One Police Plaza, where his contact at the Real Time Crime Center had been working the twelve-to-eight shift.

He had been in the diner since 2 a.m. calling back and forth to his contact at One PP. His eyes were stinging, he felt wired from too much coffee, and he felt queasy from a greasy serving of ham and eggs with home fries, followed an hour later by an order of pancakes.

As he waited for Milstein to come back on the phone he switched the phone from his sweaty left ear to his right. Tired of holding it, he put the phone on speaker and set it down on the Formica-topped table.

The work for Walter had gone in two parts.

First, finding a contact to do the research he needed. He had done that from home, calling until he had located a detective he'd worked with four years ago named Edward Ronson. Then he'd headed downtown to meet Ronson and tell him what he needed.

Ronson had made a big deal about it, even though they

both knew he'd either find what Walter asked for in about fifteen or twenty minutes or he wouldn't.

Ronson's main selling point was his availability. Most cops and more than most detectives wouldn't risk screwing around getting information from the NYPD databases and passing it on, even to a licensed private detective who was a former cop.

Ronson, however, always needed money. He had two ex-wives, two sets of children, hefty bar bills, and a habit of midweek gambling sprees at the Yonkers racetrack slot casino.

Walter made sure to tell him three times what he was looking for and to just print out everything he could find and bring it to him.

The problem was, Walter had no idea when Ronson could slip in his search requests, so he just had to wait. And wait.

When the disheveled detective finally walked into the diner, Walter spotted a large manila envelope under his arm. It looked fairly full. A good sign.

Ronson slid into the booth across from Walter, hatless, wearing a worn suit and a wool overcoat that had seen better days. He dropped the envelope on the table and held out his hand under the table.

'Christ, it's a shitty walk over here. Fucking cold enough to freeze dog shit out there. Feels like snow any minute. Come on, I gotta get back.'

Walter ignored Ronson's lack of greeting. He wasn't in the mood for pleasantries anyhow. He tapped a fold of five hundred dollars in twenty dollar bills against Ronson's knee under the table.

Ronson slid out of the booth as soon as he had the money in his hand. Maybe he really did need to get back to his desk at the RTCC. Or maybe he had done a lousy job and wanted to get out of there before Walter had time to check what he'd brought and refuse to pay him.

Ronson hadn't bothered to collate the pages he'd printed out. It took Pearce nearly an hour to sort through everything. When he was satisfied he had something worthwhile, he called Milstein.

Milstein had kept Walter on hold until he had settled in his chair out in the living room.

'Okay,' he said.

'Right,' answered Walter. He picked up the phone, took it off speaker, and spoke directly.

'So I got the information we want. It's pretty much what I expected. Maybe a bit worse.'

'What do you mean, worse?'

'These are bad people, Mr Milstein. The one with the neck tattoo is named Ciro Baldassare. He has a long record. Two incarcerations. He's connected to organized crime. Most of the names I see on his sheets are based in Staten Island. Among other things he's a bone breaker. His last bit was for assault in connection with collecting money. Don't know what kind of debt it was, gambling or loan sharking, but whatever it was wasn't pretty. He broke up two guys pretty bad. Sentence was three to eight. Would have been worse if it hadn't been two against one.'

Milstein interrupted him. 'Okay. Okay.' He didn't want to hear too many details. He already had enough trouble sleeping. 'Anything on the other two?'

'Nothing on the black fellow who passed us. I never got a good enough look at him to describe him. But I got lucky on the one who confronted you at work and took you off in the park. About a year ago, Baldassare got pinched driving a car he didn't own. That same guy was with him, and went through the arrest process with Baldassare. Nothing came of the arrest, but I have the report. The man with Baldassare then is the same one we saw. His name is James Beck. Very interesting story.'

'Meaning?'

'First of all, he's a cop killer.'

A chill went through Milstein that had nothing to do with his cold living room.

'What? A cop killer walking the streets; how's that happen?'

'It's not quite what it sounds like. About ten years ago, Beck got into a fight in a bar in downtown Brooklyn. I know the place. Used to be a lot of cops went in there. It's close to the courts and detention complex. It's the usual mess with cops and booze sometimes. Cop actually got shot in there long time ago, and that pretty much put the place out of bounds for years.'

'Who shot him? This guy?'

'No, no. It was another cop who shot him. I don't remember the details, but somebody's gun went off. Hit a guy in the leg. Drunken accident. Just telling you what kind of place it was. Anyhow, apparently this fellow Beck got into a beef and punched out a cop. Cop hit the floor. Busted his skull in three places. Died three days later.'

'Died?'

'Yep. One punch. Dead.'

'Must have been some punch.'

'A hard punch, a harder floor. It can happen if you land wrong. So Beck gets charged with murder. Gets convicted of first-degree manslaughter. Judge sentences him ten to twenty-five.

'That's hard time. Maximum-security prisons. But Beck appeals. Gets a new lawyer. There's a lot of background on this, bottom line the lawyer appeals based on procedural errors. Cited all kinds of shit, but mainly he found out the prosecutors suppressed a witness. Another cop in the bar who apparently was willing to verify Beck's claim that the other guy started it.

'Takes eight years, but Beck finally gets out. Sues for unlawful incarceration and so on. Settles with the City and State for a little over two million bucks. After that it gets shady. Not much information to be found.'

Milstein closed his eyes, seeing what he was up against. 'Anything else?'

Walter continued. 'My guess is Mister Beck made some nasty friends during those eight years in prison, including Ciro Baldassare. It must have been a really tough stretch. You go into prison labeled a cop killer, life is not going to be easy. On the other hand, he certainly would have had some status with other prisoners. Kind of a good-news, bad-news thing.'

'Okay, Walter. Good work. What are your conclusions?'

Walter Pearce paused before he spoke, gathering his thoughts. He wanted to tell Milstein to get as far away from these people as fast as he could, but he knew it was too late for that.

'Like I said before, Mr Milstein, these fellows are not

your usual bad guys. They're more sophisticated. Certainly Beck is. He's clearly got a lot of enemies in law enforcement after what he pulled off, but he obviously has resources on the other side. I need to find out a hell of a lot more about him. Where'd he come from? What he was doing before he went to prison. Anything I can get on his prison record. But frankly, I don't know that it will make much of a difference.'

Walter paused and then continued. 'There are a lot of questions to answer, Mr Milstein. What's this man's connection to Olivia Sanchez? How does she know Beck? Why did she send him after you? What exactly does she want? And if she gets it, does he go away? Or is it just the beginning of a long extortion that goes on and on until he gets everything he can? For sure, you don't want to go up against this man until you know more about who he has behind him.

'I'm not saying these guys aren't vulnerable. They have prison records. We could get this Baldassare fellow arrested for assault with a deadly weapon. He pulled a gun on me for chrissake. But then what? How many more are behind him?

'As for Beck, did he do any real damage to you? We can get him arrested, too, but proving something might be awful hard.'

Milstein thought about it. Beck hadn't done anything that would show. There were no witnesses. But maybe he could still file a complaint. Have him arrested.

Walter interrupted Milstein's thoughts. 'I'll answer my question. The answer is no. Beck has resources. Access to a good lawyer, for one. And remember, he's in a weird category. As far as the legal system is concerned, he doesn't even have a traffic ticket. He had no criminal record before the bar fight, and the conviction was overturned. Expunged. They paid him damages. It's like the crime never happened. It's like he never served time. You can't even use anything he might have done in prison.'

Milstein looked out at the dark night. Dawn hadn't even begun to lighten the sky.

'Shit.'

Milstein wasn't about to discuss Olivia Sanchez with Walter. What Walter had said was logical. Find out the connection, see what she wanted and all that. None of this was good news, but Walter had no real proof Beck was working for organized crime. Nevertheless, he had to find out more and hope Markov could convince Beck to take the payoff and leave.

'Okay, Walter. That's very helpful.'

'Thanks.'

'I want you to messenger what you have to my building. Leave it at the concierge desk.'

Walter shook his head in dismay. Where the hell did Milstein think he was going to get a messenger at five o'clock in the morning from a diner in downtown Manhattan?

'I'll drop it off myself. Then I'm going home to sleep.'

'Right. Okay. Fine. Listen, after you sleep, I want you to stay on this. See what else you can come up with on Beck. I want to know where he lives, how to find him. Anything else you can find out about his associates. Anything you can uncover.'

'All right,' said Walter. 'I did some preliminary work.

There's no trace of Beck in any of the five boroughs looking through the usual resources. But I haven't done a deep dive. I'm sure I can find him.'

'Good.'

'By the way, there are some expenses I'll want you to cover, Mr Milstein. Cash outlays. I'm not comfortable with waiting until my end-of-the-month bill.'

Milstein automatically wanted to argue about it, but was too tired. 'How much?'

'Five hundred for the cop I hired to go into the department databases. And about seventy-five bucks for cabs I'm taking to get all this done.'

'Five seventy-five. I'll leave an envelope for you with the concierge. When will you be back at this?'

'Sometime after two.'

'Fine.'

Milstein ended the cell phone connection. He looked at his watch. Laid his head back and closed his eyes. No question he had to unleash Markov. Olivia had gone way overboard. She couldn't be allowed to get away with this. Beck had to be handled. Made to forget about threatening anybody, or demanding compensation. But would Markov see this his way?

And it wasn't just Beck. What about that other guy? The ties to organized crime. Christ, that's all I need, thought Milstein. Well, this Beck character seems to be the leader. Take care of him and maybe this mess could be put behind them.

Great, thought Milstein, all this shit and I'll still be left with that maniac Crane. He'll be worse than ever after this.

14

Markov dozed in his car after talking to Milstein. He woke as Vitaly pulled up to an old five-story apartment building on Brighton 4th Street that housed a Russian restaurant on the ground floor.

The south side of the building faced the ocean. The restaurant, however, had no view of the boardwalk. It was blocked by a decrepit one-story structure.

Markov owned several apartments in the building and held a long-term lease on the restaurant. He rented the restaurant space to a Ukrainian family he didn't particularly like, but the family accommodated him whenever he wanted to come downstairs for a meal. Even at six o'clock in the morning when he felt like having blintzes and coffee.

He'd slept a few more hours on the living room couch in one of the apartments he owned, but wasn't occupied at the moment. Now he sat downstairs in the restaurant eating cheese blintzes and slurping black coffee, thinking about the plan he had formed.

Stupid fucking Milstein, thought Markov.

As soon as Milstein had finished telling him about what Crane had done and the trouble the woman was making, he knew what he had to do. He didn't need any more details about who did what to who.

He knew as sure as he knew his heart was beating that

the fucking jackals were always lurking. Watching, circling, ready to tear off a bite for themselves. And another and another until you had nothing left. Now they were getting ready to tear into him and his money.

Alan knew it. He had seen it. Why else go after that woman? This fucking bitch, whoever she was, circling around, trying to make a name for herself, trying to get ahead using my money to do it. To justify her existence. Goddamn selfish cunt.

Crane was right to come down hard on her. To fend her off. But what an idiot, breaking her fingers. There were so many better, easier ways to take care of a nosey bitch before she went out and got some criminals to help her. Markov pictured this damn woman in a business suit mincing around trying to show everybody how smart she was. How diligent. With somebody else's money, the arrogant fucking piece of shit opportunist cunt.

And now this evil bitch gets some mafia, some set of criminals to come after Milstein and Crane and his money.

What? Did Milstein think for a second that criminals live to perform some noble act to save the honor of a woman? Idiot. No, this was an attack on the money. My fucking money. The woman was just an excuse. An opportunity. A way in.

Like all fucking jackals they start with a negotiation. Come at Milstein like it was a business discussion. And Milstein believing it. Negotiating.

Markov shook his head.

There's no negotiation. Not one fucking dime. Not a penny. Negotiate with jackals and you soon have nothing to negotiate.

He shoved another chunk of his cheese blintz into his mouth and slurped from his mug of hot coffee.

And then, just as he was sleeping soundly upstairs, fucking Milstein calls him again, like a big hero with more information about the criminal, James Beck. Who gives a shit? All he had to know was that Beck would be coming to see Crane at noon.

Markov picked up his phone, scrolling to find the first number he would try for Gregor Stepanovich. His call was answered on the third ring.

He gave Gregor Crane's address in Tribeca and told him to be there no later than eleven-thirty. Bring two of his best. He gave him more instructions, making sure Gregor understood what he needed to plan for.

Markov finished his third blintz and drained the coffee. Six forty-five. The clothes he'd slept in were a mess. He knew his armpits stank. He felt as if the residue of the drugs were leaking through his pores. He needed a schvitz. Steam. And fresh clothes.

He went over everything in his mind once more. First, deal with Crane. Teach him some sense. Then, take care of this man Beck, whoever he was. But first, find out everything about the woman from him, and everything about who he was and who was with him. Markov wasn't sure if he needed to kill him. Maybe hurt him enough to teach him a good lesson. Gregor was good at that. Gregor could spend all day and all night hurting someone and never tire of it. Never get sickened by it. Gregor would extract whatever information he needed from Mr James Beck.

After that, the woman. He'd heard she was good-looking. He'd see about that. See about enjoying the beautiful woman before he ended her life. Fucking miserable bitch starting all this trouble. Who did she think she was? He'd let Gregor in on that. He'd never seen Gregor rape a woman, but he'd heard Stepanovich and his men talking about it. They talked about it like they used their cocks as weapons. It was more than just sexual. Much more. How many had they done that to in Bosnia? Markov was sure it was many. As many as they could.

He thought about what they would do to her as he picked the residue of the blintz from his back teeth. But then decided no, just get rid of her. Cleaner. He knew Gregor stopped being normal in Bosnia during the atrocities. Unleashing Gregor into certain activities was dangerous. He could become uncontrollable, like a mad dog junkie on drugs.

Markov pushed back from the table. He started planning how to refresh and revive himself. He wanted to be sharp for this day. There was much he needed to get done. In addition to this mess with Crane, he had two shipments that had to be taken care of by nine or ten o'clock tonight.

Okay, Markov told himself, step by step. He relished figuring out each single step in a plan, and then executing everything in a precise sequence.

First, call his driver, Vitaly. Then, back up to the apartment. Fill a garment bag with fresh clothes. He even pictured each piece of clothing. Blue shirt. Gray slacks. Brown jacket. Earth tones to go nicely with the blue. Then, his jewelry. Watch, ring, gold neck chain. Gold to set off the blue shirt. Socks, shoes, underwear. He pictured each piece. All of it custom-made to fit his large, flabby body. And a camel hair overcoat. Everything top of the line. Cut to make him look prosperous and respect-able.

He'd have to make sure to stay far enough away so no blood spattered on him.

Beck sat in the Mercury Marauder, engine running, heat on, parked facing south at a fire hydrant on the corner of Greenwich and Hubert streets. This gave him a clear view of Alan Crane's loft building a half-block west on Hubert.

He'd been sitting there since just before eleven, sipping a coffee now gone cold, listening to 1010 WINS, the New York twenty-four-hour news station.

Crane's building appeared to be a typical renovated Tribeca loft building: six stories, not including the ground floor, arched windows, recently sandblasted brick. There was a commercial space on the ground floor empty at the moment.

He'd scoped out the building before finding his parking spot. Next to the entrance doors a stainless steel panel was set into the wall. On the panel were nameplates, buzzers, and a fish-eye camera lens. The front entrance opened onto a locked foyer with an identical panel, nameplates, buzzers, and another camera. Crane's outside nameplate was labeled PH TOP FLOOR.

This was a secure building. The tenants most likely controlled access to their floors from their own apartments, for even more security.

From his vantage point on Greenwich, Beck watched people enter and leave the building.

A mother, or more likely a nanny, backed out the

entrance pulling a stroller; a twentysomething man dressed in black jeans, a sport coat, a long red scarf, and a porkpie hat came out and shoved on a pair of sunglasses. A woman bundled against the cold in a red woolen coat emerged and immediately looked for a cab. She kept walking and looking until she flagged one steps from where Beck sat.

Shortly after the nanny exited, an old Mercedes S-class pulled up to Crane's building. Beck figured the car for an eighty-six or -seven. Its pearl black finish gleamed in the sun. The car appeared to be in perfect shape. The man inside had to push himself out of the backseat with both arms. He was short, wide, wore no hat or gloves. A stubble of gray hair covered his round head. He wore a voluminous camel hair overcoat big enough to hide what Beck estimated to be about 250 pounds of bulk. He pushed a button on the outside panel and was promptly buzzed in.

Next, a cab pulled up on Greenwich kitty-corner from Beck. A tall man talking on a cell phone got out. He was bald, carrying a gym bag, wearing black sneakers, jeans, and a black leather coat. Beck figured him for a personal trainer. He hit a buzzer and was quickly given entrance to Crane's building.

Beck checked his watch. Eleven thirty-two. The trainer was late for his eleven-thirty appointment.

Five minutes later, the woman with the baby and stroller returned. A bag of groceries hung from the arm of the stroller. She let herself in with a plastic key card she waved in front of the nameplate panel.

A few minutes later, a FreshDirect food truck pulled up in front of the building; blocking Beck's view. A deliveryman got out of the truck and hauled out a bin of food.

Beck fired up the Mercury and drove around to the parking garage just north of Hubert. He hadn't seen anything that piqued his interest or set off any alarms.

Beck had tried to get more information about Crane's hedge fund from Olivia before he'd left Red Hook, but she hadn't had much to add. Then again, after they'd agreed on what Beck had negotiated with Milstein, they hadn't had much time to talk about anything else. She'd shown up later than he had hoped, but he wasn't surprised. Most people had a hard time finding his place.

Beck thought about whether or not he should have told Milstein to come to this meeting. Get everybody involved to agree. No, he thought. Milstein might get in the way or waffle in the presence of his head trader. Better to be alone with Alan Crane. Take his measure. Let him know the deal was already set. See if there was any defiance in him, and beat it out of him without any witnesses.

It would have been better to find out more about Crane, but what was there to find out? This was a Wall Street guy, who maybe had delusions because he thought his client had connections. Let's see how tough he is after a fist in the face. Or maybe after a few broken fingers. Fuck it, thought Beck. Time to find out where this is going.

16

They had put Alan Crane in a chair at the end of his beautiful cherrywood dining room table. Then they had firmly duct-taped his left arm to the table.

Markov watched while his man Gregor Stepanovich used yard after yard of tape, wrapping it all the way around the end of the rectangular table.

Crane hadn't put up any resistance. He knew enough to avoid getting punched and kicked into submission. But as the tape wound around and around, more tightly securing his arm to the table, he tried to get some reaction from Markov.

'What are you doing, Leonard?'

'Be quiet and listen.'

Stepanovich's gym bag sat on the dining room table. When he finished with the duct tape, he dropped the remaining roll in the bag and took out a 32-ounce ball peen hammer. The head was high carbon steel. The handle fiberglass. A well-made, nearly indestructible tool about to be used as a weapon.

Crane had never seen a ball peen hammer that large. Stepanovich sat down on the other side of the table, hammer in hand, staring at Alan Crane.

Crane worked out four times a week with a personal trainer. He was scrupulous about what he ate. Took care of his skin. Got regular massages and the occasional facial. He visited his personal physician regularly. He cared for and pampered himself, was proud of his body, and the thought of that hammer being used on any part of it made him feel like he might lose control of his bowels.

He still couldn't believe that Markov was going to do anything more than threaten him, but looking at Stepanovich he wasn't so sure. Stepanovich leered at him as he slowly massaged the round end of the hammer in the palm of his left hand, as if he were deriving sexual pleasure from it. Crane could see him imagining and plotting out the damage he would do with the hammer.

What the fuck were these two planning? Was this going to be some sort of sick lesson because of Olivia Sanchez? He'd gotten Milstein's voice mail, but hadn't bothered to call him back. What was going on?

Crane started to sweat. He turned again to Markov, who sat at the head of the table. He started to speak, but Markov interrupted him.

'Open your hand,' he said to Crane.

'Leonard, what are you doing? This is crazy. Why are you . . . ?'

Markov suddenly screamed at him, 'Open your fucking hand flat on the table.'

Crane spread his left hand flat, but immediately started talking again.

'Leonard, hear me out. You owe me at least a minute to tell my side.'

Markov got up, walked around the dining table, grabbed the hammer from Gregor and smashed the round end onto the solid cherrywood, an inch from Crane's hand.

Crane recoiled, gritting his teeth. There was an ugly dent in his precious table.

To his credit, Crane did not yell or scream, or struggle against the duct tape. He closed his eyes, calming himself. Gathering his resolve. Telling himself this wasn't going to happen. He was too valuable to Markov.

Markov pulled out a dining chair and shoved it next to Crane. He sat, and without warning he slapped Crane across the face, hard. Harder than Crane had ever been hit in his life. The stinging pain made his eyes tear up. He squeezed them shut. Steeling himself.

Markov dropped the hammer on the table, not caring that he put another dent in the flawless cherrywood.

Stepanovich quickly picked up the hammer.

Markov leaned closer to Crane.

'Listen to me now.'

Crane, through clenched teeth, said, 'I never touched her.'

Markov answered. 'I don't fucking care. It's too late. You went after her. She accuses you. She alerts police. District attorney office. She calls in criminals. They make threats. They extort compensation. I should fucking kill you, but you know I can't. You know I need you to get me my money.'

'Leonard . . .'

'I said for you to listen to me. Then you talk.'

Crane pursed his lips, forcing himself to remain quiet.

Markov continued. 'First, you close out all my positions. You start transferring my money, in cash, to my accounts in Cayman. Understand?'

Crane said, 'No. I don't understand. What criminals? Are you talking about this guy supposedly coming at noon? What happened? And do you understand what you're asking me to do? If I close out your positions now, you'll lose money. A lot of money.'

'No. You know how to do it. You make sure any losses are small.'

'I can do that. I can. But I need time. And if you let your maniac hit me with that hammer, how much do you think I'll be able to work?'

Markov patted Crane on the cheek. 'You can work with your right hand. You make me money in the past. You going to make me more. But you have to learn a lesson here, Alan. You let things get out of hand. I don't know what is going on, but I know someone comes to Milstein and demands money. You think I should leave my money where it is? Where some criminals can try to extort it?'

'I'm not letting Milstein take one penny of your money. Nobody is going to extort money from your funds.'

Markov shook his head, looking at Crane like he was making a huge, unfortunate mistake.

Crane immediately backpedaled. 'No, no. You're right. I understand. You don't want to be anywhere near this. I understand. I'm sorry. If I'm the reason for this trouble, I'm sorry. I went overboard with that woman. But I never thought . . .'

'That's the problem, Alan. You don't think. But after today, you will.'

Markov looked at his watch.

'This fucking criminal she sets on us is coming here to talk to you.' Markov checked his watch. 'Fifteen minutes.'

Crane heard the elevator open, and thought it might be the man Markov was talking about, but it was Gregor's men. Two of them. Markov watched them enter the apartment and motioned them over.

He turned back to Crane. 'Listen to me. He comes here. I tell him there is no money in this for him, or this woman. Not a fucking dime. Not a penny. I tell him I never want to see him, or hear from him again. Or from the woman.'

Crane nodded.

Markov raised a finger. 'I watch him. I see if he understands me. Then, I ask him who is behind him. I ask him questions. If he doesn't answer me or if we think he is lying, then we tape him to the table and Gregor takes the hammer to him. And you watch and see what we do. Not just a hand. Gregor breaks as many bones as I need: hand, arm, knees, face. Every part of him until I learn who he is. Who is behind him.'

Crane swallowed and listened.

'Then, when I know everything, I have Gregor put a bullet through his head.' Markov put a fat finger on the top of Crane's head, pointing down. 'Gregor has figured out to shoot down this way, so the bullet doesn't come out of the head and make a mess. We chop him up and put him in garbage bags and take him out of here. And you, you clean up the mess, and you get me my money. And maybe, maybe if I see you have right attitude, I let you clean up with both hands.'

Crane nodded. This was a fucking nightmare. This had gone somewhere he couldn't believe. Why had he had anything to do with Olivia Sanchez? He was beginning to wish he had never seen her.

And then the buzzer from the street pierced the silence.

17

As Beck pressed the buzzer for Crane's apartment, he thought he saw a change in the fish-eye lens set into the panel, as if the camera were focusing on him. He expected a voice to ask his name or something, but he heard nothing other than an electronic click that released both the front door and the inside lobby door.

As he waited for the elevator, he slipped his Bucheimer sap into the back pocket of his black jeans, unbuttoned his shearling coat, rolled his neck.

Beck had been in a few of these loft apartments, so he wasn't totally surprised that the elevator opened directly into the apartment rather than into a common hallway. That small bit of knowledge saved his life.

Because he expected to be entering directly into the loft apartment, Beck had his head up ready to see what was inside.

It took him less than two seconds to see everything:

The tall bald guy Beck had thought was a personal trainer, pointing a gun at him.

Behind the gunman, two others.

To his left, a large open kitchen, granite counters, gleaming appliances, bright white overhead accent lighting.

To his right, a living room/dining area. A man whose left arm was taped to the dining table, and the fat guy from the Mercedes splayed on a couch.

Beck saw all of it, but didn't process any of it. Didn't

analyze. Maybe somewhere in the back of his mind he realized the tall guy had positioned himself near the elevator so the gun would be pointed right at his face, terrorizing him, intimidating him. But the man had made two mistakes. First, Beck wasn't at all intimidated. And second, he was way too close to Beck.

Beck went for the gun, fast. Springing forward, both hands rising up, left hand slapping the inside of the gunman's right wrist, right hand grabbing the barrel of the automatic, lifting it, twisting it out of the shooter's hand. Then he pivoted, slammed the back of his head into the gunman's face, stunning him, pulling away, taking the gun with him.

Beck never stopped moving. He turned spinning into a crouch, bringing the gun up in a two-hand grip, finger on the trigger, pulling the trigger back past the safety pull, firing at the first body closing in on him.

Two shots. Fast. Deafening. The body coming at him flew back away from Beck.

Beck continued turning to find the third attacker, but he was too late. He slammed into Beck's left side, knocking Beck off his feet, getting his arms around Beck, locking onto him.

Beck held onto the gun, a Glock, managed to twist to his right in midair, just before he landed. He hit the floor sideways, crashing down on the arm of his attacker. Beck heard a grunt, but the grip around him didn't break.

The bald one was already back on his feet, his nose bleeding, a small cut just over his right eye. He had a weird grin on his face, as if he were both pleased and surprised that this had turned into a fight.

He ran three steps to where Beck was trapped on the floor and launched a fast sweeping sidekick at Beck's hands.

The instep of his foot caught Beck's wrist. The Glock flew across the floor, skidding and spinning toward the living room area of the loft.

Christ, thought Beck. He came right at the gun. Never hesitated.

The tall one reversed the circle of his kick and aimed his heel at Beck's solar plexus.

Beck managed to twist right, pulling the left elbow of the attacker over to block the bald guy's stomp kick – which hit the elbow of the man holding Beck – a blow so hard that Beck felt the impact. The man under him grunted in pain. The bear hug around him loosened, but he still held on.

Beck's legs were free, so he pistoned a kick at the bald attacker's shins, grabbed the middle finger of the man holding on to him, pulled it back until the finger broke with a crack. The man under him finally let go.

Beck rolled to his feet, turned toward the tall one, shaking his right hand, trying to dispel the stinging pain from the kick that had sent the Glock flying.

He crouched over and backed away.

Gregor Stepanovich, nodding and grinning even more now, spread his long arms wide as if to both welcome Beck and corral him.

Stepanovich slid one step toward Beck, forcing Beck to step back, herding him toward the wall behind him.

Stepanovich was patient. No rush. He pictured his first move once he had Beck positioned. Fist to his face, hard so that the head would bang into the wall, stunning him enough so that he could grab the head and slam it into the wall, hard and fast, again and again until he heard the sound of the skull cracking. He pictured the blood on the wall, the feel of the back of a human head turning to pulp.

Beck kept his eye on the bald one, but also on the man who had grabbed him in the bear hug. He'd managed to get up and began closing in on Beck's left. He held his right hand open, unable to close it into a fist because of the finger Beck had broken. He also bent his left arm back and forth, still numb from Stepanovich's heel kick landing on his elbow.

The two of them worked together, forcing Beck backward.

The taller one smiled at Beck, as if to say, checkmate. Two against one. It's over.

Beck took a long, slow breath. Off to his right, he could hear the man he'd shot struggling for breaths in painful gasps, but he didn't dare look over at him.

Everything had slowed down. Nobody in a hurry now. Gregor and his partner would get this done, but carefully.

As Beck stepped back another pace, the man he'd shot came into view, lying in a fetal position, a pool of blood forming underneath him. Nobody paid him any attention. They were intent on finishing this.

Another step back. On his left, Beck's peripheral vision caught sight of an open space, desk, expensive exercise equipment. To his right, he saw the man with his arm duct-taped to a large rectangular dining room table. A ball peen hammer on the table. Was that Crane? Had to be. What the hell was going on?

'Come on, Gregor,' the man on the couch snarled. 'End it.'

Gregor didn't respond to Markov, but the command reminded him that he had to take this one down alive. He watched Beck carefully. He saw that there was no fear in his face. He had survived this far. Clearly this required caution. Maim him first, thought Gregor. Get him down on the floor. Beat him. Break his radius bone or the ulna, or both, grind them together, then he will talk. He will beg.

They had Beck backed up almost to the wall. Stepanovich reached behind his back and pulled out an expandable steel baton from his rear pocket. He extended it with a quick snap, giving himself sixteen more inches of reach. At the same time, his partner pulled out a combat switchblade knife, razor sharp with a serrated edge on top.

Beck had to constantly look right and left to keep them both in sight. No wonder they were taking their time. Not just two against one. Two with weapons against one without. Or at least that's what they thought.

Beck knew when they moved, they would move at the same time. He had to choose one, the moment he ran out of room. The choice was easy. The steel snap baton would be brutal. But the knife could be deadly. Beck had seen too many knife wounds in prison. It only took a second to stab a hole into a liver or heart, or slash through a tendon or major artery.

Another slow step back. He could sense the wall looming behind him. He reached behind him, touching a shelf or a windowsill, his hand felt something. A book. Too light to do any major damage, but enough. Without hesitating he whipped it into the face of the one with the knife. At the same time, he pulled the sap out of his back pocket, took three fast steps and slid on the polished wood floor toward the knife wielder.

Beck nearly skidded past the man, but at the last second, just after the knife blade passed inches over his head, Beck jackknifed into a sitting position and whipped the Bucheimer into the side of the knife man's left knee.

The collateral ligament ruptured, the right side of his femur shattered, and the fibula cracked three inches from its top. The knife wielder fell to the side as his leg collapsed. He toppled across Beck's torso, blocking the first baton blow coming from Gregor, but still managed to stab his knife down, slicing through the outside of Beck's left thigh and burying the point an inch into the wood floor.

The wound stung and burned deep. Beck slapped the Bucheimer into the knife wielder's face, causing an explosion of pain. The lead weight cracked the supraorbital bone above his right eye, crushed the lacrimal bone, and split the nasal bone, knocking the man out cold.

Beck shoved the man off him and tried to roll away from the baton blows whipping down on him, but his pant leg was pinned to the floor by the knife.

Beck caught stinging blows on the shoulder, left arm, his back. Without his heavy shearling coat the baton would have broken bones.

Beck blindly whipped the sap sideways at Gregor, connecting with his right shin. That stopped the blows from the baton. Beck finally pulled away from the knife pinning his pants down, ripping the thick denim to get free. He scrambled to his feet. Gregor had gone down on one knee, but now he was up and limping toward Beck.

Beck backpedaled, slipping on blood.

Gregor kept coming. Beck overhanded the Bucheimer at Gregor, hoping to catch him in the face or head with the lead weighted end.

Gregor just managed to duck under the spinning sap. It flew past him and hit the frame of a window, cracking the thermal pane.

The fat man at the other end of the loft finally managed to push himself up off the couch, looking around for the Glock that had been kicked in his direction.

Gregor slashed the baton at Beck's head. Beck leaned back, barely avoiding getting whipped in the face by the steel tip, and immediately lunged forward, catching Gregor's arm before he started a backhand slash. He punched hard under Gregor's armpit. The blow cracked into a bundle of nerves at the top of Gregor's rib cage, paralyzing his baton arm, but Gregor retaliated with a hard left fist to Beck's ear.

The blow caused instant, searing pain. Beck saw black for a moment, but the pain fueled him. He punched hard into Gregor's ribs. Once, twice. Gregor dropped the baton, but managed to grabbed Beck's coat with both hands, immobilizing him. He lifted a knee aimed at Beck's ribs.

Beck twisted and caught the knee on his hip, countering but paying the price in pain. Gregor drove Beck backward, trying to trap him against the elevator.

Beck chopped both arms down to break Gregor's grip,

145

but only managed to break free from one hand. He twisted an elbow into Gregor's jaw, tried to push Gregor off, but Gregor hung onto Beck's coat with his left hand. Beck twisted around and slapped the elevator button behind him, turned back to punch Gregor in the face, and hit him a perfect shot in the temple which nearly cracked three knuckles on his bare fist.

Gregor sagged, but still hung on to Beck's coat.

The elevator door started to open. A gunshot suddenly exploded, followed by a sharp splat of metal on metal as the bullet hit the slowly opening elevator door.

Beck flinched and ducked.

He thought he heard the fat man yell, 'Stop!'

The elevator door opened. Beck grabbed Gregor's right hand with both of his, turned the hand back, twisting Gregor's wrist until his grip broke, then Beck pushed the hand straight down, bringing Gregor to his knees.

He jammed a foot into Gregor's chest and shoved him away, sending him down onto the floor. Gregor still tried to grab for Beck's leg, almost catching his foot as Beck fell back. Two more shots sounded. The elevator doors started to slide shut.

Beck pulled his legs into the cab, barely clearing the closing door. He slammed his palm onto the elevator buttons, not caring which floor it took him to, just trying to get the damn elevator moving.

The door shut, another shot rang out, the fat man yelled something, the elevator descended.

18

Gregor was on his feet banging the side of his fist against the elevator, cursing, screaming, hitting the call button. Markov finally reached him, wrapped both arms around Gregor's right arm and pulled him back.

'Stop. Stop it!'

Gregor could have easily put Markov down, but he let Markov pull him away from the door.

Markov cursed. 'Christ, you with the fucking guns all the time.'

Gregor turned to Markov, testing his jaw where Beck had elbowed him, rotating his arm to get the feeling back. He walked slowly away from Markov, limping because of Beck's sap hitting his shin.

'A gun in the face stops any resistance.'

'Except this time,' said Markov.

'Who is he? Why did he come up here ready for us?'

'Ready for you?' said Markov. 'How? He had no gun. Comes alone. Now he's fucking gone. Idiot!'

For a moment, Gregor looked as if he might go for Markov. The Russian saw it in his eyes and yelled at him.

'Gregor, calm down. Come, we have to figure out what to do with your men.'

Gregor struggled to contain himself. Clenching his jaw, making guttural sounds, he followed Markov over to the man Beck had shot. He lay in an enormous pool of blood.

They slowly lifted him into a sitting position and propped him against the base of the kitchen counter. The man gritted his teeth and hissed at the pain moving him had caused.

Gregor squatted down and began pulling his shirt up to find the wounds.

Markov muttered a Russian curse as Gregor checked the bullet wounds.

'Fucking guy wasn't even looking. How does he get the gun from you, much less shoot one of you?'

Gregor ignored Markov.

There were two bullet holes, one three inches above the bottom rib on the left side. One two inches below.

Gregor squinted at the wounds. He gently pulled the wounded man forward so he could see his back. The two bullets had exited so close together that the exit holes had merged into one large, ragged wound.

Gregor had seen many bullet wounds. His man wasn't coughing up blood, so he calculated that the bullets hadn't pierced a lung. But there had to be massive damage to his stomach and liver and spleen.

Gregor told Markov, 'We get him to hospital, and they stop the bleeding, he'll live.' But he'd said it only to give the wounded man false hope. He could see a gray pallor coming over him. With the enormous blood loss and traumatic shock, he estimated only a twenty percent chance this soldier from his old brigade would live.

The other soldier had made it up onto one foot, keeping himself up with a hand on a chair. Markov turned to him, 'Can you drive?'

He could not stand on his right leg, his face was lopsided from the fractures under his left eye, which was completely hidden by grotesque swelling, he had only one useable hand, but he nodded at Markov and said, 'For a while. Not too long.'

Markov knew Stepanovich and his men were beyond tough, but it was hard to believe either of the two wounded men could get very far. But that didn't matter. All Markov wanted was for them to get far enough away that they wouldn't be his problem.

'Where's the car?' asked Markov.

'Across the street.'

'Legal?'

'No.'

Markov hoped to God the car hadn't been towed.

'Okay, Gregor will help you down. You drive away from here with your comrade. Don't try to make it to hospital. Go north.' Markov tried to think of a neighborhood where a carjacking might be possible. 'Try to make it into the twenties. Off the highway. There's a project over there. The story is, you and Igor got hijacked at a stoplight. They pulled you out of car and beat you. Igor fought back. They shot him and ran. Blacks. You can't identify anyone. You call nine-one-one. Wait for ambulance. That's it. You don't remember anything else.'

Markov turned to the man who had been shot. There was no point in telling him the story.

Markov turned back to Gregor. 'Can you carry Igor down to the car?'

'Yeah.'

'Wrap a towel around him, so you don't leave blood everywhere. Then bring it back up. We'll leave everything for Alan to clean up.'

Crane turned to yell at Markov, 'For chrissake Leonard, get this fucking tape off me.'

Markov turned to him and suddenly something snapped. He moved quickly to Crane, picked up the thirty-two-ounce hammer, and began smashing it into Crane's precious cherrywood dining table.

He hit the table over and over and over, banging divots and dents into it, all the time yelling, 'Shut up, shut up, fucking shut up.'

Crane kept his head down, trying to cover his face with his right hand so he wouldn't get hit by flying chips of wood. He couldn't look. He had his left hand in a tight fist, steeling himself, hoping the hammer didn't land on him.

Finally, Markov's rage ended. He dropped the hammer on the destroyed wood and muttered a final curse.

He turned away to watch Gregor lift Igor to his feet. He then moved to the third man, who put his good arm around Gregor's shoulder. Stepanovich was strong enough to get them both as far as the elevator door, but Markov saw they might never make it to the car. He would have to go down with them and bring the car to their side of the street.

He shouted for them to wait as he made his way toward the elevator. There was an astounding amount of blood where the fight had taken place. Puddled on the floor, splattered on furniture. Counter stools had been turned over. Books had been knocked off shelves. Chunks of Crane's carefully plastered walls were gouged out from bullet holes.

What the hell had just happened, Markov wondered.

*

The elevator stopped on the ground floor. Beck dug in his coat pocket and found a knit watch cap. He wedged it into the bottom of the elevator door to prevent it from closing, so it couldn't return to Crane's apartment.

He limped out onto Hubert Street, blood squishing in his left shoe. He checked his leg. The pants were torn, exposing a ragged knife wound oozing blood. He tried to calculate how much attention he would attract trying to get the Mercury out of the garage versus the mess he would make in a taxi.

He decided to get the Mercury. Blood all over a cab would attract too much attention.

He walked as quickly as the pain would allow him to the parking garage on Greenwich. Just before he entered, he plastered the loose flap of black denim against the wet knife wound, hoping the cloth would stick. The blood didn't show much on his dark jeans. Maybe the garage attendant wouldn't notice. Unfortunately, Beck saw he was making bloody left footprints on the garage's concrete floor.

He reached the attendant's booth and slipped his ticket under the Lucite barrier. A tired-looking, small Hispanic man time-stamped Beck's ticket, took his money, then came out and hustled off to get Beck's car, too busy to even glance at Beck.

As he waited, Beck called Manny.

'It's me. Your cousin still there?'

'She's just leaving.'

'Don't let her go. Tell her she has to stay.'

Manny knew by Beck's tone not to ask any questions.

'Okay.'

'I'll be there soon.'

Beck hung up. The blows from the steel baton were beginning to hurt now that the adrenaline had burned off. Beck tried to remember where else he had been hit. His right wrist, below the back of his hand. Elbow. Knee. Nothing felt broken, but it was going to be hell getting out of bed for the next week or so.

The Mercury came.

He tipped the garage attendant, who hustled back to his booth.

Beck slid into the driver's seat, furious at how much he had misjudged the situation. Milstein had double-crossed him. And he never envisioned the arms dealer stepping in so quickly with fighters of that caliber. But was he protecting Milstein? No, more likely all he cared about was his money. It looked as if he was about to begin torturing Crane when Beck walked in.

Beck took a quick look at himself in the rearview mirror. There was a red welt forming on his jaw just under his left ear. His hair was disheveled. He was flushed and sweating. But there was no blood or noticeable bruises on his face that would attract undue attention.

He took a deep breath. Ran a hand through his hair. Told himself to take it easy. Use the ride back to calm down, plan what to do. As he drove the Mercury out of the garage and took the right turn that would take him past Alan Crane's block, he thought to himself, man, the next time you get surprised like that . . . you're dead.

19

By the time Beck had reached the Brooklyn Battery Tunnel exit onto Hamilton Avenue, he had called everybody he needed to come to the Red Hook headquarters.

By the time he pulled up in front of the bar, he still hadn't figured out exactly what to say to Olivia.

He double-parked the Mercury next to Ciro Baldassare's Cadillac Escalade.

He limped into the bar. Only Demarco was downstairs, leaning against the back bar, in his usual spot.

Beck tossed the car keys to Demarco and said, 'Put it in the garage, will you D? Sorry, but there's some blood on the front seat and the floor mat. I don't think there's any on the carpet.'

Demarco's eyes widened. He came out from behind the bar, heading for the front door, checking Beck for obvious wounds as he passed him.

'Who's here?' asked Beck.

Demarco paused at the front door. 'Manny and the lady, Ciro and Alex. All upstairs.'

'Okay.'

'And the doctor called. Said he'd be here soon. Said to clean out anything that's bleeding before he gets here.'

'Right.'

Beck's left leg hurt with every step up the back stairs.

He didn't bother to stop on the second floor. He kept

going to the third floor, the drying blood on his left shoe sticking to the wooden stairs with every other step. He didn't stop in his bedroom for clean clothes. He went right into the bathroom to strip off everything, get in the shower, and go to work on himself.

Beck's shower had a tiled ledge big enough to sit on. He sat for ten minutes, letting the hot water wash over him and his knife wound and bruises. He'd taken 800 mgs of ibuprofen and much of the pain and stiffness had begun to ebb.

The first five minutes, he'd just let the shower wash off all the blood. Then he'd turned his left thigh into the spray, letting the water stream into the wound, gritting against the pain.

He'd brought a squeeze bottle of Betadine scrub into the shower. He turned away from the water and covered the wound with the sterilizing scrub, then worked it into the torn skin and muscle. After a minute, he let the shower rinse it away. He did this three times. Then he turned away from the shower water again, picked up another bottle and poured hydrogen peroxide into the wound, watching the liquid bubble and foam.

Beck knew there was no way he could tend to this wound.

By the time he stepped out of the shower, Brandon Wright sat waiting for him in Beck's bedroom. Without a word, he stood up when Beck entered, waited for him to put on fresh shorts and a T-shirt, then led Beck to the large room at the west end of the third floor that served as Beck's workout studio.

Beck lay down on a massage table in a corner of the

large room. Wright said nothing. He just started working. Beck closed his eyes, listening to the sounds of surgical supplies being torn open. A needle being threaded. The quiet hiss of Lidocaine being sprayed on his wound.

He felt the coolness of the numbing spray. He ignored the insistent pricks and pushes and pulls as the doctor began stitching. Beck figured the wound would need at least thirty stitches to close it.

Wright continued to work without comment. Beck endured the silent reproach.

For a moment, Beck thought about saying something to his doctor friend. But instead he continued to think about what he was going to do once he was stitched up.

Wright worked quickly, deftly, but the procedure took nearly twenty minutes. As he finished up bandaging the wound, he finally broke the silence. 'Do you know why I do this for you, James?'

'Because you're a good man.'

'No, because you're a man who helps people nobody else will.'

Beck didn't respond.

'How many men have you and Walter Ferguson and this network of yours helped once they are out of prison?'

Beck didn't answer.

Wright slipped off his latex gloves, dropped them on the floor with the used surgical supplies, and packed his bag. He grimaced a bit in frustration. Started to leave. Stopped. Turned to Beck and said, 'Would telling you to be careful have any effect?'

Again, Beck didn't answer.

20

Gregor Stepanovich stood waiting for the elevator to return to Crane's floor, holding up the bleeding, dying Igor, while Markov held the other man. And waited. And waited.

Finally, he had to lay Igor onto the floor and walk down six flights of stairs to find out what was wrong with the elevator.

When he saw the knit cap Beck had wedged into the elevator door, Stepanovich cursed and pulled it out.

On the ride back up to Crane's apartment, Stepanovich held the knit cap in his hand and pictured punching Beck's face again and again and again until bones broke under the skin and teeth cracked, until skin split and blood flowed.

He kept control of his rage until he and Markov got their wounded men into the car and sent them off, knowing he would most likely never see them again.

As he walked back to Crane's building, Stepanovich vowed to himself that he was going to kill that bastard who had done this to him and his men. Slowly, if he could. Quickly, if he had to. But he would find out who he was and kill him. That was it. Markov's orders no longer mattered.

When they came out of the elevator, the rank metallic odor of putrefying blood and acrid gun smoke filled

Crane's loft. The stench did nothing to improve their moods.

Stepanovich looked over at Crane who sat on his couch, his shirt torn from removing the duct tape, massaging his left shoulder, staring at his ruined fifteen-thousand-dollar dining table.

Markov walked to the couch, pulled out his cell phone, and began dialing.

When Markov finished the call, Gregor asked him, 'Tell me, Leo, who was that fucking balija?'

'Criminal.' Markov answered. He turned to Crane. 'Tell us. What do you know about that son of a bitch?'

'Me? Absolutely nothing. No idea. Ask fucking Olivia Sanchez. Or Milstein. Milstein told him to come here, right? Go ask him.'

Markov held up his cell phone. 'I already ask him. He tells me he finds out this morning that he's a bad guy. Convict. His name is James Beck. He tried to extort money from Milstein for the bitch. I told Milstein to send him up here. Milstein told him he should talk to you. What do you think he does to you, we're not here?'

Crane looked at Markov like he was speaking a foreign language. 'How do I fucking know what he would have done? What did he do to Milstein? Obviously not much. Maybe if your attack dog hadn't stuck a gun in his face he wouldn't have done anything. How much do you want to blame me for, Leonard? All I'm trying to do is protect your investments. And make you money. I haven't done a fucking thing wrong, and you come in here . . .'

Markov snarled, 'Stop being ridiculous, Alan.'

Crane changed the subject.

'Leonard, why are we arguing? I'm on your side. What's going on? Are you really serious about cashing out? You're going to lose a good deal of money.'

'What? You ask me this after a fucking criminal shoots my man? Comes up here to do who knows what? Are you fucking crazy? You think I leave my money with Milstein's business, with this bitch causing trouble? Talking to police? Bringing in convicts? Thugs? You ask me this?'

'All right, all right. Forget it. Whatever you want. You want your money, fine. But if I'm going to do this, I have to start as soon as I can. I have dozens of positions I've got to start moving on. I have index hedges, options that aren't close to being where I expect, currency contracts.'

Markov pointed a thick finger at Crane. 'You don't have time. You get it done. Now. Fast.'

Crane mustered his courage. 'I'll get it done as quickly as I can. But I'm not going to let you get reamed, Leonard. I'll need a few days. You should trust me when I tell you this. How long have we worked together?'

Markov waved a hand and stood up, walking away from the dining area. 'Aaach. What does it matter how long we work together? Three years and two months, and now the jackals come after everything, so what good does it do me?'

'Nobody is going to take your money. And I've made you plenty. Well over forty percent year over year. You know anybody who's even come close to that?'

'Fine.' Markov turned and faced Crane. 'But what about now? Now you bring this shit down on me. Stop talking. Get it done. I have work to do. I have two fucking shipments going out of Albania tonight. I still don't have the right certificates. And now I have this mess. So, do we understand each other?'

Crane had been distracted. He said, 'What?'

Markov pushed himself off the couch and stepped toward Crane. 'Are you not listening to me? Did you say "what"? What? You fucking motherfucker. You answer me like that? Maybe I should have Gregor take his anger out on you for an hour or so, you worthless piece of shit.'

Crane raised a hand. 'Jeezus Christ, Leonard, take it easy. I'm sorry. I'm sorry, I'm trying to figure out . . . Christ, I don't even know what the fuck is going on.'

Stepanovich had moved closer to Crane, drawn to the possibility of violence, hoping Markov would unleash him.

Crane dropped his head and said to Markov, 'I'm sorry this happened. I'll start closing down your positions. What else do you want me to do, Leonard?'

'I need to find the woman. Milstein gave me her home address. You think she might be there?'

'I don't know. Why not?'

'Why not? Because that guy who got away from us will be warning her, that's why. You know anywhere else she might be?'

'I have no idea.'

'Get an idea.'

'Well, I think she has a mother in the Bronx somewhere. I can try to find out.'

'Good. And I need to know the connection between the criminal and the woman. I need to know that by end of day today.'

Crane answered without knowing at all how he could

find that information for Markov. 'I'll get everything I can for you. By end of day.'

What was Markov going to do with Olivia Sanchez? If they hurt, or worse, killed her, that could be a problem. The police had already talked to him about her. About her accusations. As did an assistant district attorney. If something happened to her, he would be a suspect. Not good, he thought. And he wasn't going anywhere until he had unwound Markov's complex portfolio and delivered the proceeds, so he wouldn't be around anyone who could give him an alibi.

Worst of all, the last three months of trading had been bad. Not crazy bad, but his ratio of losers to winners had shifted against him. And he'd chased after his losses. A stupid move. He wasn't out of the game by any means. One, two big hits could bring him within reach. But he needed time to unwind his positions, which he didn't have. He'd already warned Markov he would lose money, but how much of a loss could he incur before his body would be in the pile with everyone else Markov was going after?

Crane realized that Markov and Gregor were still staring at him. He lifted his head and asked, 'Is there anything else, Leonard?'

'Yes.'

'What?'

'Get me my money.'

And with that Markov turned and Gregor Stepanovich followed him out of the loft, leaving the blood and the stench and the mess behind for Alan Crane to clean up.

21

The new stitches in his left leg pulled as Beck walked down the back stairs of his building.

The blows from the steel baton were making his upper back and left shoulder stiffen with pain. The knuckles on both hands throbbed.

But surprisingly, the worst pain was in his right wrist. Whenever he pushed against something that bent back his wrist, like using the handrail as he walked down the stairs, a searing pain shot through his hand, making it nearly impossible to use that hand for five or six seconds. He wondered how long that was going to last. He hadn't bothered to ask the doctor about it.

At Beck's large desk sat a tall man, thin to the point of looking nearly gaunt. He was in his early forties, with unruly black hair, three days' worth of dark beard, wearing glasses in thick black frames that dominated his face. He wore a wrinkled red-and-white-checked shirt that didn't reach his wrists. He sat bent over Beck's keyboard, checking two twenty-four-inch computer monitors, intent on a task Beck didn't bother to guess at.

Beck checked his watch. Two-twenty in the afternoon. The foreign exchange markets were winding down in New York, opening in Europe. Alex Liebowitz was probably checking the price action. He had taken over the management of Beck's portfolio, which meant the management of the finances for all of them.

'Alex.'

Alex Liebowitz looked at Beck over the two monitors and asked, 'What's up?'

'What are you doing?'

'Getting ready to trade currency pairs.'

'Intervals?'

'Fairly long. Between two and fifteen minutes. Although I doubt I'll get confirmation any sooner than two minutes. So let's say five to fifteen.'

'Be careful.'

'Always.'

In the middle of the second floor, Manny and Olivia sat opposite each other at the long rectangular dining table that occupied a good deal of the space opposite the open kitchen.

Past the dining room, at the far end of the floor, Ciro Baldassare sat on one of the couches reading the *New York Post*, his feet up on the coffee table, moving only occasionally to turn a page.

Beck looked at Olivia. Her lustrous dark hair was loosely piled on top of her head, making her look younger than when he'd last seen her. She wore blue jeans, leather sneakers, and a crisp white shirt, everything quite simple.

As he stepped toward Olivia, Beck imagined her walking into a party looking the way she did at that moment, and effortlessly attracting the attention of everyone in the room.

Beck nodded in their direction, pulled out his cell phone, and walked into the kitchen area where he began loading the coffeemaker with one hand while talking on his phone with the other.

He finished his call. Shoved the cell phone in his pocket. Pulled open the double doors on his refrigerator. He was hungry. Actually, he was hungry to the point of feeling deeply depleted. He had expended an immense amount of energy fighting for his life. And he was still burning energy.

From the refrigerator, he pulled out sliced turkey, Jarlsberg cheese, bread, mustard, romaine lettuce, tomatoes. He didn't bother to make a sandwich. He just assembled food on a plate and poured himself a mug of coffee, not bothering with milk or sugar or anything that would soften its taste.

He stood at the counter, his back to everybody, and ate. More refueling than eating. He washed the protein and carbohydrates down with swigs of hot coffee. Nobody in the loft said anything, the silence broken only by the occasional mouse click or keystrokes from Alex, sitting in his own world, staring at computer screens.

Finally, Beck left his food, refilled his coffee mug, and came over to sit with Manny and Olivia.

Manny sat in his infinitely patient way, saying nothing. Olivia took his cue and remained silent.

Without preamble, Beck said to Olivia, 'Do you know a tall guy, bald, looks Eastern European? Name is Gregor.'

She answered, 'No,' without hesitation.

'How about a heavyset man? Maybe five six. Dresses well. Gray hair. Cut to a stubble. He strikes me as Russian, but who knows, could be Ukrainian, Turkish, probably been in America for a while?'

'No. Why?'

Beck stared at her for a moment. It felt like she had answered too fast. And he didn't like that she'd answered his question with a question.

'Okay, let's go a little slower here. Listen to me carefully. The people I just described were in Crane's loft waiting to kill me when I arrived.'

The word *kill* startled Olivia. It certainly caught the attention of Manny and Ciro. There was no perceptible reaction, but their focus intensified.

Beck continued. 'It would be very reckless and very stupid if you didn't understand that you are next on their list.'

Beck waited for a response from Olivia. She stammered, 'I, I don't know what you mean. What do you mean? What happened?'

Beck paused. Concentrated on being precise. 'When I arrived, there were the men I described, plus two others. The heavyset man was in charge. I'm assuming that was Markov. The other three were fighters. Probably ex-military. Lean. In shape. My impression is they were Eastern European. Slavic. The tall, bald guy was their leader. He was very fast, without any fear, and able to take an enormous amount of punishment. The other two also took a great deal of damage, and none of them quit. Men like that are very dangerous and very rare.'

Beck paused, watching Olivia, carefully gauging her reaction.

'They were, what? You say they were waiting for you?'

'Yes.'

'What about Crane, was he there?'

'Yes, but forget about him for now. What I'm trying to tell you is that if they tried to kill me, we have to assume they'll try to kill you, too. Two of the three are too damaged to come after you. But don't think for a minute that there aren't more ready to take their places. Are you listening?'

Olivia seemed frozen in her seat, her brow furrowed in concentration. Beck and Manny were on the same side of the table, so Beck couldn't see him, but he knew that Manny would be watching Olivia as carefully as he was, and at the same time watching him to make sure he didn't go too hard at his cousin.

Olivia answered, 'Yes. Of course.'

'Good. So, I'll ask this a different way. What is Markov's connection to men like that? Does Crane know? What's going on?'

Beck continued to carefully watch Olivia. She sat quietly, pursing her lips slightly, looking down.

Beck saw that Ciro had put down the paper and was also waiting, listening. Ciro was like Manny. Generally extremely calm and contained. But unlike Manny, when Ciro Baldassare moved, there was no going back. There was nothing between static and full blast. If Ciro suddenly went after Olivia, nothing was going to stop him. Not Manny, not Beck, not anything or anybody within ten miles of Red Hook.

Beck also caught the motion of Manny crossing his arms. He could feel the tensions rising.

Finally, Olivia spoke. 'I told you before that the kind of people who have money invested with Crane were ... were not legitimate.'

Beck interrupted her. He did not want her to go off somewhere she could hide out. He wanted the truth. He spoke slowly and quietly.

'Let me repeat back what you told me when we first met. Or, at least my impression. You described the people who would invest with Crane as unscrupulous, as people who wouldn't give a shit about Crane manipulating the market in order to bring down investments he's shorted. You didn't say they were killers.'

'I didn't know that.'

Beck leaned forward. 'But you told me that Crane threatened to kill you. You described it word for word. I couldn't see how some hedge fund asshole would be capable of actually following through on a threat like that. So when I pressed you on it, you told me about Markov and about him being an arms dealer. I got the feeling Crane knew Markov had men who would be capable of killing. Do you know anything about these people? We need to know, because now we have a much bigger problem than Crane and Milstein and your job. These people with Markov, they will kill you in a fucking heartbeat, Olivia. Who are they?'

'All right.' She said the words abruptly. In a way so that Beck would stop talking about men who wanted to kill her. 'I don't know. I mean, I don't know who they are exactly.

'I told you yesterday, I've only heard vague references about Markov. I've heard that he is some sort of arms dealer. And yes, he's Russian. And yes, a connection to Eastern Europeans seems possible. But I'm just speculating. Wall Street money managers don't give out information about their clients. I don't know where Markov made his money. Could he have connections to ex-military types? I would think that's possible. Do I know who they are? No. I don't. I know he's not wanted for any felonies. I know there aren't any outstanding IRS cases against him.'

Beck sat back, looked away from Olivia. He exhaled.

She sounded like a fucking lawyer. Maybe that had to do with her corporate background. Or her job as someone who made sure people followed regulations.

Manny shook his head slowly, repeating her name in quiet admonition. 'Ah, Olivia, Olivia.' As if to say, what have you done to us?

'I'm sorry,' she said. 'I didn't know.' She turned to Manny. 'I never wanted to come to you, Manny, but you always told me, if I needed you . . .' Her voice trailed off. 'I didn't know what else to do.'

'All right,' Beck said. 'What's done is done. Right now we need to find out everything we can about these people.'

Olivia leaned forward across the dining table. 'I can help. I can find out.'

'How?'

'I still know everybody at Summit. I'll call people I know and keep asking around. Maybe someone knows more. If I have to, I'll confront Milstein. He might know, even if he keeps Crane's operation at arm's length.'

Beck said, 'Don't call Milstein. You can't have any connection to him whatsoever. None. If we need to get information from him, we'll get it.'

Manny broke in.

'Olivia, listen to James. You don't call anybody, *carina*. We take this from here.' He turned to Beck, 'Time to go after this Crane asshole. Straight up. He knows who these fuckers are. We work on him until we get every last fucking thing we need. Or Milstein.'

Beck answered, 'We will if we have to. Trouble is, it's not going to be all that easy to scoop Crane up. I don't see him being alone now, or maybe even alive much longer. Last I saw him, his arm was taped to a table with the biggest fucking ball peen hammer I've ever seen next to him.'

Olivia looked up at that. She started to ask Beck a question, but stopped.

'What?' asked Beck.

'Why would Markov want to hurt Crane?'

'I assume he blames Crane for setting you off.'

'But he can't . . .'

'Can't what?'

'He can't hurt Crane. Crane runs his investments. He needs him too much.'

'For now.'

'What do you mean?' she asked.

'How long do you think somebody who has as much money as Markov is going to leave it at risk with a brokerage company that let this situation get so out of hand?'

'I don't know. But I know one thing for sure,' she said.

'What?'

'If he wants his money out of Summit there's only one person who can unwind all those trades. Especially if he wants it done quickly.'

'Crane?'

'Absolutely.'

'Okay,' said Beck. 'So Crane is the key right now.' Beck turned to face Manny. 'As for Milstein, I just got off the phone with the Bolo brothers. I told Ricky and Jonas to keep an eye on him. I assume he's at his office. If not, they'll know how to find him. He won't be anywhere we can't get to him if we need to.'

'Okay,' said Manny.

Beck gave Manny a look and said, 'Hey, I know you've been thinking about what guys you might need to do what you were thinking about. You know, before.'

'Uh-huh.'

'Maybe now is the time to reach out. Just to have a little manpower if we need it. No need to bring them in now. Just to have things in place.'

Manny nodded. He stood up without a word and headed for his kitchen downstairs, leaving Olivia and Beck at the dining table.

When Manny was out of earshot, Beck leaned forward, arms on the table.

'Okay, listen to me. You and I are going to sort this out. I don't have time to explain the whys or whatevers behind the things I need to do. Okay?'

Olivia nodded.

'You understand why we said you can't have any contact with Milstein or Crane now, right?'

'I think so.'

'Something happens to either of them, you don't want to be near it. Clear?'

'Yes.'

'All right. Considering what they tried to do to me, keep in mind – without me and Manny and our crew you might very well already be dead.' Beck paused, giving what he said time to sink in. 'When I ask you a question, I need careful answers.'

'Okay.'

Before Beck continued, he looked past Olivia at Ciro. The big man had settled back on the couch, leaving it up

169

to Beck for the moment. Manny was gone, which enabled Beck to talk freely.

Beck looked at Olivia, making sure to put aside enjoying her exquisite face. Or looking at the spaces between the buttons of her white shirt. Or anything that had to do with her being desirable in any way. He looked only at her eyes, looking past the flecks of gold in the deep browns and shades of ocher that gave her eyes their nearly mesmerizing color, hoping to see fear in them.

He began his questions carefully.

'How do Milstein and Crane know each other?'

'As far as I know, just from being in the business. Crane has always had a reputation as a moneymaker, but someone who takes risk. A lot of risk. But risk is what creates reward. Like I said, Milstein needed revenue. Somewhere along the line, I assume Milstein reached out to him. Could have been the other way around, but I'd say Milstein made the deal.'

'So they have no past history together?'

'Not that I'm aware of.'

Christ, thought Beck, she's back to hedging her answers. He decided he'd better get to the heart of it.

'Is Crane making money now? Is he underwater, or in the green?'

'I don't know. He did well last year, but now, honestly, I don't know. The fund managers don't report numbers until they absolutely have to.'

'What happens to Summit if they lose Markov?'

'My opinion, if they lose Markov, the firm might go under. Milstein needs the income Crane's bringing in. He might muddle through. I can't be sure.'

'How long has Crane been running Markov's money?'

'I don't know about before Summit. A little over a year at Summit.'

'So he has to have made money for him in the past. Nobody is going to stick around with somebody who's losing.'

'Absolutely. But like I said, his risk profile is very high.'

'Even if he's pulling all kinds of shit to bring down the value of stocks he's shorting?'

'The market is way bigger than one guy and one hedge fund. A few wrong moves can really hurt.'

'Where's Milstein on this?'

'Hoping the money keeps coming in and Crane doesn't blow up.'

'What about Markov? Does he think Crane can keep this going?'

'My experience is, unscrupulous people like being with someone who is stealing for them. Doing it straight is for suckers. But guys like Markov, they can sense when it's time to pick up their chips and leave.'

Beck nodded.

'You said, you estimated Markov's holdings are over a hundred million.'

'Yes. Although, like I said, I don't see the day-to-day numbers.'

'How's one guy amassed that much?'

Olivia gave Beck a confused look. 'Do you know how many people out there have amassed that much and more?'

'No.'

'Thousands. Tens of thousands. It takes a lot of people

to make up the one percent, Mr Beck. From what I hear, Markov has been at this for a long time.'

Beck changed the subject. 'How much time would Crane need to liquidate everything?'

Olivia frowned and shook her head. 'It all depends. If Markov pressures him to do it fast, it could be within a couple of days. I'm sure Crane is in a bunch of different markets. But I don't know his positions. A lot of his trades are options. He might be underwater, waiting for stocks to gap up, or more likely down. If so, he'll push for more time. It depends on how much Markov pushes to get out. And how much it will cost him.'

'Give me an outside time. Your best guess.'

Olivia looked up, thinking it through, talking out loud. 'I don't know, what's today, Wednesday? Markov doesn't seem like a very patient man. Probably end of the week, Friday latest.'

Beck nodded. Lost in thought for a moment. 'I don't suppose you have any extra clothes with you.'

'No.'

'Did you drive here?'

'Yes. Manny said parking wouldn't be a problem, so I drove.'

'What kind of car do you have?'

'A Porsche SUV.'

'The Cayenne?'

'Yes.'

'You can't go back to your apartment. It's too dangerous. And this place could be as much a target as your apartment. It know it's an expense, but you should check into a hotel for a few days.'

'Really?'

'Yes. Really.'

'Okay. I know a place where I can get a good rate.'

'Where?'

'The Four Seasons on Fifty-seventh.'

'Little close to Summit, don't you think?'

'What difference does it make? It doesn't sound like I'll be going out much. I like the hotel and I have a connection there.'

'You're not using some corporate rate are you? Something that could get back to Milstein.'

Olivia smiled. It was the first time Beck had seen her smile. It was a beautiful smile.

'No, nothing will get back to Milstein. Summit has no connection to that hotel. Out-of-town clients stay wherever they want. I just know one of the managers from going there for lunch a lot. If the hotel isn't full, I'll get a better rate and a better room than I could get anywhere else.'

'Okay, so do you mind if we borrow your car while you're there?'

'Of course not.'

'I would prefer you get out of here sooner rather than later. I'm going to ask Manny to take you to that hotel. Maybe stop somewhere you can buy some clothes. Enough for a few days.'

'All right.'

'And try to be fast about the shopping. Manny doesn't like hanging around anywhere.'

'I understand.'

Beck stood up abruptly and said, 'Okay. I'm sure there's

more that I'll need your help on. This is going to go where it goes. I can rely on you to help us, right?'

'Anything. I got you all into this.'

'Good.'

Beck walked over to the front of the loft where Ciro sat. Olivia headed downstairs to meet with Manny.

'Ciro, we might need some firepower on the home front.'

'Yeah, sounds like it. You want a few of my guys to bunk in?'

'I prefer to keep the psychopaths to a minimum. Manny is talking to some of his people if we need them. So, for now, you should plan to be around here, and how about your cousin Joey? Is he available?'

Ciro pulled out his cell phone.

'I'll find out. How long should we plan on?'

'For now let's say two, three days.'

'So, James . . .'

'What?'

'We're still following the usual playbook, right?'

'Always. The game might be a little different on this one, but yeah.'

Ciro nodded. 'Understood.'

Suddenly, without warning, a voice sounded from out on the street, yelling Beck's name.

One second Ciro was on the couch. The next he was at the second-floor window, his .45 in his hand.

Beck yelled out, 'Easy, Ciro. I know who it is.'

22

Beck parted the heavy curtain just enough to see outside.

He stepped back and told Ciro, 'Take it easy, I got this.'

Willie Reese stood across the street next to a plate glass installer's truck.

Beck parted the curtains and cranked open his casement window.

'Quiet down, Willie. I'm coming. Don't move.'

Willie Reese turned to the man behind the wheel of the van. 'Don't move.'

Beck went downstairs. Manny and Olivia were in the downstairs kitchen. Demarco stood at his usual spot behind the bar. Beck pulled open the front door and motioned Reese inside.

'You got something against knocking?'

'Not on this fuckin' door. Too many damn shotguns on the other side.'

Reese stepped into the bar and stood near the cracked front window. He looked even more frightening than before. His nose was grotesquely swollen, splinted with adhesive tape across his forehead and cheekbones. Both nostrils were filled with gauze. There was an eye patch that Reese had flipped up for the moment, showing the white of his left eye still filled with blood. He wore his usual bad guy clothes, huge arms folded across his chest.

'You're on the case,' said Beck. 'That's good.'

'Yeah, so look here, this guy talkin' mad money for this shit. For a fucking window. But he's sayin' I should ask you if you got insurance.'

'I do.'

'I didn't know nuthin' about that.'

Reese had anticipated some kind of reproach, but instead Beck responded, 'No reason you should know.'

'Yeah, okay. So, how's that work? I mean, can I use it?'

'Yes. Don't worry. You got this far. The rest is easy.'

Beck walked behind the bar and opened a drawer under the old National Cash Register that dominated the back shelf. He pulled out a folder and shuffled through papers until he found the insurance policy issued to the real estate partnership that owned the property. He handed the policy to Reese.

'Take this out to the window man. Have him take the information he needs. It's on the front page there. Then gently persuade him to file the claim, or have his office do it so you don't have to bother with it, and then suggest that he go ahead and replace the window, or wait here for the authorization from his office if he has to, and then replace it. There's a two-hundred-fifty-dollar deductible. That's out of your pocket.'

'What's a deductible?'

Beck liked the fact that Reese wasn't embarrassed to ask about something he didn't know.

'It's the part the insurance doesn't pay. They pay everything after two-fifty.'

'Well, he's sayin' it's a lot more than two-fifty.'

'Thus the need for insurance.'

176

Reese nodded, while he looked at the form. 'Yeah, but hold on. How much you payin' for the insurance?'

Beck turned to Reese, pleased by the question. 'That's the next logical question. But for someone like me, I'm ahead. Stay with your guy until the job is done.'

'Okay.'

'Part of that is so you get it done today and don't have to bother with it, and part is because I want you around.'

'What do you mean?'

'It means you're hired.'

Beck bent back down and pulled open another cabinet under the cash register. He opened a safe built into the wall. He pulled out a stack of hundred dollar bills and counted out ten of them, stood up and turned to Reese.

'Here's a thousand. Normally, that would be pocket money for a month to keep an eye on things. You hit it lucky. That's money for a week, not a month. We might have trouble coming our way. I want you and your boys to be on the lookout. All eyes open.'

As Beck talked, he wrote down cell phone numbers on a bar napkin.

'You see anybody coming through the projects headed this way, you or your guys start calling those three numbers until you get someone. If you get voice mail, hang up and call all three numbers again. If you get nobody, double back and leave messages. You don't stop anybody; you don't jump in unless we talk that over. Just call and give us a heads-up. After this week, the fee goes back to normal.'

'What's normal?'

'Like I said before, a thousand a month. How's your nose feel?'

'Like shit. Can't breathe through all this packing.'

'Yeah, you're going to be a mouth breather for a week or so. But make sure you leave it in. That gauze in there holds the shape of what's healing around it. You take it out, it'll collapse. Keep it in and you'll be breathing better than you have in years once it all heals.'

'So you did me a big favor busting it up.'

'Funny how it works out that way sometimes.' Beck came out from behind the bar, pulling out his cell phone again. 'So I'll leave you to get the window done. Who's going to paint the bottom?'

'Probably me.'

Beck headed back toward the kitchen. 'Flat black. Same height. Straight line. Call me when you get your crew organized.'

Reese called out to stop Beck. 'Hey, what we lookin' for?'

Beck stopped and turned back.

'White guys. Eastern Europeans. Military types. You know, like short hair. In shape. Dressed in clothes that won't slow them down. I don't know what they'd be driving. It may be other types, I don't know. But people who don't look like they belong in the neighborhood. Probably moving in pairs. Maybe three at a time. Okay?'

'Yeah.'

Beck continued to the back of the bar, listening for his call to go through.

Brandon Wright answered without any preamble, 'I see you're still alive.'

'So far. Thanks. I think of you every time I take a step.'

'Leave those stitches alone.'

'I will. I need another favor.'

'What a surprise.'

'I need medical information on a woman named Olivia Sanchez. About two weeks ago, she showed up at the emergency room at Lenox Hill Hospital.' Beck took a moment to calculate the date. 'Sometime around February second or third. Around seven p.m. She had two broken fingers on her left hand. Little finger and ring finger. They set the fingers in the emergency room. Can you look into it? You know, like you're her primary care physician or something and you're following up.'

'What do you mean by look into it?'

'Find out what happened. The circumstances. Get whatever records they have. X-rays, whatever.'

'Can you get me a copy of her signature?'

'Why? Can't you just scribble something on your usual form?'

'Not if you want it to match the five or six signatures she had to sign in the emergency room at Lenox Hill.'

'Who even looks at that shit?'

'The person in charge of medical records. Get me a signature. You won't get two chances.'

'All right. Thanks.'

Beck cut the call and continued on into the kitchen, trying to think of how the hell he could get Olivia Sanchez's signature.

23

'Look, Pearce, I don't need his goddamn life story. I just want to know how to find him and what his connection to Olivia Sanchez is,' said Milstein.

Milstein had just gotten off the phone with Leonard Markov, who had spent most of the call snarling threats into his ear, while Milstein kept wondering how they let James Beck get away from them.

Markov pressed Milstein, so now Milstein pressed Walter Pearce, getting more and more frustrated by what he heard.

'I know what you want,' said Pearce. 'I'm working on it. But you have to understand, this is no ordinary guy. So far I don't see any address, anywhere in the five boroughs, or Connecticut or Jersey, that would match the James Beck we're looking for.'

Milstein sat at his desk on the twenty-eighth floor of Summit Investing, wearing his phone headset, staring out at a view north and east that made up for his otherwise modest office. Milstein could see across Manhattan over into Queens. He enjoyed watching planes depart and arrive at LaGuardia Airport. The distance made them look as if they were moving so slowly that they appeared to be suspended in the air. The sight usually relaxed him. But the more he listened to Pearce, the less calm he felt.

'I've gone through five databases. I have his arrest record, court proceedings, but after his case was settled three years ago there's nothing. It's like he disappeared. No car registration. No voter registration. No property records. Nothing. He's out of the system. He's not on parole. He has no record of any arrests. No liens. No court cases. Not even a traffic ticket.'

'Goddammit, Walter, listen to me carefully.' Milstein made a concerted effort to lower his voice and speak calmly. 'I know you have your procedures. Your methods. But this situation is quite different. Every hour that man is out there – look, I'm not going to explain. I'll explain some other time. This Beck fellow is causing us real trouble. If you can't find him in your usual way, try another way. He's connected to that Baldassare guy, right? Take that angle. Find him and maybe you'll find Beck. Or maybe you can find him through his lawyer. You must have that name in his files.'

'All due respect, Mr Milstein, I doubt his lawyer is going to be handing out any information on him. As for Ciro Baldassare, I've already checked on him. The only connection to Beck that I can see is that they were in Dannemora at the same time. His last known address is on Staten Island. But if I find him, he's not going to tell me anything about Beck. All that would do is warn Beck, and he'll go even deeper into hiding. If you want to try the Baldassare angle, the best way is to put men on him, tail him, and hope he will lead us to Beck. But that will take a lot of time and will cost significant money.'

Milstein hated hearing reasons why something couldn't be done.

'All right, all right, Walter, I'm just making suggestions. You're the detective, not me. Just fucking do whatever you can to find him. As fast as possible. Stay in touch.'

Milstein hung up before Walter could tell him any more reasons why he couldn't find James Beck.

Beck walked into the downstairs bar kitchen, holding the insurance form Willie Reese had given him.

'Olivia.'

She had her coat and hat on, ready to leave with Manny.

'Do me a favor. Sign this form for me, will you. It's to get my window fixed. It'll be better if it looks like someone from the property manager's office signed it instead of me.'

She made a confused face. It didn't make much sense to her. She stared at the form, a set of three pages in three different colors. She scanned it. Decided it made no difference if she accommodated Beck's request.

'My name?'

'Yeah. Why not? Yours is as good as any.'

'That'll work?'

'Sure.'

She signed the form.

'Thanks.' Beck quickly picked up the form and said to Manny, 'You guys are getting food first, right?'

Manny said, 'Yeah. Then we'll take care of what Olivia needs. Then I'll do that other thing and be back.'

'Okay.'

Beck limped up the back stairs with the form, came out on the second floor, and handed the signed form to Alex Liebowitz.

'Alex, scan that signature, clean it up, and send it to Brandon Wright. Please.'

Liebowitz took the form, turned to the scanner on Beck's desk, and started doing what Beck had asked. Beck waited until Alex completed the scan. Then he pulled the form out of the scanner and under Olivia's signature printed 'for J. Beck.' He hurried back down to the bar, handed the form to Reese.

'That should do it. Don't let glass man leave until there's a new window in here. If it gets late, don't let him tell you some bullshit about it being too dark. He has work lights.'

'He ain't going anywhere.'

Beck looked at Willie Reese. He had no doubt that the plate glass repairman would not be leaving until the job was done.

Markov had reserved a room with his usual online shopping routine, using another stolen credit card number. The room was at the Waldorf Astoria. He arrived at 3:30 p.m., the earliest check-in time.

Markov wasn't surprised that it was a small room with no view. He didn't care. It had a bed, a desk, and outlets for his phone chargers and laptop. He could work and sleep and plan.

Markov was very good at planning. It made him feel in control. He could spend uninterrupted hours at it. The mess with Crane and Summit had put him behind schedule. Time to catch up. He already had a checklist in his head.

First, contact his sources in Albania. His masters at US Military Intelligence had ordered up a roster of small arms for militant factions trying to overthrow the Assad government. Markov could not have cared less who the arms were for. He only cared about the amount and the logistics. And the price.

The order was somewhat flexible. Markov already knew how he would configure it.

He would make a deal with his Albanian suppliers for five to ten thousand AK-47 rifles, at least two million rounds of ammunition, and as many rockets and launchers as they would sell him. Markov estimated he'd probably get about a hundred of the launchers.

The weapons were part of the stockpiles assembled for sale by a company created by the Albanian government called MEICO. The sale was perfectly legal in Albania. However, the stamps and end-user certificates he needed would not be. He would have to assemble a mix of genuine and forged documents. His sources in Albania would provide both.

He had started the process three weeks ago. Now he would finalize everything.

He worked for two hours, nailing down loose ends, and then placed a series of calls to numbers connected to US Army Intelligence. Within forty minutes, Markov received a callback through the hotel phone lines from his contact, a Colonel Mark Redmond, who told Markov to log on to a secure website where they could conduct a live video chat.

Markov used the first part of the chat to report the progress of the arms shipment, outlining how it would be flown first into Beirut and from there to Al Thaurah Airport in Syria.

Redmond told him that from Al Thaurah US Army contractors would truck the weapons to their final destination. Markov had no concerns about what happened to the weapons after he completed his part of the delivery, but he knew Redmond gave him that information so it would be clear that the shipment would have to be packed in a way to hold up under transit by truck.

The video chat was mostly one way, with Redmond responding in short sentences.

Once their business was concluded, Markov asked Redmond for a favor, explaining that he was having trouble with a criminal group in New York that was using extortion to impede his operations.

For the first time during the live video chat, Redmond looked directly into the computer webcam.

Redmond was central casting for an Army operative. All-American Big Ten football boy, aging into a hardened man, close-cropped hair going gray at the temples.

'What kind of favor?'

'I may need your help finding some people.'

Redmond paused. Calculating his answer. There was always the possibility of blowback if he agreed. But he was under enormous pressure to deliver the arms shipment. Anything that took Markov off track couldn't be tolerated. Markov had been known to disappear for weeks or months at the first hint of trouble.

'Why?'

'They are causing me trouble.'

'Is it jeopardizing our contract?'

Markov thought carefully before he answered. If

Redmond had any doubts about his ability to deliver on his commitment it could be very costly to him.

'Not yet. And rest assured, this is a problem caused by someone else. Not me. But if I need your help, I want you to know in advance. And I won't ask unless it's necessary.'

Redmond pursed his lips, nodded, and limited his response to, 'Duly noted.'

'Thank you.'

Markov ended the connection. He would have to use Redmond very carefully. He had Milstein, for whatever that idiot was worth. He had Gregor and his men. And he had another resource he could use, Ivan Kolenka, but only if it became absolutely necessary. Right now, he would put pressure on Milstein and Gregor.

24

Beck had been hunkered down next to Alex Liebowitz feeding him information, providing descriptions, looking at pictures Alex brought up for identification, in between making phone calls to the Bolo brothers, getting up to check with Ciro, and looking outside to see how Willie Reese was doing with the window repair.

Liebowitz listened, typed in data, manipulated the mouse, shifted his gaze back and forth between two monitors. Ran through databases. Pulled up information.

After about an hour, Alex leaned back and announced, 'Okay, so here we go. We've got the arms dealer. And we've got the fighter.'

'How'd you find out?'

'Started with Elizabeth Stern's ID and password to get into the NCIC database. And then from there to other sources, some of which I have my own ways into. I mean, sometimes it's like the NYPD antiterrorist group is doing it, sometimes not. Some of it was just public sites. It's really just a matter of ...'

Beck gently interrupted Alex before he began with a long lecture. 'Great. Great. I'm glad the thing with Elizabeth is still good.'

'You like her, don't you?'

'Very much.'

'I have to remember to set up a wormhole in case she

moves on. But that might be very tough. They use automatically regenerated six-digit randomized numbers every sixty seconds, so I'd have to get hold of at least one functioning sequence that I could . . .'

'Alex.'

'Yeah?'

'What have you got?'

'Right, right. So . . .'

Liebowitz sat back and linked his hands behind his head, propped a foot on the handle of Beck's bottom desk drawer, folding into himself. His face went blank. The only movement was from his slowly blinking eyes.

Beck had seen this before. Sitting while Alex zoned out was like waiting for a massive file to download. The only difference was that no computer could match the processing being done by Alex Liebowitz's brain: sorting, comparing, pulling together a lifetime of information and coming to conclusions in seconds that might take others days or weeks, if they were lucky.

Alex took his foot off the desk drawer, tipped forward and began pulling up information on his monitors.

'Okay, the fat guy as you call him is Leonid Markov. Also known as Leonard Markov. Also known as Leonyti Sergeyevich Markov. Also known as Sergey Markovich. He's Russian. But where he was born is a little vague. Best guess he came out of Perm. There's a lot of old mob based there. Before Perestroika.'

'Vory-v-Zakone?'

'I'd imagine he has connections, but he's not one of them. He comes on the scene as an arms dealer pretty far back. Looks like Leonyti goes where the fighting is. Africa, mostly Liberia. Then he pops up in Yugoslavia during the Bosnian-Serb mess in the late nineties. There are records of him being in Bulgaria, Ukraine, Albania, Syria, lately Israel and Brighton Beach, New York. And a lot of time in Moscow.'

'Any arrests or anything?'

'The Belgians put out a red alert for him with Interpol in 2008, but apparently nothing came of it.'

'Why?'

'Who knows? If he's based here now, my guess is he's working with US intelligence. Maybe the Israelis, too. If he's running weapons where they want weapons to go, he's most likely got a lot of protection. These guys are part of a system, and ultimately the big boys run the system. Who do you think makes most of the weapons in the world?'

'We do,' said Beck.

'And the Russians, China, Israel, Great Britain, France. But you're right. Nobody comes close to us.'

'Where'd you find this stuff?'

'A lot of it in DEA files. They have more foreign bureaus than the CIA. Plus in a bunch of other unknown fucked-up subagencies inside Homeland Security. Anybody supplying arms to anybody gets on their radar.'

'What about the other guy?'

More screens and mouse clicks.

'He's a Bosnian Serb. Gregor Stepanovich. Ex-military, but not from any standard army. Nasty fucker. Twenty counts of crimes against humanity, violations of laws or customs of war, and grave breaches of the Geneva Convention, including leadership responsibility for crimes against Muslims in three locations in Bosnia-Herzegovina, specifically expelling Muslims to various camps, killing, raping, and torture.'

Alex turned away from the computer monitors and looked at Beck.

'Guys like that who come out of places like that, the shit they've done, you realize how bent they are.'

Beck didn't answer.

Alex turned back to his keyboard and brought up a photo. 'As for the others, you picked this one out. The one with the knife?'

'Yeah.'

'Krylo Bartosh. Charged with participating in the beating and mass killing of two hundred sixty-one non-Serb men removed by force from Vukovar Hospital. I don't know what his connection to Stepanovich is exactly. Their paths must have crossed somewhere. Your description of the other guy was pretty vague, but I can pull up a bunch of mug shots the United Nations commission pulled together.'

'No. I didn't get a good enough look at him to ID him.'

Alex leaned back. 'Okay.'

Beck thought for a moment.

'So you figure Markov and Stepanovich are now based here?'

'Seems that way. But *here* covers a lot of territory. Is it New York? The East Coast? I mean, there's no way these Bosnians got into the United States under their real names. All of 'em are on U.N. lists of war criminals. Plus other lists.'

'So how did they? Can't be that easy.'

Liebowitz shrugged. 'If Markov is running weapons for the US, maybe we let them in.'

Beck thought for a moment. 'Great.'

'It's just a guess.'

'You think the Vory would have anything to do with these guys?'

'Maybe not directly, but if Markov is Russian and he's based here, and he's into this kind of shit, they will definitely know about him.'

Beck nodded. 'Okay. Thanks. Good.'

Alex asked, 'What's next?'

Beck checked his watch. Nearly four o'clock.

'I think we probably want to start with the money.'

Alex leaned back. 'And how do we go about that?'

'Couple ways. If I were you, though, I'd take a nap. You might not be getting too much sleep later.'

Beck headed back to the ground-floor bar.

Demarco and Willie Reese sat at one of the tables in the front, waiting for the plate glass repair to be finished. The temperature in the bar had plunged while the glass frame was empty, but neither Demarco nor Willie seemed to mind.

Beck said to Demarco, 'Time to head out.'

He walked behind the bar and took out his gun lockbox. He removed the Browning and pulled out an extra clip. Beck didn't have to ask if Demarco was armed.

Willie Reese watched them leave. Nobody said a word.

Demarco waited until they were in the Mercury before he asked where they were going.

'Brighton Beach,' said Beck.

25

Beck had been out to Brighton Beach twice before. Once on an all-night tear with a Russian woman he had become involved with. And prior to that to meet with an old Vory gangster named Ivan Kolenka. He had been summoned to meet with the gangster to receive his personal thanks for protecting an associate while he served time in Sing Sing. There was a long and complicated story behind all that, but the Vory treated the episode with such formality that Beck would have preferred to skip the meeting entirely.

Apparently, Kolenka was one of the few genuine adherents to the 'Thieves Code.' A set of rules developed in the Russian gulags. It amounted to rejecting everything that had anything to do with normal society: family, all authority other than the internal authority of the crime group, and all income except that which came through criminal activity.

The life of a true Vory-v-Zakone seemed a bit mythic to Beck, until he met Ivan Kolenka in the private back room of a large restaurant. Kolenka appeared to be a man entirely self-contained. A withered, hunched over, almost emaciated man, dressed in a black suit and white shirt that were both too large for him, chain-smoking nonfiltered cigarettes, surrounded by minions. Big, thick-necked stereotypical Russian wise guys, other men who were either relatives or worked the restaurant, women who seemed to run the gamut from waitresses and fat wives to overdressed mistresses and pampered whores.

Food and drink and people swirled around Kolenka like the cigarette smoke that filled the back room of the private restaurant, but nothing seemed to affect him. He didn't seem to care about, recognize, or interact with anybody. When the emissary who had persuaded Beck to come to Brighton Beach to see Mr Kolenka escorted Beck into the back room, Kolenka stood to greet him. The moment the old man stood, everyone in the room stopped moving. Apparently, Kolenka stood for very few and certainly bowed to no one.

Beck felt the charisma of the man, but also felt acutely ill at ease. Certainly, there was the assumed power and ruthlessness. But something more sinister or perhaps frightening lurked underneath. Beck sensed it might have been Kolenka's ability to endure pain and loneliness.

Beck instinctively wanted little to do with Kolenka. They sat in a velour-covered booth, an iced bottle of Russian vodka in front of them. They shook hands. He felt the wiry strength of the man's bony grip.

Beck had to lean toward Kolenka to hear his heavily accented English. Beck listened to Kolenka's thanks for taking care of Mister Cherevin, but responded very little. Kolenka said something about if Beck ever needed help, Beck should come to him. But the way he said it felt like an enunciation of policy. It didn't feel personal.

Beck thanked Kolenka back, politely refused the offer of food and drink, remained deferential, mindful not to offend the man. But he felt out of his realm and wanted to be done with the stiff, back-room, Russian ritual.

Kolenka hadn't gotten to where he was by missing the signs and signals around him. He sensed Beck's discomfort. He didn't seem to take offense or require that Beck put it aside. He allowed Beck a graceful exit. Beck nodded once more in Kolenka's direction, turned and walked out to the bar area in front, followed by the dark-suited emissary who had taken him out to Brighton Beach in his limo.

He climbed into the Town Car limousine and rode back in silence to the midtown hotel in Manhattan where he was staying. Back then Red Hook had been in the planning stages, and Beck moved around quite a bit, enjoying his freedom as much as possible after eight long years in prison.

The trip back out to Brighton Beach, this time with Demarco driving, seemed longer. They were caught in the rush hour flow of traffic out to the Island, moving slowly along the BQE to the Belt Parkway. Traffic finally opened up a bit when they made it past the Verrazano Bridge.

Kolenka had no phone, no means of contacting him except via a personal connection. Beck knew this trip might be fruitless, but he was fairly sure that an attempt on his part to contact Kolenka would get a fast response.

The first stop was the well-known Ukrainian Café Glechik.

Coney Island Avenue seemed foreboding. Dark and dingy as the winter night set in. It was nearly six o'clock when they pulled up in front of the café. On the commercial block with most of the storefronts closed for the night, the brightly lit and bustling café seemed like a welcome oasis.

Beck walked into the restaurant, while Demarco sat double-parked in the black Mercury.

The heat, the steamy air filled with the pungent smells of traditional Ukrainian spices and food filled Beck's head the moment he walked in the door. He seemed to remember that this place had gone down in reputation from its heyday, but he couldn't have cared less. Nothing on the menu appealed to him, and wouldn't have when it was more authentic.

He found the manager after questioning a disinterested waiter. When Beck told him his name and leaned in closer to say he needed to see Kolenka, the man's eyes actually opened wide.

'Tell him I'll be parked outside for the next half hour. If he can see me, I'll assume he'll get back to me by then. If he can't, ask him to call me at this number.'

Beck had written his cell phone number on the inside of a matchbook with a plain, white cardboard cover.

Beck didn't wait for any denials or refusals. He stuck the matchbook in the manager's shirt pocket and walked back out to the Mercury.

Eleven minutes later, a black GMC Yukon pulled up close behind them, and a battered Lincoln Town Car veered in front of them and backed up, trapping the Mercury Marauder between the two vehicles.

Demarco Jones already had his Glock resting in his lap. He calmly pointed it toward the driver's side door, keeping it low and out of sight.

'Easy,' said Beck. 'Let me talk to them.'

Beck stepped out of the Mercury at the same time a large man in dark clothes came out the front passenger door of the Yukon.

Beck tried to remember the last time he'd seen a normal-size Russian doing crime in the New York area.

He kept his hands where they could be seen and took a couple of slow steps toward Kolenka's man, who held up a hand indicating Beck should stop.

'I'm Beck.'

'Vassily. Okay, you come with me. Tell your friend you be back soon.'

Beck thought about that for a second and said, 'No. Let him follow you. He'll stay in the car.'

'I don't want a fucking parade.'

Beck said, 'Then let one of your men ride with him and leave his car here. I'll ride with you. Two cars. Your man goes with you, I go with my guy. I don't want to waste time coming back here after I talk to Mr Kolenka.'

Vassily screwed up his face. He wasn't pleased.

'You want to explain to Mr Kolenka why I never showed up?'

Beck waited.

Vassily took time to think it through.

'Okay. But can't have anybody but you around the boss. One of mine goes with your driver. They park a couple of blocks away. We go see Mr Kolenka. Takes one minute to get you back to your driver. That's fair.'

Beck thought about it. There shouldn't be any reason he would need Demarco. Mostly, he just didn't want to be bossed around by Kolenka's man.

'Fine.'

Vassily nodded toward Beck's car. 'Go tell your man.'

Beck stepped back, leaned into the open window on the passenger side and said to Demarco. 'Hey driver, you heard?'

'Yes, sir, boss, I hear you.' Then Demarco said quietly, 'You need me, hit your speed dial. I'll get rid of their guy and get to you as fast as I can.'

'Good enough.'

Everybody took their seats. Beck in the Yukon next to the driver. Vassily sitting behind him. The gangster from the Town Car next to Demarco in the Mercury.

Demarco pulled in behind the Yukon and the two cars headed down Coney Island Avenue toward the boardwalk. Vassily's driver drove nearly fifty miles an hour until Vassily told him to pull over. Demarco, following behind, slid the Mercury to the curb behind the SUV. Vassily turned and saw Demarco stopped where he wanted him, and told his driver to go ahead.

They continued four blocks straight down Coney Island until they came to a five-story apartment building about two hundred yards from the boardwalk.

The driver double-parked the Yukon in front of the building, which surrounded a small courtyard set in about twenty feet from the curb. Beck saw Kolenka in the courtyard, hunched over on a bench, in the bitter winter air, smoking. Kolenka wore no hat or gloves or coat, only a well-worn white cable-knit sweater about two sizes too big for him. The old man seemed impervious to the freezing night air made more penetrating by the damp coming in off the ocean.

Beck turned around and noted that Demarco was still in sight back on Coney Island Avenue.

As he was about to get out of the Yukon, Vassily's heavy hand dropped on his shoulder. He asked Beck, 'You have weapons?'

Beck's survival instincts kicked in. The dark night. The out-of-the-way location. Strangers all round. There was no way he wanted to be completely defenseless, but he also needed to make the meeting happen.

'Yes,' he answered.

'Can't have them around the boss.'

'Okay.'

Beck opened his coat and reached around to pull the Browning from under his belt near his right hip. He made sure to pull out the gun very slowly. He leaned forward and placed the Browning on the dashboard.

'That everything?' asked Vassily.

'I have this.' Beck made a show of pulling out a Kershaw folding combat knife and setting it next to the Browning.

But what Beck didn't show was the gun in a holster strapped to his right ankle: a Smith & Wesson 637 Airweight five-shot revolver with a light aluminum alloy frame and a two-and-a-half-inch barrel. Beck had taken it out of the glovebox of the Mercury and strapped it on his ankle on the way out to Brighten Beach.

'Let's go,' said Vassily.

Beck slid out the passenger door. Vassily came out from the backseat and gave Beck a perfunctory pat down.

'Okay. Go talk.'

Beck walked into the courtyard, noting that Kolenka

had one bodyguard standing in the shadows of the court-yard about six feet left of Kolenka. He never took his eyes off Beck.

Kolenka looked even more wizened and thin than the last time Beck had seen him. He seemed completely disinterested in everything around him, his men, the twenty-degree cold, even Beck.

Beck sat down on the bench next to the old-school Vory. Kolenka nodded, not bothering to turn in Beck's direction, and said, 'Beck,' as if to confirm Beck's identity to himself.

Beck said, 'Good to see you again.'

Kolenka nodded, but said nothing.

'I came to ask for your help.'

'What kind of help?'

'I need information. On two men. Leonid Markov and Gregor Stepanovich. Markov is Russian. Originally from Perm. Stepanovich is Bosnian.' Beck pulled out pictures of them from the inside pocket of his coat that Alex had printed.

Kolenka barely glanced at the pictures. He took a long drag off his cigarette. It had burned down to a nub. He reached into the pockets of his well-worn pants and pulled out a battered pack of unfiltered Lucky Strikes. He lit a fresh cigarette from the burning tip of the smoked-out butt.

Beck waited while Kolenka mulled over the request, feeling the cold air, smelling the stale, pungent cigarette smoke. Kolenka stank of it, even in the open air.

Kolenka's silence worried Beck. If Markov had established himself in Kolenka's backyard, one way or another whatever Markov did passed through or around Kolenka. It might not be in Kolenka's interests to help Beck.

Kolenka swallowed, smoked, looked left at his bodyguard, and then out to Vassily standing near the Yukon. Was this a signal of some sort?

Finally, the old gangster spoke. 'I have conflict here.'

'All I'm asking for is information.'

Kolenka raised an eyebrow and tipped his head.

Beck waited for Kolenka to decide.

Another puff. More acrid cigarette smoke.

Kolenka stared straight ahead as he talked.

'The man doesn't use the name Stepanovich. Although you are right. That is his real name. He is scum. A pervert. The other one, Markov, different story.'

'How so?'

'He's more businessman than criminal.' Kolenka shrugged. 'But he is criminal, too. You have to understand that.'

Beck cut right to it. 'I know he deals arms. I know he is based in the US now. I assume here, in Brighton Beach.'

Kolenka interrupted. 'And other places. In Virginia.'

Beck thought about that for a moment. 'Near Washington?'

'Yes.'

Beck realized Kolenka had just confirmed that Markov was dealing arms for the US

Kolenka pursed his lips, frowning. He took a deep drag from the Lucky, inhaling it so deeply that the smoke seemed as if it would be absorbed into his bones. Beck weighed his next question.

He decided he might as well come right out and ask. 'Do you have business dealings with him?'

Kolenka moved the hand holding his cigarette in a gesture that seemed to indicate his surroundings.

'He pays his respects.'

Beck nodded at Kolenka's euphemism.

Kolenka asked, 'What is your business with him?'

'It's complicated.'

Kolenka frowned at the evasion. 'You have a problem with him?'

'Indirectly.'

Kolenka nodded. 'Problems with one usually cause problems with others.' Beck realized Kolenka was giving him a warning. But about what, exactly? 'You are a smart man, Mr Beck. There are people he does business with who will protect him.'

Shit, thought Beck. Now what? Does that include Kolenka protecting him? And what branch of government?

Beck said, 'I appreciate the information. I don't want to trouble you anymore. But I'm going to ask a favor.'

'You mean more than just information?'

'Yes. Are you willing to deliver a message to Markov for me? For his own good. And, of course, mine.'

Kolenka turned to Beck, for the first time looking directly at him. 'What message?'

'Tell him he should talk to me. Tell him, he has a problem that I can fix. Can you do that? Can you get that message to him without any risk to yourself?'

'Is this the truth or a lie to get advantage?'

'It's the truth.'

'What's in it for me?'

Beck shrugged. 'I solve one problem, maybe I'll prevent other problems.'

'Ah.'

Beck watched Kolenka's skeletal face with its map of lines and wrinkles etched by the light and shadows as the old gangster thought through how to play the situation.

Beck's request was mostly an attempt to defuse any alarm he'd caused with Kolenka. Kolenka would certainly contact Markov to let him know about Beck's inquiries.

After about ten seconds, Kolenka nodded. 'If Markov wants to talk, how can he reach you?'

Beck pulled a dollar bill out of his pocket and wrote down a phone number that his lawyer Phineas P. Dunleavy had set up for him. The number went to an answering service. Any message would be relayed to the lawyer. And only then to Beck.

'Someone will answer this number 24/7.'

Kolenka took the dollar bill from Beck without looking at it and stuffed it into the same pocket where he kept his cigarettes.

He looked away from Beck and said, 'Good-bye, Beck.'

Beck nodded, stood, and headed for the Yukon parked out on the street.

As he walked out of the courtyard, Beck pictured the ruthless Vory giving Vassily a signal behind his back. Would it be a classic thumb across the throat? No, thought Beck. He won't take the risk. But the isolated location, the cold, the aura of decay and lassitude that surrounded Kolenka all combined to create a sense of ugly foreboding.

By the time he reached the double-parked Yukon, Vassily was on his cell phone, presumably calling his man sitting with Demarco. Or was he giving him instructions to take out Demarco. If so, thought Beck, fine. He'd never get the drop on Demarco Jones. And if gunfire erupted down the street, Beck knew he could get to the Smith and Wesson on his ankle and take out Vassily. But what about Kolenka's bodyguard? And the driver?

As Beck approached, Vassily opened the passenger-side door with his right hand. Beck noted that the big Russian held his Browning and knife in his left hand.

For a moment, Beck hesitated. It would be easier for them to shoot him in the SUV. But then he saw that the lights of the Mercury had come on and Demarco was making a U-turn back on Coney Island, positioning the car in the right direction.

'Let's go,' said Vassily.

Beck climbed into the Yukon.

The Yukon pulled up behind Demarco, Beck slid out of the passenger seat, Vassily following, still holding Beck's gun and knife.

Vassily motioned for Beck to get into the Mercury. Beck passed Kolenka's third man heading toward the Yukon, Vassily following behind. Before Beck climbed into his car, Vassily handed him the Browning and his knife. Then reached into his coat pocket and pulled out the magazine and the bullet he'd taken out of the chamber.

Beck didn't say thanks. Vassily didn't say good-bye.

26

Demarco made his way toward the Belt Parkway.

'Shit,' said Beck.

'What?'

Beck grimaced. 'Good news, bad news.'

'Meaning?'

'I got information on Markov I didn't know, but it's not good news.'

'Why?'

'He's greasing Kolenka to let him operate in his backyard, and he's running arms for some US agency, which means he probably has connections I didn't count on.'

'Well, better you found out now,' said Demarco.

'True, but now we have to do something about it.'

'Why? Your beef isn't with Markov.'

'That's before I shot one of his guys, maimed another, and pissed off some freak who seems to be in charge of his security.'

Demarco shrugged. 'So then we do what we have to. You worried about Kolenka?'

Beck thought it over. 'He won't get involved unless he has to, but if he does . . .' Beck's voice trailed off. He grimaced. 'It could get very bad.'

'I wouldn't mind putting a bullet in that fat boy of his who took you in the Yukon.'

'Why? What did he do?'

'He was yelling on his cell phone to the guy sitting with me while you were talking to the head Russkie.'

'Saying?'

'Something about *glupo chertovski negr.*'

'What's that mean?'

'Stupid fucking nigger.'

'That's not nice.'

Demarco turned to Beck. 'Moron. I gotta take that from some fat Russian slob?'

Beck nodded. 'What's worse? That he called you the N-word, or stupid?'

Demarco considered the question seriously. 'Stupid.'

'Hey, next time I see him I'll tell him you're smart enough to know Russian.'

'Tell him after I give him a beating.'

'Where'd you learn Russian?'

'Playing chess with the Russians in Dannemora. Believe me, they had a very limited vocabulary.'

Beck lapsed into silence. Demarco slid onto the Belt Parkway heading for Brooklyn. After a minute, Beck looked at his watch and pulled out his cell phone, starting a series of calls.

The first call was to Ricky Bolo.

'Ricky, Beck – how's it going on that surveillance I asked you to set up?'

'Peachy.'

'Have any trouble finding Milstein?'

'Nope. I'm parked on Seventy-ninth in the warm, comfortable Bolo-mobile, and Jonas is outside watching the back exit on Eightieth, freezing and bitching like a whiny little girl.'

'Good. Drive around and pick up your brother and head over to Hubert Street in Tribeca between Greenwich and Washington. Check out the neighborhood and call me back.'

'On it.'

The next call was to Manny.

'Manny, did you get Olivia set up in that hotel?'

'About an hour ago.'

'Okay, we need her locked-down tight. Markov may have resources that can find her. So call and tell her to shut off her cell phone. No calls, no e-mails, no Internet, no texts, nothing. She didn't use her credit card when she checked in, did she?'

'No.'

'Good. Get a woman you trust to go sit with her and make sure she doesn't leave her hotel room. For sure. No slippage. She stays put until I get there. I have to talk to her.'

'Okay. When you figure?'

'Couple of hours. Did you line up your guys?'

'Four of them. Dudes we can trust. You want them on board now?'

'Not yet. But tell them they should be somewhere we can reach them if we need them. Are you back at the place?'

'Yeah.'

'Did Ciro get his cousin Joey?'

'Supposed to be on the way.'

'Good. Get the shotguns out and keep watch. I don't think anything is coming our way tonight, but be ready.'

'What happened with Kolenka?'

'He may have a dog in this fight.'

'How?'

'Markov is paying him to operate in his backyard.'

Manny made an unintelligible noise, but didn't comment beyond saying, 'Anything else?'

'Stand by.'

Next, Beck called Alex Liebowitz and told him to gather what he needed for a black bag job and to be ready to go within the hour.

Beck checked his watch. Seven-thirty.

Demarco asked, 'Now what?'

'Now we go on the offensive. Fast.'

27

Alan Crane spent nearly two hours cleaning up after the bloody fight in his loft, followed by an hour at his computer identifying positions that he could close out without taking significant losses.

But he couldn't really concentrate. He kept imagining a ball peen hammer smashing into his hand with the same force that Markov pounded it into his dining room table.

Crane paced back and forth, barefoot, on the Calamander hardwood floors of his Tribeca loft trying to convince himself that Markov wouldn't make good on his threats of violence if he succeeded in keeping the losses to a minimum.

Unfortunately, there were too many of his positions underwater. He was going to have to monitor every holding closely, take advantage of every uptick, and close out anything immediately that turned south. It would mean constant attention over as many days and hours as he could get from Markov.

Crane kept pacing, trying to figure out his alternatives. He needed to know how this thing had suddenly blown up. What had Milstein told Markov?

He picked up his cordless phone and pulled on his headset so he could keep pacing. He punched a speed-dial number. Milstein answered on the second ring.

'Alan.'

'Yes. So Frederick, do you mind telling me what the fuck is going on?'

'Don't shout at me.'

Crane shouted even louder. 'I'll fucking shout at you all I want. Markov almost took a hammer to me, and his goons tried to kill that guy you sent up here. Who the hell was he? He shot one of Markov's men and crippled another before he got away. They practically destroyed my place. It took me two hours to clean up the blood.'

'What!?'

'You fucking heard me, Frederick, goddammit, or have you gone deaf?'

'All right. Calm down, Alan. Calm down. This is crazy. He was just supposed to go up there and hear your side of the story. Markov was supposed to explain to you the deal I made to pay off the woman, get you to agree to back off, and convince that thug to go away. What the hell happened?'

Crane took a deep breath.

'Christ. Tell me exactly what happened to you and what you told Markov. Then I'll explain what happened here.'

It took five minutes for each man to fill in the other. Finally, Milstein said, 'Alan, this is completely out of hand. We've got to contain this. We have to shut this down.'

'Forget it. You're not shutting down Leonard Markov. Not after what happened up here.'

'What's he going to do?'

'He wants to kill Olivia and Beck. And if I don't close out millions in positions without incurring big losses, he's going to kill me, too.'

'I can't believe this is happening. Is Markov really threatening to kill you?'

'Yes. No. Not exactly. But he's doing a good job of terrifying me into thinking anything is possible.'

'What do you want me to do, Alan?'

'Has Leonard called you?'

'Yes. I'm supposed to locate Olivia Sanchez for him.'

'So do it. What about Beck?'

'He wants me to find him, too.'

'Good. Find them and let Leonard take care of them.'

Milstein's voice dropped into a tense whisper, 'I'm not in the business of getting people killed, Alan. I didn't even start this.'

'Neither did I. That bitch started it. And made it worse by sending in her tough guy threatening to kill you. And I'm sure he came up here thinking he could do the same to me. And now they're both going to get what's coming to them. It's out of our hands.'

'This is going to cost us millions.'

'Maybe not, Freddy. I'll get Markov his money. Hopefully, he'll see how stupid it was demanding we close out his positions so quickly. Maybe I can talk him into putting everything back.'

'You really think so?'

'I don't know. But I'm not giving up without a fight. You do whatever Markov wants. Keep him off my back while I squeeze everything out of his portfolio I can. We'll see where it comes out. That's all we can do.'

Milstein winced. 'How bad is it going to be?'

'The portfolio could take a twenty, thirty percent hit.'

'Jeesuz.'

'Look, stop worrying about it. It's my job. Just make Markov believe you're doing everything you can for him.'

'Where's Markov now?'

'How the fuck should I know? Probably gathering a million of his Bosnian ex-militia so he can go kill everybody in sight. Stay with it, Freddy. Markov is going to do what he wants to do. You do what you can to help him.'

Crane hung up.

28

Beck and Demarco arrived back in Red Hook just before 9 p.m. The bar downstairs was dark. They parked the Mercury Marauder across the street, stepped out of the car, and waited a few moments so they could be seen, just to make sure they wouldn't be shot as they walked in the front door.

Beck wasn't worried about Manny or Ciro, but he wasn't taking any chances knowing that Ciro's cousin Joey B had arrived to help guard the headquarters. Joey had a unique ability to act unencumbered by thought.

Beck and Demarco stood outside the front door, waiting. Beck took note of his new front window, the bottom third painted black exactly the way it had been. Ciro popped open the front door. Beck and Demarco entered quickly. Sure enough, Joey B had been planted in the bar downstairs with a shotgun. Beck greeted Joey B. He always got a kick out of trying to get his arms around Joey while receiving a bone-crushing hug from one of Joey's huge arms.

Beck broke away from Joey B's one-arm bear hug and asked Ciro, 'Is Manny upstairs?'

'Yeah,' said Ciro. 'Alex, too.'

'Okay, let's go upstairs and talk. Joey, come with us and keep watch from the window up there. You can hear the plan.'

They quickly assembled around the coffee table. Joey stood at the second floor window looking out at the street, looking back at the others, walking from one end of the drapes to the other.

Just as Beck and the others sat down around the big coffee table, his cell buzzed.

'Yeah.'

Ricky Bolo's voice asked him, 'So we made it over to that Tribeca address you gave us.'

'Good. You have time to check the area?'

'Yeah. Did you figure the street in front of that address was gonna be filled with hard guys?'

'Shit.'

'Whatever you're interested in on that block, somebody else is, too, Jimmy boy. There's two gangster SUVs, one at each end of the block. Tinted windows, the whole nine yards, but we caught looks at the inside through the windshields.'

'What's going on?'

'Each of the SUVs has a driver and a bad guy in the front seat and more hard cases in the backseats. But they're still coming into the neighborhood. Every once in a while someone gets out of a taxi or shows up on the street and joins the party in one of the SUVs. The one near Washington Street should be about full. We saw four bozos get into that one. Only two so far in the one near Greenwich.'

Beck thought about what Ricky was telling him. Clearly, the Bosnians were gathering the troops. But why? To protect Crane? Seemed like an awful lot of men for that. What then? Had Kolenka located the Red Hook headquarters for Markov? Were they gathering to mount an attack?

He thought about how he should respond. It didn't take long.

'Okay, Ricky, here's what I want you to do.'

Beck gave instructions while the others watched and listened. The tension in the loft cranked up significantly. By the time Beck stopped talking, everyone knew what was next.

Beck hung up. Ciro asked, 'So?'

Beck didn't say anything. He sat, lost in thought. Finally after about twenty seconds, he spoke. 'Okay. I don't have time to fill you in on all the background. There's someone on Hubert Street in Tribeca I needed to talk to tonight. And maybe some other shit. But now it looks like he's either being guarded, or the guys watching him are gathering up enough strength to hit us tonight. Or both. I figure they didn't know where we were, but now, or soon, they might get our location. So, we have to hit them first.

'We've got to move now. Manny, Ciro, you go with Demarco. I'll take Alex and Joey in Olivia's car. Everybody arm up. By the time we get to Tribeca, I'll have it figured out what everyone should do. Alex, make sure you have your bag of tricks. You're going to be doing a break-in.'

Everyone stood up and moved. No questions. No comments.

Beck was back on his cell phone before he hit the back stairs.

29

When they'd first arrived, Ricky and Jonas had driven around the Tribeca neighborhood in their nondescript van getting a general sense of who was on the streets. After Beck talked to them, the Bolo brothers circled the blocks from Hubert to Greenwich to Beach and back, on foot. They checked for any security cameras that might catch images of what was to happen.

Ricky and Jonas were experienced burglars, safecrackers, and locksmiths. They knew whatever there was to know about CCTV cameras, alarm systems, sensors, locks, and surveillance techniques. They were experts at breaking and entering. They knew the policies of every major security company that offered service in New York City, including response times, patrol habits, radio frequencies, and more. They were wraiths. They were a protected place's worst nightmare. And their last name was not Bolo. Very, very few knew their real last names. Bolo had come from Ricky's penchant for bolo neckties.

James Beck had met Ricky in the Eastern Correctional Facility in upstate New York, a facility that had originally been known as the State Institution for Male Defective Delinquents, a name that seemed appropriate for Ricky Bolo, even though he had reached the age of thirty-seven. His brother Jonas had been incarcerated at the same time, having been arrested for the same complicated theft as his brother. But the prison authorities wisely kept them separated, so Jonas served his time in Ossining.

Upon their release, the Bolo brothers had resumed their life of crime literally within hours. However, they now specialized in casing targets for other criminals.

Still, Beck's assignment for them was a bit unusual. They only had a vague idea of what he planned. And he had asked them to essentially blind an entire neighborhood.

Ricky was the flamboyant one. Jonas, serious and studious. They made a good pair as they walked the neighborhood seeing things most people never even thought about. Both wore overcoats that hid an array of equipment. Ricky spoke on his cell via a Bluetooth earpiece, giving Beck a continuous narrative as Beck headed for Tribeca.

Jonas walked next to Ricky, hands in pockets, ready to pull out whatever was needed for a given task, pointing out anything Ricky missed.

The area had much more surveillance in place than most neighborhoods. Almost all the restaurants had cameras. Most of the loft buildings had cameras on their intercom panels as well as cameras watching the sidewalks in front of the buildings. The block-long parking garage on Greenwich had cameras covering the entire front of the garage. The Smith Barney building had all entrances and most of the space occupied by their wide plaza under camera surveillance.

The trick was to eliminate as much of the surveillance as they could without causing too much attention. Street-level fish-eye lenses were easy. They covered them with a stick-on reflective material of their own design. It took about a second. The only image visible was a silver blur. The material caused no permanent damage, and had been designed to fall off in about an hour.

Most of the cameras were at the one-story above-street level. Anything beyond that height wouldn't give much of an image. The Bolos used telescoping poles retrofitted to hold spray paint formulated to cover plastic. It took about ten seconds to pull out a pole from under their overcoats, extend it, and spray the camera lenses with gray paint.

By the time they'd circled the area twice, they'd degraded eleven security cameras to the point where they'd be useless, decided four others wouldn't be a problem, and obliterated the lenses of seven more.

The only other variables were people on the street and onlookers glancing down from apartments who might see something. But that wasn't their problem. Beck and his men would have to deal with that.

During their circuit, the Bolos also got better looks at the two SUVs the Bosnians were using: an Escalade and an old Chevy Blazer, parked near Crane's Hubert Street loft. One at each end of the block.

They reported all this to Beck and then headed back to their beat-up white van parked on Hudson Street. Beck told them to stick around somewhere they wouldn't be noticed and monitor police broadcasts.

The last thing the Bolo brothers did before going back to their van was to stop in front of Crane's loft building. Ricky stood near the buzzer panel firing up a cigar, while Jonas, who looked like he was texting a long message on a smartphone, scanned the electronic lock system that secured Crane's front door and elevator. His scanner broke the code in thirty-seven seconds. They both resumed walking. Ricky leaving billows of smoke in his wake.

Jonas sent the data he'd secured to Alex Liebowitz riding in the backseat of the Mercury Marauder. Alex pulled something out of his backpack that looked like a portable hard drive, followed by a keypad he attached to it. Within seconds, he started fabricating a passkey to open Crane's front door and lobby door. By the time Beck drove into the Battery Tunnel, Alex had entered the last bits of information he'd received from Jonas Bolo.

Demarco, driving the Mercury, arrived in Tribeca about five minutes ahead of Beck driving Olivia's Porsche. Demarco found a legal parking spot on Hudson Street. Beck parked the Porsche illegally in front of the fire hydrant on Greenwich where he'd parked before.

Beck called Demarco's cell and told him to bring the others and meet him on Greenwich. All the men wore long coats and some form of cap to obscure the view of their faces. All of them had shotguns under their coats.

When Demarco, Ciro, and Manny arrived at the Porsche there was only room for Ciro and Demarco in the car since Joey B took up most of the backseat. Manny drifted off toward a building nearby. He leaned against a wall hidden by shadows, watching.

Beck checked his watch. 9:15 p.m., Wednesday. It seemed like an awful lot had happened since yesterday morning.

*

Alan Crane realized he hadn't eaten since breakfast. There was no more work he could or wanted to do on the investments. The coffee he'd gulped throughout the afternoon had worn off and his appetite had surged back.

He checked his watch: 9:30 p.m. There should be some empty tables at Harrison.

Beck had just worked out his plan. He motioned for Manny to come near the open passenger-side window and listen up.

'Okay,' said Beck. 'Here's how it's going to work.' He pointed toward Crane's building west of them on Hubert Street.

'Alex, the computer you have to rig is in the top floor apartment of that building. It's an open loft. Elevator opens directly into the apartment. There's an office area near the east end of the floor, past the kitchen. Computer, four monitors, clearly set up as a trading station. We need to know every move Crane makes on that computer.'

'Right. Is the place empty?'

'I'm assuming Crane is home. I'll convince him to come out and talk to me.'

'You sure he'll do that?'

'I doubt he wants me to come in after him. I'll be nice. When you're done, you call me, and I'll bring him back. How long do you think you'll need?'

'No telling. I have no idea what's going on up there. If he leaves his computer on and doesn't have any security systems running, it'll take about fifteen minutes. If not, who knows?'

'All right. Once I get him out, use the key card to get in.

You do your thing. We'll make sure he doesn't get back in until you're done.'

'Okay. What about the bad guys outside?'

Alex hadn't taken his eyes off Crane's building the whole time Beck spoke.

'We'll take care of that, too.' Beck turned to the others. 'While I'm with this asshole Crane, the rest of you get into position to cover those two SUVs. Ciro, you and Joey take the one at the west end of the block. Manny and Demarco, you do the same for the one at this end. If they try to stop me from taking Crane, or follow us in their cars, or make any move to go into the apartment, you make sure they don't. Clear?'

'No,' said Ciro. 'Stop how? You want us to take them out, or just the vehicles?'

'Let's try not going to jail tonight. Blast the crap out of their tires. Maybe pump a few shots into the engines, a couple over the roofs to keep them in the cars, and then disappear. Don't get into a gun battle. Position yourselves near the corners so you can take a fast fade.

'The precinct is just a few blocks away so the cops will show up quickly. Figure around three, four minutes after you start shooting. That should give you enough time to make it back to the cars, or jump in a cab, or just walk out of here. I'll leave the keys to this car under the floor mat.'

And then, Beck's plan evaporated.

Up the block Alan Crane walked out of his building, heading their way. Gregor Stepanovich emerged from the SUV parked east of Crane's building and intercepted him in the middle of the block.

30

Gregor asked him, 'Where you going?'

'To eat. What am I now, your prisoner?'

'Mr Markov thinks you might need someone to watch out for you. You should be grateful.'

Crane rolled his left shoulder and said, 'Yeah, I'm real grateful. I can hardly use my fucking arm thanks to you. Exactly what do you mean by "watch out" for me? If you want to watch out for me, you can come watch me eat.'

Crane stepped around Stepanovich and continued walking.

Gregor fell in next to Crane.

'I asked you once, now I ask again. Where you going?'

Crane stopped and pointed south. 'Jeezus fucking Christ, Gregor, a couple of blocks. Over to Harrison. It's a restaurant over there.'

'I walk with you. Make sure you get there safe.'

Crane shook his head. 'Unbelievable.' They started walking together. After a few steps he said to Stepanovich, 'You're not really planning to sit with me while I eat are you?'

'Don't worry.'

Beck watched them talk, and then continue walking together toward Greenwich Street. Crane didn't look very happy about Markov's man walking with him.

As they approached, Beck said, 'Guys, hunker down. Better they don't see us.'

Manny sauntered off away from the Porsche.

Demarco said, 'How the hell is Joey going to get out of sight?'

Ciro started to laugh. Beck started to laugh. Joey B gamely tried to hunch down in the backseat, which made everyone laugh harder.

Luckily, Stepanovich and Crane walked past them on the other side of Greenwich and never bothered to look at the Porsche.

Still smiling, Beck said, 'Okay, calm the fuck down. So much for that plan. Alex, take off now. Get into the building with your passkey. Get to work on that computer.'

'I should go into the basement. Check his alarm system first.'

'Okay, whatever. Just go now. Work as fast as you can. Demarco, go follow those two and call me when they end up wherever they're headed.'

Alex and Demarco left. Beck slid over to the passenger seat. He looked out onto the street to find Manny, who was leaning back in the shadows on Hubert Street. He motioned for Manny to get in the Porsche.

As Manny slipped behind the wheel, Beck turned in the passenger seat so he could talk to everybody at once.

'Okay, you guys, hang in here. The goal is the same. Give Alex enough time to do what he has to. Position yourselves near those SUVs. If those guys make a move, stop them.'

'What are you going to do?'

'Go wherever that fucker ends up and keep him there

until Alex is done. Maybe we can pull this off without shooting up the neighborhood.'

Manny asked, 'You going to pick up Alex, or you want me to?'

'We'll see. You guys might be busy keeping those assholes in the SUV out of play.'

Beck watched Alex slip into Crane's lobby. With his long herringbone overcoat, Buddy Holly glasses, and backpack, he looked like he belonged in the trendy loft building.

Beck's cell phone rang. Demarco told him, 'The guy from the building just settled in at a table near the front of a restaurant called Harrison. Place is small, but a shitload of people in here. He ordered a drink. He's checking out the menu. Looks like he's going to take his time with his meal. Baldy walked him to the door and left.'

'Okay, good. See if you can get a seat at the bar where you can keep an eye on him. When it looks like Crane's ready for dessert, call me. If Alex isn't done, I'll come to the restaurant and sit on him. I'll tell Alex to call you when he's finished. You stay at the bar and signal me when Alex calls you.'

'Got it.'

Beck scanned the street for Stepanovich. The tall man's head appeared from the south bobbing above the few people on the street. Beck rolled his shoulders, feeling the stiffness and pain from the blows Stepanovich inflicted with his steel baton. He pictured walking up to Stepanovich in the middle of the block and shooting him in the face. It might save him a lot of trouble later, but murdering someone in the middle of Tribeca wasn't part of the plan.

Stepanovich crossed Greenwich in the middle of the block, angling toward his SUV, talking on his cell.

31

Demarco Jones's seat at the crowded bar gave him a sidelong view of Crane. Demarco was sure Crane had no idea he was watching him, mostly with his peripheral vision.

Jones sat quietly sipping Grand Marnier and coffee, attracting attention from a few of the restaurant patrons who decided he was probably some sort of pro athlete. Crane was too involved in his dinner and his own thoughts to notice anything around him.

At ten-twenty, Beck's phone rang. It took two seconds for Demarco to give Beck the message. It took Beck about three minutes to arrive at the restaurant and slip into the empty chair opposite Crane.

Crane had just been served coffee and one of the house-made éclairs for dessert. He stopped the coffee cup midway between the saucer and his mouth.

'Oh, Christ,' he muttered.

'Nice to see you, too. How're you doing, Mr Crane? Last time I saw you, you were taped to a table. This looks a little more pleasant. Mind if I join you?'

'You just did.'

'Yes. I did.'

'What do you want?'

'Well,' said Beck, 'I guess I want to help you. Or, you

know, I want you to help me help you. Like the line from that Tom Cruise movie. How's that sound?'

'It sounds stupid. What the hell are you talking about?'

Beck leaned across the table, ignoring Crane's question. 'What was the deal with that hammer? Were they going to use that on you?'

'What do you want?'

'Let me ask you something. Those guys with the hammer and tape, those were the same ones who tried to kill me. I got a goddamn knife wound in my leg and about a thousand welts on my back where that bald fucker hit me with a steel baton, not to mention that fat guy trying to shoot me.'

'I don't hear a question.'

'Yeah, so I intend to do something about that. I would imagine you'd be in favor of that, wouldn't you?'

Crane gave Beck an appraising look. He had to admit, the man had impressed him with how he'd handled Stepanovich and his men.

'I might be.'

'That being the case, how about giving me a little information where I might find your buddies. Let 'em know it's not something they can get away with.'

'Really?'

'Yes. Really.'

Crane sipped his coffee, took a bite from his éclair, and continued to study Beck.

'Let me get this straight. You're the one who goes to Milstein about that fucking whore Olivia Sanchez, and threatens to kill him so he'll pay her off. Then you come to my place, intending to do what? The same thing, right?'

'Not necessarily. Milstein just said I should get your reaction on the severance package he agreed to with me. And something about getting your side of the story.'

'Severance package?'

'That's what it's called, isn't it? And, oh yes, he wanted me to convince you to lay off with the threats and the lawsuits and blackballing her.'

'What world are you living in?'

'Yours, my friend. That's the way things are done in your world, aren't they? Everybody gets a golden parachute, or whatever.'

'Uh-huh. Meanwhile, Milstein calls Markov and gets him all riled up, knowing Markov would probably show up with his Bosnian army to threaten me and do whatever they intended to do to you.'

'So you're saying Milstein purposely killed the deal? Okay, so Milstein goes on the list, too. But I know where to find him. I don't know where to find the fat guy and the others.'

'And what makes you think I want to have anything to do with you? You're working for that crazy bitch who started all this shit. I have nothing to say to you.'

'Hey, let's not get bogged down on who started what,' said Beck.

'Yeah, let's not. How about you just get the fuck away from me and leave me alone?'

'Alone to do what? Have Markov and his buddies torture you? Why not let me get between you and them? Tell me who they are, and where I can find them.'

'Who they are? They're bad fucking news, that's who they are. They're crazy. That moron Olivia sets everything off. You start making trouble. Freddy Milstein the idiot panics. He calls the client. A man you do not want to call about any trouble, because Leonard Markov is someone who lives in a paranoid drug-addled world of craziness. Milstein sets Markov off like a bomb, and now everything has gone to shit.'

Crane leaned across the table toward Beck.

'I don't need your help. I don't want your help. There's nothing you can do but make my life worse. So stay the fuck away from me. You're part of the reason I'm in this mess.'

'You're telling me they're going to leave you alone.'

'Are you deaf or stupid, or both?'

Crane motioned for the check. 'Listen to me, and then never talk to me again. Olivia stuck her nose into something she had no business getting involved with. And I wouldn't be surprised if Milstein encouraged her to do it. I set her straight. She kept pushing it. She got you involved, whoever the fuck you are. You obviously scared the shit out of Milstein. He goes to the client, Markov. Markov loses whatever little sense he had to begin with. His only response is . . . shut it down and give me my money.

'Okay. Fine. He's going to lose a shitload. Not my problem. I do what he says. I'll try to minimize the damage. I'll try to do it in such a way that maybe Markov won't break every bone in my body and have his insane enforcer Stepanovich put a bullet in my head. But the bottom line is, it's all gone to shit. And there's not a fucking thing you can do about that!

'Milstein loses the only investor that might have kept that bust-out brokerage of his afloat. Sanchez loses any chance she'll ever have of working in finance. As well she fucking should. Forget Milstein's bullshit about paying her off. The place probably won't be in business six months from now. Me, I'm the only one out of all of them who can make money out of money, and trust me, there will always be a place for me to land.

'So Mr Beck, or whatever the fuck your name is, I don't need you, I don't need Milstein, Markov – any of you. So fuck off and good-bye.'

Beck glanced over at Demarco, sitting at the bar. He saw Demarco on his phone. Demarco shook his head slightly, indicating that Alex Liebowitz wasn't done.

Just then Crane's phone, which had been sitting on the table, buzzed. He checked the number and answered it.

He listened for just a moment, then said, 'I'm leaving now. No, you don't have to.'

Crane hung up, dropped his phone back on the table, and muttered, 'Asshole.'

The waiter brought the check and turned away without a word. Crane stuffed cash into the check folder, stood, and leaned in close to Beck.

'And one more thing, tough guy. Markov is going to squash you like a bug. Trust me. If they'd wanted to kill you, Stepanovich would have had orders to shoot you the minute you stepped off my elevator. They wanted to find out who you are and what you were up to, until you went all commando on them. So now they won't hesitate, and I for one don't want to be around you when they pull the trigger. So do me a favor and stay the fuck away from me.'

32

Beck watched Crane leave. He stood up and pantomimed steering a car to Demarco, indicating he should get the Mercury. He walked out after Crane.

Beck checked his watch. Nearly 10:40 p.m. Crane was about twenty feet ahead of him.

It was cold, damp, windy. There were still people in the bars and restaurants along Greenwich Street, but there was no one on the street within view.

Beck closed the distance between him and Crane. When he was within six feet, he called out. 'Hey, Crane.'

Crane had just wrapped a long red scarf made of fine Peruvian alpaca around his neck and was still buttoning up his expensive cashmere overcoat. He turned at Beck's call, exasperated. He stood there watching him approach, shaking his head.

Beck closed the distance between them in two strides and buried his right fist into Crane's solar plexus without any extra motion or warning. He held back on the punch, because he didn't want to knock Crane out completely. Crane crumpled and would have gone down on his knees if Beck hadn't grabbed his arm and eased him into a sitting position on a raised platform outside a restaurant where they were standing.

'Have a seat. Just for future reference, you ever talk to

me like that, I'll beat you so bad you'll spend six months in a hospital and never be the same.'

Crane remained doubled over, barely able to suck in a breath. He wavered between throwing up and passing out.

Beck took a quick look around and spotted Stepanovich coming into view on Greenwich. He crossed the sidewalk and slipped between two parked cars out into the street.

A more reckless man might have been tempted to play the hero and face Stepanovich straight on. Not Beck. He wasn't taking any chances. He had no idea what weapons Stepanovich might have on him.

Beck walked north on Greenwich, bent over so the parked cars would block Stepanovich's view of him. He kept sight of the Bosnian through the car windows by raising his head just high enough to see him pass by.

The moment Stepanovich passed him, Beck slid in between cars, walking lightly, slipping into position behind Stepanovich, ready to take the tall man down.

But Beck had underestimated Stepanovich. Either he had seen Beck moving around behind him, or heard him, or perhaps Crane had signaled him, but without any hint of stopping or turning, Stepanovich spun and whipped a closed fist at Beck's head.

Beck's reaction time saved him from a knockout blow to his temple. He just managed to duck under the blow, which clearly demonstrated Stepanovich's reach advantage.

Stepanovich didn't hesitate; he continued his spin and launched his left knee into Beck, who barely managed to block it with his forearms. The blow didn't hit anything vital, but it knocked Beck into the side of a building.

Gregor closed in on him. Beck fired a hurried, off-balance front kick at Stepanovich, ramming his right heel into the taller man's left kneecap.

Stepanovich flinched backward, lifting his left foot off the ground, skipping back a step to keep his balance.

Beck surged forward, slapped aside Stepanovich's raised hands, rammed his left elbow into Stepanovich's head, banged his right fist into Stepanovich's left temple, followed by a rapid set of six punches to the Bosnian's face, throat, and chest.

Stepanovich blocked most of them and tried to head butt Beck in the face. Beck dodged it but felt the bristles on the Bosnian's head scrape across his left cheek.

Beck hadn't planned on being in a fight like this. It had only lasted about ten seconds, but two people had already stepped out of the restaurant where he had put Crane. Beck was sure someone was already dialing 911.

Stepanovich made a grab with his long arms for Beck's head, getting two huge hands around the back of his neck, pulling Beck toward him, his mouth open trying to take a bite out of Beck's face. Beck jammed his hands against Stepanovich's chest to hold him off.

Stepanovich, snarling and grunting, tried to pull Beck to him.

Beck kept his hands on Stepanovich's chest, holding him at bay, but not so far away that he didn't smell the sour stink of his breath. The thought of Stepanovich biting him made Beck furious. He suddenly brought two fists up hard into the underside of the Bosnian's mouth, slamming his jaws shut and snapping his head back. But Stepanovich still held onto the back of Beck's neck, launching three fast knee kicks to Beck's ribs and hip.

Beck tried to twist away from the strikes, to block them with his elbows, but the Bosnian's arms and legs were too long and the blows landed causing sharp, nearly paralyzing pain.

Beck cursed to himself, intent on ending this now. He focused, shifted away from another kick, timed his move, reared back slightly, not giving the Bosnian any warning, just enough to seem like he was trying to avoid the knee kicks, and then he snapped his head forward with enormous force into the center of the Bosnian's face. He caught him perfectly, and heard the muffled crunch as Stepanovich's nose cartilage split like shattering bamboo.

Beck felt the Bosnian sag. He let Gregor's grip around his neck stay, so that the Bosnian remained close to him and twisted fast, hard right and left hooks into his chest and ribs with as much force as his hands could stand. The blows lifted Stepanovich off his feet. He was half conscious, immobilized by the body shots. Beck punched hard into both of Stepanovich's arms, broke the grip around his neck, and shoved Stepanovich away from him.

Stepanovich staggered back and would have gone down, but he fell against the wall behind him. His broken nose streamed blood. He was doubled over in pain, and yet in a perverse way he seemed to relish the feeling. He spat a mouthful of blood and saliva at Beck, grinning at him, daring Beck to come finish him off.

But police sirens were sounding in the distance.

Beck couldn't afford to get arrested for brawling. Clearly, he wasn't going to finish off Stepanovich quickly.

He turned away just as Demarco pulled up in the black Mercury. He slid into the passenger seat, and they accelerated away from the scene, heading downtown, away from Crane, his apartment, and Gregor Stepanovich.

Demarco said, 'Can't leave you alone for a minute without you getting into a fight.'

'Next time I'll let you do it.'

'No thanks. Alex is done. He's waiting around the corner on Washington.'

'That's good. The next move would have been to just go and shoot those two pricks, which would have defeated the whole purpose.' Beck pointed down Greenwich and said, 'Make your way around all these fucking one-way streets and come in from the highway side.'

Beck pulled out his cell phone and called Manny.

Manny listened carefully to Beck, said, 'Okay,' and hung up.

Manny turned to the others in the Porsche and said, 'Okay, *maricóns*, listen up.'

Manny turned the Porsche onto Hubert Street, heading west. He passed the first SUV parked near Greenwich, giving instructions as he drove slowly up the street.

Suddenly, he pulled up next to the SUV at the far end of Hubert near Washington Street.

Ciro and Joey got out first, moving very quickly.

Ciro went to the driver's side and smashed the butt of his shotgun into the window, immediately flipped the shotgun around and placed the barrel against the driver's head.

Joey B smashed the passenger window behind the

driver, reached in, unlocked the door, and pulled it open. Holding the shotgun in his right hand, he grabbed the closest body with his left, pulled one of the men out of the SUV, and shoved him down to the street with enough force to ensure he didn't get up.

In the meantime, Manny slipped out onto the street, a large knife in his hand, and punched holes into the two rear tires of the SUV.

Ciro stepped back, keeping his shotgun aimed at the remaining men inside the SUV.

Joey did the same as he dragged the man he had pulled out of the SUV with one hand and tossed him into the back of the Porsche. He shoved in after him, pinned him against the far door, and jammed the muzzle of his shotgun into the underside of the hostage's chin.

At the other end of the street, the other SUV started to head toward Washington, but Manny and Ciro were back in the Porsche turning onto the West Side Highway and heading for the Brooklyn Battery Tunnel and Red Hook before any of the leaderless Bosnians processed what had happened, or figured out what to do about it.

The only Bosnian who knew what to do, Ahmet, did so because Joey B told him. Keeping his shotgun firmly under Ahmet's chin, Joey said, 'Don't move.'

33

Alex Licbowitz slid into the backseat of the Mercury. Demarco drove north along the dark side street to Laight Street, then headed east, figuring he'd catch Varick Street and head for the bridge.

Alex said, 'That wasn't too bad. I was right to check the basement first. That dude's apartment is like a satellite trading office. There's a ton of security wiring going up to that apartment. He even has motion detectors up there.'

'So?'

'I worked around it. Got into the place, but there wasn't too much I could do. At first, I thought I was going to get lucky. His computer was on. But he's got a RAZ token password that prevents logging on. Thing changes every sixty seconds. I looked around for it, but couldn't find it. I blind downloaded the hard drive and put a keystroke program on his computer. It'll activate the next time he types in his pass code. Then I linked his Wi-Fi into a transponder in the basement that will send everything he does to a secure website I've set up. When he starts working, I'll just shadow him and work it from there.'

'How long until you figure he finds out he's been compromised?'

'I don't know. Depends on his firm's security protocols. I would imagine they run checks once a week. If not, I doubt he'll notice anything if we just shadow him. If we start making moves in his accounts or anything, he'll catch on at some point. 'Course if he has a regular security company that shows up in person and does a physical check, they'll find out.'

'Nobody is going up there. What if he decides to work from his office?'

'Anything he does there will eventually show up when he logs in from his apartment.'

'But he has to log in from his apartment.'

'Yeah. But all he has to do is log in once, and we're in.'

Based on the way Crane had talked about Milstein, Beck didn't think he'd be working at the office any time soon. But he needed more information. He needed Olivia's help so he could find out everything possible about Crane's portfolio and anticipate his moves.

Beck said, 'Okay you guys, head home. But first take me over to Church Street. I'm going to head uptown.'

Demarco said nothing. Just kept driving east.

'Alex, when you get home, see if anything shakes out.'

Beck hit his cell phone while Demarco maneuvered toward the uptown street.

'Manny?'

'Yeah.'

'Where are you?'

'I'm in the Battery Tunnel.'

'You pick up that package?'

'Yeah. We got what you asked for.'

'Good. When you get home, just put him in the basement. Don't say anything to him. Put a bag or something on his head from now until then. Check him for weapons and all. Leave a jug of water with him. Nothing else. No lights. No talking.'

'Okay.'

'Demarco and Alex are heading back, too. I have to go check on Olivia. This thing has got to blow apart at some point. They have to organize and come at us, so hunker down and make sure Willie Reese has his boys out watching the streets.'

'I'll call him.'

'And call Olivia. Tell her I'm coming. What room is she in?'

'Forty-oh-one.'

Beck had the cab drop him off on the Fifty-eighth Street side of the Four Seasons Hotel so he could get to the hotel's elevators without walking across the huge open lobby that faced the main entrance.

As he walked toward the double bank of elevators in the center of the hotel's mezzanine level, he could feel the pressure of time, fatigue, and the growing burdens of pain plaguing him.

The knife wound on his leg throbbed, made worse by Stepanovich's knee kicks. He could barely close his hands, and by tomorrow he'd be feeling another set of bruises and strains.

He decided that his move against Markov's men in Tribeca had probably delayed any attack on them, but for how long? And how many men could Markov send against him? And what if he called on Kolenka for help?

Beck stood in front of the elevators that would lead to the fortieth floor. He thought about hotel security. The doormen on Fifty-eighth Street had greeted him and held open the door, but barely glanced at him. It was after eleven, but the bar and restaurant on that side of the hotel were still open. He could be a guest, a diner, someone stopping in for a drink, or a hired assassin.

There was a single corridor in the middle of the hotel which occupied a section of the block between Fifty-eighth and Fifty-ninth streets where the elevators were located. There were six elevators. Three on the south side of the corridor that went from the fifth floor to the twenty-ninth floor. Then three on the north side that went from the thirty-first floor to the fifty-second floor.

Beck waited in front of the north-side bank of elevators. An elevator opened and he stepped in. The car was empty.

The elevator rushed him to Olivia's floor without stopping. He stepped out into a surprisingly small foyer, lit with discreet overhead accent lighting. Small brass plaques to the right and left indicated which rooms occupied each corridor. There was a small Léger print above each plaque.

Beck called Manny once more.

'Okay, I'm at the hotel. Call your woman who's watching Olivia and tell her I'm heading toward the room now. Tell her what I look like and to open the door for me.'

'How soon you gonna be there?'

'Thirty seconds.'

'Okay. Give me a minute before you knock.'

'Sure. Demarco back yet? You get that guy squared away?'

'D's not back yet. Yeah, we got the guy set the way you asked.'

'One last thing, after you talk to your gal, call Ricky and Jonas and tell 'em to get some sleep, then get back on Milstein in the morning.'

'Got it. What are you gonna do with the one we snatched?'

'Pump him for information. Maybe trade him for something. I don't know. Just leave him alone to wonder what's next.'

Beck broke the connection. He relaxed for a few moments, standing motionless in the quiet opulence of the fortieth floor, giving Manny time to call the woman guarding Olivia.

He wondered how much a room went for at the Four Seasons.

He inhaled slowly and held his breath for a moment, listening, feeling for a sense of the city just outside. He felt nothing, heard nothing, but it seemed as if he could still sense something out there. A hum? A pulse of the city? He wondered if he was imagining it.

He thought for a few more moments how hotels were able to create such a cocoon of peace and security like the one that surrounded him. How the careful lighting high-lighted certain areas while leaving other sections in soothing shadows. How the plush carpets absorbed sound and the tasteful decorations gave an impression of opulence.

Beck looked at the calm subtle colors surrounding him. He considered how important it was for guests to feel like they had escaped from the discomfort and tension of a sometimes frantic, often inhospitable city into a refuge where they could feel warm and safe and protected. Was it true?

No, thought Beck, it was an illusion.

34

Markov had sweated through his clothes in the cramped back room at the Waldorf. It had nothing to do with the hotel's ventilation, which worked fine. He always sweated when he concentrated and pushed and cajoled and manipulated and calculated until he had accomplished what he'd set out to do.

The acrid odor he exuded actually comforted him. It made him feel not only productive, but protected in a perverse way. The fact that he was repugnant empowered Markov. He extracted pleasure from it. He reveled in exercising his entitlement to cause discomfort in others. As if it were his right.

The people who dealt in selling weapons that could kill, that could create a chain of incalculable misery, almost always made some effort to rationalize it. As did thieves and exploiters of all types. The rationale ran along the usual line – if I don't do it someone else will, so why not me? Markov never rationalized. He created misery and pain without a second thought. As if it were his natural right. And because it brought him power and privilege, which he deserved to have. Why did he deserve it? Markov didn't need a reason why.

No one had the right to prevent Markov from getting whatever he wanted. And yet, at the moment, his will was being thwarted. His entitlement obstructed. He had not yet succeeded in overcoming his biggest challenge: obtaining end-user certificates for his arms shipment. In this case, he needed end-user certificates to get his shipment of arms someplace where they could be trucked into Syria. Flying directly into Syria was out of the question. There could be no trail connecting him and his masters to where the arms had been obtained, or to where they would end up in Syria. There had to be a destination in between that would allow plausible deniability.

He had planned on Beirut. But as so often happened, his suppliers knew the game, and knew the end-user certificates represented an opportunity for profit. In order to squeeze more money, they had to claim more difficulties. There was always a tipping point between the costs versus the trouble. And Markov never went into a negotiation without options.

So, he considered Turkey. Gazientep Airport was a good choice, but Markov knew from experience the bribes needed were astronomical. Not that US Military Intelligence couldn't afford it. He just had to calculate the cost of Redmond complaining about the rise in price.

Markov played chicken or egg for three hours, trying to work around the problem of end-user certificates. He finally realized his first plan was the only way possible and spent an additional half hour forcing his Albanian connection with a combination of threats and bribes to come up with the documents he needed.

Many would have given up, or at least taken a break, but not Markov. He thrived on the effort.

He began to strip off the sweaty clothes, until he was

sitting on the upholstered desk chair in only his socks and underwear.

He checked his watch. Nearly eleven o'clock. He had been working since just before four. He retrieved the cell phone he used while in the United States and turned it on, having kept it off while he was working.

As the phone booted up, he absentmindedly fondled his penis, thinking about which escort service to call after he finished his work. He'd decided on negotiating for some desperate Russian girl that would keep doing whatever he asked as long as he kept handing her hundred-dollar bills.

He began to fantasize about how far he could take her. Which humiliations he could get her to agree to. He knew his body would disgust her. Fat, hairy, too many creases and crevices producing body odors that would sicken her. He pictured her – thin, bleached blond. Her pubic region shaved completely. The fun would be to see how far he could go. How long he could keep things hovering on the edge of fear and disgust and shame, giving her just enough additional money so she wouldn't rebel.

Maybe take a half a Viagra. A few pulls of marijuana. Nothing too extreme. He'd rummage around in his laptop bag and see what he had.

And then a big dinner. Steak. Where? Smith & Wollensky? What restaurant would still be open when he was done?

In the middle of his musing, his cell phone began to signal the missed calls alert.

Three missed calls from Stepanovich.

Markov's alarm instincts fired. He felt a pang of dread in his gut.

He dialed Gregor's number. The call went directly to voice mail. He left a message. Waited. Waited.

'Fuck.'

He continued to wait.

Finally, Stepanovich returned his call. Markov's face darkened the moment he heard Stepanovich say, 'Trouble.'

'What kind of trouble?'

'That asshole from this afternoon showed up again.'

'What! Where?'

'Near Crane's apartment. He must have been waiting for him.'

'You sound strange.'

'He broke my fucking nose.'

Markov looked up, shaking his head. '*Chyort voz'mi.* What did he want with Alan?'

'He wanted Crane to tell him about us. He told Crane he would help him against us.'

'And what does Crane say he told him?'

'Crane says he told him to fuck off. Told him to leave him alone, and that we would crush him.'

'Do you believe Crane?'

'Yes. When I went to the restaurant to pick up Crane, the guy had roughed him up. Left him doubled over outside a restaurant.'

'What did you do?'

'I tried to beat him down. Break his face. Bite his fucking nose off and kill him.'

'But . . .'

'But I fucking didn't. He got away.'

Markov cursed silently, thinking, Again he gets away.

'What's Crane doing now?'

'He's in his apartment. Said he had to work. Shouted at me to keep that guy away from him. I have men with me. We have to find him and kill him.'

Markov paused. 'Forget it.'

'What are you talking about? Why?'

'No. You failed twice. I need more information on who he is. How many men he has. Exactly where to find him.'

'We have to move. Fast. Now.'

Markov began shouting. 'Don't fucking tell me what we have to do. You fucked up twice already. I tell you what to do. I tell you what I want you to do, or you can take your crew of idiots and go fuck yourselves off back to fucking Bosnia. What's the matter with you?'

'Sorry.'

'Sorry, sorry. What fucking good does sorry do me? What else? Is that it?'

'No. He had other men with him. They took one of ours. Ahmet.'

'God Christ fuck.'

'They took Ahmet while I was with Crane, near the restaurant.'

'Why? What for?'

'I don't know. So what. Let them kill him. What does he know that can hurt us? Nothing. Ahmet won't say anything anyhow. It's just another reason to get to Beck fast.'

'How many men did Beck have?'

'I don't know. I was with Crane. What does it matter? I can get more. Ask Kolenka for men.'

Markov lapsed into silence. After a few moments he

said, 'All right, Gregor, listen to me. Right now my thinking is, go for the woman first.'

'The woman?'

Markov spoke more calmly. 'I know what you want to do, Gregor. You want to go after Beck. But he escaped you twice. How many times do you want to make the same mistake? Be patient. Do this my way. You'll have your time with him, I promise you. I'll call you back and let you know what to do. Where to go.'

Markov broke off the call and dialed Milstein's number. When he answered, Markov got right to the point.

'Do you know where I can find the woman?'

'I'm working on it. I've called her home number, her cell phone. She doesn't answer.'

'She's not at home. She's hiding somewhere by now. All right, listen. Get me all the information you have for her. Addresses. Social Security number. Bank information. If she has a company credit card, the numbers. Financials. Everything. Check your personnel records. I want it now. E-mail to me.'

He hung up before Milstein could protest about the late hour.

Yes, Markov said to himself. Find the woman. She is the key to Beck.

He'd heard from Crane more than once how astounding the woman was. He would find her, strip her naked, do things to her she had never imagined, then turn her over to Gregor and his Bosnians. They would destroy her and take their time doing it. Then they would see how good Mr Beck is at this game.

As soon as Milstein supplied the information, he would

call Redmond. Redmond would have more resources to find her than anybody. Plan it right. Move fast. No mistakes this time.

Markov spat toward the wastebasket near the small desk in his room. No whore for him tonight. But maybe something better before the night was over. Or, at least different.

35

Nydia Lopez was an attractive young woman. She was small, but she had a great figure, was strong, and moved with a natural grace. She also had an impressive collection of tattoos, including the burst of stars and lines that extended up the right side of her neck and the back of her head, made visible by the fact that her hair in back was cropped short enough to reveal the ink.

Adding to her style was a red bandana tied into a do-rag under a New York Yankees ball cap with a hologram seal, camouflage pants, boots, leather jacket, and a permanent scowl.

And, then, there was the brutal presence of her Smith & Wesson M&P .40 Compact automatic that she held in her left hand resting on her left thigh.

Nydia took pride in her knowledge of weapons and ammunition. Of all her guns, she loved her Smith & Wesson most. It looked badass. All black and tough looking. Top of the line. Small. Only a 3.5-inch barrel, but it held ten rounds in the magazine and one in the chamber, with lots of features to accommodate left-handed shooters like Nydia.

Olivia wasn't sure if the tough young woman really believed she had to keep the gun in her hand while they were alone in the room, or if she just liked holding it all the time.

Olivia sat on the hotel room bed, her legs drawn up under her as she read through the stack of newspapers and magazines she had ordered up from the concierge downstairs.

Nydia sat about as far away from Olivia as she could get, slouched in an upholstered armchair, roaming through the TV channels with the sound turned down. She surfed from a show about being locked up in the Indiana State Prison, to a fishing show, to CNN news, to snippets of movies.

It seemed to Olivia that the TV screen soothed her almost as much as the gun.

Olivia wondered what her bodyguard would do after she turned off the lights and went to sleep. Probably sleep on the couch or the floor. Holding the gun?

Clearly, Manny wanted Nydia there as much to keep Olivia in the room as to keep everybody else out. Olivia flipped through the latest issue of *Vogue*, but couldn't concentrate on anything. She kept thinking about how much events seemed to be spinning out of control.

The phone call to Nydia had been a welcome relief, even if all it did was break the monotony.

Nydia ended the call and said to Olivia, 'Manny says a dude named Beck is coming up. You know him?'

'Yes. When is he coming?'

'Like, right now. I asked Manny what he looks like, but all Manny said was he looks like a guy you don't want to fuck with.'

'Well, that's one way of putting it. He's maybe six, six one. Solid. You know, strong looking. Good head of hair. Dark hair.'

'Okay.'

'Do you know why he's coming?'

'No. All Manny said was to let him in.'

Just then, there was a light knock on the door. Followed by another. Just two.

Nydia moved quickly toward the door, the Smith & Wesson held against the side of her left thigh.

She stood in front of the door. There was no peephole. She slid the security lock into place.

'Yeah, who is it?'

'Beck.'

'Step back from the door, and don't move when I open it, or I'll shoot you.'

'Okay. Is Olivia in there with you?'

'Yeah.'

'Have her ID me.'

Nydia motioned for Olivia to come to the door. She turned the knob and opened the door as far as the security lock would allow. Olivia leaned around to see if it was Beck.

'It's him.'

Nydia closed the door, unfastened the security lock, and let Beck in as she quickly stepped back, her gun aimed at the center of his chest.

Beck took one step into the room and let the door shut by itself with a thunk.

Nydia looked back and forth between Beck and Olivia, lowered the gun, and took her seat in front of the television, satisfied she had let the right man in, and content to ignore them both.

Beck looked at Nydia for a moment, then at Olivia,

who tipped her head and widened her eyes as if to say, I didn't tell her to do that.

Beck scanned the hotel room. It was a bit smaller than he had expected, decorated in warm wood tones, browns and beige, with a queen-size bed, two armchairs, an ottoman, a round table desk with chair, and a 36" flat-screen TV.

The room occupied a corner and featured a large square window on the south wall, and a floor-to-ceiling set of windows on the west wall. Only the inner curtains were drawn, adding a gossamer layer over the lights outside and the traffic moving on Fifty-seventh Street. Beck could hear the faint hum of the city through the double-paned windows. It seemed a comforting sound.

Olivia returned to her perch on the queen-size bed. Beck kicked the ottoman toward the side of the bed and dragged the desk chair over so he could sit next to the bed and talk to Olivia.

For a few moments, Beck said nothing. Olivia waited. Beck's demeanor did nothing to comfort her.

Beck noticed that Olivia wore the same clothes he had seen her in earlier, white shirt and jeans. She still looked stunningly attractive. Beck wasn't getting accustomed to it at all.

'So,' he said.

'Yes?'

Beck sat back in the chair and put his feet on the ottoman and looked at Olivia again. She looked back at him without expression. She sat with her back against the headboard, her encased hand in her lap, watching Beck, waiting.

Finally Beck said, 'The situation isn't getting any better.'
'Why? How?'

Beck waved off her questions. 'I'm not sure how to stop this, and that makes me very uncomfortable.' Beck scowled for a moment. Shifted in his chair. 'Worse, I don't know how to stop this without risking Manny and my friends ending up back in jail.'

'I'm . . . I don't know . . .'

Beck interrupted Olivia. 'And just so you're clear, that cannot happen.'

Just as Olivia was about to respond, Beck's cell phone rang. He checked the caller ID. Brandon Wright.

He told Olivia, 'I've got to take this.' He answered the call by saying, 'Hang on.' He walked into the bathroom, closed the heavy door behind him, and sat on the closed toilet seat.

'What's up?'

'I obtained that information on the woman's injury.'

'Yes?'

'How did you say the injury occurred?'

'Somebody standing over her slammed a fist down on her hand.'

'I see.'

'See what?'

'I think this news I'm about to share is going to upset you, James.'

As he listened to the doctor, Beck noticed that Olivia had washed her bra and panties and hung them on the shower rod to dry. The bra was black, made out of a sheer lacy material. The panties were black, too, a string and a lacy triangle piece, nothing more. The lingerie seemed incredibly erotic to Beck. His mind alternated between picturing her in the sheer underwear and thinking about her sitting on the bed a few feet away naked under her white shirt and jeans. It was enough to give Beck the beginning of an erection.

'Why?'

'Are you calm, James? Seriously. Are you calm? Are you someplace where you can . . . ?'

'Brandon, for fuck's sake, you know I'm not going to be calm. But have you ever known me to do something stupid because I'm pissed?'

'That depends on how you define stupid.'

'Come on.'

Beck was already standing, the cell phone pressed to his ear, the images of Olivia in black lingerie instantly dispelled.

There was silence on the other end of the phone.

Beck spoke more calmly. 'Brandon, believe me, this isn't the time for you to second-guess me. What's going on?'

Another pause, and then Doctor Brandon began to speak.

'All right, here are the facts. Because you got me her signature I was able to get copies of the Lenox Hill records. The admission records, ER notes, X-ray report, all of it.

'James, your friend didn't sustain those fractures the way you described it.'

A cold, sick sensation hit Beck in his gut.

'Are you sure?'

There was a pause and Wright answered, 'Yes.'

'Why?'

'First, the notes from the triage nurse. Olivia Sanchez's hand came in with scrapes on the palm of her hand, embedded dirt that the ER nurse took pains to wash and sterilize. Second, the X-rays showed all the damage was done to the proximal phalanges, indicating that the fingers broke because they were pushed backward. If they had been broken like you described there would have been more damage to the metacarpal bones. The fractures were above the knuckles. It didn't happen from a blow landing down on the hand.'

'So how do you think it happened?'

'According to the notes, she told both the nurse and the surgeon that she fell on the street. Tripped on a curb or something. She fell, put her hand out, landed hard on it, bent back the fingers. She broke the little finger just above the knuckle, broke it completely, and cracked the finger next to it, the same bone, proximal phalange.'

Beck muttered a curse.

'James, I . . .'

Beck spoke softly. 'No, Brandon, you don't have to say anything more. Thank you. I'll deal with it. I had to find out the truth.'

'Yes. Of course. I'm sorry. I'm not going to ask you what this all means now.'

'I'm not sure I can tell you, but . . .' Beck's voice trailed off. 'I have to go. I'll be in touch. Thank you.'

Beck ended the call and sat back on the toilet seat, phone in hand, thinking it through. Going back over the time frame. Trying to figure out how she worked it. Roughing it out. Thinking of the angles, the motives, the possibilities.

He slowly raised his phone and speed-dialed Manny. Beck found it difficult to focus. The anger and tension nagged at him. He felt it in his neck and jaw, in the involuntary movements in his face and mouth.

The phone answered.

'Yeah.'

'Manny, what's going on?'

'Same. Nothing.'

'No sign of anybody coming into the neighborhood?'

'No. Don't worry, we got our eyes open.'

'Okay, do me a favor. I need to talk to your cousin in private. This lady you got up here, I have a feeling if I tell her to do something she doesn't want to do, she'll shoot me.'

'Yeah, that's Nydia.'

'Well, the room's too fucking small for me to talk to Olivia in private, so call Nydia and tell her to take a break for a while. Go downstairs and get a drink or something to eat. Or take a walk around the block. Tell her she should wait for me to call her back to the room.'

'What's going on, James?'

'I don't know yet. Not all of it. I have to talk to Olivia.'

'James . . .'

Beck interrupted the wariness he heard in Manny's voice.

'Manny, just let me do what I have to do. Okay? We got our fucking backs against the wall here. I have to figure this out. I just don't have time to tell you everything now. You have to trust me, partner.'

There was silence. And then Manny Guzman spoke slowly and carefully. 'She's my family, James.'

'And you're mine. Call your girl with the gun, and tell her I need some time here.'

Beck ended the connection before Manny could ask him anything more. He shoved the cell phone in his pocket, put both hands on the sink, concentrating on letting his anger recede. Brandon Wright knew him well, but Beck knew himself. He ran the water and rinsed his face, first feeling the cold water, then feeling the water when it had heated up, soothing him, calming him.

As he dried off with the plush hand towel, he heard a cell phone ring outside in the room.

He stepped out of the bathroom and stood waiting as Nydia finished her call. She looked up at Beck. He said, 'Dial my cell number so I have yours.'

He recited the number. Nydia dialed it without comment. Beck answered the call, stored the number, and said, 'I'll call you when it's time to come back.'

Olivia watched the exchange. Something had changed Beck's mood. She wondered what had happened in that bathroom.

Beck walked over to the window overlooking Fifty-seventh Street and stood with his back to Olivia while Nydia gathered herself, shoved the Smith & Wesson in the back of her camouflage pants, and left the room.

As the door shut, he turned to face Olivia, staying near the windows at the other end of the room.

'What's going on?' she asked.

Beck stared at her for a moment. Amazed that part of him was actually thinking about the fact that she was sitting on that bed with no underwear on. A rueful smile crossed his face. Maybe that wasn't such a bad thing, he thought. If I completely terrify this woman, it probably won't do me much good.

He watched her for a moment, wondering if there was any way he could see the true part of her underneath everything on the surface.

She was wary, confused by Beck, but so accustomed to controlling men that she still seemed relaxed and confident.

Beck said, 'So, I was telling you about things getting worse.'

'Yes?'

'Did you understand what I was saying?'

'I think so.'

'Just to be clear, it's important that you realize any one of us could be dead now: Manny, Demarco, me. Ciro. You understand that, right?'

'Yes, if you say so. Of course.'

'Or on our way back to jail.'

Olivia continued to give Beck her attention, but said nothing.

Beck motioned toward the door with his head, 'I like that tough little chick Manny has looking after you. But she wouldn't be much more than a small bump between Markov's men and you. You get that, right?'

'His men?'

'Yes. You have to understand who Markov has working with him. War criminals. Rapists. Killers of women and children and old people. Mass murderers. One of them, the one who seems to be their leader, is clearly insane.'

Olivia stared at him, but didn't answer.

'There are others, too. A group of hardcore gangsters.

Russian. Not the crazy loose-knit crews who flail around with dumb shit. Hardcore. Old, old school.' He shook his head, thinking about it. 'From out of the gulags. Beyond anything you know about.'

He moved away from the window overlooking Fifty-seventh Street and sat in the chair where Nydia had been, keeping his distance from Olivia, but his gaze unwavering.

'So,' said Beck, 'you and I have to talk about a few things.'

'All right.'

'And there can't be anything less than the truth. In whatever you say. So help you God.'

Olivia stared back at Beck.

'You understand, right?'

Olivia nodded.

'Let me talk you through it. You're at Summit. You've worked your way to a position of responsibility. You find out Alan Crane is being reckless. Investing money for, as you say, bad people. And he's pushing it, taking big risks. Naked shorts and all that. Manipulating stocks, whatever unscrupulous shit guys like that do.

'Milstein isn't comfortable with it. He's made a deal with the devil, but you know he's worried. Crane's too reckless. But Milstein is between a rock and a hard place because he needs the fees and the twenty percent of profits.'

Beck paused, waiting to see if Olivia wanted to say anything. Correct anything. She just continued to stare at him, composed, unmoving. He continued.

'You go to Milstein. You encourage him to put a stop to Crane's high-risk behavior. Nothing more than that. Basically pushing him in the direction he wants to go anyhow.'

Beck waited. Olivia said nothing.

'Okay. Crane gets wind of it. He goes nuts. Comes down on you. Threatens you. Bangs on your desk. Breaks your hand. Yells. Tells you he's going to kill you. Have I got it right so far, Olivia?'

'That's what I told you.'

'I know that's what you told me. Is that what happened?'

'Yes.'

'All of it? All of that is what happened?'

'Why don't you believe me?'

Beck leaned forward and spoke softly, but his intensity sent a chill through Olivia.

'This is not the time to ask me questions, Olivia. This is the time to tell me the truth. That's the only way this will work. So don't ask me questions. Just tell me the truth.'

Beck leaned back. 'It makes no sense that Crane would go off the way you described just because you gently pushed Milstein in the direction he was thinking of going. No, the truth is – you and Milstein conspired to get rid of Crane, and he found out about it. You and Milstein joined forces to shut Crane down.

'But you had to do it in a way that wouldn't upset Markov. Milstein couldn't afford to lose him. So you and Milstein came up with a plan. Milstein would drop the hammer on Crane to make him stop taking so much risk. You would step forward to monitor his trades. Why? Because you convinced Milstein you could handle Markov. There isn't a man alive you don't think you can handle, Olivia.'

For the first time, Olivia looked down, staring at her lap, looking at her broken fingers in their cast, no longer maintaining eye contact with Beck.

'You saw all that money. You saw Crane screwing it up. You knew you could twist that fat guy around your finger. So why not? Why shouldn't you get your fair share? Earn a nice bonus. Hey, Wall Street jerks a fraction as good as you are taking home multimillion-dollar bonuses like it's nothing.

'You were willing to work for it. Hell, a measly two, three million and you'd own that nice little place up in Riverdale. All you needed was a chance to make your mark. To get your wings. You could save the day. Crane was looking at huge losses. You could keep the account from blowing up.'

Beck sat forward, talking faster. Now Olivia looked up and watched him.

'But you both knew Crane wouldn't go quietly. Hell, Markov was his client. He brought him in. No way he would give up control. But you had that figured out, too.' He stopped and turned to face Olivia. 'You had Manny. What did you tell Milstein about Manny? Did you tell him you could have Crane killed?'

Olivia answered quickly. 'No. No. Absolutely not.'

Beck continued looking at her. 'No?'

'No. No way.'

'You're lying.'

Olivia's voice rose. 'No. I'm not. All right, I admit we talked about Manny. Milstein told me how volatile Crane was. I told him I wasn't worried. I told Milstein that my cousin was a man people feared. I told him that one conversation with him and Alan would fold. He would back off and let us do what needed to be done.'

'How were you going to arrange that? How were you going to get Manny involved? The truth.'

'I was going to tell Manny that a man at work was trying to intimidate me. Giving me a hard time. Bullying me. If I had to, I was going to tell Manny he threatened me.'

Beck looked at Olivia, nodded, thinking it over.

'Call in Manny against the bully.'

'Something like that.'

'Something like that? There's no *like that* with Manny Guzman, Olivia. No middle ground. No gray. He's not the kind of man who slaps someone in the head and says be nice to my cousin. He fucking kills them. Makes them disappear.'

Olivia shook her head. 'No. I mean, why would I think that? I never believed it would get to that. Milstein was too smart. He never planned on getting rid of Crane completely. We were fine with him staying around to front the business and handle Markov. We just needed him to step back, stop being so reckless, and let us cut back on his high-risk trading. It meant he had to cut me in for a share, but I was going to earn it.'

'And you were going to leave Markov to Crane?'

'No. Not completely. Sure, he was Crane's client, but I was going to be involved. I had no problem with turning on the charm to keep Markov happy.'

'So what went wrong? Why did Crane get so crazy?'

'Because he got wind of what we were planning before Milstein could pitch him. Crane heard what Milstein and me were up to and he went nuts.'

'Meaning the attack. The yelling and screaming, threatening to kill you. Breaking your hand.'

Olivia stopped. She sensed something. She watched Beck looking at her. She knew. Maybe she had known from the moment Beck started going over it all again. She looked down, than back up at Beck. She spoke slowly and softly. 'It didn't happen exactly that way.'

Beck sat back in Nydia's chair. 'What way did it happen?'

She couldn't look at Beck. She stared past him, gazing at the glow of the city lights coming in through the transparent inner drape drawn over the window.

'Everything I told you is true. Crane came in. Yelling, screaming, threatening. Pounding the desk. He really got to me. I really believed my life was at risk. I realized I may have underestimated the whole thing. Crane truly sounded like he actually could have me killed.

'I hadn't really thought about who Markov was until that moment. What he might be capable of doing. When Crane threatened to kill me, I was terrified. Then I suddenly got paranoid. Maybe Milstein had set the whole thing up knowing Crane would do this. Maybe *he* tipped off Crane. Was he using me as a stalking horse to see what Crane would do? Did he blow up everything so I would go to Manny?

'My head was reeling.' Now she turned her gaze to Beck. 'I never experienced anything like that.'

'Go on.'

'I was numb. I kept thinking, what the hell have I done? I left the office in a daze. I usually get the train on Fifty-ninth, but I couldn't. I needed to move. I decided to walk to Grand Central. It was cold out, but there were still a lot of people on the streets. People heading home. I was kind of like walking at my own pace, you know. Dazed, not like all the people walking past me.

'It was dark, I wasn't paying attention. I don't even know exactly how it happened. Or where. I was in the middle of a crosswalk. Maybe there was a little ice, a manhole, an uneven part, I don't know. I just slipped. Fell sort of to the side. Landed on my hand.'

She lifted her left hand, wrapped in the cast as if it were an exhibit. Remembering how it had actually happened. She closed her eyes. The tears were coming, silently moving down her cheeks as if something separate and apart from her.

Beck watched her. Picturing it. Listening for the truth in her words.

'I don't think anything ever hurt me as much as that did. I didn't even have gloves on. It was horrible. Horrible. I swear it seemed to be all part of what Crane had done to me. He put me in that state. He drove me out of there. It was as if he'd done it to me. Made it happen.'

She took a slow deep breath, shook her head, distancing herself from the memory. Beck sat unmoving, watching her, listening closely.

'Anyhow, I just cradled my hand in the crook of my arm. I knew the little finger was broken. It was jutting out at a crazy angle. I was crying. People helped me up, asked me if I was okay. I couldn't talk. Somebody told me to get to a hospital. Somebody hailed a cab for me. Next thing I was in the emergency room at Lenox Hill.

'They gave me a shot. The pain started to ebb. I just went with it. Whatever they said, I did. Sit here. Go there. I was drained. The time didn't matter. It took a while to get everything done, but once the X-rays came back and the surgeon set my fingers, it felt more normal. The pain shots kept it all numb. He was a very confident guy. He told me I might not need surgery.

'About the time they started to put the cast on and the pain settled, I began thinking about what had happened. I started to get furious. That fucking Alan Crane. The years I put in. His arrogance. His stupidity. His . . . his reckless-ness. And the fucking nerve to threaten me like that.'

She paused to look at Beck. He sat motionless, no expression, listening. She had to get through it now. Get the rest of it out.

'Fuck.' She shook her head. 'I was still afraid. From what Crane did. But I started wondering if Milstein had turned against me. If he had tipped off Crane. I was sure Crane meant what he said. The hate in him.

'I called Milstein from the hospital. I left a message on his voice mail. I figured for sure he'd call me back. He never did.'

Olivia paused, remembering it. She looked directly at Beck. 'That's when I decided to fight back. Sitting in that emergency room. I called the police. I started to build a case. I knew Crane would deny it. I didn't care. I was going on the offensive. They weren't going to get away with it. I waited for the police to come to the hospital. And waited. After a while I just couldn't wait any longer and I went home.

'On the cab ride home, that's when I decided to go to Manny. I think I would have gone to him whether I'd bro-ken my hand or not. I was convinced I had to have some protection. The accident just made everything more real.

Like a slap in the face to wake me up and show me where I was at.'

Olivia shrugged. Held up her hand again.

'It cost me enough pain. I figured I had every right to use it.' She paused. 'I guess I didn't think the whole thing through with Manny. I knew about you in a very vague way. Manny never talked to me about his life. When I told him a man at work had attacked me, had broken my hand, it seemed totally real to me. I swear I didn't know it was going to get this far. I was just determined to fight back. To survive.'

She paused, wiped away the tears as if they were annoying her.

'That's the truth. That's what I did.' She stopped. Beck waited. 'It's my fault Manny is involved. That you're involved. I never . . . I didn't know. I'm sorry.'

Olivia leaned back against the headboard. Relieved. Drained. Showing a terrible vulnerability that actually made Beck want to comfort her.

Finally, Beck said, 'I believe you.'

'Thank you.'

Beck nodded.

Olivia got up and walked to the foot of the bed. She sat on the bed, close enough to Beck so that she could reach out and touch his knee.

'What can I do? What should I do? How do I make this right?'

36

After he finished talking to Stepanovich, Markov began working every angle. He pestered Milstein until he received an e-mail with most of the information he demanded on Olivia.

Next, he reached out to Kolenka.

Markov had to leave messages and wait nearly a half hour for the old gangster to call him back. When he answered his phone he heard Kolenka's raspy voice growl out one word.

'Yes?'

'Ivan, I need your help.'

Kolenka muttered one word. 'Beck.'

'Yes.'

'I warned you.'

'You did. And now I'm taking steps. I want someone kidnapped.'

'Who?'

'The woman who started all these problems.'

'You have people, why call me?'

'Because your people are better.'

Markov heard Kolenka cough, the phlegm-filled hack of an inveterate chain-smoker. He pictured Kolenka hunched over, sipping strong Turkish coffee, smoking an unending chain of unfiltered Lucky Strikes in one of the shabby, barely furnished apartments that Kolenka used randomly.

Markov pushed. 'Ivan, are you thinking of refusing me?'

'You want to take the woman because you think that will draw out Beck.'

'Yes.'

'Maybe. You understand this man is someone you must be careful with.'

'Maybe I can persuade her to call him off.'

'He won't listen.'

'Then I will make sure they are both dead.'

'There are people who will try to avenge Beck.'

'They won't find me. Or maybe we take care of them, too.'

Kolenka's silence told Markov he was thinking everything through. Markov listened to Kolenka breathing on the other end of the phone. A raspy, labored sound. Breathing and thinking.

Finally, Kolenka asked, 'How will you find her?'

'My friends in Washington.'

'Ah. They push buttons and see everything.'

'Exactly.'

Another pause. Finally, Kolenka spoke. 'One condition. Everything works through your end. I will give you two of my best men. You find her. They will help capture her, and deliver the woman wherever you say. After that, we have nothing more to do with it.'

'Fine.'

'Do not take Beck lightly.' Kolenka hung up without another word.

Markov felt the sharks circling him. Coming after him and his money. But now he would strike. Capture the woman. She would either tell him where to find Beck, or Beck would come after her. He would be ready this time. And then, once he had his money safe, teach those idiots Milstein and Crane a lesson for allowing this mess to happen.

37

Olivia continued talking to Beck, sitting at the end of the bed, leaning toward him.

'I'll do whatever I can to make this right, James. I'll tell Manny the truth about my hand. I'll do whatever you say.'

Beck shook his head. 'No. Do not do that. I wouldn't be able to guarantee you would survive it.'

Olivia shook her head. 'I don't believe that.'

'I know you don't. But don't do it. And don't argue with me about it.'

She frowned, looking confused, but agreed. 'Fine, whatever you say. What can I do?'

'You sure you've told me everything you know about Markov.'

'Everything I know.'

'Do you know anything about who his customers are?'

'Just what I told you before. My impression is that Markov does a lot of shipments for this country.'

'Arms?'

'Yes. Obviously, the US does a lot of stuff that's covert. Someone has to do it. Markov is one of those someones. That's how Milstein rationalizes handling his account. He says Markov doesn't do anything the US doesn't want him to do.'

'Do you know which agency?'

'No.'

'How did Markov get a legitimate brokerage to handle his money?'

'What do you mean?'

'I wouldn't imagine someone can just hand over a hundred million dollars to you guys without triggering an inquiry.'

'Yes, you're right. It's worse than ever since the Patriot Act. But Crane and Markov have worked through it. That's one of the things Crane is good at. I suspect most of it never entered the US banking system.'

'It's hidden offshore?'

Olivia shrugged. 'All money is hidden to a certain extent. I'm sure Markov and Crane make sure nobody knows where his funds are: competitors, creditors, anybody he doesn't want knowing his business. It's only illegal if you're hiding money to avoid taxes. It's offshore because it was never onshore. Never earned here.'

'But how does he buy investments in US markets?'

'Tons of ways. And who's to say it's all in US markets? I'm sure Crane is trading in markets all over the world. That's part of how guys like Crane earn their commissions.'

'How's it work?'

'Same way hundreds of US companies do it. They bundle money in various entities. Keep the assets of that entity or corporation in an offshore bank or brokerage. Invest those assets however they want. And don't forget, money that goes into those entities is legally earned. Or in ways that look legal. Markov followed the rules enough so he can invest in whatever Crane wants to invest in.'

'The rules. Whose rules?'

'The ones written for people like Markov. And they still bend them as much as they can. Why do you think guys like Crane exist? Why are you asking me all this?'

Beck ignored the question.

'So, beyond Markov, do you know anything about the people Markov is associated with?'

'No.'

'Crane has no clue either? Or Milstein?'

'I imagine Crane knows more than Milstein, but I don't know that either of them knows as much about them as you seem to. How'd you find out about the war crimes stuff?'

Again, Beck ignored the question.

'Well, I guess you know about criminal types from your time in prison. What was it like?'

'Prison?'

'Yes.'

'That's not exactly the right question. More to the point would be what was it like going from a fairly normal civilized life out in the world into being locked up, incarcerated. There was no break-in period for me. No reform school, or minimum-security lockup. There was normal life, and then maximum-security hell.'

It was Beck's turn to gaze out through the flimsy drapes.

'Eight years I breathed that stink. Listened to the din of constant yelling and screaming and carrying on twenty-four-hours a day. Crazy, insane bullshit. The most primitive, inhuman survival behavior imaginable. Trapped in a world of constant maneuvering and conning and conniving. Surrounded by men with pathetic attention spans and zero impulse control, and stupid, dangerous rationalizations.'

Olivia listened to Beck's speech, perched in front of him at the end of the bed.

'Imagine living with people ready to kill or hurt or maim anybody at any time. Anybody.' Beck snapped his fingers. 'Without warning.'

'I can't imagine that.'

Beck leaned forward in his chair, moving closer to Olivia's so she couldn't avoid hearing what he was about to say.

'But those people I'm talking about in prison? They're run-of-the-mill criminals who live in that world. Sure, they can go off at any moment. They'll stab you, shoot you, hit you, doesn't matter. They'll end up dead or in prison, and either way, it's pretty much okay with them.

'But these guys Markov is with – they are in a whole other category. They went after whole towns and villages. Women, children, old people. They tried to wipe out entire categories of people.

'And the Russians I was telling you about? My God, they live by a code so ancient and fucked up they don't even know how to be half-human.'

Beck trailed off for a moment.

Olivia watched him shake his head and sit back in his chair.

'Why are you . . . ?'

Beck interrupted her. 'Why am I what?'

'Telling me all this.'

'So you understand how dangerous this is for you. And us. For all of us.'

'If you're trying to terrify me, you have.'

'Good.'

'Why?'

'So you understand.'

'You already told me I can't.'

'I want you to try.'

Olivia fairly shouted, 'Try? I can hardly fucking breathe I'm so scared. What am I supposed to do?'

Beck leaned forward again, sitting on the edge of his chair again, speaking low and fast and hard as he stared into her eyes.

'You know what you have to do. What we have to do.'

'What?'

'We do exactly what Markov fears we will. We steal his fucking money. The only way we survive this is to take control of that money. The only edge we have is to make him choose between us and his money.'

Olivia stared at Beck. 'How?'

'We'll figure out how.'

'No, how is that going to stop him? That will make Markov want to kill us all the more.'

'No. He kills us, he loses the money.'

'You think if we make some sort of deal he'll agree? Walk away?'

'You leave that up to me. Right now, the thing you have to do is help us get control of Markov's money. Can you do that? Can you help us?'

Olivia answered without hesitation. 'Of course I'll help you. I'll tell you whatever I know. I'll do anything I can.'

Beck sat back in his chair, nodding. 'Good.'

Suddenly, Olivia slid off the end of the bed and sat down on her folded legs in front of Beck. She wrapped her arms around his legs, holding onto him tightly. Beck felt her breasts pushing into his knees. Her face was nearly level with his. Less than six inches separating them.

He could smell that feminine soapy scent she had. He thought about her bare skin under her crisp white shirt. He stared into her gold-flecked brown eyes. They seemed luminous. Her closeness, her completely unchecked, uninhibited hold on him made the moment feel incredibly erotic.

'You have to help me. You have to, James. I won't survive this without you.'

'I know.'

38

The clock next to Walter Pearce's computer said 11:52 p.m. The caller ID on his ringing cell phone said MILSTEIN.

'It's me. What have you been doing all day? Have you found Beck for God's sake? I need results, Walter.'

Walter had no intention of telling Milstein what he had spent most of his day doing.

After he had dropped off the material on Beck and Baldassare, Walter had intended to catch up on his sleep. But he thought of a way he might find Beck, so he'd sat in Milstein's lobby using information from Beck's trial records to locate Beck's law firm, which turned out to be a mostly one-man operation run by a lawyer named Phineas P. Dunleavy. He called the office, explained to the woman that answered that he had urgent correspondence for one of the firm's clients, James Beck.

The woman told him all correspondence for Mr Beck came through their office. Pearce told her he needed to get an envelope to James Beck by end of day.

The secretary responded that their messenger service could guarantee delivery by end of day for a $150 express-delivery fee, if Pearce could get the envelope to her by three o'clock.

That confirmed that Beck was somewhere in the Tri-state area. Pearce agreed to the price of delivery and said he would have the material in Dunleavy's office in time. It was just after 2 p.m.

Pearce walked over to the Staples on Lexington and prepared an envelope. He picked one that was a distinctive color, green, and big enough to spot from a distance, ten-by-fourteen inches. He filled it with meaningless papers, drove to Dunleavy's office in Lower Manhattan, and parked at a hydrant across the street.

He was up to Dunleavy's office and back in his car before anyone had time to ticket him. He waited behind the wheel of his nondescript Toyota Camry. A half-hour later, a messenger entered Dunleavy's office building. He came out carrying the green envelope.

The messenger jumped in a cab, and Walter fell in behind it, tailing as closely as he could. The stop-and-go traffic made it easy to follow the cab.

What Pearce didn't know was that as the cab pulled away, Phineas P. Dunleavy stood at the window of his office watching Pearce's Camry slip behind the messenger's cab. Despite being just past sixty years old, Dunleavy had excellent eyesight. From the second floor he was able to see the license plate on the Toyota, noting it down on a yellow legal pad, wondering what fool was trying to find James Beck with one of the oldest tricks in the book.

Dunleavy frowned at the departing car. He had given the messenger an address in the opposite direction of Beck's location, a restaurant on City Island up in the Bronx.

Dunleavy was a sturdy man with a head of thick white hair and a booming voice made pleasant by the hint of an Irish brogue. He was well practiced at playing the role of a friendly scoundrel who loved his Irish whiskey. But underneath the hale-fellow-well-met act, Dunleavy was a shrewd, tireless, implacable advocate for his clients.

Watching the clumsy ruse set against Beck made Dunleavy more than slightly angry. Angry because one of his clients appeared to be in some sort of danger. But even more angry because whoever was behind this thought Dunleavy was stupid.

The lawyer set about finding out who owned that car. He didn't intend to take long doing it, or in letting Beck know what was afoot.

Nor did it take Walter Pearce much time to realize after following the messenger for nearly an hour that James Beck had no connection whatsoever with a City Island lobster restaurant shut down for the winter.

Beck had already made him feel incompetent and ashamed. Being sent on a wild-goose chase had only added to the sting. It made him more determined than ever to find James Beck. The minute he got home, Pearce immediately got on his computer and his phone searching for James Beck, only stopping when his phone rang.

Milstein's rude insistence only increased Walter's anger. There was no way Walter was going to tell him that he'd wasted most of a day on a wild-goose chase. Instead he answered, 'I spent most of the day following a lead that went nowhere. I've been working nonstop. I'll call you when I find something.'

'No. You pick me up at seven tomorrow, first thing in the morning. I want a full report on everything you've done. I have to make some decisions. Fast.'

Walter didn't have time to protest or answer before Milstein hung up on him.

Pearce's failure stood in contrast to Redmond's success. Within two hours after Markov's request to find Olivia Sanchez, he called Markov's secure cell phone line.

'We've located the individual. We have her credit card charged for two nights at the Four Seasons Hotel in New York, starting tonight. I went ahead and found out her room for you. Four-zero-zero-one.'

'Wonderful. Thank you. I knew I could rely on you.'

'You also e-mailed me that you want to contract a team with black-ops capabilities.'

'Yes.'

'I'm sending you encrypted information on that. I suspect you want a standard team of three?'

'Yes.'

'Don't tell me what it's for. Discuss it with their representative. I'm sending you information on one source. The best. The man you call will go over backgrounds and capabilities. These men are very, very serious. Don't compromise them. Don't renege on your agreement in any way. Don't fail to pay them in full. Any misrepresentations or failure on your part will reflect badly on me, and result in serious consequences. Do you understand?'

'Yes.'

'I hope so.'

'What do you mean by that?'

'It means I know you. Pay the price they ask. Don't try to bargain. And don't ask them to do anything more than you agree on.'

'All right. Of course. How soon can I get them?'

'If you need someone who can be at your location quickly, make that a requirement.'

'Right.'

'Is there anything else?' asked Redmond.

'Yes. Your shipment is leaving in seven hours. Arrival at the agreed-on place approximately fifteen hours from now. Have your people in place for transit to wherever you want the shipment to go.'

'They already are.'

Redmond cut the call without further conversation.

Markov checked his watch. Nearly ten-thirty.

So, first the woman. She was smart to hide in a hotel. But not smart enough. He would call Gregor, tell him to take one of his men and meet Kolenka's men outside the hotel.

By this time tomorrow his shipment for Redmond would be completed. Beck and the woman would be history. Which would certainly help motivate Crane.

Markov heard his computer sound a tone that signaled an e-mail had arrived. A series of letters, numbers, and symbols appeared when he opened the e-mail.

He used the encryption code Redmond had given him and a single phone number emerged with a name. Wilson.

He checked his watch again. First, get Gregor and Kolenka's men going. Gregor plus one of his, and Kolenka's two. That should be more than enough for one woman. Then hire the contract team.

They were usually ex-Special Forces, of some country or other. He knew he would have to carefully plan the negotiation for the black-ops team. What exactly did he want? Foremost above anything, he needed protection for Crane. Gregor would not agree to watch Crane. He probably preferred beating Crane to death after what had happened to his two men. Gregor was now completely focused on eliminating Beck and the woman. Good. But if something happened to Crane, none of it would matter.

Markov also knew that at some point there was going to be a war. There might be a way to use their military skills, at least at the planning stage. But Markov had to be careful. He knew hiring such men would be very costly. He knew he couldn't involve them in anything that would cause trouble for Redmond and jeopardize that relationship.

But mostly, he had to get them on board quickly.

Markov dialed the phone number of Wilson.

A recorded message started abruptly, stating, 'Please leave a clear recording stating the following: number of personnel, time and dates of employment, place of employment, skills required. Also, leave a secure contact number. If we can fill the requirements, you will receive a callback within thirty minutes, confirming personnel and price. Thank you.'

Markov had been jotting notes. When the electronic tone beeped, he cleared his throat and recited the information in order, 'I need three men, starting as soon as they can arrive in New York City, until approximately 4 p.m. Friday. I need experts in surveillance and personal security.'

Markov gave his cell phone number, hoping he hadn't been too vague. If they wanted more details, he would just emphasize they would be guarding one man who was working for him. He couldn't think much beyond that.

He had completely sweated through even his underwear. His empty stomach grumbled. He reached for his attaché case laying on the bed and removed a gram of cocaine from the lining. He snorted a small pile into each nostril from his thumbnail. He sniffed at the sting in his nose and the back of his throat and blinked away the tears that filled his eyes.

The cocaine picked him up considerably, but it would be wearing off soon. He rummaged around in the side pocket of his attaché case, looking for his Adderall. He would be working for a few hours more, at least.

39

Olivia continued to stare at Beck, unblinking, with such intensity that it sparked something in Beck beyond desire.

Power.

She was making him feel incredibly powerful. As if he had total dominance and control over her.

Until that moment, he had not fully understood how dangerous Olivia Sanchez could be. Or how devious she actually was.

The temptation to exercise control over such an astonishingly alluring woman actually made it difficult for Beck to breathe. Beck's eyes narrowed. He let the fear of how much control *she* was about to obtain over *him* penetrate into his gut, actually feeling his stomach tighten.

She didn't move.

She didn't waiver.

She continued holding on to his legs, pressing herself into him, staring at him.

Beck pictured what would happen if he simply reached out and touched her, ignited the fire by making her believe he was comforting her.

They would be on each other in a heartbeat. A literal heartbeat.

She still wore nothing under her white shirt and jeans. It would take seconds for her to be naked. Beck pictured her standing in front of him without clothes. Without guile. He felt his erection grow, adding an excruciating insistence.

He imagined the feel of her bronze, flawlessly smooth skin. Even smoother and softer over her breasts. He had stared at them long enough when she was clothed to be able to imagine them uncovered. Full, perfect teardrops. Perfect. The thought of cupping those beautiful breasts, feeling them, running his hands around to her back and down to her ass, around her hips, in between her legs; feeling for the wetness made him clench his jaws, but he didn't back off from the fantasy.

That was the thing. The intriguing thing about her body. Full breasts and rear, but long limbs with fine wrists and ankles. And the skin, that amazing skin. And her mesmerizing eyes. And a mouth he wanted to feel against his. Passion he wanted to experience as he slid into her. Feeling the silky tightness. Hearing her gasp. He was actually sweating slightly under the sexual tension. The offer of sex, the contest of power and control, the temptation to say fuck it to everything to experience her – he was in a battle of wills he was losing.

Christ, Christ, stop it, he told himself. What a fucking disaster.

He swallowed hard. He forced a mantle of deception over himself. He continued to look into her eyes, intent on preventing her from deriving any satisfaction from making him look away. He leaned forward in the chair, using the force of his larger physical presence to impose on her.

The moment passed. The power of her seduction, her intensity, were diverted into a part of Beck that nobody could touch. A part that had emerged in the hard, cold hell of his incarceration. Something that he shared with Ivan Kolenka, and Gregor Stepanovich, and Manny and Ciro and Demarco. A part that even the power of Olivia Sanchez couldn't penetrate.

'Okay,' he said. 'Okay.' He reached out and took hold of her forearms, firmly, with purpose. He slowly pulled her arms away from him.

He stood and lifted her to her feet. Holding her forearms, controlling her, he pivoted quickly, like a boxer who had been maneuvered into the corner of the ring, slips a punch and twists away, exchanging the cramped, tight area of confinement for the open space that allows maneuvering.

He let go of her and sidestepped deftly to the other side of the room, leaving her alone near the end of the bed. But he had done it with such agility and quickness that she couldn't pretend he was fleeing from her. He had achieved a separation from her completely on his terms.

Just then, his cell phone rang.

At one o'clock in the morning, Beck knew there was very little chance this would be good news.

He answered quickly. 'Beck.'

It was Nydia. 'Yo, I was you I'd get the fuck out of that room. Hard guys on their way, man. Two coming at you, two down here covering both ends of the elevator bank.'

'Fuck! Do what you can to help when we get to the lobby.'

Beck shoved the phone in his pocket. Olivia had heard him. It immobilized her.

'Quick, Olivia – we have to get out of here.'

For just a beat, perhaps two seconds, Olivia didn't move, trapped in fear and confusion. And then she reacted with surprising speed. She didn't say a word, no questions, no comments. She moved fast toward the head of the bed, picked up her bag from the floor, ran to the bathroom without hesitating, and pulled her underwear off the shower curtain rod.

She was at the doorway grabbing her coat from the closet before Beck had on his own coat.

He opened the door. Checked the corridor. Motioned her out of the room. She followed with her bag over her shoulder and her black underwear clutched in her hand.

He moved cautiously out into the hall, peering around, standing in front of Olivia until he saw that the hallway was empty. He quickly tried to locate the stairs, but gave up on the idea. He didn't want to set off any alarms, or be trapped in a stairwell.

He hurried toward the elevators, sensing more than seeing Olivia behind him.

He pulled out his Browning Hi-Power, racked a bullet into the chamber and released the safety, holding the automatic pointed down next to his right leg.

Beck thumbed both the up and the down elevator buttons. Whatever elevator came first, they were getting on it. Hopefully, not the one bearing the hard men coming for them.

40

Nydia Lopez had returned from a quick meal of eggs, bacon, toast, and coffee eaten at the counter of a diner down the street near Lexington. But when she had left the hotel for the diner, she'd made sure to stop and speak to the doorman on duty.

The fact that he was Hispanic helped. The fact that underneath the tattoos and rough clothes Nydia Lopez had a killer body and sharp, attractive features helped more.

'Yo, homes,' she had said. 'What up?'

For a moment, the doorman hesitated, as if he were deciding whether or not to acknowledge being referred to as somebody's homeboy while on duty at the prestigious Four Seasons Hotel. But then Nydia flashed a smile accompanied by a sly wink that said volumes.

The doorman, Caesar Gascon, melted. He smiled back.

'What's up with you?' he said, posturing a little, his macho side coming out.

Nydia shrugged. 'Not much. I'm taking care of a white lady up on the fortieth floor.'

'Taking care how?' asked Caesar.

Nydia pulled back her jacket and turned just enough so that Caesar could see the butt of the Smith & Wesson tucked in at the small of her back.

'You know,' said Nydia, as if she didn't need to explain it to him, making Caesar a co-conspirator.

'I didn't see that,' said Caesar.

'No doubt,' said Nydia. 'But you see anything, you know, like any nefarious types hanging around, you let me know, huh?'

'Yeah, sure. Where you going?'

'Got to eat. My partner is upstairs covering until I get back. Watch things for me for a few, okay?'

'Yeah, sure.'

Nydia placed a forefinger under her eye, then pointed around, and flashed her killer smile as she slid into the revolving doors.

When she returned, Caesar quickly opened the front door for her and said, 'Check out the front desk. Four guys, only one big rolling bag? Don't feel right.'

Nydia muttered, 'Thanks,' and focused instantly on the men at the top of the landing. They had their backs to her, taking no notice of her in the huge, multistoried lobby.

The four stood in pairs of two.

Nydia didn't have to look at them for more than a second to know they were trouble. She angled to her right, quickly stepped up a half flight of stairs, making sure to stay far enough away so she wouldn't catch their attention. She pulled out her cell phone and slid into a chair, keeping the men in her peripheral vision.

One man stood talking to the hotel clerk at the main desk. He was tall, bald, and looked ready to kill someone, perhaps because someone had recently broken his nose. There was adhesive tape across the bridge and both eyes were blackened. On his left, stood a man with a large rolling duffel bag.

Two others stood as a pair off to the right of the bald man talking to the clerk. They both wore dark overcoats, good shoes, dress pants. One of them leaned in between the bald man with the broken nose and the hotel clerk to ask something. She pointed toward the rear of the hotel. Both men peeled off, leaving others with the rolling bag at the desk.

Nydia guessed he had asked for the men's room, but as soon as the two of them reached the middle section of the hotel where the elevators were, they stopped, looking to see which set of elevators to take.

Nydia had already dialed Beck. Listening to the phone ring, she said to herself quietly, 'Pick up, motherfucker.'

41

There were two elevators that opened onto the fortieth floor. Beck waited and waited. He pushed the buttons again. It seemed like minutes had passed, but it was closer to thirty seconds. Finally, Beck felt more than heard the air being pushed ahead of the elevator rising to their right.

The elevator door vibrated. Beck reached behind him for Olivia, feeling for her as he faced the elevator. And suddenly, he cursed.

'Shit. We've been out here too long.'

He moved Olivia to the left, away from the corridor where they'd come from. He backed up quickly, gently guiding Olivia to the east corridor while he faced the elevator, gun ready as they moved out of sight around the corner.

Just as they made it into the east corridor, the elevator door opened and Beck heard somebody step out of the elevator. He craned his head around just enough to see two men in dark clothes head in the direction of Olivia's room.

Beck moved very quickly, trying to remain completely quiet on the hallway carpeting. The elevator door had almost closed, but he just managed to get four fingers between the closing doors and force them open.

Olivia was right behind him. They slipped into the

elevator, the doors closed, and before Beck could press any buttons, the elevator started to rise.

Beck snarled, 'Shit.'

Beck's agitation made Olivia nervous. She backed into a corner of the elevator.

The elevator stopped on the forty-fifth floor. A hotel waiter stood in the corridor with a room-service cart. He hesitated. Beck said, 'Come on in. There's plenty of room.'

Beck expected the elevator to reverse, but again it went up. He checked the digital numbers showing the floors the elevator serviced. This one served floors thirty-one to fifty-two. They rose past fifty, without slowing. The hotel waiter stood with his back to Beck, watching the floor indicators. Beck slipped the Browning into the pocket of his shearling coat.

One of Kolenka's men pressed his ear against Olivia's door, trying to hear movement inside the room. Nothing. He took out a small crowbar from underneath his overcoat and began to pry open the door just above the lock. It took a good deal of effort, but when the door popped free of the frame, it made surprisingly little noise.

The room was unoccupied, but the magazines and wrinkled bed top showed that someone had been in the room. They quickly searched for luggage or anything that might indicate the occupant would be returning, but there was nothing.

On the way up, Beck calculated how to play the situation.

If the two who had come up for Olivia got back on this elevator, what would they do? Would they know it was

Olivia? Would they risk a move with a hotel employee on the elevator? What would happen when they hit the lobby? And who were they? How the hell had they found Olivia?

Beck's thoughts were interrupted when the elevator stopped on fifty-two. There was nobody there. But just as the doors started to close, a woman appeared. She stopped the doors and stepped into the elevator. She was blond, dressed in a fake fur coat. She wore high heels and a blue dress that barely reached mid-thigh. She carried a large handbag on her left shoulder.

Hooker, Beck thought. And not a very expensive-looking one at that. She stepped to the back of the elevator, avoiding eye contact, hardly moving.

Her perfume filled the elevator, but it didn't give the impression that she was clean and fresh. She looked worn out. Intent on leaving the hotel without causing any notice.

The elevator started down. Christ, thought Beck, if things go bad, if shooting starts, now there were two more people who could get hit. The complications had escalated exponentially.

But then again, the more people who got out in the lobby, the better their chances of getting to an exit before the two waiting downstairs could sort out who was who.

Then the elevator slowed down and stopped on forty, and all of Beck's calculations changed.

42

Gregor Stepanovich checked his watch. One-forty in the morning. Kolenka's men were to secure the woman in her room, then call him. He and his partner would go to the room he had rented for an outrageous price with the large rolling bag. The bag contained everything he needed and would be used to remove the body from the hotel.

Kolenka's men were to deliver her to Gregor's room and leave. That was the agreement. Which was fine with Gregor. He and Josef would have the woman all to themselves. Once they were in the room with the woman and secure, he would tell his driver to leave, call Markov, and the fun could begin.

He waited at the west end of the elevator bank. His man Josef at the east end.

Gregor checked his watch again. What was taking so long? She was probably sleeping. They should be in before she even woke up. Ah, he thought. They have to get her dressed before they take her out of the room. That must be it.

The elevator door opened on two men. Both were medium height. Both wore long, dark wool overcoats, dark slacks, and decent tie shoes. One wore a blue button-down shirt. The other a white shirt.

They had the hard-edged look of Slavs. Both grizzled.

Thin and sinewy and feral. The good clothes couldn't hide their predatory air. When the man in the white shirt reached to hold the elevator so his partner could enter, he revealed a tattoo of a Russian Orthodox cross on the back of his right hand.

Shit, thought Beck. Vory-v-Zakone. Definitely Kolenka's men.

Between the four people already in the elevator and the hotel waiter's food cart, there wasn't much room for the Russians, but the hotel waiter said, 'Please, come in. I'll take the next one.'

He wheeled his room service cart out of the elevator, and both men stepped in.

Beck had been standing in front of Olivia. Now he moved to his left so that he seemed even more apart from the two women. Give the hunters the impression that the blonde was with Olivia. Two escorts working as a pair. But would they believe Olivia belonged in the same league as the blonde?

Beck made sure to not even glance at the two women behind him. He was certain Olivia had figured out these two were after her. Could she mask her fear? Would they sense her apprehension, like animals closing in on prey?

The Russians briefly checked out Olivia and the hooker, ignored Beck, turned to face the front of the car. The elevator started its descent. Beck gripped the Browning in the right hand pocket of his shearling coat.

He considered the situation. Maybe they would make it to the lobby. After all, the elevator had come from a different floor. There were two women instead of one. They hadn't connected Beck to either of the women.

But what would these two do when they reached the lobby? What made sense?

Step out and confer with their partners, Beck supposed. Could they slip out unnoticed while that happened?

Beck made no move to look at the men on his left. He didn't want to distract them from doing just what they were doing: standing still, facing front, looking at the numbers flashing by on the elevator's display panel.

And then the Russian farthest from Beck did what men do. He turned to look over the blonde once more. He stared at her, blatantly, without apology, as if she were sitting in a store window. She completely ignored him. She stood in the back of the elevator, staring past him as if he weren't there. And then he looked over at Olivia.

No, thought Beck. No. He felt the atmosphere shift. The Russian in the white shirt stared at Olivia a beat too long. Then his partner turned. They both stared at her, stared for way too long.

Beck had to move. Now. Hard and fast and now.

In the cramped space, Beck leaned right, raised his left foot, and stomped the side of the Blue Shirt's right knee, driving the leg down to the floor of the elevator. As he collapsed in Beck's direction, screaming, Beck rammed his elbow into the man's right temple, knocking him out, and driving him toward the second Russian.

As Blue Shirt crumpled to the floor, Beck whipped the barrel of the Browning into White Shirt's face, cracking open his forehead and sending a spray of blood spattering against the rear wall of the elevator.

White Shirt fell back into the blonde, who couldn't avoid him, but she was tough. She stifled a scream and shoved him away, which kept him on his feet. He lunged for Beck, blood pouring into his eyes, obstructing his vision, trampling his partner still on the floor, managing to get his arms around Beck's waist.

Beck let the standing attacker drive him into the side of the elevator. Beck knew he wasn't going down. There was no room to fall. White Shirt was bent over, arms around Beck, his face on Beck's chest. He reared up and tried to ram the top of his head into Beck's chin.

Beck turned away, but the man's head banged into the side of his jaw. Before White Shirt could do any more damage, Beck leaned over him and drove the butt of the Browning down into his spine, liver, kidney – shot after vicious shot, again and again and again with as much leverage and strength as he could muster. His attacker let out guttural grunts of pain. He was paralyzed, but Beck didn't let up. He kept hitting him until he felt the man's grip loosen, then he kneed him in the chest, driving him off, and kicked him to the other side of the elevator. White Shirt fell over his comrade on the ground, but still grabbed for Beck's leg.

Beck rammed his foot into his face, breaking White Shirt's jaw, and knocking him out. He fell in a heap, half on top of his partner, who screamed at the added weight on his torn knee. The pain revived Blue Shirt. He reached for his gun. Beck backhanded the butt of the heavy Browning into his temple, knocking him unconscious, just as the elevator landed on the ground floor.

But the elevator door wouldn't open fully because White Shirt's body was jammed against it. Beck pulled him off the door, maneuvering him out of the way so he and Olivia could get out.

Olivia seemed frozen in the corner, but the hooker moved, deftly stepping over the Russians. She muttered a curse as she made her way out of the elevator, touching her face to feel for any blood spatter, intent on getting the hell out before hotel security arrived.

Beck shoved one of the inert bodies farther into the corner and pulled Olivia toward the open elevator door. He leaned out to see who was in the lobby. The blonde had already walked past the bank of elevators, turning toward the Fifty-eighth Street exit.

He spotted two men, one at each end of the elevator area. On the west side stood Gregor Stepanovich, with a large rolling luggage bag. At the east side, stood his partner.

Beck didn't linger. He pressed the elevator button for the fiftieth floor, stepped off, and led Olivia toward the east corridor in the direction the hooker had taken, figuring she had momentarily distracted Gregor's partner on that side. She had, but not enough to prevent Gregor's man from seeing Olivia, clearly terrified, and Beck with blood smeared on the side of his face and chest.

He raised a gun in Beck's direction. Beck had the Browning down against his leg. Beck stopped, pushed Olivia away from him, raised the Browning, knowing he would not get the first shot. His only hope was that the man would miss at ten feet. And then, Nydia Lopez appeared out of nowhere behind the gunman. She jumped to gain height and leverage, and came down with a smashing overhand blow across the back of his head. She hit him so hard that he flew forward and fell flat on the marble floor, out cold, his face smacking into the lobby's marble floor.

Just then a gunshot shattered the two-o'clock-in-the-morning serenity of the Four Seasons.

Olivia ran toward Nydia. Beck dropped into a crouch, turning to face Gregor, who had already twisted around the corner, taking cover from Beck and his Browning.

Beck didn't fire. He immediately turned back and ran around the corner for Olivia and Nydia. Nydia held Olivia's arm with one hand and her compact Smith & Wesson M&P .40 with the other.

'Go!' Beck shouted, pointing toward the Fifty-eighth Street exit. Even if Gregor ran after them, they should be able to make it out the door.

Beck shoved the Browning into his coat pocket, ignored everyone and everything except Nydia and Olivia. He ran ahead of them toward the back of the hotel, sure that they would be running right behind him.

As they reached the far end of the hotel, he slid around the corner, and hustled down the steps to the ground floor exit. Outside, Beck could see a doorman and someone who looked like a hotel security guard struggling with a large man trying to get into the hotel.

There was a Cadillac Escalade parked in front of the hotel. The driver's-side door was open. The SUV was empty. It had to be the driver fighting to get into the hotel. He had already tossed aside the doorman. The security guard, a young black man who nearly matched the driver's size, was clearly have troubling grappling with what Beck figured was the last of the team sent to get Olivia.

Beck turned and told Nydia, 'Get her into that SUV.'

Beck burst out of the exit door and jumped into the scuffle without breaking stride. He pulled the driver's head back with his right hand and punched him in the throat with his left.

Beck didn't even pause to see the result. If the security guard couldn't take him down now, he didn't deserve the job.

He ran out into the street and jumped into the driver's seat of the double-parked SUV. Keys were in the ignition. He turned over the engine, shoved the gearshift into drive, and accelerated east on Fifty-eighth, tires squealing, the trucklike SUV fishtailing down the street.

Police sirens were already converging on the hotel. Beck turned left onto Park Avenue, blasting through a red light, just missing a cab.

The light ahead was green and Beck floored the accelerator. The four-hundred horsepower engine hesitated, and then the massive torque kicked in and he streaked through the intersection as the light turned red. He continued accelerating, catching green lights one after the other until the light on Sixty-sixth turned red while he was a half block away from the intersection.

He braked hard, hoping Nydia and Olivia had had time to get their seat belts on. He hadn't, but braced himself on the steering wheel. They slid into the intersection. Luckily there was no cross traffic. Beck managed to wrestle the big SUV into a right turn and headed east on Sixty-sixth. He braked hard at Lexington, peered to his left looking for empty cabs. He didn't see any, the light changed and he continued east at a normal speed, stopping at Second

Avenue. He pulled the SUV into an empty space near a fire hydrant, shut everything down, took a deep breath, and turned to Olivia and Nydia seated behind him.

'Fuck. You two okay?'

Nydia said, 'Yeah.'

'What'd you hit that guy with? Couldn't have been your fist.'

Nydia pulled out a set of brass knuckles.

Beck pictured the blow. Thought for a second how hard that man's face smacked into the marble floor when he went down.

'Thanks. You saved us.'

'No problem,' said Nydia.

'Olivia?'

'Yes?'

'You okay?'

'When I stop shaking. God, what happened back there?'

'You guys almost died,' said Nydia.

43

Gregor Stepanovich knew after missing with his first shot that he wouldn't get another. He had to leave. There was no point. The police and hotel security would be on him before he could kill Beck, or capture the woman.

He had turned and walked out of the front entrance of the Four Seasons as fast as he could, nearly shrieking with frustration that Beck had gotten away from him yet again. It took every shred of his willpower not to chase after Beck, shooting at him until his gun was empty.

What the hell was he doing here? Guarding the woman, obviously. Even so, Gregor couldn't believe Beck had wiped out three men he couldn't have known were coming. How does this fucking guy keep doing this?

He had lost another man. He assumed Kolenka's two men were also lost.

Markov would be furious. Kolenka? Who knows? This might send the old Vory over the edge. Good, thought Gregor. Kolenka has plenty of men. Maybe this will persuade him to send them against Beck.

Stepanovich vowed never to go after Beck, or anybody connected to him, without enough men to crush him. Next time, there would be no chance for Beck to fight him off. Stepanovich vowed to literally shoot Beck into unrecognizable pieces.

No one tried to stop the tall, raging Bosnian from

leaving. He walked straight out the door, hailed a cab, and was gone before anybody could identify him as the man who had shot off a gun in the lobby of the Four Seasons.

They'd all piled into a cab on Second Avenue. Nydia directed the driver to her neighborhood up in East Harlem. Beck thanked Nydia again, dropped her in front of her apartment building, and then gave the driver directions for the long ride to Red Hook.

He sat on the right side of the cab's backseat. Olivia to the left. Beck didn't much want to talk, but he had to know how they had found her. Manny wouldn't be stupid enough to check her in under her real name. And Beck was sure he had rented the room for cash.

'You checked into the hotel with Manny, right?'

'Yes.'

'Then how did they know your name?'

Olivia paused. For the first time Beck heard her curse. 'That fucking idiot, Raymond.'

'Raymond? Who's Raymond?'

'The manager.' Olivia turned to Beck. 'Look, I know him. He comes on to me every time he sees me. Offers me discounts at the spa. Preferred rates at the hotel. I have lunch in their lobby café a lot. He saw me check in.'

'So you asked him for the preferred rate?'

'No. No. I specifically told him that' – Olivia made a quotation mark in the air – 'I wasn't supposed to be there. That I was checking in under a different name.'

'What name?'

'I told them to put the room under the name Ellen Grey.'

'Ellen Grey?'

'I was thinking of Earl Grey. The tea. So I changed it to Ellen.'

Beck asked just to make the point. 'Do you have a credit card under the name of Ellen Grey?'

'No.'

'He has your card on file?'

'I don't know. I've used it enough times in there.'

'For hotel rooms or the restaurants?'

'Both. I've stayed there a couple of weekends. And I've used my rate for friends. What does it matter? Manny paid cash. I told them I'd pay cash for incidentals. Told them I wanted privacy.'

'He probably used your card to credit you back the difference, trying to score points with you when you saw the nice surprise on your next statement. That automatically checked you in under your real name. Using a phony name for people calling around trying to find somebody doesn't change the hotel billing system.'

'Christ, I can't believe it. I could kill that idiot.'

'I should have made you go to a hotel where nobody knew you. It's my fault.'

'No. It's mine. But how did they find me?'

'Obviously Markov has connections to people who can access credit card records. And phone records and e-mails and blah, blah, fucking blah.'

Beck shook his head in disgust and slumped down in his seat, doing his usual inventory of where it hurt. His left elbow was going to be sore. There'd be the usual aches and strains in the aftermath of yet another fight. At least he hadn't hit anything with his hands. Just the butt of his gun.

When they arrived at the safety of the Red Hook

building, Beck let Manny find a room for Olivia on the third floor and settle her down. He went straight to his room, showered off the sweat and blood from his two fights, took four ibuprofen, and collapsed into bed.

Markov had continued to work and wait for Gregor's call to verify they had the woman. It was nearly two-thirty when his phone's ringtone pierced the quiet of his room at the Waldorf. Too long. Markov knew Gregor had failed, but he waited to hear the words, 'They got away,' and then he cut off the call without saying one word in response.

He muttered a stream of Russian curses. And then his phone rang again. He was about to throw it against the wall rather than speak to Gregor, but the caller ID showed it was Ivan Kolenka. Kolenka sounded very calm, which made it all the worse. He told Markov, 'We are going to solve this Beck problem now. Come see me.'

Markov checked his watch. Two thirty-seven, Wednesday morning.

'When?' he asked.

'Two hours. The place near the boardwalk where we met last time,' said Kolenka. 'I want to know exactly how many reliable men you can put into this. Exactly.'

Kolenka broke off the call.

Markov called Gregor back and told him to come to the lobby of the Waldorf in one hour and wait for him.

Sixty minutes later, after showering, shaving, and changing into his last set of clean clothes, Markov walked out of his room, towels on the floor, toilet unflushed, his clothing bag over his shoulder, heading for the lobby.

44

Beck slept a dreamless sleep for just over five hours before his cell phone woke him.

He recognized Ricky Bolo's voice. Ricky always spoke in a low voice, out of the side of his mouth. He could have been in a secure facility in a sound-proof office with an encrypted scrambled phone, and he would still talk as if someone were standing right behind him.

'You up?'

'I am now.'

'Your boy just walked out of his place. Front door. Got into a Town Car driven by a big guy.'

'Milstein?'

'Yeah, you told us to look out for him.'

'What time is it?'

'Little before seven.'

'Okay,' said Beck, sitting up. The pain immediately sent him back down on his bed. 'Okay, good. But right now I'm more interested in his driver. I expect them to go into that building on the corner of Fifty-seventh and Lex. The one with that plaza outside.'

'You want I should go in and see where he ends up?'

'No. I already know. Where's Jonas?'

'With me. He's driving the Bolo-mobile.'

'You still using that same piece of crap van?'

'Hey, it blends in anywhere. It's practically invisible.'

'What'd you guys do all night after you left Tribeca?'

'Had some fun. Grabbed a couple of hours sleep. Then came over here to check up on your guy.'

'Okay. Follow him and verify he's going to work. Then stay with his driver.'

'Will do. Kisses.'

Beck set down his cell phone and remained flat on his back.

Kisses indeed, he thought. Images of Olivia Sanchez filled his mind. He wondered if he'd ever get out from under what was beginning to feel like an obsession.

He checked the time on his clock radio. Ten minutes to seven. He rolled onto his side, gritting his teeth against the pain and stiffness. He sat upright slowly, wincing as his weight pressed down on the stitches in his left thigh. Everything hurt. The room was cold. Dark. It all reminded him of prison.

Prison. Trapped by endless restrictions and circled by enemies. Much of the time you lived within the bubble of a tense truce. But if the truce broke down, and you knew you were a target, the key to survival was knowing who would be coming for you, and striking first. And you couldn't make a mistake or you'd create another set of enemies.

Beck had survived by quickly learning the process. Build an alliance with people who could supply you with intelligence, arms, and backup. Strike first and hard, but always make sure you had a way to end the feud. Ending it was the difficult part. It had to be in everyone's interest that you survived. There were two ways to make that happen. Make it too costly for your enemies to kill you by proving to them you would kill or maim as many as it took to survive, and if you didn't survive, your allies would avenge you. Or, make sure your enemies would profit if you were alive and well. Generally, that meant sharing whatever drugs or money or power you had. And that, of course, meant you had to maintain your efforts in another whole realm.

It was exhausting, and you had to work at it continually.

He might be outside, be free to move, have access to more, but the rules were essentially the same. The big difference was that inside prison the population was limited and the geography tightly defined. Outside there were way too many people you didn't know about who could be set against you. Worse, they could come at you from anywhere.

There was a soft knock on his bedroom door.

Beck knew by the sound that it was Manny.

'Yeah.'

The door opened. Manny stood at the threshold, making sure not to encroach on Beck's personal space, an old habit from prison where you never stepped into a man's cell without being invited.

Beck sat in his underwear on the edge of his bed, feeling the cold air around him, gently rolling his head, flexing his hands.

'You okay, James?'

'Okay enough.'

'I hear you had trouble at the hotel. I'm sorry, man. I should have made it clear to her.'

'You did. Some friend of hers at that place screwed it up for her. Good thing you picked the right person to bodyguard her. That Nydia saved us. She spotted the bad guys in the lobby when she came back from eating. It was close, but she gave us just enough warning. And she took down one of the fuckers in the lobby. Without her, we were dead.'

'Good. She's a tough kid. Good in the pocket, as they say.'

'She is.'

Manny smiled.

'What?'

'You can't have no shoot-up in a fancy hotel like that, man. It's all over the news.'

'What's the big deal? Nobody died. I'll bet there were gunshots all over the city last night. Nobody gave a shit.'

'I hear you. So what's the next move?' asked Manny.

'I fucking shower to get myself loosened up enough so I can move, and we start in on everything. Is Olivia still sleeping?'

'Yes.'

'Where's Alex?'

'Downstairs. He's sleeping on the floor by the computers. He gets a signal when Crane gets on his computer. He was at it until a little while after you all got back. Nothing since then.'

'What about you?'

'I'm just waiting, *jefe*. Not sure I want to wait much longer.'

Beck stood up and moved stiffly toward his bathroom. 'Don't worry. You won't have to.'

'By the way . . .'

Beck stopped.

'What?'

'You got a message from Phineas.'

'Oh?'

'Said a guy named Walter Pearce tried an old scam to find out our location.'

'Christ, that guy?' Beck stood for a moment shaking his head.

'You know him?'

'Works for Milstein. Where's D?'

'He just got up. He's in the bar. Like usual.'

'Ciro and Joey still here?'

'Watching in shifts. Except for Joey B. Seems like he don't sleep. I never seen a guy that size so buggy. You know what kinda drugs he's on?'

'The kind that make you big and buggy, I guess.'

'Everybody is restless.'

'Good.'

Beck was thinking about what to do with Manny. When to tell him about Olivia. The trouble was, he wasn't sure how or when would be best. Or, what Manny's reaction would be. Instead, he decided to give Manny something to do.

'Hey, about that guy Pearce.'

'Yeah.'

'Check with Phineas. See if he can find out where he lives.'

'Okay.'

'You got coffee going?'

'Sure.'

'I'll meet you and D in the bar in a few.'

45

Olivia lay wide awake.

By the time they got back to Red Hook, the adrenaline and fear had washed through her and she'd fallen asleep almost as soon as her head hit the pillow. She'd slept soundly. But she had awakened at her usual six o'clock and remained in the strange bed in the small room at the east end of the third floor.

She listened to sounds from the house. The steam hissing and softly banging through the old pipes. Muffled male voices from the floors below her. An occasional sharp sound coming from the big kitchen on the second floor.

She felt trapped and surrounded. She didn't want to be in this house with all these men. Beck made her uneasy. She hadn't thought about him nearly enough before this had started. How could she? She knew so little about him. She had mostly thought about Manny.

Beck was the only man she had ever met that made her unsure of herself. On one level, he was doing exactly what she wanted him to do. But there was too much that he wouldn't reveal to her.

She was as sure about Manny Guzman as she had ever been. He hadn't taken all that much effort. Mostly just time and persistence. Something she was very good at. It had been easy. She had played the role of his one, loyal relative perfectly. It was kind of like training an attack dog. Feed it. Be the only one kind to it. Let the dog feel loved.

Manny loved her. He'd let her know it the only way he could. By telling her if she ever needed him, just reach out.

She had never asked him for anything. Ever. But she had kept careful track of him. The days and years left in his prison sentence. The dates of his parole hearings. The likely time of his release.

When she offered to help him get settled outside of prison, he'd gently refused her. That was when she'd found out about Beck and the place in Red Hook.

And now she was inside the Red Hook headquarters, most likely for the duration. Right where she wanted to be. So why didn't it feel better?

She stared up at the plaster ceiling. What was it that made her feel uneasy? On one level it seemed obvious. She was surrounded by killers. Maybe not the computer guy, but all the others. She'd manipulated men all her life, but never men like these. Never men who could or would kill. And never a man like James Beck.

Manny would never let anything happen to her. Never. And Beck had made it clear that he needed her. He would protect her. So why was she worried? Because the violence had spun out to terrifying levels. Olivia winced when she thought about that fight in the elevator. She touched her cheek where the blood had spattered. She remembered the sound of Beck's gun butt smashing into that man's body.

Beck was unbelievable. To be so close to somebody doing what he did to those men. The power excited her.

The strength. She'd been attracted to Beck almost from the moment she first saw him. It was easy to come on to him in the hotel room. But he was too smart, too disciplined. Now she wanted him even more, but she crushed the idea. Not now.

This was going as planned. She was exactly where she needed to be to push everything along in the right direction.

The predawn gray slowly crept into the small room.

The room reminded her of her small bedroom back in the projects. She had lived with her mother and her *abuela*. The household was all women. Her father disappeared when she was two. Her grandfather had died of alcoholism when she was eight. Her mother and grandmother raised her, scraping by on food stamps, dependent-child payments. And the numbers.

Her *abuela* was a tough old bird. She'd run the numbers in their Mott Haven neighborhood for years.

Olivia shook her head and blinked away thoughts of the past.

She felt tired. More weary than tired. But she couldn't afford to be slow or lacking now. She had to keep up. Right now, most of what was going to happen depended on Crane. And on how well Beck could hold off whatever Markov would be sending at him.

They'd almost had her at the hotel. That fucking idiot manager Raymond. Well, she told herself, it's my fault. I never stopped him from giving me discounts before. He was one of those stupid grinning men waiting to be smiled at and patted on the head for his favors.

Markov clearly had connections to powerful resources.

How much time would it be before they found this place? How long before they stormed in here?

Surely Beck had a plan for that. Beck was the key. Thinking of Beck again sent another pulse of desire through Olivia. This time she didn't push it away. She let the feeling blossom. Something she hadn't felt about a man in a long, long time.

She felt the ripple of desire just in the pit of her stomach, pulsing down between her legs. She let her right hand slide under the flimsy black triangle of her thong. Her middle finger slipping into the warm space between her labia. She moved her finger further so that the heel of her hand pressed into her clitoris, sending a pulse of erotic sensation flooding through her.

She grabbed herself and squeezed, pulled her hand away, and moved it upward to cup her left breast and pinch her hardening nipple between her forefinger and middle finger.

She wondered what kind of lover Beck would be. On the couple of occasions when she'd touched him or bumped into him, she could tell he was solid. No fat on him. And God, he moved fast and with such sureness. Again she thought about the elevator. Those two he went after — it was like they'd found themselves in a cage with a wild animal. They never had a chance.

When the first one turned to look at her, she'd been sure he was going to kill her. Just pull out a gun and shoot her. But Beck got them both. He didn't hesitate. If he ever made a move for her, she imagined it would be fast and hard and without any bother to seduce.

The thought excited her. He'd resisted her, but it only

showed her how much she would have to do. Olivia Sanchez had never met a man she couldn't seduce, and James Beck wasn't going to be the first.

46

Leonid Markov sat with Ivan Kolenka in a dirty kitchen in the building on Coney Island Avenue where Kolenka had met Beck. Kolenka chain-smoked his unfiltered cigarettes, which made the small, overheated space almost unbearable for Markov. Even if Kolenka had noticed, he wouldn't have cared. All he cared about was killing James Beck.

His calculations had been swift. His conclusion immutable.

Two of his men out of action, who would have to be killed because he couldn't take any chances that the police would use them to penetrate his operation.

There was clearly a serious ongoing threat to Markov, a man who was a source of significant sums of money to him.

But above all else, Kolenka was certain that Beck realized he had aligned with Markov, and would therefore try to kill him.

Conclusion: Beck had to be eliminated. And all his men, whoever they were. Anything and everything that had to do with James Beck had to be eliminated from the face of the earth. Executed, burned down. Buried and salt poured in the hole.

Along with Kolenka and Markov sitting in the kitchen were three of Kolenka's men plus Gregor Stepanovich, who had come with Markov.

Finally, Kolenka spoke.

'We must eliminate Beck.'

'Agreed.'

'You understand he's not alone.'

'How many men does he have?'

'I don't know. I expect he's gathered his men at his headquarters in Brooklyn. I have made inquiries, and now I have the exact location.'

There was a street map of Brooklyn laid flat on the kitchen table. Kolenka pointed a bony finger at a spot on Conover Street. He had studied the streets around Beck's building, which was located right near the water at the far western edge of Red Hook. Kolenka believed they could trap him in that location by blocking only two streets: Van Brunt on the south side and Van Dyke on the east side. Once trapped, they would kill everything that moved in that building. But Kolenka had to be sure Beck was in the building and find out how many men were with him.

'We need to do this very soon,' said Kolenka.

'Yes.'

But even as he agreed, Markov began to calculate the time he would need. It was Thursday, a little before 6 a.m. Crane would certainly want Friday to trade. He imagined Kolenka would want to strike at night. So, earliest would be tonight, more likely early Friday morning.

For sure, there would be a massive police investigation. Markov could not be anywhere in New York when that happened. But if he closed out all his positions by the end of trading on Friday, assembled all the cash in his Cayman bank by the end of business Friday, he could fly out of New York Friday night. Meet in person with the Cayman bankers on Saturday to transfer the money someplace only he knew about. Set up the funds on the Isle of Wight, or maybe Andorra. Or Lichtenstein. Or maybe all three. No point leaving everything in one basket. The Syrian arms shipments should all be in place by then. Handle everything with the bank in Cayman and the transfer banks, leave Grand Cayman the same day to a place outside the US, but civilized. Disappear. Settle in Prague, perhaps. Perhaps Sicily. Just lay low. Stay out of circulation as he planned his next moves.

Beck would be eliminated once and for all. And in all likelihood, the woman was with Beck, so she, too, would die. But if not, if she was hiding somewhere else, he would find her and take care of her later. For now, Markov knew he had to gather his assets and disappear.

This was going to cost him. Certainly Kolenka would demand a large payment. Speculating with his investment would cost him millions. But there were always reversals in business. He told himself to never look back. Crane would preserve enough to meet his obligations, and be ready for the next deal. There was always another deal.

'Agreed,' said Markov. 'Thursday night, early Friday morning.'

Kolenka asked Markov, 'And how many men can you give me? Good men,'

'How many do you need? For what?'

'To wipe this Beck and all around him off the map of life.'

'I'll give you whatever you need. What is your plan?'

'I'll tell you after I send men in to look around. To see exactly what is where.'

Markov asked, 'Do you have men that can do that? Without being spotted?'

Kolenka shrugged.

Markov said, 'I have the best. Three men. Highly trained. They will be meeting me at JFK in a few hours. We can send them into Beck's neighborhood. Nobody will connect them to us. They know how to fit into any area. They are experts, I guarantee it. They'll get whatever intelligence you need.'

'Fine. Have them go in this afternoon. We'll see what we have to do. We make a plan. We end this, now.'

'Agreed.'

'Yes, and then you and I will agree on how much you will be paying me.'

47

Milstein and Walter Pearce were the only occupants in the Summit offices at 7:10 a.m. on a Wednesday morning.

They sat in Milstein's office, a surprisingly small space, situated in the southeast corner of the twenty-eighth floor. The building at that height was oddly shaped, so that Milstein's office didn't occupy a full corner, but rather a section of a triangle. Milstein liked the shape of his office because with him sitting behind his desk, anyone else in his office was relegated to the cramped and disorienting space on the other side of his desk.

Although it was a workday, Milstein wore casual weekend clothes. Brown corduroy pants, open-collar blue button-down shirt, a tan V-neck cashmere sweater, all of it about a size too big for his small frame.

Pearce sat uncomfortably at the side of Milstein's desk. His rumpled suit, white shirt, and blue-striped tie looked like he had been wearing them all day.

A large Styrofoam cup of coffee from the office kitchen sat on the floor next to his size fifteen shoes. He needed it. His frustration, anger, and Milstein's insulting phone call had kept him from sleeping soundly. He'd finally gotten out of bed at around four and stubbornly continued to work on finding James Beck.

He used a lawyer friend's subscription to LexisNexis and kept pounding away at legal and public records that had any connection to Phineas P. Dunleavy, his enmity at the lawyer's dirty trick fueling him. He tracked through one paper trail after another until he found the name of a James Beck listed as a managing partner buried in closing documents on one of the properties Dunleavy's law firm had acquired. Bingo. Pearce knew he would have to take a quick drive to the building to verify that Beck actually lived at that address, but his gut told him he had succeeded in finding out where James Beck lived.

He sat waiting for the right moment to let Milstein know the information he had uncovered, which would be the moment when Milstein lodged his next complaint. Told him how incompetent he was, or threatened him.

Milstein shifted in his seat. Working himself up to something.

'So, Walter, I asked you up here so I could tell you face-to-face.'

Instead of waiting for it silently, Walter pushed it.

'Tell me what, Mr Milstein? How disappointed you are in me?'

Walter's directness surprised Milstein. 'Well . . .'

'Well, what?' pressed Walter.

'Well, uh, yes, actually. It's been days since I asked you to find out about those men and you seem to be completely stuck.'

Walter interrupted Milstein. 'It's been about thirty hours since we walked out of Central Park and you told me to find those men, Mr Milstein.'

'What? Oh, well, it certainly seems longer. You know, I hired you mainly as my driver and to watch out for me. But the reason you got the job was because you were a cop. A detective. Someone who could find things out for me if I needed it. I'm overpaying you as a driver, Walter.'

'And way underpaying me as an investigator, Mr Milstein. Although I'm sure you figure to get the best end of it however it works out.'

Milstein squinted at Walter Pearce. This wasn't going as he expected. He started to respond, but Walter held up his hand to stop him.

'The fact is, Mr Milstein, this fellow Beck and his associates have gone to a lot of trouble not to be found.'

'I don't like excuses.'

'Not an excuse. Just a fact. But I've been working on this nonstop and I've succeeded. I identified the one who held me at gunpoint in the park. I identified Beck. And now I know where we can find Beck. I doubt anybody else could have cracked this sooner than I have.'

'You cracked it?'

'Don't look so surprised.'

'You're sure?'

'Ninety-nine percent. I just have to drive out to the location and verify it.'

Milstein sat motionless. Walter watched him go through a calculation. And then it hit Walter. Milstein had called him up to his office not to complain, but to fire him. Son of a bitch.

'Well, that's good news, Walter. I'm glad to hear it.'

Goddamn this fucking Milstein. Walter had to force himself to stay in his chair. This little snake, cocksucker, just sitting there waiting to drop the hammer. He was tempted to get up and leave. No, no way. He'd put in too much work. Better to play this right, cash in, then walk out on this fucking asshole when it suited him.

'I would hope so,' Walter said. 'Like I said, over thirty hours pretty much nonstop. Cashing in a lot of favors people owe me.'

'I see.'

Walter asked, 'So, do you have an idea how you want to use this information?'

'As a matter of fact, I do. That's why it was so frustrating not to have what I need.'

'What's your plan?'

'I've been talking to someone at my law firm. A man I trust. A man with connections to the NYPD.'

'So you want to call in the police?'

Milstein leaned back. He had no intention of explaining his thinking to Walter Pearce. He had decided not to leave this up to Markov. A murder investigation into Olivia Sanchez or James Beck would surely implicate him. He had to get it on record that he had done the right thing. Reported his part of it to the proper authorities. And if the police took Beck out of the picture, Markov would thank him in the end.

'Yes,' he answered. 'I think that's the best course of action now. Especially since you have solid information we can give them.'

Walter shrugged. 'All right.'

Milstein tipped forward, put his elbows on the desk, assuming the role of a decisive C-suite executive.

'Here's what I want to do, Walter. I've spoken to a contact at my law firm. He knows a high-level police official that he says can help us. We've got solid information on who assaulted me. It was assault, right?'

'You said the man threatened you. And tried to extort money from you. That's felony assault.'

'Yes.'

'A known felon pulled a gun on me. That's a ticket back to prison right there. You have plenty to bust these guys on. Plus, when the cops hit them, I'll bet a dollar to a donut they'll find weapons and probably more.'

'Exactly. And all we have to do is give my contact at NYPD the information, and he'll take it from there.'

'And how much juice does your contact have?'

Milstein shuffled folders and papers on his desk and uncovered a legal pad. 'He's a bureau chief.'

'Do you know which bureau?'

Milstein looked at his notes. 'Patrol.'

Walter nodded, relieved. Milstein had no idea how the NYPD was organized. There were dozens of senior police officials in divisions that wouldn't be able to do much for them. But someone high up in Patrol, that would work.

'Okay,' Walter said. 'He'll have to run it through borough command in Brooklyn, but that shouldn't be a problem if he wants to help us.'

'Good. Good. So I'll arrange a meeting with him. Today.'

'If you can.'

'Oh, trust me. I can make this happen.'

Walter looked at his watch. It was an old digital Casio that showed the time and date. 'What is it, not even eight?

Still early in the day. I'd say the sooner I meet with him, the better.'

'I'll set it up. How soon do you think they can arrest these men and put them away?'

'Well, if I talk to your bureau chief today and he kicks it into gear, late tonight, early Friday morning sometime. But you have to file a complaint, and get a court to issue an arrest warrant.'

'Don't worry about that. My lawyer said he can get that done in a matter of hours.'

'Good. You want me to drive out to the location, verify that Beck is there?'

'No. We don't have time for that. As soon as I get the warrants I want you to meet with this bureau chief.'

'What's his name?'

Milstein looked at a legal pad near his phone. 'Waldron. I want the cops to take over now.'

Walter figured he'd teed up Milstein just enough.

'Well, that's all fine, Mr Milstein, but you and I have to come to an agreement.'

Milstein's brow creased. It took him a nanosecond to know that Walter was about to put the squeeze on him.

'What do you mean?'

Walter laid his big arm on Milstein's desk and leaned toward him. 'Let's not bullshit each other. You were about to drop the hammer on me, Mr Milstein. You've never brought me up here before. You were about to fire me.'

Milstein frowned. He had underestimated Walter Pearce. He'd grown accustomed to seeing him as a big slow plodder. He'd made a mistake. Walter might be a lummox physically, but there was nothing slow about his brain.

'Is that what you think?'

'Yes.'

Milstein narrowed his eyes. If Walter was going to walk, he would have already done it. So now it was just a matter of negotiating.

'I see.'

'Apparently there's not a lot of job security around here.'

Milstein settled into his negotiating stance.

'You have an employee contract with us, don't you?'

'And it says I can be let go with two weeks' notice. And vice versa.'

Milstein nodded. Might as well get right to it.

'So what are you saying here, Walter? You saying you're not going to give me the information I need until we come to some sort of agreement? The information that I paid you to get. The information obtained while you were drawing a salary from me.'

Walter didn't hesitate. 'That's what I'm saying.'

Milstein said, 'Are you looking to get sued for breach of contract, Walter?'

'Sure, why not.' Walter laughed. 'Sue me. That'll get you what you need.'

Milstein let out a slow breath. 'All right, Walter, before this gets any more acrimonious, tell me what you want.'

'Everything I can get,' he replied.

'Oh come on, Walter. Don't play the tough guy asshole. It doesn't suit you.'

'I always heard, whoever says the first number is the loser.'

'Not when the first number is the last and final number. You really want to play this game with me?'

Now Walter leaned back.

'All right. Here's where I stand. First, I've got information that cost me a lot. A lot of time and wear and tear. But it also cost me putting myself at risk. Getting information out of NYPD databases is a risk I don't need in my life. I get caught at that, I could lose my PI license. Maybe even my pension.

'As far as getting a high-up bureau chief to help you, you might like it, but I don't. The minute he sees what I have, he'll suspect I tapped into inside information. Maybe this chief won't have any cause or chance to do anything to me about that. Maybe he will. Bottom line, it doesn't help me.'

'So then I'll meet with him,' said Milstein.

'We both know that's ridiculous. You won't know where to start. You won't know if he's just bullshitting you. And he'll know you didn't do the legwork. Which means he won't trust you, and he'll do nothing for you. Certainly not until he vets everything you tell him, and you want this taken care of now.

'Lastly, you were sitting here ready to dump me if I hadn't come up with the information you wanted on Beck.' Walter raised his hands. 'Hey, that's your prerogative, but I end up with nothing after a lot of sweat and putting myself on the line for you. How is that fair?'

Milstein started to speak, but Walter cut him off.

'On the plus side, except for your idea that I should be at your beck and call 24/7, you gave me a cushy job for about eighteen months, and fairly decent pay.'

'Are you done?'

'No. Here's how I see it.' Walter lifted his big hands

palms up, weighing each option. 'On one hand, I walk out of here, you get nothing about Beck, and I get nothing from you. Clearly, you wouldn't even pay me the lousy two weeks' severance. But I'm free and clear, and that would mitigate the risk that anybody in the department finds out that I dipped into classified information.

'On the other hand, I give you the information on Beck, you thank me, and wait for the right time to fire me. Either way, I'm screwed.'

Milstein nodded. 'Now are you done?'

'Last point, I've demonstrated to you that I'm not a dumb fuck that can be exploited, which ultimately makes me a much more valuable guy to have around.'

'So again, what do you want?'

'Again, what are you offering?'

Milstein could see Walter had maneuvered him into making the deal so he got to it.

'Okay, fair enough. How about this. I give you a fifty-percent increase in salary. Your contract goes until April, if I remember right.'

'End of April.'

'Right. End of April. I'll make the increase start first of April, and guarantee to renew your contract for another year, at the increase. It's a very good deal, Walter.'

'It is. I appreciate it. But I also want a twenty-thousand-dollar bonus for this year's work. That's chicken feed for a year-end bonus around here. And just so you don't get second thoughts, you guarantee if you fire me, for any reason, you have to pay off the balance of the new contract.'

'You realize I'm losing my biggest client.'

'Hey, that's the whole point here. This information on Beck will go a long way toward showing your client that you're taking care of him. You tell me, is that worth twenty grand or not?'

Milstein needed Beck out of the picture. And he had to at least try to keep Markov from leaving Summit. Or give him a reason to come back.

'Fifteen thousand, plus the increase in salary and guaranteed contract extension, and we have a deal. But only on the condition I keep this client. If he goes, the firm will either close or cut staff drastically.'

Walter shook his head. 'No deal. That leaves me taking all the risk.'

Milstein pushed. 'Well I can't take all the risk either, Walter.'

Walter paused. 'Okay, here it is. I get the bump in salary. If the firm goes south, I get three months' severance, plus the twenty-thousand signing bonus, and you cover two grand in expenses today, which you owe me anyhow.'

'Walter, come on, you have to do better than that.'

After a pause, Walter said, 'Shit. Final offer, or I walk. I'm already tired of this. I'll agree to the fifteen bonus, in my next salary check. You pay me the two grand in expenses today. And you start my salary increase today. Not at the end of the month.'

Milstein immediately did the math in his head. He wondered if Walter had actually figured it out. Starting the salary increase two weeks earlier just about met him halfway on the fifteen versus twenty thousand. Milstein made a note to watch Walter Pearce much more carefully.

He put his hand out. 'Okay, we have a deal.'

They shook.

'I'll get this set up for you as soon as I can. Be ready to meet this fellow at police headquarters.'

'And my check for the two grand? Unless you want to give me cash.'

Milstein frowned and pulled out a desk ledger checkbook from his top drawer and wrote Walter a check against the firm's petty cash account.

48

Beck took the back stairs down to the ground floor, past where he knew Ciro Baldassare and Joey B were on watch, through Manny's kitchen, stepping out into the downstairs bar shortly before 8 a.m.

Manny Guzman sat at a table near the front door with his 12-gauge Winchester Model 1300 shotgun. Demarco stood behind the bar in his usual spot. An assault shotgun had been placed within reach on top of the back bar cabinet. An AA-12 loaded with a 20-round drum box filled with 12-gauge shot.

'Morning,' said Beck. 'I'm going downstairs.'

Without saying any more, Beck went through a door near the front of the bar and walked down a flight of wooden steps to the basement under his building. He turned on overhead bare lightbulbs as he walked through the musty space, making his way past the detritus that had accumulated over the decades: old radiators, shelving, boxes of junk, half-filled cans of old paint, rotting documents that nobody would ever bother to look at, old restaurant dishes and cookware. He went past the boiler room and continued on to almost the back wall.

On his left, a nine-foot set of metal shelves was set against the north wall. The shelves were crammed with more junk.

Beck braced himself and carefully pivoted the shelves

away from the wall. A close look at the wall showed that part of it wasn't completely solid. Beck worked his fingers into two small indentations, and gently but firmly pulled back a four-foot-square slab of plywood, plastered over so it looked like the rest of the wall. He slid the plywood to his right, just enough so that he could step into the opening and enter a passageway about five feet long connecting Beck's building with the building next door. Bending low, Beck made his way into another basement, much newer and about four times the size of his. The area was clean and empty except for machinery in the far-west corner, and a free-standing one-man prison cell in the east corner.

The machinery consisted of a long steel table under a rotary saw. The powerful saw had been mounted on an aluminum frame so it could slide back and forth over the table. Just past the table sat a large industrial-strength meat grinder. The machine could grind a hundred pounds of meat and bone into paste in about five minutes.

All the equipment could be seen by whoever occupied the prison cell. The entire basement was dimly lit by sparsely spaced fluorescent lights that stayed on 24/7.

Upstairs was a warehouse, empty except for the first floor where a garden equipment business stored mostly stone and gravel. Beck had a twenty-year net lease on the building.

Ahmet Sukol sat on an iron bench that was chained to the bars of the cell. The temperature in the basement hovered around a perpetual fifty-five degrees. Not cold enough to freeze somebody, but cold enough to make any extended stay nearly unbearable. Over the course of days or weeks, without winter clothing and enough food needed to maintain a body temperature of 98.6 degrees, a person would gradually die of hypothermia.

Sukol wore his winter coat, a knit cap, and gloves.

Beck's men had given him only water and one cold cheese sandwich.

Beck checked his watch. The man had only been in the cell about nine hours, but Beck knew that it probably felt more like fifteen or twenty.

He approached the cell, stopping about five feet from the iron bars. He looked at what he assumed was another Bosnian Serb. The man stared back at him.

Beck didn't utter a word. Neither did the Bosnian. That told Beck this wasn't the first time the man had been imprisoned. Beck preferred that the man had done time. Especially if he had ever been placed in solitary confinement. It didn't much matter where or what type of cell. The horror of solitary derived from two things: no contact with the outside world, and no way to tell time.

If his prisoner had been in solitary before, the prospect of suffering it again would terrify him. Solitary confinement was one of the worst tortures ever conceived.

But that required this Bosnian tough guy to truly believe that it was happening to him. Suddenly. Out of nowhere.

Beck waited a few more moments to see if the man would ask him a question, curse him, yell at him, plead with him. Nothing.

Shit, thought Beck. He doesn't believe it.

Beck put it aside. He concentrated on looking at the man in the cell as someone who had been part of a force gathered to kill, or maim him. Or do that to his friends.

Beck pictured the man attacking him. Shooting him. Or striking with a knife or bat. He worked at connecting the man in the cage with pain that could have ended his life. Or the lives of the others.

Beck stared at Sukol and imagined the Bosnian kicking him in the face. Breaking his teeth. Maybe stomping out an eye. He thought about fists and feet slamming into his back, ribs, head. Beck thought about the pain. About the number of agonizing days he might have suffered. About the certainty of permanent damage.

The hate welled up. The mercy leached out. And the Bosnian saw it happen right before him. He saw Beck's face. He was ready to believe it now.

It seemed that the man was about to say something, but right at that moment Beck turned and walked back toward the opening in the far wall, his footsteps echoing off the concrete floor, filling the cold, forlorn, unidentifiable space behind him with the sound of his retreating steps. Empty save for the dim lights and the meat-grinding equipment.

When Beck reached the opening in the wall, he stopped to place four fingers over four light switches. With one move, he flipped all of them down.

The fluorescent ceiling fixtures all went off, plunging the entire space into darkness so deep and profound that he knew Gregor's man would not be able to see his hand in front of his face.

As he ducked into the opening Beck heard the man cry out, 'Wait. Stop.'

Beck grimaced. Nope. No stopping now.

49

By the time Beck had made his way back to the bar, Manny, Ciro, and Demarco had assembled around the big petrified wood coffee table on the second floor. Joey B remained downstairs watching the street.

Manny and Demarco had their shotguns within reach. Ciro had a semiautomatic version of the M-16 assault rifle, a weapon designed to fire bullets at very high velocity.

Alex Liebowitz sat at the other end of the loft, eyes glued to his computer monitors. Apparently Alan Crane was back at work.

Beck asked. 'Where's Olivia?'

Manny answered. 'She's keepin' to her room. When are we going to move, James? Sitting here waiting for the shit to fall on us is a bad idea.'

'The list of shit about to fall is going to take me some time to explain. Let me talk to Alex, first.'

Beck headed to the other end of the loft. Liebowitz leaned back in his desk chair, arms crossed over his chest, eyes half closed staring at the computer monitors in front of him. Each monitor was divided into four segments, so Alex was watching eight different images simultaneously.

'Your hack is working?'

'Not exactly a hack. I'm not controlling anything. Yet. But the malware I implanted is humming along nicely.'

'So I was only half-listening to you last night, what exactly did you end up doing with Crane's setup?'

'I spent a chunk of time in the cellar tracing his phone wires. His Internet connections, luckily, ran through the basement, too, instead of just along outside walls. They wired the whole building when they renovated it. But his wiring is special. He's got a full 4nx T-1 line in there. No fractional. Plus, four different phone lines. Plus . . .'

Beck interrupted, 'So did you get everything done you wanted?'

'Close enough. Hard to tell when you don't know everything he has in that apartment.'

'What happened with his computer?'

'After I disabled and rerouted all his alarm shit with some routing boxes Ricky lent me, which are tricky because you have to get all the interfaces wired in before you reroute . . .'

'Uh-huh.'

Alex could tell Beck was being patient, so he tipped forward in the chair and tried to be more specific, but he just couldn't avoid talking about relays, codes, information packets, Internet protocol, radio frequencies, access controls, identity management, and alarm systems.

Beck gave it a minute, then carefully interrupted and said, 'So, Alex, did you get what we needed to find out about what Crane is doing and where he has the hedge fund money?'

'Yeah. As far as it goes.'

'What do you mean, as far as it goes?'

Liebowitz talked to Beck while glancing intermittently at the images on the computer screen.

'Like I said, after I overrode all the alarms and security, I went up into the apartment. His computer was on, but of course access had shut down and I didn't have time to get through his pass code. I suspect he has at least two layers. Long story short, I just bypassed everything and copied the entire hard drive.'

'And?'

'And I've been spending the last six hours unbundling everything, while I'm key-tracking everything he's doing when he's online. I've got just about everything opened. But, it's only current from the time he shut down last night. He started up again about a half-hour ago. I'm still catching up.'

'And you can do that how? The short version, Alex.'

'Short version, I loaded a sniffer program into his computer. Routed it through his T-1 line to a VPN connection that is hooked into this computer which is maybe an hour from being a full twin of the one in his apartment. Mostly. Whatever he does on that computer, he does it on this computer.'

'Okay.'

'Thing is, I can see what he's doing, but that doesn't mean I completely understand what I see. He places his trades through a very high-end platform. It's been customized a hell of a lot.

'From what I've tracked so far, he has four or five different accounts in his fund that he trades through leased servers. Those servers connect to six or seven electronic exchanges. He routes every trade into the exchange that gives him the best price, so it's a lot to keep track of.'

Beck nodded. Alex had spoken rapidly, but he still

thought he had absorbed the gist of it. 'Okay, so how long before you see everything?'

'About an hour to get one hundred percent tracking. But it's like he's fluent in a language that I only know the basics of. I guess I can just follow along with his trades until the money starts getting assembled. But I'd like to know exactly what he's doing, you know, what trading strategy he's executing so I can get out far enough ahead of him to set up a snatch.'

Beck nodded. 'You really think you're going to figure out his strategy?'

'Not completely. Unless we can get somebody who knows how he operates. At the very least I'd like to be able to predict a little bit when he's ready to finish up.'

'Okay, I'm figuring Olivia should get on this with you. She'll know more about his trading methods than any of us. And what he has to do to get Markov's positions closed out.'

'That would definitely help.'

'I'll get her down here, but where is he right now in the process? As much as you can tell.'

Alex leaned forward and grabbed his wireless mouse. After some sliding and clicking and typing, screens of financial data bloomed on yet a third monitor. A desktop trading platform filled the central twenty-seven-inch monitor with a set of preconfigured screens.

Beck leaned forward to watch the blur of action in cyberspace that moved tens of millions of dollars. He saw columns of numbers and currency amounts and symbols. The numbers changed continuously in color-coded columns. It all seemed totally disconnected to the world around him.

Alex answered Beck as he squinted through his black-framed glasses at the screens. He pointed to images on his monitors.

'Okay, Summit Investing runs the fund. Or Crane does. The fund has several brokerage accounts for Markov. All the investment vehicles are in these accounts. As Crane closes out trades the cash goes into various sweep accounts.'

Alex pointed to different segments on the third monitor, pointing out the separate trading accounts.

'But there are also bank accounts, aside from the brokerage accounts. Summit isn't a chartered bank so there's tons of money in accounts scattered around in different banks. Some US banks: JPMorgan, Wells, B of A. Also, a handful of offshore accounts. Four of them in Nevis. Two in Isle of Man. Two in Geneva, Switzerland. And four in Grand Cayman. There are probably more. But I only see these accounts when Crane transfers cash into them.'

'How much has he assembled?'

'In cash?'

'Yes.'

Alex leaned closer to the monitor. Moving his mouse. Clicking his keyboard.

'I count just over thirty million. But he's only closed about twenty-five percent of his positions.'

Beck thought about the amount. Crane had been at this less than a day. If there was another hundred million or so, the pace would have to accelerate very soon.

'Okay, Alex, can you keep going for a couple more hours?'

Alex's long arm reached amidst the clutter on his desk and rummaged around until he found a small energy drink bottle. Liebowitz gulped it down in one swallow.

'Of course.'

'Good. I'll have Olivia walk you through all the separate accounts and look over the assets. I suspect she'll know how he'll sequence his trades to close things out. At least some of it.'

'Okay. But I'll tell you, from the looks of it, a lot of his trades are automated. Running on bracketed conditional orders.'

Alex clicked through more screens and pulled up a tool that looked like a spreadsheet.

'His trading platform has a function that pulls in algorithms right off Excel. My hope is that even if he's not running it himself, there's a bunch of trades that will cycle through and he'll just sit and oversee it so he can pull out the cash as it comes in. Or bust a trade if he doesn't like it.'

Beck nodded. 'He may have his conditional orders in, but if the numbers don't hit fast enough, he'll have to step in and override the orders. He's got to. I don't think Markov is going to wait around for his money.'

'Why doesn't he just move the assets as is?'

'Because Markov can't manage those investments. He has a very complicated, volatile portfolio.'

'Makes sense,' said Alex. 'But remember, once Crane's got everything assembled, there's no guarantee I can hack into the bank accounts it ends up in, and take it out. That's movie stuff. It doesn't work that way in the real world. The banks will shut down access to accounts if anything starts tickling that money.'

'I know. We'll do that another way.'

'Really? How?'

'Don't worry about that now. You just let me know where it is as soon as you can.'

'When he starts to run out of time and starts pulling the plug, James, there's going to be big tranches of cash flowing in. If I'm fast enough I can see where it goes. But I won't know what happens to the cash after that. Once it's all assembled, I won't be able to track it unless Crane moves it.'

Beck stared at the screen and nodded. 'Understood. Just try to get a sense from Olivia when he's approaching the finish.'

Beck patted Alex on the shoulder and headed up to the third floor.

The knife wound in his left leg twinged with each step up. He emerged on the third floor and walked to the east end of the building. He found her room. The door stood open; she sat on the end of the bed combing her thick black hair. She looked like she had just showered.

'Good morning,' she said with a quick, half-smile.

Her diffident smile seemed out of character. Beck couldn't interpret it, so he stood in the doorway and asked, 'You sleep okay?'

'Not bad.'

'You feel all right?'

She stopped brushing her hair and looked up at Beck still standing in the doorway.

'I guess. I don't know. I never experienced anything like last night. I don't know how I feel.'

Beck nodded. 'I understand. So, you still ready to help?'

'Of course.'

'We're into Crane's computers. Can you help Alex understand what he's looking at?'

'I'll try.'

She placed the hairbrush down on the bed, leaving it there as she stood up. She walked toward the doorway where Beck stood. He watched her. He decided that he could spend a lot of time watching this woman and never get tired of doing it. He didn't move. She stopped in front of him, so close to him that her breasts nearly touched his chest. She looked directly at him. Beck returned the look. Neither of them moved.

And then, suddenly, Olivia stepped into him, grabbed him by the head, and kissed him hard and fast on the lips. Just as quickly as she had done it, she released him and stepped back.

'Get out of my way,' she said, smiling at him as she walked past him.

50

Beck had left Olivia and Alex alone to work uninterrupted for an hour. It was now nearly noon. He couldn't wait any longer. He stood up from the couch at the west end of the second floor and headed back to speak to them.

As he approached, Alex told him, 'He's moving a lot faster now. He's liquidated more in the last couple of hours than since he started last night.'

Beck didn't bother to sit. He asked, 'How much?'

'Over fifty million.'

'How much more is left?'

'Depends on how the markets move. About seventy mil. Assuming all the accounts are appearing on this computer. If he hasn't opened one or looked at one since I rigged his setup, I won't know what the total is.'

'How much you think isn't showing?'

Olivia answered. 'Not much. Maybe ten million or so.'

'Okay, keep on it. Where is it looking like it's going to end up?'

Alex answered, 'Grand Cayman. He's sweeping the cash into a Summit account in the Grand Cayman branch of HSBC. That account is actually five accounts, all in the bank, but it looks like one.'

'Why?'

Olivia spoke. 'It makes it easier to see which accounts are up or down. At some point Crane will assemble everything in one account at HSBC. That way Markov can transfer it out faster and easier. How are you going to . . . ?'

Beck interrupted her before she could finish the question. 'Okay, I got it.'

Olivia dropped her question and said, 'I suspect Crane is going to start slowing down a bit soon.'

'Why?'

'He's going to wait as long as he can before he takes down his options that are underwater. There isn't much time decay on those contracts. If the underlying stocks pop, he could make a good deal.'

'But what if the market turns against him more?'

'Then he's just going to lose more. He'll have stop-loss orders in. But it's worth the chance in case any of those positions gap up.'

'Okay,' said Beck.

Just then his cell phone rang. He didn't recognize the caller ID phone number, but answered it anyhow.

'Yeah?'

The sound of a voice talking through a plugged-up nose identified the caller as Willie Reese.

'Beck.'

'What?'

'Just spotted some unfamiliar-looking white dudes who came into the neighborhood.'

'Really?'

'Yeah. Thought they might be some hipster types that got lofts or studios around your neck of the woods. But they arrived in a car. A new car. My boys on the street say it's a rental.'

'Interesting.'

'Yeah. So I ask myself, what some strange-looking ofays doin' rentin' a car to come into this hood?'

'And the answer?'

'Ain't no answer.'

'Right. How many of them are there and where are they now?'

'Three. They just rolled through the projects. Heading your way on King Street. Looks like they trying to find a place to park.'

'Where are you?'

'Sitting upstairs in a crib across from the park. My boys have been passing them off.'

Beck heard the sound of a cell phone ring in the background.

'Hold on a second.'

He listened to Willie talking to one of his spotters. He came back on the phone and told Beck, 'They just got out of their car. Three guys. Average size. They got out and split apart, one walking on one side of King, two on the other. Just about to come out on Van Brunt.'

'How are they dressed?'

'Hang on.' Willie asked his man on the street. 'Two dark coats and one wearing like a silver down coat. One of 'em has a beard.'

'Okay, thanks Willie. Good job. Tell your guys to back off. We'll handle it from our end.'

Beck moved fast. He motioned for Ciro to keep an eye at the window and hustled downstairs into the kitchen.

'Manny, let's go. Grab a coat.'

Manny turned off the flame under a pot of something,

grabbed his Navy-surplus peacoat and followed Beck out to the bar. Beck just motioned with his head for Demarco to come with them. Both men knew by the look on Beck's face that something was up.

In less than a minute they were out on the street.

51

The point man for the team was Ralph Anastasia. Ex-US Army Special Operations Forces, a man with a long list of military missions, mostly direct-action and counterterrorism, mostly in the Mideast.

Anastasia hadn't particularly liked serving in the military, but he was proud of his skills. He had been the right type for a Special Forces fighter. Compact. Unemotional. Resourceful, with more endurance that he'd ever actually needed on a mission. He had zero inhibitions about using deadly force. Ralph Anastasia had been told more than once that he lacked empathy, which he took as a compliment.

He also lacked tolerance for the military command structure. The long leash allowed on most Special Forces assignments helped, but there was always somebody above him to answer to. So as soon as it was feasible, Anastasia mustered out with an honorable discharge and went freelance.

He had been quickly hired by private military contractors. At first, most of the assignments were like the ones he participated in while inside the military. The big difference was that Anastasia operated as an independent contractor. He was given an assignment, whatever reasonable support he needed, and allowed to decide how to complete the mission.

He worked in Sudan, Libya, Iraq, and once in Guatemala on an antidrug assignment which did not go well.

After Guatemala, he went with private security companies. He was the leader of his current team, which consisted of Anastasia, an ex-Army Ranger called Harris, and a South African Special Forces brigade member turned mercenary called Williams.

Anastasia didn't know if those were their real names, and he didn't care. He knew something about Harris's training and almost nothing about the South African's. None of that bothered him. He considered both men about as expendable as paper plates.

Their first assignment on this particular job on this particular winter afternoon was pretty standard stuff. Find a location based on an address he'd been given. Survey the surrounding area. Attempt to find out who was at that address. Lay out attack options. And do it without attracting any attention.

Piece of cake.

But as he walked through the Red Hook neighborhood, Anastasia became increasingly concerned about being spotted. From the moment they parked their rental car, he had an uneasy feeling. He wasn't worried about being attacked. Any of the locals who might attempt anything along those lines wouldn't last ten seconds. All three men were armed with Beretta 9-mm automatics, and various other personal weapons. Harris, the Army Ranger, had a supercompact MP5K fitted with a fifteen-round magazine concealed under his winter coat. He also had a spare magazine in each pocket for a total of forty-five rounds, more than enough to shoot their way out of a problem.

Anastasia's main worry was the lack of pedestrian traffic. They'd passed pockets of black guys near a bodega. And hanging out near a park. But there were almost no people walking on the streets they could blend in with. He had no idea that this section of Red Hook was so industrial.

He'd told Harris and Williams to pair up, and walk together. That would attract less attention than a group of three.

He split off and moved out ahead of them by about a block as he made his way to the location on Conover Street where the target was located. Anastasia walked with purpose, without hesitating or looking around or trying to find a street sign, a sure tip-off that he was a stranger to the area.

Beck walked with Manny and Demarco, north along Conover. He walked slowly and talked softly.

'So our friend Willie Reese spotted some boys who don't look like they belong around here. Supposed to be coming our way.'

Beck described them and what they were wearing. Both Demarco and Manny were already looking ahead, trying to spot them.

'I don't want to take them out. I want to see what they're here for. It'd be best if we got behind them. They should be crossing onto Van Brunt around now. D, you head over to Van Brunt and hang out by the pharmacy or a little south and see if any of them pass you by. Then fall in behind and see if they keep heading toward our place.'

Demarco drifted left on Coffey Street, while Manny and Beck continued up Conover.

Beck said, 'Manolito, let's split up. You take the other side of the street. If they show up, let 'em pass between us. Then I'll figure out what to do from there.'

Manny nodded.

Under his peacoat Manny wore his apron and work clothes. Beck watched him slip his Charter Arms Bulldog into his right coat pocket. If it came down to it, he knew the gun's short four-inch barrel would mean Manny would have to get close to make sure he hit his target. Beck also knew that Manny wouldn't hesitate to do just that.

The heat of the kill fairly radiated off Manny. He'd been seething for days.

Beck blinked, tensing up. If the men Reese had spotted were here to attack Beck's bar, he knew it would get very bloody, very fast. They'd walk into shotgun blasts from Joey B and a steady stream of rifle fire from Ciro. And if they tried to escape from that, Beck knew they'd be running into Demarco and Manny, and himself.

But that didn't mean Beck and his men would escape unharmed. The last thing Beck needed was gunfire and dead bodies. That would bring cops. And cops would mean endless trouble.

He put the thought out of his mind and concentrated on finding out who these men were, and what they wanted.

52

Walter Pearce walked through the familiar doors of One Police Plaza. He'd been in the building enough times to know his way around. Other than promotion ceremonies, it wasn't a place that any cop really wanted to be. One PP was the house of the bosses. And no cop in his right mind wanted to be around the brass. Not much good ever came from it.

He showed his identification, checked his gun, went through security, and got a visitor's badge at the reception desk. He was four minutes early for his appointment, but as he turned from the desk, he noticed a young woman dressed in a conservative skirt, jacket, and white blouse waiting for him. A civilian.

She smiled and explained that the chief would be meeting him on the third floor.

Walter smiled back. They rode the elevator to the third floor and she escorted him to a small conference room.

'Can I get you anything? Water? Coffee?'

Walter could have used more coffee, but he was un-accustomed to being treated like a guest at One PP, so he declined.

She left him sitting in a small meeting room with space for a table and four chairs.

He patted his jacket pocket and pulled out the information he had on James Beck and Ciro Baldassare. He wondered how this was going to go. He told himself that he should stop worrying so much. This wasn't his idea. He was just the messenger.

Bureau Chief Martin Waldron appeared suddenly at the doorway of the small room. An aide was right behind him, a young man in a brown suit who looked even younger than the woman who'd escorted him.

Chief Waldron had the look of a lifelong NYPD cop. He was stuffed into his dress white shirt and black tie, the shirt decorated with collar bars and a badge plate with all his decorations.

Waldron looked annoyed. Clearly, this meeting was not something he wanted to be doing.

He dropped a thin manila folder on the table and sat across from Walter. He turned to his aide and said, 'Come back and get me in ten minutes, Ernie.'

The young man left without a word.

Waldron turned back to Pearce and said, 'Why am I here?'

Walter suppressed the urge to say, If you don't know, why the fuck should I? He dropped his paperwork on the table.

'I work for a man by the name of Frederick Milstein. He's runs a small brokerage firm.' Walter pushed the paperwork he had for James Beck toward Waldron. 'This is information on a man named James Beck. He assaulted Mr Milstein in Central Park Tuesday night. He threatened him and tried to extort a large sum of money from him.'

'How large?'

'Over six hundred-thousand dollars.'

Waldron squinted at Pearce. 'Who did you say did this?'

349

Walter pointed to the folder. 'Name is James Beck.'

'How the fuck did he expect to get six hundred grand from, what's his name?'

'Frederick Milstein. He claimed it was compensation for a woman that Milstein fired. He threatened to kill Milstein if he didn't pay.'

'Who can corroborate that?'

'I was there, but they were too far away for me to hear the threat. Mr Milstein will testify on the extortion, plus he'll testify that the man choked him until he nearly passed out and threatened to kill him if he didn't pay. You'll note that James Beck was incarcerated for killing a police officer.'

That got Waldron's attention. 'What?' He grabbed Beck's folder and started skimming through the pages.

'He was eventually found not guilty, but the fact remains, he killed one of ours.'

'Who the hell is this guy?'

'He's someone associated with known felons.' Walter pushed the second folder across the desk. 'Including this man. Name's Ciro Baldassare. He's organized crime. Record goes back to when he was a teenager. He held a gun on me while Beck threatened Milstein. Told me he'd blow off my head if I moved. He's a convicted felon. Long record of assaults and weapons charges. He can go right back to jail just on possession of a firearm. I'll testify to that.'

Waldron was still thinking about Beck.

'What the fuck is a cop killer doing out on the streets?'

Walter shrugged. 'Like I said, his conviction was over-turned. Brady due-process stuff. Apparently, not only did the DA's office withhold exculpatory evidence, they actually suppressed a witness. Plus, the judge overreached on the jury instructions. It was a manslaughter charge. A bar fight. Beck didn't know it was a cop. They took it to trial. Nailed him, but his lawyer got the conviction overturned. Beck did eight years of hard time before he was released.' Walter decided not to mention Beck's successful lawsuit against the city.

Waldron squirmed in his chair. He frowned, stared at the documents on the table.

'We have warrants?'

'Milstein's lawyers already got it done with Central Warrants.'

Waldron watched as Walter laid the arrest warrants on the room table as if playing his final cards.

'You know why I'm talking to you?'

Walter shrugged. 'Milstein said somebody in his law firm is a friend of yours.'

'Not anymore he ain't. Dumping this crap on me. All right, stop bullshitting me . . .' Waldron squinted at Walter's visitor's pass. '. . . Pearce. What the fuck is really going on here? And what's your involvement? You retired as what, detective?'

'Yes. Three years now. My involvement is simple. I work private security. I'm Milstein's driver/bodyguard.'

'Why's some Wall Street hump need a bodyguard?'

'He doesn't. At least not until now. He just likes the idea of someone with a gun driving him around. This is the first time anything like this has happened to him since I've been working for him. My two cents, these assholes are bad guys and it's a good thing you got an excuse to put them back in jail.'

'We got plenty of bad guys we can put in jail.'

'So these two made it to the top of the list. But no bullshit – they aren't choirboys. I saw them operate this extortion. They worked it smoothly. So I wouldn't plan on just knocking on their door and bringing them in. I'd be prepared.'

'That's what you think?'

Walter gauged Waldron's comment for animosity and didn't quite know how much was there. The chief seemed to be a man who was perpetually pissed off. He answered simply, 'Yes, sir.'

Waldron softened. He seemed to have realized he was going to have to take care of this and figured he'd better get what he could from Pearce.

'So you wouldn't recommend this just be a regular Warrants Squad.'

'No, sir. I would plan on more than that.'

'Fuck.'

Walter was about to say more, but he kept his mouth shut.

The chief checked his watch, gathered up the documents, and stood up to leave.

'Both of them are at this address.'

'That's how it looks.'

'How it looks?'

'That's where Beck lives. I'm pretty sure you'll find Baldassare there, too. And there's a good chance a few others that you can arrest.'

'Tell your boss we'll serve the warrants. If they're at this location, we'll arrest them. If not, tell him he can go fuck himself.'

Walter ventured a question.

'When do you think you'll do it?'

'What? You pushing me now?'

Walter shrugged. 'I just need something to say to Milstein. He'll be pushing me for an answer.'

Waldron looked at his watch again. 'I don't want this hanging over me. I'll put the word out now. We'll do it wee hours of the morning, Friday. Hopefully these knuckleheads will be tucked in sleeping.'

'I'll tell Mr Milstein.'

'Yeah, you do that.'

Waldron left without another word.

Walter decided he'd call Milstein from where he sat, then get a steak downtown somewhere. Have a couple of glasses of wine, go home, and sleep. It was out of his hands now.

53

Demarco Jones spotted two men about a block away coming toward him on Van Brunt. He slipped into a neighborhood bar, not worrying if they had seen him. He knew the bartender, Jimmy, who stood behind the bar, bored, arms crossed. At this time of day, his only customers were two young guys sipping pints of beer and an old crone hunched over a white wine spritzer.

Demarco nodded at him and pantomimed a cup of coffee. He took a seat at the long shelf that ran along the bar's front window. Jimmy placed the cup of coffee at Demarco's elbow, just as two men appeared outside the bar.

Demarco lowered his head as he sipped the coffee and watched them with raised eyes as they passed by. The one closest to the bar turned to look inside, but didn't seem to see anything of interest.

The coffee wasn't very hot, so Demarco took a long swallow, laid down his cup, and stepped out of the bar. He didn't pay for the coffee because he knew Jimmy wouldn't charge him.

Demarco hung back in the doorway of the bar, letting the two men get out ahead of him. He pulled out his cell phone and called Beck.

Beck's phone vibrated in his coat pocket. He answered, 'Yeah.'

'Two of 'em just walked past Dikeman. On Van Brunt. My guess is they keep going then come around on Reed and get on the far side of our place.'

'Right. Manny and I are on Van Dyke. Manny's making like he's helping some guys unload a truck.'

'That would be worth seeing.'

'Yeah, I think he might actually pick up a box. I'm standing behind a van on the other side of the street. If the third guy comes this way, we'll drop in behind him. You do the same with the pair.'

'All right.'

Beck slipped his phone back into his pocket and kept watch through the windows of the van. He saw a man that fit Willie Reese's description walking with his hands in his coat pockets, slow and steady. Eyes watching straight ahead of him.

Beck crouched down below the windows and stayed out of sight until the intruder had passed. Then he looked out from behind the van, still low, and watched the man as he continued up Conover: beard, no hat, silver down jacket that looked like it had been worn a long time, still walking easy with his hands in the pockets of his coat.

Beck knew the man's two partners were walking parallel one block over. He figured they were almost certainly going to meet in front of his bar.

Silver Jacket didn't look like one of Kolenka's Russians or Markov's Bosnians. He appeared to be much more relaxed and comfortable on the streets of Red Hook. Relaxed, but at the same time alert. The man's build, his size, demeanor, the beard, the confident way he moved convinced Beck he was military. Most likely Special Forces.

Apparently, Markov had brought in mercenaries, most likely through his government connections. This could change everything. The three men would be armed, and very dangerous. They wouldn't panic if shooting started. They would stand and fight with discipline. But Beck found it hard to believe they'd send just three men to take down his base.

Beck slipped out from the cover of the van and moved cautiously in the direction of the bar. The bearded leader in front of him continued walking like he belonged in the neighborhood. Nothing tentative about him. No glancing around. No looking for an address.

Beck was curious what he'd do when he arrived at the bar. There certainly weren't any address numbers to confirm the location. He'd pulled them off the front door years ago. And from the building next door.

Beck instinctively dropped back a few paces, deciding that if they did attack, the right play would be to lay back and let Ciro and Joey B blast them from inside. Then move in from behind to finish them off. But how the hell was he going to explain that to Demarco and Manny in time?

The interloper crossed Van Dyke. Now there was no doubt he was headed for the bar. There was nothing on Reed, and Conover Street ended in a dead end.

Beck sensed movement from across the street. He turned to see Manny cross Conover to his side of the street, falling in about ten feet behind Beck. Good, thought Beck. He'll be harder to spot and I have a better chance of holding him back if this goes off.

The bearded guy hadn't looked back once. That didn't

mean he was unaware that he was being followed, but if he knew or suspected, he was showing a lot of discipline and control.

And then the other two turned onto Conover from Reed Street. One of them wearing a backpack.

Now what? Beck pictured these three dropping into some sort of attack formation, shooting out his front window and lobbing a bomb-filled backpack into the bar.

Boom, mission accomplished.

54

Olivia Sanchez had noticed Beck's fast exit. The one they called Ciro took up a position watching the street and told the huge guy to do the same. She decided to use the situation to her advantage.

She'd been sitting next to Alex for almost two hours, mostly watching Crane adjust conditional sell orders. Some of them executed, others didn't as the market fluctuated. In many cases, Crane shifted them with a series of limit orders shaving the spread until he hit the prices he wanted. Or at least the prices he could live with. She knew what Crane was doing took enormous concentration. She wondered how long he could keep up the pace.

Alex, too, had been working nonstop for hours. He was a quick study, and his attention never flagged. But he could certainly do with a shower, a shave, and a set of clean clothes.

'Is there a bathroom on this floor?' she asked Alex. 'I've had about a gallon of coffee.'

Without looking away from the screens, Alex pointed toward the kitchen. 'Off the kitchen over on the left.'

'Thanks.'

She headed in that direction, making sure her cell phone was in her pocket. She made it to the bathroom without attracting any notice, locked the door, confident it would block the sound of her conversation.

She pulled out her phone and dialed Crane's number from memory. She'd made sure not to store his number on her phone. And was going to be sure to erase the call from her phone log.

She waited anxiously for him to answer. She didn't want to be in the bathroom for too long.

After five rings she heard Crane's voice. 'Finally. Talk fast, I'm tracking a ton of positions. What's going on?'

'I'm at Beck's place in Red Hook. As predicted, Beck is going after the money.'

'Good. What's he doing about Markov?'

'Like we figured. He's going to try and buy him off with his own money. Where's Markov? Is he watching you?'

'No. I haven't seen him since Wednesday noon. My bet, he's busy trying to track down Beck.' Olivia didn't mention anything about how close Markov had come to getting both her and Beck at the Four Seasons. 'Beck had another run-in with Markov's security goon. Beat the crap out of him. They want to kill Beck in the worst way. Your buddy better stay alive long enough to make his move on the money.'

'Well, I can tell you he's got a lot of tough guys here with guns and rifles.'

'Good. You know how he's going to go for the money?'

'Not exactly. But he has a first-rate computer guy who knows a lot about trading tracking all your moves. And I'll help them over any bumps.'

'Yeah, that guy must be pretty good. I didn't make it too easy so they wouldn't get suspicious, but Beck's guy made it through all my security. What's he got on my computer?'

'I think he downloaded your entire hard drive, and put

some sort of tracker program in. Then he tapped into your Internet connection somehow. Whatever he did, they see what you're doing, so just keep going however you want. When do you intend to close out the last positions?'

'Exactly when we planned. What's your cousin doing, by the way?'

'Whatever Beck tells him. Beck runs the show.'

'Okay. And you can make sure they stay with my moves?'

'Definitely. But why are you slowing down the transfers in the consolidated account?'

'No need to put things in there before Markov pushes me. I want as much time as I can to close out some of my options contracts. Every tick down on my puts cuts my losses. I'm still under fucking water on a lot of this. He's not going to be very happy.'

'Wait until he sees Beck stole it.'

'You sure he's going after the money?'

'Absolutely. Trust me, he figured this out himself. I didn't even have to suggest it.'

Crane laughed. 'The goddamn fox in the chicken coop. This is really something.'

'I wouldn't play this so tight, Alan. There's plenty of money. Just get it assembled.'

'Hey, every fucking dime I make is a dime we keep.'

'All right, all right. Just remember, it's going to be me who has to make the last move here. Give me enough time.'

'Second to last move.'

'Right. Right. You're set in Switzerland?'

'Yes. It's not the most secret place anymore, but it'll be fine for what we need to do. And it's the most fucking civilized. A great jumping-off spot for us.'

'Okay. Gotta go.'

She broke the connection, but sat in the bathroom, running over everything one more time. She was sure that Alan Crane wanted her with him, just like every man she'd ever gotten close to. In fact, not only did Crane want her, he actually thought he deserved her.

She finished up in the bathroom and went back to her seat next to Alex Liebowitz. She sat down, wondering how she might convince him to let her track Crane's transactions while he took a shower. Then again, she thought, if this geek doesn't have any clean clothes, it's not going to make much of a difference.

Thursday trading would close soon. Then one more day, Friday. Thirty hours or so and she'd be set for the rest of her life.

If they weren't all dead by then.

55

Beck slipped out of sight behind a panel truck a little less than a block away from his building.

He watched the bearded mercenary meet his two partners right in front of the bar. Manny slipped in next to Beck behind the truck. He already had his Charter Arms in his hand. There was no sign of Demarco.

The bearded leader motioned for the others to spread out. He sent one across the street and one back to the corner of Reed Street. They took up positions so that they could spot anyone approaching on any of the streets leading to Beck's building. Beck's tension dropped several notches knowing that backpack wasn't near his bar anymore.

It seemed obvious to Beck that they weren't here for an attack. They were here to plan one.

Okay, let them plan.

Beck pulled out his cell phone and dialed Ciro as he watched the bearded leader shield his eyes and try to look into the bar through the front window. Willie had painted the bottom third of the new front window. There was no way he could get a quick view inside, unless he stretched his full height to see over the black paint.

Ciro answered. 'Three guys, right?'

'Yeah. Listen, I don't think they're here to start anything. So what I want you to do is let them see people inside. I want these fuckers to think they're finding shit out.'

'You sure? Why not take them out now? Less trouble later.'

'No. You stay upstairs. If they make any noise or knock on the door, you peer out from behind the curtain. Everyone stays inside. Don't open the door. Just let them see that you're watching.'

'Okay.'

'If they take out their guns or make a move, I'll let you know. Put your phone on speaker and keep it near you, but don't let them see you talking.'

'All right.'

'Make sure Joey B has a good shooting angle in case I'm wrong, and they decide to rush the place. Tell Alex to go downstairs and move around behind the bar like he's looking for something, then go back upstairs.'

'Got it.'

'Keep your rifle ready, Ciro, just in case.'

Beck's phone started signaling another call coming through.

'Shit.' Beck had never figured out how to keep one call on hold and take the incoming call, so he just pressed talk on his cell phone.

'Yeah.'

'Interesting news, James.'

'Jeezus, now what Ricky?'

'We tracked that big dude from Lexington and Fifty-seventh. Guess where he went?'

'I'm not in the mood for guesses. We got armed visitors in front of the bar.'

'Fuuuuuck. Sorry. Okay, big boy went to One Police Plaza. Was inside about an hour. Came out. Now he's walking downtown. Jonas is trailing him on foot.'

'Shit, fuck.'

'Yeah, shit fuck.'

'Okay, I'll call you back. Stay on him.'

Christ, thought Beck, that's all I need: the fucking NYPD joining forces with everybody else. Had to be that asshole Milstein. He couldn't worry about it now.

Beck tried to see if Ciro was still on the line, but the phone was dead. He shoved it into his pocket.

'What's up?' said Manny.

'More fucking trouble. I'll tell you later.'

Beck watched as the bearded leader checked out the industrial buildings on either side of his building. Then the empty lot across the street. He peered out into the harbor. Clearly getting the lay of the land.

Anastasia motioned for his men to follow across the street into an empty lot. The three disappeared off Conover Street and hunkered down behind a pile of derelict shipping skids.

Anastasia pulled out a small but powerful set of binoculars and focused on Beck's building. It seemed to be locked up tight and empty. He peered at each window, looking for any movement at all, and then just as he was about to look away, he saw a curtain move on the second floor. Somebody was checking him out.

From his seated position behind the skids, Harris asked, 'What do you think?'

'There's no number on the door. None on the buildings

on either side, but GPS says this is the place and the building outlines match the 3-D map. It looks empty, but it's not. There are people in there. They don't want anybody to think there is, but they're watching the street.'

Harris said, 'Yeah, I saw those drapes move up on the second floor. At least I think I did.'

'You did. Notice anything else?'

Williams answered in his clipped South African accent. 'There was a black man behind us for a block or two as we walked over here, but he turned into a pharmacy before we came this way. I doubt if he was trailing us. Don't think he took any notice.'

Anastasia looked around one more time. 'Well, I got that eyes-on-us feeling. My money says they're in there, which is most of what we need to know. Let's hang out here for a bit and see what happens.'

Beck stayed on the west side of Conover behind a panel truck, down on his knees, the cold and wet penetrating though his jeans, watching the three mercenaries disappear into the lot across from his building.

Beck pulled out his phone and speed-dialed Demarco.

'Where are you, D?'

'I'm sittin' in the Merc. In the garage. Got a feeling you might need the car. At least more'n you need me walking all the way around and letting those fellows see me again so they know they've been made.'

Beck smiled at Demarco's smarts.

'You think they spotted you?'

'Of course. They haven't seen someone as good-looking as me maybe ever.'

He told Demarco, 'Okay, D, I want to keep track of these fuckers. If you try to follow them they might spot you. Certainly if you try to trail them back to their car. Willie said they parked over by the ballfield just past the projects. Those three have to be connected to Markov. Markov is connected to Kolenka. So roll out ahead of them. Drive back to the area around that building on Coney Island Avenue where we met Kolenka. Just park around there and see if they show up in the neighborhood and follow them to wherever they land.'

'Will do. Even if they don't show up, I'll see what's doing around there.'

'Good.'

'Can you get a description of their car?'

'I'll call Willie now. Head out whenever you want. I'll have it for you before you reach the area.'

Beck cut off the call and thought through the situation. Clearly Markov and Kolenka were getting ready to attack. Beck decided to make sure they did.

He called Ciro.

'You see where those guys ended up?'

'Across the street behind some skids.'

'Okay. I'm coming in. If it looks like they might take a shot at me, try to shoot 'em first.'

Beck got up off his knee.

Manny reached for his arm.

'You sure?'

'Yes.'

56

Detective First Grade Jeffrey Esposito had planned on using the last part of his shift to catch up on his paperwork. He'd set up at his desk in the Brooklyn South 76th Precinct with all his case files, assorted memos, and papers piled on the left side of his desk, and various reporting forms, logbooks, and notebooks on the right side.

He figured he would put in two or three solid hours and get it all done. Until one of the civilian clerks came up to his desk and said the precinct captain wanted to see him in his office.

Not good, thought Esposito. He checked his watch. Nearly four o'clock. He asked the clerk, 'He's still here? He's doing seven-to-three shifts these days, isn't he?'

'He came back.'

Uh-oh. Definitely not good. What the hell was going on?

As the head investigator for the precinct, Esposito ran a detective squad of six men. The Seven-Six offered a good mix of crimes and very few homicides. Esposito liked the precinct. He didn't like surprises. Whatever this was about, it had already been kicked all the way up to the top guy, and Esposito knew from experience that rarely meant anything good.

Captain Peter McManus was young for his rank. He'd earned it with a bachelor's degree from John Jay, a master's from Fordham, and from being a whiz on the civil service exams.

Thin, tall, angular, short hair, the captain sat at his desk dressed in his civilian clothes. McManus had a look on his face that Esposito couldn't quite interpret. Is he pissed off or merely annoyed? Or is it a fake expression of concern to cover what he's about to dump on me?

The captain nodded for Esposito to sit. He had both hands on top of a thin manila folder.

'What's up, skip?' Esposito asked.

'Detective Esposito, I'm sure you have heard the technical expression, shit rolls downhill.'

Here it comes.

He answered, 'I have, sir.'

McManus continued. 'Subparagraph one says the higher the shit rolls from, the faster and harder it lands.'

Esposito frowned, saying nothing, the best course of action at this point.

He looked at the folder under McManus's hands. Clearly, the answer was in that folder. Although it couldn't be much of an answer. The folder wasn't very thick.

'How high up are we talking about?'

'You want to know how high up?'

'Sure.'

'Borough Command.'

'That's high.'

'It is. And I got the feeling that Borough Command is just one stop on the way down from even higher.'

'Shit.'

'That's what I said.'

McManus slid the folder toward Esposito. Esposito didn't look at it. Didn't touch it.

'I don't know who called who or what or why. All I know is that somebody with a good amount of juice wants us to arrest two bad guys.'

'For what?'

'Assault.'

'Of who?'

'Of somebody with a lot of juice.'

'What'd they do to him?'

'Don't have the details. Something bad enough so that the brass wants these guys brought in.'

'When?'

'As soon as you can get organized. Like now.'

'Seriously?'

'Absolutely.'

'We know where to find them?'

'We know where to start. Someplace on the ass end of Red Hook.'

'So they gave it to the Seven-Six and not some regular Warrant Squad.'

'Correct.'

'And after we arrest them?'

'We get them into Central Booking and the higher-ups will take care of the arraignments, or whatever they want to do from there. Presumably burying these guys in a very deep place which will take a very long time to crawl out of.'

Esposito opened the folder.

There were two warrants. One for Ciro Baldassare.

369

One for James Beck. Behind the warrants were a few pages of arrest records for both men and prison records. Baldassare had six pages. Beck, two.

This was a shit assignment. Outside of his normal duties. Way outside the normal chain of command. He had very little background on the assailants, and apparently he wasn't going to get any. Plus, it looked like the whole thing had to be done on the quiet. But with all the brass connected to this, if he fucked up, things would get loud and angry very fast. This was all risk and no reward.

'What's the story on these guys?'

'Assume they are armed and dangerous. Assume there may be others at this location also armed and dangerous.'

'Great.'

'Do they know we are coming for them?'

'Assume they know. How quickly can you get organized?'

'To do this right?' asked Esposito.

'I sure as hell don't want you to do it wrong.'

'It feels like we should pull together some decent backup. Come in hard.'

'I don't think you have time to get a lot of backup or tactical guys. Go in fast. Get out fast. Don't make a big deal out of it. But don't get caught with your pants down.'

Typical command bullshit. McManus wanted it done *right*, but he wanted it done fast. The two rarely went together.

Esposito knew he would have to organize a decent-size show of force. You didn't go to an unknown location where there could be unknown firepower without as many bodies as you could muster.

But he'd have to do it within the precinct. He didn't have enough time to liaise with other divisions for personnel. Nor was he going to get the command backup to pull that off.

McManus sat staring at him. Esposito sat thinking it through. Start with the precinct sergeants to get squads organized. Get the patrol guys to provide bodies. Gather up as many from his detective detail as possible. Then get everything coordinated and go hither and yon out to Red Hook to arrest two guys on chickenshit warrants who were clearly way more dangerous than the charges made them seem.

Esposito picked up the folder.

'I want to do this right.'

McManus gave Esposito a look that said, don't fuck with me, and asked, 'How much time?'

Esposito checked his watch. 'It's going to take me a few hours to find the bodies. Get everybody organized. Coordinate shifts. Absolute soonest I can do it is tonight, late. Actually, early Friday morning. You know the drill. Two, three in the morning. Go in hard and fast, put guns on people, haul these guys out, and get the fuck away as fast as possible.'

'Sounds good,' said McManus. 'Let me know if you need anything.'

Esposito didn't even want to think about the list of things he needed or would like. He stood up, picked up the folder, and left.

57

It was nearly dark by the time the three mercenaries left and Manny came back into the bar.

Beck told Manny, 'You could have come in the back way.'

'I wanted to wait until they left.'

'What did they do after I let them spot me?'

'Took pictures of you walking in, then walked around the area, and drifted off. I guess back to their car.'

'Sounds like they were pretty thorough.'

'I suppose.'

'We should eat soon.'

'All my prep is done. I'll move everything up to the big kitchen. 'Bout a half hour.'

'Thanks.'

Demarco settled into a parking space on Coney Island Avenue, just past the elevated subway tracks, a few doors south of the restaurant where they had first sent word to Kolenka.

The nearest streetlight was almost a block away on the other side of Coney Island Avenue, so the black Mercury Marauder sat in a pool of darkness. Demarco cranked back the seat and positioned himself low and even with the doorpost. Nobody driving by would spot him, but he could easily see passing traffic.

*

Beck headed upstairs and called back Ricky Bolo.

'Ricky, sorry I had to cut you short.'

'Don't worry about it. I get it.'

'How are you holding up?'

'I'm a fuckin' iron man, dude. Don't worry.'

'How's Jonas?'

'He's sleeping like a baby.'

'Good. Make sure you switch off and get some sleep for yourself.'

'Don't worry. We'll stay sharp, even if we need a little magic potion.'

'Don't get too cranked.'

'I already am.'

'So what happened with Milstein's bodyguard?'

'We trailed him out of One PP. He settled in a restaurant about five blocks away. Big boy is chowing down.'

'Okay, here's the deal. Phineas sent me the bodyguard's address. It's over in Clinton. I'll text it to you. My bet is our friend Walter heads home after he eats. So you two either hang with him, or just head over there now, and make sure he ends up at home.'

'Done.'

'Then swing back down to Tribeca and get somewhere you can see Crane's building on Hubert.'

'Okay. You expect him to be on the move?'

'No. He's holed up in his place. But I want you to look out for three guys who might show up at his building. They're all about the same size. About six feet or a bit under. In shape. My guess is ex-military. Not your usual Tribeca hipsters or upscale types.'

'Who are they?'

373

'Bad news. Keep your distance. They're driving a blue Ford Taurus rental. License plate BLU2711. Two are wearing dark coats, one of them has a backpack. The other is wearing a silver down jacket. He has a full beard. Just hang somewhere you can see Crane's building and tell me if they show up. I have to know what those three are doing.'

'Got it.'

'Then see if you can grab a little sleep and come out here to my place by ten o'clock.'

'What happens at ten?'

'I need you to take someone someplace.'

'And after that?'

'We'll see.'

By seven o'clock, six people sat around Beck's large rectangular dining table on the second floor. There were two large bowls of salad, one at each end of the table. A large bowl of French fries and a large bowl of steamed broccoli. Two bottles of Spanish Rioja and two six-packs of toasted amber lager in bottles. Every person had a broiled sirloin strip steak on their plate.

Manny and Beck sat at either end of the table. Joey B occupied most of the middle on one side, Olivia next to him. Ciro and Alex on the other side.

It could have been a rather hip and eclectic dinner party, except for the various shotguns and Ciro's assault rifle propped against the dining table.

Beck waited until all the bowls were passed and drinks poured, and until everyone was well into their meals. They ate like it would be their last meal for a while. Even Olivia filled her plate and went at the steak like she was going to finish every last bite.

Beck ate slowly and methodically, limiting himself to one glass of wine, thinking over all the angles.

Finally, he said, 'Okay, listen up.'

All heads turned toward Beck.

'As soon as we finish, I want you all to find a place where you can catch a few hours' sleep. There are four beds upstairs. Plus couches on this floor. If you can't sleep, just lie down and zone out somewhere.

'Alex, you take one of the beds upstairs. You've been at it a long time. We're going to need you to follow this thing right to the end, so try to grab as much sleep as you can until we wake you.

'Olivia, you slept last night, so you keep tabs on what Crane is doing with the money while Alex is resting.'

'Okay.'

'We'll all help Manny clean up. Then rack out. We meet back at this table right at midnight. By then, hopefully, I'll know what our next moves are. If you have any questions, save them until later.'

There were nods and words of assent around the table. Everybody finished up their food and set to cleaning up. Olivia rose and started clearing the table, but Beck touched her arm and motioned for her to sit down in the chair closest to him.

He spoke to her in a quiet voice the others could not hear. 'Listen, about ten o'clock, two men are coming to take you out of here.'

Surprised, she asked, 'Why?'

'Because there's a good chance we're going to be attacked tonight, and you can't be here.'

Olivia blinked and stared at Beck when he told her that. 'Who's coming? Markov's men?'

'Doesn't matter.'

Olivia hadn't planned on being taken away from the computer, away from where she could track the flow of Markov's money.

For a moment, her control slipped. 'What am I supposed to do when I leave here? Where am I going? What's going on?'

'Just keep working until about ten. See if you can get a bead on when Crane will be finishing. Once you leave, Alex will take over.'

'Okay, but about tomorrow?'

'We'll take care of tomorrow when tomorrow comes. We're going to take you to Nydia's place in East Harlem for tonight so you can get some sleep and be ready for the last push.'

'Okay. My guess is Crane is going to have everything consolidated in one account by end of day tomorrow. Probably sooner. Have you figured out how to get it out of Markov's account?'

'Tomorrow is tomorrow. Let's just take it one step at a time. First, we have to survive this night. That includes you.'

'Where are you going to be?'

'Wherever I have to.'

Olivia nodded. Clearly, Beck was keeping information from her. Was it because he no longer trusted her?

Or because he just didn't have the time to explain things?

It didn't matter. It sounded like he was getting her out of harm's way just for tonight. She could deal with that. If she was back tomorrow, she could make this work. She decided to push a little.

'I need to be back here before the market opens tomorrow, James.'

'I understand,' he answered.

He hadn't quite agreed, but it was the best she was going to get. If she had to, she'd somehow convince Beck. She wasn't going to lose now.

Just then, Demarco Jones appeared on the second floor, in his usual manner, suddenly, almost as if he'd been there all along.

Beck looked in his direction. Demarco gave him an almost imperceptible shake of his head and sat down on one of the couches at the far end of the loft.

Beck told Olivia, 'Better get back on the Crane watch, okay?'

'Sure.'

She headed off to the other end of the loft. Beck went over and joined Demarco.

'Those guys never showed?'

'No. At least not anywhere near where I was watching for them.'

'You check out Kolenka's building? You cruise by before you came home?'

'Absolutely. And around. And behind. He's in there. Saw two SUVs outside. Couple of big bodies in the lobby. Has to be more inside. He's getting ready to make a move.'

'It'll be tonight.'

'Yep,' said Demarco.

'Get something to eat. And get some sleep if you can.'

Demarco stood up and headed for the dining table. Manny had already put down a plate of food for him.

Beck left Demarco to his steak and headed downstairs. As he walked, he dialed Ricky Bolo's number.

'Anything?'

'Yeah. We just got down here. I haven't seen those guys, but the blue Taurus you described is parked over on West Street. So it looks like they are up there with your boyfriend Crane. Unless they know somebody else in this nabe.'

'Pearce ended up home?'

'Yep.'

'Okay. See you at ten o'clock.'

58

Beck shoved his phone in his pocket and continued through the front bar and down the stairs leading into the cellar. He went through the same routine he had before. Walking to the back, moving the shelves, carefully sliding back the plastered plywood cover, and walking through to the basement of the building next door.

As he passed through the opening in the wall, the smell of body odor was palpable. The darkness still impenetrable.

Even though it was cool in the basement, and it had only been about twenty-four hours, his prisoner had started to stink from worry and tension.

Beck stood at the doorway, motionless, waiting in the dark for any sound that his prisoner was awake and moving.

He'd picked up a Maglite they kept hanging on the wall near the entrance and turned it on, aiming it at the floor so he could follow the circle of illumination and still remain concealed by the darkness.

When he arrived at the cell, Beck stopped about five feet away from the iron bars. Slowly he aimed the beam of light into Ahmet Sukol's small prison cell. He carefully moved the bright light toward the bunk where Sukol lay, and shined the beam on his face.

If Sukol had been sleeping, he wasn't now. He immediately covered his eyes with the crook of his arm.

Beck waited. And waited.

Finally Sukol broke and said, 'I need food. Or are you going to starve me?'

His voice sounded raspy, and he seemed to be slightly out of breath. Like he'd spent a few hours shouting for help. He spoke with a Slavic accent, but his English was good enough to make Beck think he had been in the US for a long time.

'So far, that's the plan,' said Beck.

'What?'

'Just let you starve to death.'

'You are serious?'

'Of course I'm serious. The easiest thing is to just leave you here in the dark and let what happens, happen.'

'Why not just shoot me?'

'I'm not going to splatter blood all over the place. You can't believe how hard it is to get all the traces of blood out of a porous surface like that concrete block wall, or the floor. Much easier if I just let you wither away in the dark and die. Then all I have to do is get rid of your body. Plus, by then there'll be a lot less fat on you.'

Sukol cursed quietly in a Slavic language Beck didn't understand, and didn't take much notice of. Beck continued speaking as if talking to himself as much as to the prisoner.

'Not that getting rid of a grown man is all that easy.'

Beck swung the light away from Sukol's face and aimed it at the large commercial meat grinder in the opposite corner.

'That thing helps. It can grind up a body in about fifteen minutes. I mean, first we have to cut you into pieces, which is a lot more difficult than most imagine. Takes about half an hour. That's with two guys. We use hacksaws. We don't use the circular saw on that rack. That thing throws shit everywhere. Blood and bone and flesh. Cleaning that up is impossible.

'We do it by hand. First the arms, they're pretty easy. Just have to get through the shoulder joints. Then your head. Easy. Legs are a bitch. Big bones up near the hip sockets. Then we still have to cut them at the knee joints. Not easy.

'Then the fucking torso. That's the hardest part. That's when you're tempted to use the electric saw. Got to cut it in sections. All those ribs and the spine, and all the fucking intestines and big organs. But once that's done, the hard part is over. That damn grinder goes through everything fast: bones, meat, everything. Made in China.'

Beck paused. Waiting to see if the prisoner said anything, but Sukol remained silent, which was fine with Beck.

'We push the paste into heavy-duty twenty-five-pound plastic bags and feed it to a pack of dogs a crazy lady around here keeps. Big mongrels. Pit bulls. Shepherds. Rotties. All mixed up and inbred. Those dogs can eat a couple hundred pounds a week, easy. We burn the bags and you end up as big piles of dog shit.'

Beck paused. Letting the prisoner think about it.

'I suppose once you're dead, you really don't care how you end up. I wouldn't. But some people don't like the idea of the dogs.'

Beck paused again.

'I admit the dog thing is disgusting. And it takes time. We don't give her everything at once. We want to make it look like we've accumulated restaurant scraps. So, we have to keep the bags in the walk-in refrigerator until she's done. About three weeks.

'I sometimes wonder if that woman has figured it out. It's not like we give her a steady supply.

'But like I said, she's crazy. Nobody can figure out what she's talking about half the time.'

Beck stopped talking for a while. Feeling the fatigue and stress of the last days coming over him. But he kept the Maglite shining on the meat grinder.

'Cleaning that grinder is no picnic. Doable, but has to be done right. Cold water first. Then laundry detergent. Then ammonia. Then bleach on the concrete surfaces. I think there's some other stuff the guys use. Enzymes or something to break down the protein. Everything washes down the drain, then we pour a bunch of bleach in the drain to get rid of any blood traces or scraps.

'We don't keep the hacksaws. They end up in the bay.'

Beck paused, letting the circle of light from the Maglite rest on the floor drain.

'Doing it all down here is safer than hauling you out and dumping you someplace. A lot more work, but way more safe. No chance anybody sees us loading your body into the trunk of a car or something. Most important, zero chance anybody finds a body.'

Beck remained in the dark, just a matter-of-fact voice reciting the truth with the Maglite again shining steadily on the industrial meat grinder.

Finally, Sukol said, 'Like you say, who gives a shit once you're dead.'

'I agree. But trust me, some guys really freak out at the idea of getting eaten by a bunch of filthy mongrels and mastiffs. I'm like you. It's the dying that I'd worry about. Just withering away down here in the dark. You've only been here about a day.' Beck shook his head, thinking about it. 'You ever starve for a long time? You start really going nuts.'

Sukol had to concentrate on not screaming at Beck to shut the fuck up.

Beck let silence fill the dark basement as the Maglite beam drifted back toward Sukol's cell. And then he said, 'You're thinking about how you can persuade me to kill you some other way instead of letting you just lay in there and die. Something quicker. You're also thinking, fuck him. Markov's men will be here some time or other. They'll find me.

'But I won't kill you any other way, because there's no percentage in touching you. Or getting close enough so that you can touch me. I won't put a bullet in you because that causes lots of other problems.

'And as far as waiting for that bald motherfucker or anybody else, forget it. This place isn't anywhere near where they think I am, so even if they find me, they won't find you. Nobody knows about this place. Nobody will find you, or hear you. There's nothing above you or around you that has anything to do with me.'

Beck waited again. Letting it sink in. Then finally said, 'And face it. Who's looking for you anyhow? Who really gives a shit about you?'

After a while, Sukol said, 'Then why are you down here?'

With that question, Beck knew he had a chance. He just had to play it carefully.

He turned off the Maglite. Beck suddenly felt exhausted. He'd had very little sleep since this all started. The cold basement pressed in on him. The knife wound on his thigh ached. Every time he moved pain flashed in his upper back. There were tender bruises everywhere: his arms, hips, ribs. And the constant tension was making his lower back stiff.

There was a row of brick pillars holding up the floor above the cellar. One of them stood opposite the cell, about five feet away. Beck sidled over to it, eased himself down onto the cold concrete floor, and leaned back, arms around his knees. He felt the moist cold from the floor seeping through the seat of his black jeans. He tried to position himself so his lower back stretched out.

Beck repeated the question. 'Why am I down here?' He waited a few moments. 'Sometimes it's good to go back into the hole.'

'What do you mean?'

'You've never been in solitary confinement?'

Sukol didn't answer.

'I did twenty-eight days once. Then another time, fourteen days. The fourteen days was worse than the twenty-eight. By then, I knew what I was looking at. The first time they turned the lights off and on, I thought I might not make it. But then your eyes get used to it. Yours are all fucked up now that I've brought some light in. You won't be able to pick anything out for hours.

'And it's almost worse when the lights come on. I was never sure they weren't fucking with me. How long was it between dark and light? Eight hours? Six. Ten. A half hour. I was convinced they were using the lights to drive me nuts. But maybe I already was.'

Beck lapsed silent. Thinking back on it.

'So you come down here to remember how crazy you are?'

'You think that's it?'

'No. I think you want to use me for something.'

'What can I possibly use you for?'

Sukol sat up suddenly, swinging his feet to the cold basement floor. 'Listen to me,' he said. 'I know things. I don't give a fuck about Markov or Stepanovich. Stepanovich is a maniac. I hate that guy. I was just in it for the pay.'

And then Beck knew he had him.

'Uh, what the hell is your name, anyhow?'

'Ahmet.'

'Ahmet, why the fuck would I believe anything you say? You're with the guys trying to kill me.'

Ahmet started talking. Fast. His Slavic accent became more pronounced the faster he spoke.

'Don't believe me. Just listen to what I tell you. Then you keep me locked up here until you find out I told the truth. Once you know I tell you the truth, you let me go. Believe me, you will never see me again. I walk away. Nobody ever sees me again. For sure not that fucking piece of evil shit Stepanovich.'

Sukol waited but Beck said nothing. Beck wanted to let the man talk.

'Trust me. My best chance to walk away is if

Stepanovich is dead. He'll fucking shoot me the next time he sees me just because I've been with the enemy. I'll tell you anything I can to help you kill that fucker. If you have any brains, you kill him the next time you see him. Just kill him. If he gets you, he'll do shit to you you can't imagine.'

Beck laid his head back against the brick pillar. He could feel dried mortar and paint flecks falling against the back of his neck. He waited a full minute before he spoke. It felt like ten minutes to Ahmet Sukol.

'Where can I find Markov?'

Sukol answered without a second's hesitation, eager to prove his worth.

'You can't. You never find him. Not possible. He never stays in one place for longer than one night. Maybe two. He has some apartments and businesses scattered around Far Rockaway, Brighton Beach, but he doesn't use them much. He keeps clothes in these places. Things he needs. He stays in hotels. Usually Manhattan. He always moves around. Has a driver who fetches his clothes, picks him up, and brings him wherever he wants to go.'

'How does he work?'

'Cell phones and computer. Laptop. It's all in his head. Or on his laptop.'

Ahmet waved his hands in front of him. 'Or somewhere in the cloud. He doesn't leave a paper trail. He sleeps at night, at daytime. Always with drugs he operates. Always moving. He's not like any human you know.'

'How do you know this?'

'Everybody around him knows this. It's not secret.'

'Why does Markov need someone like Stepanovich?'

'He uses Stepanovich for personal security. Markov is paranoid. He's a drug freak. He lives in his own world. He thinks everybody is after him. Maybe it's true.'

'How does he know a criminal like Stepanovich?'

'How do you think? He sold arms into Bosnia for years. He knew plenty of men like Stepanovich.'

'That was a long time ago.'

'Not so long.'

'How do you know him?'

'Who? Stepanovich?'

'Yeah.'

'Mostly his reputation. He has a core of men who served with him. I didn't know him in the wars. Besides them, he recruits whoever he needs. Like me. There are a lot of us around. Russians, Turks, Serbians.'

'Are there any warrants out for Markov in the US?'

'I don't know. I don't think so. He seems safe in the US. I hear he runs a lot of arms for the US military. Or the government. Your fucking government is arming half the world. They need guys like Markov.'

'Stepanovich isn't going to protect Markov from a government.'

'You'd be surprised. Getting through Stepanovich isn't easy. Gives Markov time to disappear. He's the kind of guy that can walk out of a room, get on a plane, and be gone anywhere.

'But it's not governments or police Markov worries about. It's competitors. Business rivals. A maniac like Stepanovich discourages competition. Markov is always paying somebody for protection. Or bribing somebody.'

'Like Kolenka?'

'Yes. Kolenka is almost worse than Stepanovich. He will kill anybody. Very fast. He doesn't care. Stepanovich will kill you, but he'll torture you first and try to figure out ways to make pain. He lives on pain. Kolenka don't waste time. With him you are dead before you know it.'

'How many men do you think Kolenka has?'

'I don't know. The ones close to him have to be real Russian old-time thieves before he has anything to do with them.'

'What do you know about Kolenka?'

'Vory-v-Zakone. There's a lot of bullshit built up about them, but Kolenka is real. You know about how it all started in the gulags.'

'Pretty much.'

'Well there aren't many of the old ones left. But even without all the old stories, Ivan Kolenka is the real thing. He's ruthless. He does crime up and down the East Coast. Lots of money from Ukraine. Some say even Chechen money. He has gambling money. Prostitution. He runs gasoline scams. Cigarettes. Extortion. He has construction companies. Restaurants. Crime and money. Crime and money. Anything. Robberies, insurance scams, murder, anything you can think of Kolenka will do it.'

'And Stepanovich? How many men does he control?'

'It goes up and down. He likes the ones out of his Serbian brigade. From the old times. But they come and go. Lot of them end up with immigration trouble. Maybe Stepanovich can call on six good ones. Maybe ten. Kolenka, maybe the same. Do they know how to find you?'

'Yes.'

Ahmet paused. 'Then you had better run. They have many more men than you, I think.'

'Run where?'

Ahmet shrugged. 'That's for you to decide. Run far.'

'How will they come at us?'

'You think Kolenka will help Markov?'

'Yes.'

'Kolenka's men will run the show. They don't fuck around. They will surround you, burn your place down, shoot anybody who comes out. They will massacre you.

'If you don't die and Stepanovich takes you, he will hurt you for days. Maybe weeks. Trust me. Better you take the bullet or burn to death. Better you run now. But maybe there's no place they don't find you.'

'Anything else you can tell me?'

'No. Not really. Are you going to fight them?'

'I'm not going to run.'

'Then do me one favor.'

'What?'

'Give somebody the key to this cell who can come let me out if you die.'

'Sure. One last question.'

'What?'

'Where can I find Kolenka?'

'I don't know. I never have anything to do with him. I know he owns buildings in Little Russia. I don't know where he sleeps.'

Beck slowly got to his feet.

'You want the lights down here on or off?'

Sukol answered quickly.

'On.'

Beck headed back toward the entrance to the basement.

'I'll send some food down. Enough for a couple of days. One way or another, it should be all over by then.'

'And will you tell somebody about me?'

'Yes.'

As Beck approached the light switches, he heard Sukol yell out. 'Whatever happens, make sure you kill Stepanovich.'

Beck answered by flipping on the overhead fluorescent lights as he ducked back into the tunnel between the two buildings. He checked his watch. Maybe he could get two hours of sleep. He needed ten.

59

When she entered his room, he was on his back, fully clothed except for his shoes, completely motionless, having fallen into a deep exhausted sleep.

Olivia sat on the bed next to him and laid her left hand on his chest, the one with the cast. The weight of it made Beck open his eyes.

She didn't say a word. She waited, hovering over him until he focused on her face. Then she slowly leaned down and kissed him, taking her time, exploring his lips, her soft, full breasts just barely touching his chest.

She sat up and stared down at Beck.

The only light in the room came from a small lamp on Beck's night table, turned half on. He checked the clock next to the lamp. 9:30.

Beck looked back at her.

Perhaps she'd come in to wake him before ten o'clock, when she was supposed to leave.

But this was not just a wake up. They both knew what this was.

What Beck didn't know, was what he wanted to do about it. Reject her? Why? Just to show her that he was one man she couldn't control?

Still, neither one of them spoke.

Beck could have reached up and gently pushed her

aside so he could sit up. Or he could have reached up and touched her face, but he did neither.

Doing nothing ensured that something would happen.

She began to unbutton Beck's shirt with her good right hand. Her encased left hand resting on his shoulder.

Before she reached the third button, Beck got up and started undressing himself.

Olivia stood up with him. She had changed from the white shirt into a black, long-sleeved knit top. She lifted it up and over her head, taking it off and letting it fall to the floor. She slid down her jeans and stepped out of them.

As he watched her, Beck unbuckled his belt and slipped off his black jeans.

Olivia waited, letting him see her in the flimsy underwear he'd seen hanging on the shower curtain rod at the Four Seasons. She looked even better than he'd imagined she would.

Beck stood wearing only his briefs. They looked at each other's bodies, taking in the sight, both of them now seeing what they had pictured in their minds' eyes.

He knew she was going to stand there until he moved for her. It would be the first time he reached for her. And she was going to wait, standing tall, unmoving, unflinching in her sheer black bra and black lace thong.

Beck smiled. The fucking bra and panties had to be black, didn't they? He could see her nipples, dark areoles and a strip of pubic hair through the sheer material. There was no goddamn way this wasn't going to happen.

Beck stepped forward, slowly put his arm around Olivia, and pulled her to him. Her skin, unimaginably soft and smooth, felt like a balm to him. Her lush body glowed with an inner heat. She put her long arms around him, held him, and kissed him again.

Beck didn't want even the thin lacy fabric of her bra and panties between them. He unclipped her bra. It fell to the floor. He let go of her and sat back on the bed, reaching up to slide the thin straps of her thong down over her hips.

Olivia let the panties fall. She stepped out of her last bit of clothing and knelt in front of Beck to take off his shorts.

Beck lay back on the bed and lifted his hips so Olivia could strip him.

She spread his legs, and hands on his thighs, bent forward taking him in her mouth. Her thick dark hair fell over his lap as she moved. He could have let her do that for a long time, but he took her arms and pulled her up so he could see her face. Her skin glowed in the faint light from the lamp next to his bed.

For a fleeting moment, he thought about the fact that depending on what happened in the next hours, this very well might be the last woman he would ever make love to. And then he realized, no, there's no love here. This is just sex. Just excruciating lust and sex. Without apologies.

He stopped thinking about what might happen to him. He refused to think about what might happen to Olivia.

Beck moved back onto his bed, Olivia following, swinging her long leg over him, gently coming to rest on top of him, straddling his hips, her soft backside against the rigidity of his almost painfully hard erection.

There was no pretense, no guile, no preening. Just the clear naked fact of it happening, now. Finally.

She placed both hands on his chest to steady herself as she rose up.

The cast on her left hand felt rough on Beck's skin, reminding him of how unlike any other situation this was.

She maneuvered Beck inside her with her right hand, and he heard Olivia hiss with pleasure, a sound unlike any he had ever heard from any other woman.

She straightened up, then settled down even farther on him, pressing down and moving him all the way inside her as deep as possible. She pivoted her hips gently so as to completely engulf him. Beck felt her squeeze his cock, almost grabbing it, almost as if to say 'this is mine. I have you now.'

Beck watched her. He put his hands on her thighs, feeling the taut muscles of her legs, sliding his hands up to her hips, seeing the muscles in her stomach flex, watching the sway of her amazing breasts. He smiled at how absurdly perfect she was. Elegantly long and thin, and at the same time so full and feminine and sensuous. Her saw her eyes, her face, her thick gleaming hair.

She kept working him now. Pleasuring herself, pleased at knowing whatever she did, Beck would be swept up in it.

Beck let himself give in to her rhythm, timing soft thrusts into her, just to communicate that he was with her. She was clearly fucking him, clearly in charge, intent on gleaning every ounce of pleasure she could.

Olivia's taking charge, being in control, made something deep in Beck give way. After the constant tension, maneuvering, calculating, he found himself immersed in mindless moments that left him with nothing to do but go along with her. Enjoy her.

She began to grunt softly. Her eyes closed, allowing Beck to watch her in his own private way. Beck felt captured. He had never felt that with a woman, ever. The freedom of it, the pleasure of it, the erotic force made his jaws clench. She was taking him away with her.

Suddenly, Olivia reached up with her right hand and caressed her breast, squeezing the nipple. And then she grabbed Beck's right hand and forced him to do the same to her other breast and nipple.

Now she maneuvered herself so that she could stimulate her clitoris more. She held herself in position by placing both hands on his shoulders, one rough and chafing in the cast, the other soft and insistent, gripping his shoulder.

A light sheen of perspiration appeared on her chest. She was breathing harder now, giving out louder grunting sounds of pleasure. Beck squeezed her nipple, grabbed her ass.

'Harder,' she hissed. 'Harder.'

He did. Doing whatever she told him. She slowed down, somehow grinding down even more on him, burying Beck as deep and as far as she could inside her.

And now she started to climax. In waves. Suddenly sitting up straight, grabbing her vagina with Beck inside. Forming a V around his cock between her middle and ring finger, stimulating herself and him, rocking now, finishing her orgasm, pulling every ounce of erotic pleasure out of her orgasm and pushing him to come. Beck thrust up into her and released. She reached around behind her and cupped his balls, helping him with quick caresses, draining him, finishing him.

Beck muttered a curse.

Olivia smiled. Accepting it as a sound of admiration.

She had captured him. Truly. Rightfully. Inevitably.

Beck knew that she knew it, and he didn't care. Judgment and worry had already passed.

She slowly lifted off him, and lay down alongside him, rolling sideways to lie against him, now erotic in another way, giving off a palpable heat. Beck felt the fullness and length of her alongside him, felt her gently rise and fall as her breathing subsided.

Her left hand was back on his chest where it had started. The feel of the rough cast against his skin bringing him back to reality.

Beck tried to capture all the sensations, tried to inventory the whole experience, to store it away somewhere it wouldn't be sullied or destroyed by what was to come next. But he only tried for a moment. What would happen this night, would happen.

60

Beck made it down to the ground floor bar at 10:30 p.m. Ricky and Jonas Bolo were sitting at the table nearest the front door.

Beck had showered, dressed his knife wound, taken more ibuprofen, drunk more coffee, and changed into fresh clothes. He entered the bar stuffing weapons and ammunition into various pockets. His Browning Hi-Power was fully loaded with thirteen rounds in the double-column magazine and in its usual place, shoved under his belt just over his right hip.

He had two more magazines in his right back pocket. He had a Gerber guardian boot knife strapped around his right ankle and a compact Glock 26 in a holster strapped to his left ankle, so he could draw it with his right hand. The Glock 26 held ten rounds of 9-mm ammunition in the magazine, plus one in the chamber. Finally, he'd replaced the Bucheimer sap with a midget sap nestled in his front left pocket.

He went behind the bar and took out ten thousand dollars from the safe under the cash register and stuffed it into the inside pocket of his shearling coat.

'Jeezus Christ,' said Ricky Bolo, 'looks like this is going to be some night.'

Just then, Olivia Sanchez appeared in the bar. She stood with her coat open, holding her small overnight bag and purse, looking exactly like what she was – a beautiful woman who'd just had an intense orgasm, every pore of her pulsing with sexual energy.

For the first time since Beck had known Ricky Bolo, Ricky had nothing to say.

'Olivia, this is Ricky and Jonas. They're going to give us a ride.'

'Us? You're coming with me?'

'Partway. Let's go. We don't have much time.'

The four of them left and settled into the Bolo brothers' nondescript white van.

Beck sat next to Ricky in the front passenger seat. Jonas sat quietly all the way in the back of the van on a bench seat next to Olivia. The middle of the van was filled with racks and shelves and storage area, holding cases, cords, tools, and miscellaneous electronic equipment.

Nobody said much of anything on the ride into Manhattan and up the west side.

Ricky pulled off the West Side Highway at Fiftieth Street and drove to a five-story tenement building between Tenth and Eleventh avenues. He pulled over opposite the building.

'This is where he ended up,' he told Beck. 'Matches the address you gave us. His name is on one of the outside doorbells.'

Beck turned to Olivia and said, 'I'm getting out here. Ricky and Jonas will take you up to Nydia's. She has a room ready for you.'

Olivia answered, 'Okay. I'll be fine. I have one more set of clean clothes.'

'Good. That should get you through what's left. Grab

some sleep. I'll be in touch in the morning. If we're right about things, and if Alex has it figured out, tomorrow shouldn't be too hard. Keep your cell phone on.'

'I will. I have my charger.'

Beck turned to Ricky and spoke quietly.

'After you drop her off, get out to Coney Island Avenue. Watch that building Demarco told you about. It's important. We have to know when those guys are moving.'

'We're on it.'

'Thanks. You two are the best.'

'Tell me something I don't know.'

Beck nodded once and slipped out of the van.

He stood in front of a rundown building that had obviously endured while the neighborhood around it had changed. It was part of a set of old Hell's Kitchen tenements squeezed in next to one another, five stories high, four windows across. They were depressing rent controlled or rent-stabilized buildings that housed residents who had occupied the neighborhood for decades.

Beck pictured what Walter Pearce's apartment looked like.

A guy on a cop's pension, hanging on to a second-career job that wasn't much more than a glorified driver, living in that building in this neighborhood – Beck decided the ten thousand in his pocket might look pretty good to Walter Pearce.

He crossed the street and peered at the names listed next to the outside buzzers. Pearce's name was next to 3A.

There wasn't any intercom. Beck rang again. And waited. He rang again. Insistently, and waited. Finally, the buzzer sounded him in.

Beck trudged up the stairs to the third floor. The over-heated air in the stairway redolent with cooking smells, Lysol, and the faint odor of cat spray reminded Beck of his youth. He'd grown up in a building like this not too many blocks away. The old round fluorescent ceiling fixtures, the glossy paint, and the smells were all familiar.

As Beck stepped around to the third-floor landing, Walter Pearce stood outside his apartment in slippers, a white T-shirt hanging over his pants, holding a Glock aimed at Beck.

Beck stopped.

'You.'

'Yeah. Me. Sorry if I woke you. It's important.'

Walter said, 'Keep your hands where I can see them. What do you want?'

'To talk to you. It will be worth your while. Guaranteed.'

Pearce stood watching Beck. For a moment, Beck thought he might try to arrest him, but instead Pearce asked, 'You armed?'

'Of course.'

'Don't bother taking anything out. Just move slow and keep your hands where I can see them. The second I see your hands move, I'll shoot you.'

'Fair enough.'

Walter motioned for Beck to come into his apartment.

The place was like Beck had pictured it. He stepped into a dark living room straight out of the fifties, filled with old, large furniture. A big couch with a coffee table in front of it. End tables. Two high-backed upholstered chairs with a standing ashtray in between. Dark green carpet covering most of the wood floor. Gray walls that needed a paint job to cover the decades of grime that had accumulated.

The two windows facing Fiftieth Street were covered by pull-down shades, flanked by heavy curtains with a floral pattern. Beck would have bet all the money in his pocket this was the apartment Pearce had grown up in.

Walter pointed to the couch. Beck sat, sinking into the worn-out cushions. Walter sat facing him in one of the upholstered chairs resting the Glock on his knee, pointed at Beck. The only light in the room was from a floor lamp next to Walter's chair.

'Talk,' said Walter.

Beck said, 'I have ten thousand dollars I want to give you.'

'Why?'

'I'll explain.' Beck started to take out the money.

Walter barked, 'Slowly.'

Beck picked out the wad of hundred-dollar bills with his thumb and forefinger and put it on the coffee table in front of him.

Beck said, 'I had men tail you. I know you were at police headquarters. So apparently now you've got the cops on me.'

Walter didn't answer.

'Can I put my hands down?'

'Keep 'em where I can see 'em.'

'I presume Milstein used some of his leverage to get somebody high up to pull together the orders.'

Walter still said nothing.

Beck cocked his head as if to say, understandable.

'Okay. Milstein is doing whatever the fuck he's doing. My guess is he wants to make sure he never sees me again, and I suppose he thinks it will endear him to his client. But I don't think he has any idea what Mr Markov is capable of. The fact is, I'm his best chance to get this thing resolved in a way where he's not going to get hurt. Hurt badly. Or you for that matter.'

Still nothing from Pearce.

'But I can't do what I have to do if I'm locked up. Or if some cop gets nervous and shoots me. So I have an offer to make you.'

Finally, Walter spoke. 'Go ahead.'

'Whatever you got going with Milstein, I figure you more than earned your keep. You found out who we are. You used your status as an NYPD detective to talk to the bosses at One PP about us. But what has he done for you? Has he really compensated you for something very few people could have done for him? I doubt it.'

'Go on.'

'And for what? So Milstein can go to Markov and say he's taken care of me? He's a moron. Even if the cops did manage to arrest me, I'd be out on bail right after they arraigned me. So what's that buy him? Eight, ten hours?'

'What about your partner with that thirteen tattooed on his neck? He'll be violated back to jail.'

'So what. It just means he'll get out a little later. You think anybody at Rikers is going to fuck with him while he's waiting for a grand jury to indict him? And trust me, they won't because let me make something clear, Mr Pearce – nobody, and I mean nobody is going to make a case that will stick against Ciro Baldassare, or me. Not

you. Not Milstein. Not anybody. You understand what
I'm saying?'

Beck saw that Pearce was not taking the implied threat
very well. Beck waved a hand to change Pearce's focus.

'Anyhow, who gives a shit about Ciro? Not Markov.
Not Milstein. I'm the one they're interested in. And I'm
clean. I have no criminal record. Trust me, Milstein won't
ever make it to court.'

'What about me?'

'What about you? What's in it for you to back Milstein?
He's not paying you enough. And you're out there getting
the NYPD brass at One PP all worked up for what? For
that little fuck Milstein? How's that gonna help you?'

Walter said nothing, but he shifted in his chair. 'Hey, I
was just the messenger.'

'Come on, Walter, if this thing blows up the fucking
NYPD isn't going to make life miserable for Milstein. But
you, you they can fuck with. Close every door there is on
you. And if they really want to get shitty they can mess
with your PI license and maybe even your pension.'

'For what reason?'

Beck leaned forward, 'Since when do they need a reason? But getting the higher-ups to mount a big operation
against me for nothing might be reason enough.'

'Hey, you're a fucking cop killer for chrissake. They're
going to love having an excuse to come back at you.'

'Bullshit. Think it through. They fucked up before.
Everything was dropped. Plus, the City and State had to
pay me a shitload in the end. I'm fucking Kryptonite, man.
You think they want to take me on for some asshole Wall
Street prick? They're risking a lot of trouble, for what?'

Beck leaned forward again.

'Walter, I got the same crazy crusading lawyer ready to go back for round two, anytime, for any reason. Ten minutes after they arrest me, my lawyer will be suing everybody that had anything to do with this. He lives for that kind of an arrest. He'll find out all the brass that were involved. He'll turn over every fucking stone and trace back every meeting, every phone call. He'll connect every dot and name every one of those sons of bitches in an avalanche of complaints and lawsuits. And your name is going to be right in the middle of it.

'And guess what, when the shit goes down, the first fucking thing Milstein is going to do is fire you and forget your name. You'll be out on your ass, the department will blackball you, but he'll still have his business and his Park Avenue apartment and sit in Central Park smoking his fat cigar while his dog shits on the lawn. And you, you'll have nothing. No job and One PP telling everybody Walter Pearce is an asshole that caused them a ton of trouble.'

Walter snapped back, 'All right, all right. I get your fucking point. But it's already done. What the hell can you do about it?'

Beck leaned back. 'I can make everybody a hero, including you, except for Milstein. I can make all the shit fall on him. I can make you somebody the department will remember helped them.'

Walter screwed up his face in disbelief.

'Bullshit.'

'Try me.'

'How? How the hell you gonna make everybody a hero?'

404

Beck held his open hands in front of him. 'All I need is for you to find out who they're sending after me. Find out who's in charge. Find out now. Tonight. And then tell that guy what I'm about to tell you.'

'Which is what?'

'Can you find who's in charge? Can you find that out? If you can, this will work. If not, you're right. There's probably nothing I can do.'

Walter wiped his face with his big hand. For the first time in the conversation, he let the Glock point away from Beck.

'Can you find out who's coming after me, Walter?'

'Sure.'

'Good.'

'And one last thing, Walter.'

'What?'

'I don't like Milstein. He's a supercilious little fuck who let this whole stinking mess unroll. I don't like the fact that he thinks he can come after me. And I don't particularly like that he's going to use you and spit you out. If this works like I hope it will, I'll put another twenty thousand in cash on top of that ten. So, you'll not only be squared away with the department, you'll have a little cushion to tide you over until you get your next job.'

'So now you're my friend? Fuck you. I'm no charity case.'

'I'm not your friend. And it isn't charity. Trust me, you'll earn it.'

Walter pointed his gun at Beck again, this time with the butt resting on the arm of the chair to steady his aim. They were less than six-feet apart. He couldn't miss. Beck watched the anger well up in Pearce. He realized he might have gone too far. Demeaned Walter too much.

'What if I just shoot you now? You're armed. I put your gun in your hand, say I got the drop on you. Then I'm a hero for sure. Call the brass and tell them they don't have to go arrest you. Nobody gets tangled up with your lawyer. Milstein will kiss my ass. I pick up the ten thousand on the table. And I don't have to worry about your bullshit coming back at me.'

Beck nodded. 'You could do that. Yeah. Definitely. Shoot me. Take my gun and put it in my hand. Fire it off in your direction. You might make it work.'

'That's what I figure.'

'But let me ask you something.'

'What?'

'What do you think the guy with that thirteen tattooed on his neck is going to do if you shoot me? Or the other guys you never saw and don't know about? Shoot me, Walter, and you might as well put the next bullet in your head and get it over quick, because you're a dead man.'

'Oh right – your gang. Let me tell you the biggest gang in New York. The fucking NYPD.'

Beck tipped his head, conceding the point. 'Yeah, I've heard that one. Trouble is, Walter, you're not in that gang anymore. You're retired. Nobody is going to avenge Walter Pearce.'

Beck leaned forward a bit more, his hands now hanging down between his knees, his right hand inches away from the Glock 26 strapped to his left ankle. He watched Walter Pearce very carefully, spoke softly. 'Think it through, Walter. You got no chance of this working out if you shoot me.'

Beck knew it would be a very tough move to get his gun out from under the cuff of his jeans. If he moved fast, right now, he had a chance to win the shoot-out. But it would be a Pyrrhic victory. He needed Walter Pearce. He moved his hand away from his ankle and sat back.

'What the hell, Walter, why not just hear me out? You can still take your chances and shoot me. And pick up the ten grand.'

Walter Pearce stared at Beck, his Glock pointed at the center of Beck's chest.

Beck crossed his left ankle over his right knee. He rested his right hand on his left ankle, inches from the Glock, sitting back on the couch, trying to appear totally relaxed. His hand was as close to his gun as he was going to get it. He figured if it came down to it, he might win a shoot-out. It would be a mess, but as much as he needed Walter Pearce, he wasn't going to let the big, morose, angry man shoot him.

'Come on, detective. Listen to the rest of it. Then decide.'

Finally, Walter nodded, laid his gun flat on his knee, and said, 'Say what you have to say.'

Beck looked at his watch. He didn't have a lot of time. He started talking. Fast.

61

As soon as Beck got out, Jonas Bolo took Beck's place in the passenger seat, leaving Olivia to herself in the rear of the van.

Olivia laid her head back and closed her eyes. They were nearing the end. Crane was going to be moving fast now, and she didn't need to watch his trades. She knew what was left to do. Tonight he would be trading on the twenty-four-hour futures market. Some of his biggest positions were options on the S&P index. He'd be taking them down throughout the night. He also had big hedges in the currency markets which he could also trade over-night. In the morning, he'd start closing out whatever was left on the US exchanges. It would easily be wrapped up by end of trading on Friday, if not before. Alan couldn't keep going much longer. And Markov wouldn't wait any longer.

Once she got out of this horrible van, she would call him. They had to make final arrangements. She was sure it would be no problem. Nydia would probably be sleeping or staring at a television screen.

She wondered what Nydia's apartment would be like. Probably reeking of garlic and diapers, overheated, with a bunch of beat-up toys littering the place. Olivia pursed her lips at the thought. Much like the one she had grown up in. Her mother's place in the Mott Haven projects felt like eons ago, and she would die before she ever returned to that life.

This was going to work, she told herself for the hundredth time. Alan and I can pull this off. We've been through every step of it over and over again.

Beck had come to the right conclusion. He had to go after the money. And she and Crane were going to let him do just that. Crane would leave enough bread crumbs for them to follow. When Markov tried to retrieve his money, it would be gone. Gone with Beck's fingerprints all over it.

While Markov was blaming Beck, she and Alan would steal the money from Beck, and disappear.

It could work. It had to work. Olivia Sanchez wasn't going back to the projects.

62

By the time Beck returned to his bar after talking to Walter Pearce, it was 12:35 a.m. He'd finally convinced Walter Pearce to get on board.

Of course, having Walter agree to Beck's plan didn't mean he could convince the cops to play it the way Beck wanted. But that was what the extra twenty-thousand was for. To motivate the lumbering ex-NYPD detective.

Pearce would succeed, or he wouldn't. Beck would know that answer in the next few hours. If he succeeded their odds of survival increased dramatically. Either way, Beck had no choice but to go forward.

When he walked into the second-floor space, Manny, Ciro, Joey B, Demarco, and Alex Liebowitz had all taken seats at the dining table.

Beck pulled out his cell phone, rested it on the table. He looked around. Joey B seemed to have arrived at a strange state of suspended animation, finally settled in his seat, attentive, staring at nothing.

Manny and Ciro as usual displayed little emotion. Demarco, who might have raised an eyebrow or shot a look that spoke volumes, was expressionless. Alex sipped a cup of coffee, for once all his attention on one thing, Beck.

Everyone knew this was it.

Beck looked around at everyone.

He started to speak, stopped, and looked around again.

And then he said, 'Well, it's pretty simple. Men are coming to kill us tonight. Why?' He shrugged. 'We tried to help one of ours.'

Beck felt his anger swell, ignored it, and continued.

'All right. We didn't ask for it, but it's coming. What do we do? We defend ourselves. But we can't defend ourselves like others can. We can't kill them before they hurt us because that would mean there'd be a reason for the law to come at us, and that can't happen.'

Beck paused to look at the men around the table. They were waiting. Waiting for him to give them the answer. The way out.

'So we have to do this a different way. Here. On our turf, our home, we have to do it a different way. A way that can work. So, let me explain.'

He looked around the table one more time. And then Beck started talking. He talked for eighteen uninterrupted minutes. Then he listened to questions. And then he went through everything again. And then one more time.

Even after all that, he knew that maybe only Demarco had grasped the whole thing. But no matter. All Beck needed was for each man to do what was required of him. None of them had to know it all.

Beck finished by saying, 'So that's it. Obviously, I'm guessing at a lot of this. But I think I'm pretty close. So just concentrate on getting done what you have to do.'

Beck looked again at Manny and Ciro. He knew what they were thinking.

'Yes. If you can. If not . . .' Beck made a face. 'If it all goes to shit, do whatever you have to do, and we'll face the consequences.'

He got a nod from each man.

Beck said, 'Okay.'

As if on cue Beck's cell phone rang. This time Ricky Bolo didn't wait for Beck to even say hello.

'They're getting ready to move.'

'How many?'

'It's hard to tell. There's a lot of bodies moving around in front of that building. Two SUVs. They're packing men and guns into both vehicles. Figure about fifteen of 'em. About half of them with semiautomatic rifles.'

Beck grimaced at the number. 'Okay. Thanks.'

'What next?' asked Ricky.

'Call me when those SUVs leave that location, and then stay right where you are. Don't be seen. They spot you, you won't survive. If I don't call you by daybreak, disappear.'

'James.'

'What?'

'Jeezus, James, all these fuckers coming for you? Clear out, man. Just get the fuck away, now.'

'Call me when they move.'

63

Jeffrey Esposito had spent six hours pulling together the men he wanted to serve the warrants on James Beck and Ciro Baldassare.

He'd managed to get three from his detective squad who were on the four to midnight shift, and had agreed to stay on. They were reliable men, but not the bust-doors-down-shooters he would have preferred.

David Rutledge was a veteran detective. He played everything straight, went by the book. In fact, he carried a battered detective's notebook in his baggy back pocket and wrote everything down in a careful print. Everything. He referred to his notes constantly. Rutledge was over-weight and wore glasses, but of all the men Esposito knew, Rutledge was the most fearless. He'd been in a shoot-out with Rutledge and saw him do something few could: stand and shoot back, without panic overwhelming him.

The other two detectives were Tony Ball and Michael Grandon. Both were young. Early thirties. Fit. They usu-ally worked as a team. They gave the impression they were tough. Esposito didn't know if they were or weren't, but he figured at least they would be willing to act tough, and that might be good enough.

His best shot at success was Augustus Mosebee. He'd reached out to Augustus as soon as McManus had given him the assignment. They were old friends from working Missing Persons years ago. Augustus had landed on a Warrants Squad that specialized in going after serious felons. He was a six-foot-six black man who weighed somewhere around two-fifty. Maybe two-seventy. Augustus was one of those men who was so big that twenty pounds one way or the other didn't show much.

When he arrived at the precinct, Esposito was very glad to see him. There was nobody better than Augustus Mosebee when it came to knocking down people and getting handcuffs on them quickly. Especially people who didn't want to be knocked down and handcuffed.

Finally, Esposito had rounded up two patrol officers. That's all the precinct sergeant would spare him. They seemed completely ordinary. Just another pair of bodies that might either get in the way or actually help. Eight men including himself. They would have to do.

Esposito was studying a street map of the area when the call came through from the desk sergeant downstairs.

64

The back of Beck's building opened onto a small yard about eight-feet deep that ran the width of his property. The yard was overgrown and untended. There was an ailanthus tree that had grown tall enough to cover most of the back windows. An old slat-board fence ran across the back of the yard. The fence was only five-feet high. It wasn't much of a barrier, but wasn't meant to be. The fence was wired with a motion detector to warn Beck if someone tried to scale it.

On the other side of Beck's fence was an abandoned plot of land about fifty-feet deep that ran the entire width of the block. It was fairly clear of rubble, except along the back walls and fences of the buildings that faced Conover. The junk back there was completely random, everything from stacks of old shipping flats, to an abandoned Dodge Dart, to piles of old tires.

The west side of the empty lot was blocked by the two-story back wall of a warehouse. The chain-link fences at each end of the lot were topped with a single strand of razor wire.

The only entrance to the lot was through a rolling chain-link-fence gate on Reed Street, secured with a chain and a large old Master lock.

Beck figured the three scouts who had walked the area knew a killing field when they saw it. That, combined with the information Ahmet Sukol provided, guided Beck's plan of defense.

He calculated they would divide the attack into two groups: Kolenka's men and Markov's men. One attacking in the front of the building on Conover, the other group stationed in the back to shoot down anyone trying to escape the attack out front.

To cover the back, the second group would have to come in on the Reed Street side where the gate was located. The old lock and chain wouldn't stop anybody from getting into the empty lot. In the middle of a dark night, in the middle of winter, it would be easy to shoot down men stumbling over ice, junk, and snow.

Beck was betting that Kolenka's men would attack the front while Stepanovich and his men would cover the rear.

Beck knew getting into a gunfight with the attackers would cause too much damage and chaos. There was no chance that all of them would survive, and a hundred percent chance some of them would end up back in jail.

That's where his deal with Walter Pearce came in. That was the part of his plan that made him grind his teeth and wish he had never heard of Olivia Sanchez.

65

Ricky Bolo called Beck at 1:35 a.m. All he'd said was, 'They're pulling out now.'

Beck thanked him, hung up, and announced, 'Let's go.'

Within ten minutes, everyone was in place.

Ciro Baldassare and Joey B stood across the street from the empty lot, opposite the chained fence gate. Beck had positioned them behind Olivia's Porsche Cayenne, which was parked in the lot of a wholesale food store.

Ciro had his semiautomatic M-16 assault rifle set to fire in bursts of three. The 5.56-mm bullets could penetrate just about anything at the range he'd be firing from. Joey B had a pump-action Mossberg 500 shotgun loaded with Federal Flight Control LE132 12-gauge shot, a weapon with a capability pretty much the opposite of Ciro's. Each shell had fifteen pellets rather than a standard twelve. He'd be able to blast larger areas, with enough force to take someone down, but not enough penetrating power to kill.

It was nearly two in the morning. The moon had already set. The temperature had dropped to eighteen degrees with intermittent gusts of cold air coming in off the bay.

Ciro held the M-16 down low, standing motionless, wearing a dark wool overcoat that made him nearly invisible except for the wisps of condensing exhalations floating up and disappearing in the cold night air. Joey B stood next to Ciro, his broad back leaning against the rear of the small Porsche SUV. He held the Mossberg by the barrel, the butt resting on the ground in front of him. He wore a black wool coat much like Ciro's, and a black knit watch cap. He looked up at the dark night sky, trying to see stars between the scudding clouds, finally relaxed, free of any need to pace. A sense of calm came over Joey B, like a hunter waiting in the blind. He kept picturing it. Practicing in his mind what Beck had told him to do.

He would wait for Ciro. Move when he moved. Stand and shoot until he emptied the shotgun, or Ciro told him to stop.

Beck had concealed himself about a half block west of the empty lot, between a car and a wall near the corner of Reed and Van Brunt.

From there, he could spot any vehicle turning toward Conover, heading for the entrance to the empty lot. He had a Benelli M3 shotgun resting on the roof of a station wagon parked next to him, plus all the weapons he'd started the night with: his Browning, knife, sap, and extra ammunition.

Out on Conover Street, Manny Guzman stood alone, deep in the shadows of a warehouse doorway about twenty-five-feet north of the bar's entrance. An overhead high-pressure sodium light mounted above the doorway shone down brightly, illuminating the area, but creating deep shadows where Manny stood.

Manny had only one weapon. He'd substituted his Charter Arms Bulldog for a long-barrel .38 revolver. He had one shot to make. The target would be about twenty-five, thirty feet away, which was why he needed the range of the long-barrel revolver.

Once he made the shot, he could do the real damage he intended, with an item sitting ten feet from where he stood, carefully placed on the sidewalk.

Demarco Jones was also out front on Conover, but nobody quite knew where. Beck had left it up to him to pick his spot.

Beck stood motionless, hunched against the cold, waiting. Waiting for the call from Walter Pearce. If Walter failed to come through with the NYPD, Beck didn't see much chance of avoiding a bloodbath. He hated depending on a disgruntled retired cop. He hated even more depending on cops intent on arresting him. But he had little choice. They were five against how many? Fifteen? Twenty? Maybe more. He checked his watch in the dim ambient light of the dead winter night.

One way or another, it would be over soon.

66

Two things convinced Walter Pearce to follow Beck's plan.

The additional twenty-thousand dollars Beck promised him. And the absolute certainty that Frederick Milstein was going to screw him.

He figured the fastest way to make things work would be to go directly to the 76th Precinct in Brooklyn. He was certain that any police action against Beck would launch from there. It was a little after one in the morning when he walked through the double doors that led into the familiar sights and sounds of an NYPD neighborhood precinct. He presented his credentials to the desk sergeant, and did his best to convince him that he needed to see whoever was in charge of the detail heading out to serve warrants in Red Hook.

Naturally, the sergeant wanted to know more about it. Pearce told him, 'Sarge, I'll be happy for you to hear the details, but I've only got time to tell it once. So please get whoever is in charge of this thing down here as soon as you can. Bottom line, I've got information that could prevent some good cops from getting hurt tonight.'

Walter watched the sergeant think it over. He seemed a bit young to have the job. Pearce watched him check his credentials one more time, thinking over what Pearce had said. Walter knew better than to say anything more to convince him. After about thirty seconds, the young sergeant picked up the phone.

It took a full fifteen minutes for Jeffrey Esposito to appear. His opening comment was, 'Who are you, and how do you know about my warrants for these guys in Red Hook?'

Walter began by apologizing for the intrusion.

'Sorry to get into the middle of this thing, but I think I can help you. I know what's going on because I'm the one who went to the brass at One PP and got this whole thing going.'

'What thing?'

'Serving arrest warrants on James Beck and Ciro Baldassare.'

The fact that Walter knew their names told Esposito he should listen to what this man had to say.

'Go ahead.'

'It was my boss that those two assaulted. Fellow named Milstein. His law firm has connections with somebody who had enough juice to put pressure on One PP.'

'I'm listening.'

'You should know that Beck and Baldassare are not going to go quietly. They are part of a bigger crew. I've been looking into them. It's almost certain a good number of that crew will be at that location tonight.'

'Why didn't you tell that to the brass?'

'I did. Spoke to a chief called Waldron, but he wasn't in the mood to take advice from me, if you know what I mean. I started worrying that information might not filter down to you. All I'm sayin' is, if you have to serve those warrants tonight, and it seems like you do, go out there with your heads up and ready.'

'For what, exactly?'

'I don't know exactly. I just know you could be facing more than two men and a lot of them armed. Go with as many men as you can get.'

'Great, and how the fuck am I going to get that kind of backup at one o'clock in the morning?'

Walter knew this was the crucial part. He couldn't tell Esposito what to do. But he had to give him enough direction to cover what Beck had asked.

'Well, I was you, I'd grab what you can. Don't go charging into anything. Call a ten-thirteen as soon as you get there. Call it hard and loud. Wait until every cop in the area shows up before you go in.'

'Christ.'

'If you go in with enough manpower, it'll be worth it. You'll get more than just the two assholes on your warrants. If you go in aware, this could be very good for you.'

'Good for me? How?'

'You'll take down more than just those two. A lot more. And the brass will be glad you did. These are bad people.'

'How do you know all this?'

'Trust me, I know,' said Walter. 'I don't have time to explain everything, but I'm trying to help you.'

'Why? Why are you doing this?'

'Because I don't want to be the reason a bunch of cops get hurt out there tonight. I'm off the force, but I'm working in private security. I brought this thing to that bureau chief, so my name's all over this. Somebody gets hurt out there tonight, it won't go good for me. You can see that.'

'So who are you trying to help here? You, or me?'

'Both.'

Esposito nodded. It made sense, but it didn't make him happy.

'And I'm supposed to trust you, some guy I don't know from Adam.'

'If you had more time, you could check me out. I'd come up good.'

Walter watched Esposito struggling with what he had been told. Walter made his final pitch. 'It's too late to call it off. The brass will murder you. All I'm saying is, call for backup before you go in. What's the downside?'

'Me looking like an asshole.'

Walter was about to tell Esposito how bad he'd look if he didn't listen to him, but he held back. Instead, he said, 'Do what you think is best.'

It would have to do. He turned and walked out of the precinct. The last thing he had to do was give Beck the word when the cops headed out, but he knew he couldn't do much more than that. He had no idea if the precinct detective was going to take his advice.

67

Beck checked his watch. Five minutes to two. He'd received Ricky's last call twenty minutes ago. He figured with no traffic it would take about a half hour to drive from Brighton Beach to Red Hook. He called Willie Reese and told him to be on the lookout for two SUVs, as well as cops coming into the neighborhood. He'd told Willie all he needed was a heads-up, nothing more.

Beck told him again, 'Let me know what you see, but stay out of sight, man. Seriously. Don't put yourself anywhere around this.'

'I'm up in the fuckin' projects, dude. Nobody gonna see me, but I'll tell you right now, I see them.'

'Who? What?'

'Two black SUVs comin' down Lorraine, heading your way.'

'Can you spot any cops anywhere?'

'Nah. No five-oh anywhere I can see. Got some boys over by all the Hamilton Street crossings and ain't heard any word from them about cops.'

'Okay, thanks. Stay where you are.'

'I hear you, boss, but I got one request.'

'What's that?'

'Don't let any dumb-ass motherfuckers bust up my window.'

Beck smiled. 'I'll do what I can.'

And then Beck heard the far-off sound of a car engine breaking the silence of the dead winter night. The sound seemed to be coming his way, slowly.

'I think I hear 'em.'

Beck's phone signaled another incoming call. Shit.

'Take care, Willie.'

He tried to drop the call to Reese and catch the second one. He ended up with only a dial tone. 'Goddammit.'

Had to be Pearce. But what was the message? He'd made the pitch? They bought it? Didn't buy it? Were coming? Weren't coming? Fucking cell phones.

Suddenly, Beck saw the glare of headlights behind him on Van Brunt.

It was going down. A black SUV turned onto Reed.

Too late to try to call Pearce. Had to go with the assumption that even if the cops were coming, they'd be too late. Useless pieces of shit. I must have been crazy to count on them.

The SUV rolled past Beck, headed in the direction of Conover.

Beck let the SUV get about twenty feet ahead of him, then edged out into the street. He crouched down low near the front of the car he had been hiding next to so that he could have a better view in front of him.

He glanced across the street at Olivia's Porsche. No sign of Ciro and Joey B. Good, stay out of sight, boys.

Now they all had to wait. Stick with the plan until they couldn't. If the cops came in time, it might work. If not . . . Beck didn't want to think about 'if not.'

Beck watched the SUV slow to a halt a few feet before the gate. Shit. It would be better if they had stopped parallel to the gate. Fuck it. Beck eased a few feet forward, still keeping low. In the dim light Beck could make out the Chevy emblem on the back of the SUV. It was a Suburban. Big enough for a lot of men.

The passenger door of the SUV opened. One man stepped out of the vehicle. He had a two-foot-long bolt cutter. So far so good. The interior lights dimmed as he shut the door behind him, but it was on long enough to light up the inside of the Suburban. Time enough for Beck to catch sight of Stepanovich's bald head rising above the others, but not enough time to get a body count. Didn't matter. At least he knew where Stepanovich was.

The man with the bolt cutter went straight to the chain on the gate and set to work. Beck hoped he'd be smart enough to cut the hasp of the lock. The chain would be too hard for a bolt cutter. Even one that big.

The guy kept working it, grinding away, opening and closing the long handles. Finally the chain fell. He grabbed the end of the gate and tried to pull it open. Nothing. He pushed on it, leaning his weight against it. It went nowhere.

Jeezus Christ, thought Beck, you dumb son of a bitch. Slide it. Slide the damn thing. It's on wheels.

Finally, the man with the bolt cutter figured it out and started to push the gate to his right. The wheels were frozen or rusted. They wouldn't turn. Another of Stepanovich's men stepped out of the Suburban and helped him. They kept lifting and shoving the long gate over the patches of frozen snow, opening it wider and wider.

What are they doing? Beck wondered.

And then he saw what they were up to. They intended

to drive the SUV into the lot. Why? What were they thinking?

Beck began worrying that Ciro and Joey B might start shooting as soon as they saw the SUV pull in, but there was nothing he could do about it. They were across the street in the parking lot behind a tall wrought-iron fence. Too far away to signal them.

Out in front of the bar, Manny Guzman watched a second SUV, a black Chevy Tahoe, turn onto Conover. He remained back in the doorway, hidden by a small slice of shadow. Waiting. Watching.

He agreed with Beck that killing any of these men would bring way too much heat down on them. But if it came down to it, he would kill as many of these bastards as he could, and die doing it before he let anybody hurt Beck, or the bar, or any of his brothers.

The Tahoe stopped on the other side of the street, right across from the bar. Manny nodded. So far so good. If Demarco could do what he had to.

Well, thought Manny, if anybody can, it's Demarco Jones. If not, fuck it. What happens, happens.

Back by the empty lot, Beck realized it wasn't quite as bad as he first thought. He saw what they were doing. It was actually pretty smart. Once they got the gate open wide enough for the SUV, the driver made a slow Y-turn and backed it into the lot so it ended up facing out toward Reed Street.

The driver rolled the big Chevy into the open space where the gate had been, halfway in the lot, halfway out on the sidewalk, effectively blocking most of the only way in or out of the empty lot.

Out on Conover, Manny watched the passenger door behind the driver ease open. One of the men in the SUV stepped out onto the street, leaned back in the SUV, and brought out a five-gallon polyethylene gas can which he placed on the cobblestone street. Then he leaned in and brought out another five-gallon poly can.

Once the gasoline cans were on the street, the man crouched down next to them. He was short, stocky, wearing dark clothes.

Manny watched as he looked at the bar for a moment, and then unscrewed the lids on both cans. He turned the lids over, revealing the spigots, and screwed them back on the cans. The rest of the crew got out of the Chevy and took cover behind the length of the big SUV.

They moved quietly. No slamming doors. No talking. Two positioned themselves behind the hood. Two behind the roof. One crouched at the back end of the SUV. The driver stayed in the vehicle.

So far, Beck had called it right.

They all looked at Beck's building. It was dark and quiet. Either it was empty, or everyone inside was asleep with the lights off.

There was no movement anywhere on the desolate street. No sounds except a distant foghorn way out in New York Bay.

The arsonist stayed crouched down low, waiting, listening. And then he was ready. He slid one of the five-gallon containers around and grabbed it with his right hand, leaving the other for his left. He turned to say something to the men on the other side of the SUV.

Just before the attacker with the gasoline turned back to face the bar, Manny slipped out of his doorway and moved quickly for the cover of an old wooden utility pole. He reached the pole and stayed behind it, leaning his back against the rough wood. He took a deep breath, leaned out, and aimed his long-barrel thirty-eight at the red can on the arsonist's left side.

His first shot missed the poly can by a quarter of an inch, and plowed into the side of the arsonist's leg, just above the ankle. He went down. Manny fired again. This time his shot hit the polyethylene can on the left. The hot bullet didn't ignite the gasoline, but the container exploded, and five gallons of gas, probably mixed with some sort of accelerant, splattered everywhere.

By the second shot, the men behind the SUV had seen Manny and began firing back.

They were Kolenka's men. Seasoned. Calm. Shooting rapidly, but without panicking. Two were leaning flat on the hood of the Chevy, bracing their shooting arms, firing semiautomatic handguns slowly. A third held fire and watched, while the fourth fired a rifle somewhat blindly over the roof of the tall SUV. The fifth man crouched behind the back of the vehicle, fired two-shot bursts in Manny's direction from another handgun.

Manny had twisted back behind the telephone pole, standing sideways. The pole just about covered him completely, but bullets zinged past him, wood chips from the pole flying around him. He couldn't move. He was trapped. But he had just one more thing to do, and with the hail of bullets, it would be impossible not to get hit.

Shit, thought Manny. Come on, D. Get to work, man.

The gunfire over on Conover Street couldn't have been timed better. The sound forced Stepanovich and his men to get moving.

Now Beck saw how many attackers had come. Six more men, including Stepanovich, piled out of the SUV, joining the two already outside the vehicle. They all started running into the empty lot, fanning out to get in position behind Beck's building. Beck saw three with some sort of rifles. The rest seemed to be holding handguns.

Across the street Ciro had maintained iron discipline, following Beck's orders even though the SUV had ended up in a place different from what they'd planned. Exactly one minute after the last man had exited the Suburban, Ciro stepped out from behind Olivia's Porsche, walked to the wrought iron fence bordering the parking lot, and started methodically shooting rounds from his M-16 into the SUV. Joey B followed next to him and began pumping blasts of 12 gauge into the vehicle, aiming for the tires first, and then the windshield.

Ciro stood as if he were on a firing range with zero regard for the possibility of anybody shooting back. He had the barrel of the assault rifle between the iron bars of the fence, his aim rock steady. He fired shot after shot into the engine block, placing twelve bullets into an area no larger than a square foot.

Joey B obliterated the front tires and the windshield.

Within five seconds, the Chevy had become a useless wreck.

Bullets continued to zing around Manny and into the old utility pole. The pole was slowly disintegrating. One way or another, he'd have to do what he was supposed to.

Before he had taken his position in the doorway, Manny had placed a Mason jar filled with gasoline and melting mothballs next to the telephone pole. He'd punched a hole in the screw-on top and stuffed a thin piece of a dish towel down into the flammable mix.

Manny bent his knees, trying to stay covered by the pole, and grabbed the Mason jar. He managed to get hold of it and stand up without getting hit. He pulled out a cigar lighter that produced a torchlike flame.

Once, twice, three times, and the lighter ignited with a hiss. Manny hesitated, knowing that once he touched the flame to the piece of towel, he would have to step out and throw it, gunfire or not. Which meant he'd probably die throwing the goddamn gasoline. Where the fuck was Demarco? Had they spotted him? Did he go down with the first shots? Fuck it. So be it.

And then Manny heard the first scream.

Seconds can seem like an eternity when people are shooting at you. But it hadn't taken Demarco Jones more than ten seconds to make his move. He'd been concealed behind a patch of overgrown bushes and scrubby trees that ran along the fence of the empty industrial lot opposite Beck's building.

He'd waited patiently for Kolenka's men to start

shooting at Manny. Then he rolled out onto the sidewalk, crouched low, and moved quickly toward the shooters from behind, fluidly, effortlessly, unheard against the gunfire.

In his left hand he carried a Spyderco Warrior combat knife, in his right hand a crude fifteen-inch galvanized iron pipe with the bottom taped for a secure grip. A beautifully designed and expertly honed cutting tool in one hand. A crude bludgeon in the other.

Demarco moved like a wraith behind the five men shooting at Manny. They never saw or heard him. Even if they had, there wasn't much they could have done about it.

Demarco's first slash severed the thick hamstrings on the legs of the two men leaning over the SUV's hood. One fast hard slash cut through the muscles and tendons of four legs. Both men screamed, reached backward toward the searing pain, turning toward the iron pipe that smashed into their heads with two fast hits. Both were down in just under three seconds.

The third shooter, leaning over the roof of the SUV, turned toward Demarco as the pipe crunched into the middle of his forehead, splitting the skin, breaking his nose, and knocking him unconscious. The combat knife's blade swept down and sliced through the arm that held his gun, cutting through muscle and tendon, all the way into the hard humerus bone just above the elbow.

The fourth shooter holding the rifle turned it toward Demarco, but way too late. Demarco was already too close to him, the barrel of the rifle pointing past him. Demarco punched the iron pipe into his stomach and slashed the rifle out of his hands.

The last shooter crouched behind the back end of the SUV had been shooting with his left hand. He had to spin all the way around to get a shot at whoever was attacking them from his right.

Demarco wasn't even breathing hard. He spun toward the last man, his back now against the SUV. He was so calm, so fast, that he actually had to wait a beat for the man to finish turning toward him, and then Demarco slashed his blade down on the man's gun hand, cutting all the tendons running along the wrist to the thumb. Followed by a fast uppercut with the galvanized pipe that shattered the man's left mandible, knocking him unconscious. He fell in a heap, his gun hand useless.

The gunfire had stopped almost as suddenly as it had started.

Manny Guzman smiled.

He stood up, holding the Mason jar filled with homemade napalm, the soaked piece of dish towel burning and smoking.

He stepped out from behind the light pole and stepped toward the SUV, taking no chance that he would be throwing it from too far away. But Manny had forgotten about the driver. He had apparently followed orders by staying in the SUV, but now that he saw Manny approaching with a flaming bomb of some sort, he jumped out onto the street, gun in his hand.

He took aim. Manny overhanded the jar like a major league pitcher. The driver fired. Manny threw. Bullet versus firebomb.

The momentum of Manny's throw pulled him down low. The bullet missed his chest, but caught him on the top of his right shoulder, gouging out a trail of flesh and blasting through the top tip of his clavicle.

The jar shattered. The homemade napalm splattered into the gasoline. The driver pulled off a panicked second shot, but Demarco Jones had already thrown his iron pipe. It smashed into the driver's back. The shot went wide. A soft whump sounded and everything burst into a roaring black inferno of flames.

Stepanovich's men were caught between two impulses.

Shoot back at whoever had shot up their SUV. Or, keep running through the lot to get into position behind Beck's building to intercept anybody fleeing the flames clearly visible on Conover Street.

Stepanovich stood near the middle of the lot, about twenty yards back from Beck's building, yelling orders.

Beck moved closer to the gate now, to keep his eye on what Stepanovich and his men were doing.

His original plan had depended on the cops being in the neighborhood by now, responding to gunshots, while Manny, Ciro, Demarco, and Joey got the hell out of the area.

He looked across the street to make sure that the Porsche was moving. It was. Ciro and Joey B were driving out of the lot to swing around to get Manny, who should be running as fast as his old legs would carry him into the empty industrial lot opposite Beck's building where Ciro and Joey would pick him up.

Demarco was supposed to head quickly in the opposite direction and get the Mercury which was parked over on

Beard Street, meet Beck, and drive out of the neighborhood.

But there were no cops swooping in and taking out whatever was left of the Russians on Conover and the Bosnians in the empty lot.

He checked again after the Porsche. It was out of sight. Good. Manny, Ciro, and Joey would be safe. Beck wasn't worried about Demarco. He was probably already climbing into the Mercury on Beard Street.

Beck could have turned around and hustled over to Van Brunt, where Demarco would find him, but no. No way. Not now. Not with these bastards and that bald maniac alive and able to come after them.

He went through a quick calculation. His men were safe. He had all the weapons he could carry. His Browning was registered. The Benelli legal. He could hear Phineas making the argument that his client had been forced out of his home, only to be ambushed, whereupon he had no alternative but to fight to save his life.

Beck smiled in the dark red glow that pulsed on the other side of his building. It would end here and now, one way or the other.

68

Beck kept moving toward the disabled Suburban blocking the entrance to the empty lot, watching Stepanovich and the others as best he could. They were midway in the dark empty lot, having spread out behind his building.

He saw Stepanovich pointing and ordering two of his men to go back to the Suburban and see who had shot the SUV to pieces. That left six, plus Stepanovich out in the lot.

Beck watched the two come running back toward him. He slipped forward, staying low and squeezed between the SUV and the open fence gate.

He carried the shotgun in his right hand, and moved toward the rear of the SUV. If he could take out these two, that would cut his enemies to seven, but he had to do it silently or he'd lose any advantage surprise might provide.

Beck stayed where he was, watching the two men slow down and approach him across the empty lot. As they came near, they split apart so they'd approach on either side of the SUV. Beck cursed. Now he would certainly have to shoot them.

They walked bent over, wary of becoming targets for whoever had shot up their SUV.

Beck knew he could get the one advancing toward him on his side, but it would be tough taking out the second one.

Suddenly, the first of Stepanovich's men loomed out of the darkness only about three feet from where Beck crouched, his attention focused across the street trying to spot who'd shot up the SUV. He never saw the butt of the Benelli which rammed straight up into the underside of his chin. Both sides of his jaw shattered, three teeth cracked, and his head snapped back so fast that his top two vertebrae ruptured.

The sound attracted the second attacker. He spun toward Beck, aiming an assault rifle at him.

Beck saw the weapon out of his peripheral vision. No way he could flip the Benelli around and get off a shot. Maybe he could fire wild, make the shooter duck or flinch, and hit him with the second shot.

He tried to turn the Benelli so he could get a finger on the trigger. Too long, too long, the assault rifle pointed right at him, he was going to die.

And then out of nowhere the solid form of Ciro Baldassare flew between the SUV and the small opening in the gate.

The man aiming the rifle at Beck heard Ciro. He turned toward the sound as Ciro's huge right fist smashed into his face, splattering his nose and cracking his right eye socket.

Ciro hit him so hard, the man's head snapped back with such force, that Beck thought Ciro might have broken the man's neck.

Jeezus, thought Beck. Ciro. Ciro saved my life.

Ciro stomped the side of the shooter's head for good measure, ripped the rifle out of his inert hands, turned to Beck, and asked, 'How many left?'

'Six, plus the leader. Stepanovich.'

Just then, sirens could be heard in the distance. Beck listened, but couldn't tell if they were police or firemen.

'Ciro, what the fuck, man. What are you doing? You have to get out of here.'

'Saving your ass. Don't worry, I dumped all my guns with Joey. He and Manny are getting rid of everything like we planned. I'll meet 'em over by the warehouses.'

Beck and Ciro heard yelling out in the lot. Nobody had come out from Beck's building, and now the sirens were getting louder. They seemed to be coming from every direction, both the high-pitched wail of fire trucks, and the deeper pitched sirens of police cars.

There was more yelling and movement out in the darkness in front of them. Ciro and Beck saw the shapes of men running toward them, trying to get out of the lot before the cops arrived.

Ciro laid the rifle on the ground near him and yelled at Beck, 'Gimme the fucking shotgun. I'll take these guys. Go after the leader.'

Beck tossed the Benelli to Ciro and yelled, 'Don't kill them unless you have to. Keep them pinned down for the cops, then dump the weapons, and get the hell out of here!'

Beck took off after Stepanovich.

Ciro went down on one knee and started blasting shots at the men running toward the gate. Then he picked up the rifle and started shooting with that.

He aimed shots high and low, alternating between the shogun and the rifle, moving right and left from behind the Suburban, varying the angles, trying to give the impression that more than one person was firing.

The Bosnians dropped to the ground, trapped in the open. They began to return fire, even though they had little idea where to shoot.

Wailing fire trucks began arriving over on Conover. The police sirens were closing in fast on the Reed Street side.

Beck angled toward the south side of the lot so he wouldn't be seen and ran toward the middle of the field, trying to get behind Stepanovich, who was now running full blast, away from the sirens, heading toward the fence at the other end of the lot.

Beck ran parallel to him, about fifteen yards to Stepanovich's right, but far enough behind so that Stepanovich didn't yet know he was being chased.

The shotgun blasts from behind ended. Beck figured Ciro had emptied the Benelli. He hoped he wouldn't stay to empty the rifle. Get out now, Ciro, thought Beck. If you get caught by the police, everything goes to shit.

Beck closed some of the distance between him and Stepanovich, but he was still ten yards behind him.

Police cars were converging on Reed Street.

Stepanovich turned to see the first police car slide to a stop, lights flashing. Then two more. And a third. He had a Mac-10 machine pistol in his right hand. He stopped and threw it as far away as he could.

Beck closed the distance between them by a couple of yards, but Stepanovich was still out ahead of him. Beck's only hope was that the fence on Beard would slow him down.

Stepanovich ran full speed toward the fence.

Beck knew Stepanovich's goal. Get out onto the street,

unarmed, and try to walk out of the neighborhood. No way. No fucking way.

He heard a garbled voice yelling commands through a police loudspeaker. All of the remaining six men began firing. A fusillade of bullets erupted from the cops. More police cars arrived, screeching to a halt, adding to the forces.

Beck ignored everything and kept running.

Stepanovich approached the fence at a full run, jumped, and grabbed on nearly halfway up. He quickly climbed up until his waist was level with the top of the fence. A single spiral of razor wire was all that prevented him from going over. He leaned his right arm and shoulder between two loops of razor wire, pushing them out of his way.

Beck closed in on him fast.

Stepanovich leaned sideways, his winter coat protected him enough so that he managed to get one leg over the fence.

Beck ran furiously to catch Stepanovich before he made it over.

Stepanovich finally heard Beck's footsteps. He turned to look behind him.

A full-scale gun battle raged on Reed Street between the Bosnians and the cops.

Beck leaped at the fence, lunging for Stepanovich's leg still on his side.

Stepanovich lifted his right foot away from Beck and kicked downward, stomping into Beck's left shoulder. He dropped to the ground. Stepanovich made it over the fence.

Stepanovich hit the sidewalk on Beard Street. Beck

leapt onto the fence, scrambled up and jackknifed over, ignoring the razor wire, depending on his leather coat to protect him. He made it to the other side, ready to drop down when Stepanovich ripped a vicious punch into Beck's kidney. The searing pain made him lose his grip on the fence. He fell to his knees, smashing them into the hard pavement.

Stepanovich immediately tried to kick Beck in the face, but Beck grabbed Stepanovich's right leg with both arms. He stood and lifted the leg out from under the Bosnian. Stepanovich went down hard on the sidewalk, but ripped his leg free and tried to kick Beck, who backed away still grimacing from the pain in his right kidney. Beck rolled his left shoulder, swinging his arm, trying to dispel the effect of Stepanovich's kick.

Stepanovich spun around on the ground and kicked Beck's right leg out from under him. Beck went down sideways, but he was up quickly. Stepanovich made it to his feet, too.

Beck gave a quick glance over to Reed Street. The street was filled with flashing blue and red lights. The gunfire continued, but it was starting to wane. It seemed like more fire engines were pulling onto Conover. So far, Beard Street was clear. All the cops had converged on the gunfight, but Beck knew the entire area would be sealed off soon.

Stepanovich backpedaled away from the fence so that the police on Reed Street wouldn't see him. Beck followed, knowing only one of them was going to leave this street alive.

Stepanovich bared his teeth at Beck, and spit at him.

Rolling his head. Flexing his long, powerful arms, ready to do battle.

Beck bent his knees trying to dispel the pain from landing on the sidewalk. He rotated his left arm. It was still numb. Stepanovich's kick must have hit the brachial nerve bundle. Feeling was coming back, but maybe too late.

Suddenly, Stepanovich jumped toward Beck, reaching for his head with both hands to pull him in close.

Beck ducked under Stepanovich's arms and twisted two right hooks into his ribs. The Bosnian mostly blocked them with his elbow, and grabbed the back of Beck's head, pushing down hard as he lifted a knee into Beck's face.

Beck barely managed to block Stepanovich's knee with crossed forearms, but the force of it drove Beck's arms up into his face. Stepanovich tried to knee Beck in the face again. Beck countered by grabbing Stepanovich's thigh and tried to twist the taller man down onto the ground.

Stepanovich pushed Beck away and pulled his leg free. Beck lunged forward and punched Stepanovich hard in the side of his neck. He kept coming forward, banged his forehead into Stepanovich's broken nose, and hooked punch after punch into Stepanovich's face before Stepanovich landed a desperate blow into the side of Beck's head, knocking Beck four feet back.

For a moment, everything went black. Beck instinctively ducked and covered up with his forearms. Another punch landed on the other side of his head. Beck twisted a blind left hook into where he figured Stepanovich's ribs might be. The punch landed solidly. He heard Stepanovich grunt in pain. Instantly, Beck hit again, with all the force he could muster. And again. He felt a sharp pain as the impact against Stepanovich's ribs crunched his knuckles and bent his wrist. He accepted the pain, knowing he had done major damage.

Stepanovich twisted an elbow at Beck's head that would have knocked him out if it landed, but Beck just managed to duck under most of the strike, feeling Stepanovich's elbow skip off the side of his head.

Beck straightened up and backpedaled. He felt the sickening nausea from Stepanovich's roundhouse punch, but he shook his head, breathed deep, managing to dispel the dizziness.

Beck knew he had cracked Stepanovich's ribs. He knew that he'd further damaged Stepanovich's already broken nose. He circled away from Stepanovich, taking more deep breaths, blinking, sucking in the cold night air, getting his focus back, estimating how badly Stepanovich was hurting.

A nose further smashed. Broken ribs. Press him now, Beck thought. Make sure he can't breathe. Smash him. Finish him off. Get inside where the man's longer reach and advantage in size and strength wouldn't help.

Beck tried to move in for the kill, but he felt like he was moving through molasses. His legs weren't working. His focus was still hazy.

And then Stepanovich pulled the knife.

The sight of it sent a cold, sickening chill flaring in Beck's chest and stomach.

Beck backed away quickly. Shit. The thing Beck hated most. He would rather face a bullet. He'd seen too many men stabbed and slashed in prison. Memories of horrific wounds, limbs made useless because of sliced tendons flashed through his mind.

Stepanovich took a quick swipe at Beck's face, trying to take out his eyes. Beck leaned away from the blade and stepped back farther.

Over on Reed Street, the gunfire had ceased. Beck heard muffled commands sounding through a police loudspeaker telling whoever was in the lot to come out with their hands on their heads. He hoped there wasn't anybody alive to obey the order.

Stepanovich gathered himself, his blade ready, closing in.

Beck continued circling away from Stepanovich, moving out into the empty street as he pulled his own knife out of the sheath on his ankle.

Stepanovich paused to check out Beck's blade. He smiled. It didn't seem to matter to him. He knew he had a much longer reach, and in a knife fight, that was all it took.

Beck knew it, too. For a moment he thought about just pulling out his Browning and shooting Stepanovich, but that would certainly bring the cops flooding into Beard Street. Demarco was parked at the end of the block. Shooting now would trap him, too. There was only one way he could do this. And it meant overcoming the overwhelming, instinctive urge to get away from that blade.

Stepanovich slowly weaved as he carefully edged closer. Beck circled to his left, away from Stepanovich's right hand. Stepanovich looked like he had done this many times.

Beck held his knife low, at the level of his thigh. He crouched over, his left arm out in front to block

Stepanovich's knife if he could. He pictured blocking and immediately punching roundhouse stabs into Stepanovich's ribs, kidney, and liver.

But Stepanovich didn't move closer. He stood upright, slashing back and forth, without much speed, testing Beck's reaction. Beck stood his ground. Stepanovich feinted a stab, then a slash. Relaxed. Almost lazy.

Beck knew it would be coming now. The kill move. He stayed low. Blocking arm ready. And then as if powered by an electric jolt, Stepanovich leaped at Beck with shocking speed, his right hand coming down at him with a long, looping overhand stab.

It was a move intent on burying the full length of his knife into the crook between Beck's neck and shoulder.

Beck saw the knife coming down at him. But instead of reflexively turning away from the blow, or stepping back, he did the opposite. He moved straight into the oncoming blade's downward path, completely surprising Stepanovich, who tried to change the angle of his downward stab. But Beck had gotten too close. The blade came down, just past Beck's left shoulder, slicing through Beck's coat, cutting into his upper back.

Stepanovich let his momentum carry him forward, turning away, but Beck spun right with him, turning clockwise, almost as if he were attached to Stepanovich, flipping his knife into an ice pick grip, and stabbing the point of his blade into the left side of Stepanovich's neck, quickly, precisely, and without hesitation.

The knife punched through the carotid artery. Beck spun away from Stepanovich's counterthrust like a matador avoiding the horns of a bull.

They ended up five feet from each other. Both still standing. Both bleeding. But only one dying. Stepanovich stood stunned, grabbing at his neck, trying to staunch the massive spurts of arterial blood his racing heart pumped out onto the dark Red Hook street. There was very little pain. Just the paralyzing terror of knowing he was going to die.

Beck backed away from the spurting blood.

Stepanovich wobbled. He swiped his blade at Beck in a desperate, hateful attempt to hurt one last time. Beck stood fast, staring into Stepanovich's eyes, watching until they glazed over and his enemy slowly folded to his knees, and then fell over onto his side, eyes open, his life draining away.

Beck ignored his own warm blood seeping into his coat. He knew the slice in his back was long, but not deep. There were no arteries or veins back there that could have been severed. He hoped Stepanovich's knife hadn't cut through too much muscle. He rolled his shoulder. It was all right. It hurt, but he could move his arm without too much trouble.

He stepped around Stepanovich's body, watching the last slow pulses of blood turning the remnants of snow and ice on the street into black slush.

Beck began shivering. He crouched down to fight a wave of nausea that hit him. Get to the car, he told himself. Have to get out of the neighborhood. Can't be caught on the street with this corpse. But he knew he wasn't done yet.

All right, he told himself, you have to do this. He looked

at the corpse of Stepanovich. Concentrated. He had a chance to make the death look like an accident.

Stepanovich had fallen fairly close to the fence.

Beck walked hunched over, and grabbed Stepanovich's right foot. He pivoted the body around so the feet faced the fence and dragged the body just a foot or so closer, estimating where Stepanovich would have landed if he had fallen back off the fence, and how far he might have staggered back. The blood everywhere could make sense, because it would have taken some time to collapse and bleed out.

He positioned the body. Looked at the fence one more time. Close enough.

Beck quickly made his way to the far end of the fence.

The cops now had spotlights glaring into the lot at the Reed Street end, illuminating everything for about twenty yards out into the field, but leaving the Beard Street end well in the dark.

At that end of the lot, it looked like one of Stepanovich's men had surrendered. Beck could see him laid across the hood of a police car. Hopefully, that would keep their attention off what he was about to do.

Beck climbed up at the far corner where the razor wire ended. He managed to pull a bit of wire free, and used the serrated edge on the top of his knife blade to bend and rip off a piece with a razor edge attached to it.

He dropped off the fence. The impact sent pain through his bruised knees and body. The cold was making his hands numb. He was already stiffening up from the blows Stepanovich had landed. He crouched low and quickly made his way to the body. He didn't have much time.

He went down on one knee and bent over to examine the wound in Stepanovich's neck. His knife hadn't gone in too deep. He took the razor wire, tried to picture the angle. There were rips on the right side of Stepanovich's coat from the razor wire. Beck's knife had punctured the left side of his neck. Beck imagined the tall man at the top of the fence, trying to push the razor wire away, stepping over the top of the fence, which would turn his left side toward the wire that had cut the right side of his coat. Beck pictured him falling sideways and backward, catching the left side of his neck on the razor wire.

Beck placed the sharp edge of the barb in the wound and carefully pulled the edge through the flesh.

He then laid two fingers in Stepanovich's blood, again painfully climbed the fence just high enough to dab blood on the razor wire to make it look like it had cut the dead Bosnian.

Done.

A searchlight from the police cars over on Reed flashed across his end of the lot.

Beck dropped down from the fence and crawled out of sight. Crawling was about all he could do.

Black smoke rose over the buildings on Conover. Flashing lights illuminated the area. Two more cop cars raced past up on Van Brunt.

Beck told himself, Got to get the fuck out of here, now.

He pocketed the piece of razor wire he'd used to cut Stepanovich, stood up, but the quick move made him suddenly dizzy. He had to go back down on one knee. He felt exhausted, enveloped by pain now, stiff and weak.

He cursed, forced himself to stand again, determined to make it down the block to where the Mercury was parked. And then he saw the black car, backing up toward him, all the lights off, coming for him like a dark ghost vehicle in the night.

69

Beck slid into the open passenger door of the Mercury.

'I was about to climb into that lot and pull out your body,' Demarco said.

'No. I wouldn't want you to risk hurting yourself.'

Demarco sped away, steering the Mercury straight through the intersection of Beard and Van Brunt. He avoided turning on Van Brunt. He kept the car headlights off, racing along the dark street until he was well past the intersection.

Beck sat back in the passenger seat, closing his eyes, pressing his shoulder against the seat back to help stop the bleeding from his knife wound. The warmth in the car making him sleepy.

Demarco wore a light down jacket. Black. Black wool pants and black suede shoes with rubber soles. He had a black Kangol fur cap turned backward on his nearly bald head so the brim wouldn't bump into the windshield as he peered out, finding his way along the dark streets with his lights off.

He asked, 'Whose blood is that on you?'

'His, except for in back.' Beck turned so Demarco could see the slice through his coat.

'Bad?'

'I don't think so, but I don't want to look just now.'

'I take it you won?'

'You take it right. If there's a hell, that bald bastard is in it.'

'What happened to the rest of them? The cops get them like you planned?'

'I saw them arresting one of them. Hopefully, they wounded or killed the rest. Cops arrived way too late. Ciro came back and saved my ass.'

Demarco smiled and shook his head in admiration.

'He get away?'

'I hope so. If he could climb that fence in front of the food store, he did.'

'Good. Where'd the bald fucker end up?'

'Out on Beard Street. I tried to make it look like he ripped his neck open getting over the fence. How'd you and Manny do?'

'Got 'em all. I think Manny wounded one guy. I don't know how many of them got burned up. Hopefully, all of 'em.'

'And Manny got away?'

'Far as I know, he and Ciro and Joey followed the plan. Left all the guns in the Porsche. Left the Porsche parked in the food store lot, then went down to the warehouses on Van Brunt to make believe they're unloading trucks. The crew there will cover for them if the cops come looking.'

'Good.' Beck felt himself succumbing to the exhaustion.

He relaxed now. He knew if anybody could maneuver the confusing streets of Red Hook to avoid whatever cops were descending on the neighborhood, it was Demarco. He tilted back his seat and stretched out. It felt like the wound in his back had stopped bleeding, but if the cops stopped them, there'd be no hiding the blood on him. Demarco would just have to deal with it. It was in his hands.

Beck took a last look out his window. They were already on Bay Street. If Demarco could maneuver around and get on the Gowanus Expressway, they'd make it out of the neighborhood.

'You okay?' asked Demarco.

'Yeah. Just let me close my eyes.'

'We got some killing to do, James.'

'I know. Wake me when we get there.'

70

Alan Crane took another Ritalin and continued scrolling through his positions for what seemed like the thousandth time. He pushed himself, knowing that in these last hours the difference in working every trade rather than giving up and closing out positions could amount to tens or even hundreds of thousands.

He checked his watch. Three in the morning.

Markov's minders were working in shifts. The one with the beard was up now, watching him while the other two slept.

Fucking ridiculous, thought Crane, but who cares. Let Markov waste his money, and these bozos waste their time. At least they had enough sense to keep their mouths shut while he worked. Crane wondered what their exact orders were. Probably something simple, make sure he doesn't go anywhere and keeps working.

As if I weren't going to do that anyhow.

Crane sat back and rubbed his face, trying to focus on a one-minute-interval candlestick chart showing the creeping spread between the US dollar and the euro.

He stared at the Bollinger Bands beginning to bulge in the direction he wanted. Crane found himself pleased that he was still able to maintain his discipline. At this stage, Crane believed ninety-nine percent of traders would be pulling the trigger too soon, too weary to eke out the last bips. But he had a big position to close out and right now the bips were going in his direction. He willed the next candlestick to turn green.

The minute interval felt like ten. The chart blinked. The candlestick moved up.

Got it. Crane calculated an eighty percent chance the trend in the next few minutes would continue up. He clicked his first sell order, grabbing the first tranche. Then he quickly pulled up his order ticket and typed in sell orders in ascending values, hoping the trend would last for a few minutes.

He was on a roll. He knew he'd grab each price. He felt it. He'd make a profit on this position. And not for you, Markov, you fucking Russian cunt. Putting these assholes on me. Having them snoring and shitting and sleeping in my house. Bringing their mess and their stink and their bullying. Fuck you, Markov.

Crane pushed back from his desk. He turned to Anastasia. He made a point of not asking permission or informing him of what he was doing, and went to the kitchen.

Ralph Anastasia sat in one of Crane's custom George Smith chairs and watched him without comment. He had concluded early on that Crane wasn't going to present any problems. It was just a matter of keeping an eye on him and killing time, not something that Anastasia found hard to do.

He could hunker down and wait for days doing essentially nothing. Ralph Anastasia had been shot at enough times to appreciate an opportunity to get paid for hiding out and laying low.

Harris and Williams were a bit more restless, but every once in a while Anastasia would send one of them out to walk the neighborhood and look for anybody lurking or watching Crane's building.

As Crane walked barefoot to his kitchen, his Bluetooth earpiece buzzed. He continued walking, headed for the bathroom in the main area of the loft, and waited until he was out of sight before he tapped the on button.

'Hold on,' he said. When he had the bathroom door closed, he continued talking. 'Yes?'

Olivia Sanchez spoke in a soft voice, obviously somewhere she didn't want to be heard talking on her phone.

'How's it going?' she asked.

'It's going. What about you?'

'They've got me stashed away up in East Harlem.'

'Why?'

Olivia lied, 'Beck's place is getting too crowded. There's nowhere for me to sleep. One of Manny's gang people is watching over me at this place. Luckily she prefers watching TV to watching me. Where are you at?'

'Closing out everything I can. Grabbing profits, minimizing losses. Same thing I've been doing for days. I'm planning to have everything closed out by ten, eleven o'clock this morning. I won't make it much longer. There isn't much left.'

'Good. When is Markov going to take over the account?'

'I don't know. I haven't heard shit from him. He must be busy with something else. Drugs, whores, or presumably killing Beck. You sure your guys are going to survive this?'

'Well, nobody is going to take them by surprise, that's for sure.'

'If Beck doesn't make it, you realize, we're fucked.'

'No, we just go to plan B and take it ourselves.'

'And be on Markov's kill list for the rest of our lives?'

'We're not giving up now, no matter what happens.'

Crane said, 'Agreed.' But he was thinking it through. Realizing now that he had to have a plan in case Beck and his men didn't make it.

He asked Olivia, 'Where are you going to be when the market opens?'

'Hopefully back at Beck's.'

'Hopefully?'

'He said I would.'

'You've got to be there to see where they put the cash.'

'I will. I will. Just hang in. Eight more hours and it's done. If you don't hear anything from me by nine-thirty, you'll know I'm back there.'

Crane calmed himself. 'Fine. You keep them pointed in the right direction. I'm assuming Markov will show up to look over my shoulder and breathe his stink all over me sometime soon. When I start consolidating everything in his bank account I'll do it fairly fast. I'll make the amount of the last transfer about five million, so hit it when you see it going in.'

'Got it.'

Olivia cut the connection.

Crane splashed his face with cold water, washed his hands, and headed back to his computer.

Anastasia stared at Crane when he returned.

Crane stared back at him, almost daring him to say something. He didn't.

Crane asked, 'You hear from Markov?'

Anastasia shook his head.

'When is he going to show up?'

'No idea.'

Anastasia continued staring at Crane. For the first time since they'd been guarding him, Crane wondered, is this guy just trying to fuck with me, or could Markov be paying these thugs to watch me until he has his money, and then kill me? No. He'd made money for Markov in the past. If he made him almost whole this time, there'd be little reason for Markov to kill him, but still – definitely got to think about a Plan B. There's no downside having a Plan B.

All right, Crane told himself, keep going. Make this work. Cover your bases. First, get the fucking money. Money can solve anything, even this hard ass watching him like he was a target.

As Crane settled behind his keyboard, he had a disturbing thought. If these guys did manage to kill him, Olivia could very well end up with everything.

For a moment, Alan Crane tried to calculate the possibility that Olivia Sanchez had planned it that way from the very beginning.

71

It took Jeffrey Esposito and his men two hours just to square away the bodies and arrest the survivors.

They'd left the Seven-Six in four cars. Esposito and Augustus Mosebee in the lead, driving an unmarked squad car. Behind him the three detectives from his precinct squad in another unmarked. Behind them were two patrol cars. He'd managed to wangle one more than he originally planned after talking to Pearce, both cars with a team of two uniformed cops.

They'd heard the gunfire and seen the light from the burning gasoline five blocks away. Esposito stopped and immediately called for support. All police personnel in the area were told to respond to gunshots at Beck's location.

Esposito sent one patrol car to investigate the fire on Conover. He and his detectives and the other patrol car converged on the gunshots on Reed Street.

By the time Esposito screeched to a halt near the bullet-ridden SUV blocking the empty lot, the gunshots had ceased. He flooded the SUV with his high beams. The unmarked and the patrol car pulled in next to him and did the same. That's when he spotted the two men Beck and Ciro had knocked out lying on the ground.

Everyone stayed behind the cover of their open doors.

Esposito got on his loudspeaker and ordered, 'Police. Anybody in there, come out with your hands up.'

Immediately, shots rang out, bullets hitting their cars. Esposito and his men returned fire, but the advantage of the two remaining assault rifles almost outweighed their superior number of handguns. Two patrol cops taking cover behind car doors were hit. One in the hip, the other in the lower part of his bulletproof vest.

By then, more police flooded into the area and joined the gunfight.

Eventually, the overwhelming firepower of the cops prevailed. Of the six remaining Bosnians, three were killed, two seriously wounded. The sixth evaded injury by taking cover in a dip in the ground behind a pile of discarded tires. He surrendered babbling unintelligible English.

Before it was all over two more cops were hit, both in the lower legs.

Everybody was half deaf from the gunshots.

On Conover, the first fire truck had arrived before the cops. Two more were on the scene by the time the flames were extinguished.

Three more patrol cars arrived on that side of Beck's building, but they had stayed well back of the billowing fire, even though they saw bodies on the street and sidewalk.

All five men that Demarco had wiped out had survived the fires because they were on the far side of the SUV. Four suffered extensive burns when the SUV went up in flames, but by then the firemen were on the scene and had dragged them away.

The driver died from inhaling superheated air and burns over most of his body. The arsonist that Manny had shot had managed to roll away from the flames, but he was badly burned and unmoving.

Once the paramedics loaded ambulances with the survivors, all under arrest and escorted by police, the Crime Scene Unit teams began securing the area, waiting for the Medical Examiner personnel who would investigate and handle the dead.

While all that was going on, Esposito and Mosebee pounded on Beck's front door. Alex Liebowitz appeared in his pajamas, looking bewildered and somewhat terrified at the gunshots and fires.

Of course, he had been prepped by Beck.

All the computer equipment and files had been locked and secured behind a fake back wall.

Whatever questions the cops asked him, he answered, telling Esposito that James Beck was not around, he didn't know where he was, or when he might return. As for Ciro Baldassare, Alex told the cops he had never heard of him, but that James Beck might know him.

He volunteered that they should contact Beck's lawyer, who he was sure would straighten everything out.

Alex kept jabbering at Esposito and Augustus Mosebee, distracting them, trying to hand them a piece of paper with the phone number of Phineas P. Dunleavy.

When they asked Alex for ID, he presented it. When they asked why he was at this address, Alex said he was staying there while his place was being renovated.

Esposito finally grabbed the piece of paper Alex kept trying to give him and threw it on the floor. Knowing the building would be empty, he and Augustus did a cursory search and stormed out.

Esposito realized this was now out of his hands. His only course of action was to stay out of the way of McManus and the other higher-ups now on the scene. He and Augustus trudged back to his car. They'd already given their preliminary interviews. Now they would have to wait for their union delegates, and start the long procedures that were standard.

While he waited, Esposito tallied the damage. He counted seven out front, eight in the back lot. All of them either dead or out of commission. As far as Esposito could figure, the only ones dead had been killed by police gunfire or by a gasoline fire that looked like it had been started by the men who had been burned.

A sixteenth body had been found out on Beard Street. A preliminary investigation concluded that he had cut his neck on razor wire trying to escape over the fence at that end of the lot. Probably while Esposito and the others were emptying their guns at the other end.

The sky was beginning to lighten.

Augustus had somehow obtained a pint of Johnnie Walker Black. He took a long pull and handed the bottle to Esposito, who shook his head.

'Fucking mess,' said Augustus.

'Goddammit.' Esposito shook his head.

'What?'

'We got played.'

'What do you mean? How?'

'That retired cop who came to see me.'

'What about him?'

'He told me to come out here heads up, ready to call for backup because there would be more than the two guys on our warrants at the location.'

'Well, he fucking got that right.'

'No. I thought he was talking about Beck's crew.' Esposito motioned toward Conover and the empty lot. 'You think any of these guys are in Beck's crew?'

Augustus shrugged. 'Who gives a shit? It still turns out good for you. You took down a bunch of bad guys. Armed. Trying to kill cops. End of story.'

Esposito shook his head. 'I don't like being played.'

Augustus waved a hand, too tired or uninterested to argue the point.

'Think about it. Beck had to have planned this whole thing. Sixteen men show up here with guns and gasoline. Why? To take down Beck and whoever else was here. Sixteen of them. None of them even got near the place. They didn't firebomb it. There's not even a bullet hole in that building. Beck, and whoever he had with him, somehow got the drop on all sixteen. They fucked some of 'em up pretty good, but didn't kill them. So there's no murder investigation. That takes most of the heat off this. The only ones who killed anybody is us. We're the ones who are going to be investigated.'

'Correct. And we'll get medals for it. It was a righteous shooting.'

'Probably. But where's Beck? Who helped him? How many of them did it take to do all this damage?'

Augustus took another pull of Scotch. 'Don't know. Don't give a fuck. I'm gonna rack out in the backseat of your car. Let me know who we have to talk to, and when I can get the fuck out of here.'

'Go ahead.'

'And one more thing, Jeffrey.'

'What?'

'If you still got to serve those warrants after all this shit, don't call me.'

72

Beck's phone woke him from a nearly comatose sleep. Demarco was just exiting the Belt Parkway, headed for Coney Island Avenue. Beck fumbled for the TALK button and croaked, 'Hang on.'

He took a deep breath, trying to come fully awake, to focus.

'Go ahead.'

Ricky Bolo muttered into the phone.

'Congratulations. You're still alive.'

'So far. What's happening?'

'Things have been quiet since that group headed out. About thirty seconds ago, a black Tahoe pulled up. It's sitting right in front of the entrance to that apartment building.'

Beck said, 'Hang on.' He turned to Demarco, 'How far away are we from Kolenka's?'

'About five minutes.'

He turned back to the cell phone. 'Can you see into the Tahoe?'

'No. Tinted windows.'

'Anybody getting out?'

'No. Looks like they're waiting for somebody.'

'You're not anyplace you'll be spotted are you?'

'Nah. We've been in the same spot for hours. Engine's off. It's like we're parked overnight. We got a little space heater running off the battery. We're good.'

'Okay. Call me if something else happens.'

Beck hung up and turned to Demarco, 'How long since we left Red Hook?'

'About a half hour. What are you thinking?'

'Kolenka knows by now something went wrong. He's got to get somewhere safer. Somewhere we don't know about.'

Demarco continued down Coney Island Avenue. He was three blocks from Kolenka's building. Beck's phone rang.

'Yeah.'

'Another car pulled up behind the SUV. Cadillac. XTS. Three hard types got out. One went into the building. Two are standing guard just outside the entrance, guns out. A big meatball got out of the passenger side of the SUV. He's got a piece in his hand, too.'

Beck told Demarco, 'Pull over, D.' Then he told Ricky, 'Shit. Looks like they're getting ready to take our guy out of there.'

'Yep.'

'All right. Can you tail them?'

'Traffic is dead. It's not rush hour yet. We'll have to lag way behind, but it shouldn't be hard.'

'Okay, we'll trail you and then probably switch back and forth so they won't spot you. You in the white van?'

'Still in the Bolo-mobile.'

'Stay on the phone and tell me what's happening.'

'It's like they're moving the fucking president.'

'They are.'

'All right. Here we go. There's a small old guy coming out now. Raggedy-ass suit coat over a white sweater, baggy pants, smoking. Everybody's looking around. The one who went in for him is on one side. Another guy on the other. The third one is leading them to the Cadillac. Everybody has guns out. They're putting him in the back of the Cadillac.'

'Who's in which car?'

'The big guy and I'm guessing just a driver in the SUV. Can't see through the windows. The boss man and two bodyguards in back of the Cadillac. Another bodyguard and driver in front. Cadillac leading. SUV trailing.'

'Stay with 'em. Keep your phone on.'

Beck put his phone on speaker and placed it in the Mercury's ashtray so Demarco could hear Ricky Bolo's running narrative. Kolenka's cars were on Neptune Avenue headed east.

'Now what?' asked Demarco.

'Pray we get lucky. I've got my Browning. You have your Glock, right?'

'Plus my AA-Twelve. It's on the floor in the back. I put a thirty-two-round drum on it.'

'Loaded with what?'

'Mostly twelve-gauge shot. But every fifth or sixth shell is a single slug. Big ones.'

'Well, maybe we have a chance.'

Beck was stiff and sore all over, the long knife wound on his back was only oozing blood. He downed a five-hour energy drink from the pocket of his coat. Grimaced through the pain and reached over the backseat for the assault shotgun.

Ricky Bolo's voice came over the cell phone speaker. 'They're gettin' on the BQE.'

'Still heading east?'

'Yeah.'

'Fall back a little more. We'll overtake you and follow them.'

Demarco asked, 'What do you think?'

'If he stays on the BQE, my bet is he's heading for JFK.'

Demarco nodded. 'Makes sense. Fly out to somewhere we can't find him. Maybe the homeland.'

'We aren't chasing this fucker to Russia. Gimme your phone.'

Beck used Demarco's phone to get online.

Demarco eased past the Bolo's white van and spotted Kolenka's caravan of two cars about a hundred yards ahead. The van fell back. Demarco took its place and followed from well behind. Both of Kolenka's vehicles were in the far left lane, going about sixty.

Beck was bent over Demarco's phone.

'There aren't any flights leaving at four in the morning. Where are we?'

'Just past Floyd Bennett Field.'

Beck pulled up Google Maps and searched for motels near JFK.

'I'm saying he's heading for Kennedy, but he'll have to hole up somewhere until planes start flying. There's a lot of motels around the airport, but there are five that are the closest. Three in one cluster, two a block away. I guess we'll have to roll the dice and cover the cluster of three.'

Demarco thought it over. 'Or we split up and cover all five.'

Beck thought it over. 'No, that could mean one of us against six. There's a better way.'

Beck picked up the cell phone and took it off speaker. 'Ricky, there's three streets just past the JFK Expressway. One Hundred Fifty-third Place, Hundred Fifty-third Lane, and Hundred Fifty-third Court.'

After a moment, Ricky responded, 'I see 'em on my GPS. What genius came up with that?'

'There's two motels on One Hundred Fifty-third Lane. Three on the corner of One Hundred Fifty-third Court and South Conduit.'

'I see 'em.'

'Demarco and I are going to find a spot midway between all five. Can you lay back and follow them until they turn off, then let us know which street they take?'

'Not without them spotting us. How bad do you need to get this guy?'

'We don't get him now, we'll never get him. He could send gunmen after us forever.'

'Shit. James, there's hardly anybody on the road. They spot us, it's over.'

'Fuck.'

Beck thought it through. He was almost positive Kolenka was going for a flight out of town. That meant JFK. Would he go straight to the airport? They'd never be able to take him there. And then Beck thought, no. He's not going to sit for hours in the airport. He can't smoke in the airport.

'Okay, here's what we do.'

Beck laid out his plan.

'All right, man, we got to hustle. Right now.'

468

Demarco slid into the far right lane. Two minutes later, the white van pulled up in the middle lane blocking any view of the Mercury because Beck feared the big Russian in the SUV was Vassily, and he might remember it. Both vehicles gradually sped up and past the Kolenka two-car caravan. Once past, they continued accelerating. The van topped out at ninety miles an hour. It took Jonas Bolo's full concentration to keep the van under control.

The van nearly spun out when they hit the exit.

Jonas braked hard and parked the van on South Conduit Avenue where they had a view of all three streets. Beck and Demarco continued on, found a spot in the middle of 153rd Court, and parked the Mercury, shutting it down.

Beck said, 'There have to be security cameras around these motels.'

Demarco spun his Kangol hat around to cover any view of his face from above. He reached into the glove compartment and pulled out a NY Knicks ball cap for Beck.

'They're mostly covering the entrances.'

'Let's get into that lot connecting the two blocks. Try and angle away from any cameras we spot. Once they turn onto one of these two streets, we'll have to run to get in place. We have to take them outside. Can't let them get into the motel.'

Demarco popped open his door and headed into the dark night without a word, Beck following close behind. Within seconds, they were hunkered down between two parked cars in the lot of the motel facing South Conduit.

Beck handed Demarco his Browning. 'Take my

469

gun.' He held up the AA-12. 'I'll need two hands for this fucker.'

'Don't worry. It doesn't kick much at all. But be careful. It shoots fast and does a hell of a lot of damage.'

Beck worked the headphones for his cell phone into his ears. The phone had been on the whole time.

Beck asked over the phone, 'Any sign of them?'

'Not yet. I didn't think the old Bolo-mobile could go that fast, but they should be here pretty soon. If they're coming here.'

Beck turned down the volume on his phone. Suddenly, everything seemed quiet. All he could hear was the whoosh of occasional traffic out on the BQE. A gust of cold wind blew through the parking lot.

They didn't have long to wait.

Beck heard Ricky Bolo's voice in his ear. 'Here they come.'

Beck felt a spasm of emotion run through him. He'd won half his bet. He stood up, moving out from between the parked cars. He did two quick half-squats, trying to loosen his sore knees, getting ready to run.

And then Ricky's voice. 'They just turned on . . . on . . . what the fuck is the middle street called? Goddamn it, is it Court? Lane? Whatever, it's the middle street.'

It took Beck a split second to figure he had to run left, Demarco drifting easily behind him, guns in both hands.

They came out onto 153rd Court just as the trailing SUV drove past. The Cadillac was heading for the motel near the end of the block.

Beck took in everything. Across the street was a long-term parking lot filled with cars dropped off by airline passengers. A six-foot chain-link fence surrounded the lot, covered by a green plastic mesh.

Beck started running as fast as he could toward the lot. Demarco could see Beck was taking the high ground. Beck rolled under a locked double-wide gate and ran toward the fence bordering the motel parking lot.

Demarco raced up 153rd Court, closing the distance between him and the slowing SUV.

The Cadillac turned into a narrow lane that led to the parking area behind the motel, the SUV following. Demarco dug in and ran full blast.

Beck slipped and stumbled across the parking lot, but hit full stride and made it to the last row of cars parked parallel along the chain-link fence. He scrambled onto the roof of the nearest car, leaned over the top of the fence, and found himself ten feet above the motel lot as the big Cadillac slowly eased between the concrete wall that supported the parking lot fence, and a car parked against the motel wall in a handicapped space.

Beck opened fire. Fully automatic bursts of 12-gauge shot. In five seconds, he took out the front passenger tire of the Cadillac, and both front tires of the Tahoe. He then shifted and blasted the back windows of the Cadillac. The driver floored the accelerator and the car leaped forward on the shredded front tire, sending up sparks as the rim spun against the asphalt.

Out on the street, Demarco stood behind the SUV shooting nonstop with both handguns through the back window. The driver tried to accelerate between the wall and the car parked on his right, but with two flat front tires, he veered into the wall.

Beck fired a blast into the Tahoe's engine, stalling the SUV.

The driver was too close to the wall to open his door, but the big Russian, Vassily, fell out of the passenger side, landing hard on the asphalt, gun in hand, firing back at Demarco.

Demarco calmly shifted aim and fired both guns at the downed Russian. After six shots, the Russian stopped firing back.

The panicked driver of the Cadillac tried to turn left, but without a front tire, he smashed into a parked car.

Beck blasted five quick shots into the back of the Cadillac, obliterating the trunk and tires. Everything went silent.

Demarco calmly walked to Vassily, who had been hit four times: his left arm, chest, right shoulder, and a grazing shot that had taken off most of his right ear. He leaned down, put his gun against Vassily's head, and said, 'Who's the *glupo chertovski negr* now, fat boy?'

Vassily's mouth moved like a fish gasping for air. Demarco put him out of his misery with one shot.

Beck had no choice but to climb over the fence. It seemed to take him forever to lower himself to the ground and slide down off the four-foot concrete wall that bordered the parking lot while still holding the shotgun. He had never fired it before and could hardly believe the damage it did. He started limping toward the Cadillac.

Demarco looked inside the open door of the SUV. The driver had fallen over the steering wheel. He looked dead, but Demarco put one shot into him to make sure.

Beck had to be certain Kolenka was dead. He moved as

quickly as he could toward the Cadillac. When he was ten feet away, the back door opened and one of Kolenka's bodyguards leaned out and shot at him. Beck lurched right and fell to the ground, but could not get the AA-12 out from under him to fire back.

Demarco, still back at the SUV, fired off wild shots at the bodyguard over the open door of the Tahoe, until both handguns clicked empty, giving Beck enough cover to fire the AA-12 from a prone position, cutting down the bodyguard with two shots.

Demarco stepped over Vassily, slammed the Tahoe door in his way and ran to Beck, lifting him to his feet. They both walked to the Cadillac, Demarco reloading his Glock. The carnage inside the car was nearly complete. The driver and remaining bodyguards were dead. Kolenka was pitched forward against the passenger seat, blood across the top of his head.

Beck leaned into the car and pulled Kolenka back off the seat. He had a massive head wound, but he was still breathing. Beck placed the muzzle of the AA-12 into Kolenka's side.

'You should have stayed out of it, Ivan.'

He pulled the trigger.

The entire gun battle had taken less than three minutes.

Demarco helped Beck limp back to the Mercury as quickly as he could. He wasn't sure if Beck had been shot, but he couldn't waste time on the street finding out.

The Bolo's white van was long gone. By the time they crossed over to get onto the BQE heading west, they still hadn't heard a police siren.

73

Phineas P. Dunleavy loved battling law enforcement. Good, bad, competent, indifferent, it didn't matter. Cops. Judges. Assistant district attorneys. It didn't matter. He would even badger a court clerk or a corrections officer if he felt he had to. He didn't waste energy being mean or vindictive about it. He just took it as his mission in life.

For Phineas it came down to a visceral reaction against bullies. Maybe it was his too often drunk and angry father who demeaned Phineas as a kid, or the fearsome nuns that tried to terrify him in parochial school, or the tough older boys who took shots at him because they didn't like his looks or his brogue. Or maybe it was just some deep dark Irish DNA that rebelled against oppressors. Whatever it was, Phineas P. Dunleavy was hardwired to fight against anybody who thought they had the right to push other people around, and Phineas never had to look far to find those people. The legal machine that ground out its merciless work 24/7 teemed with tin-pot tyrants who assumed they had a right to ruin the lives of thousands who had neither the education nor the resources to do much about it.

Which stoked Phineas's ire sufficiently to keep him in battle mode perpetually.

When he knocked on the side kitchen door of Beck's bar after coming in through the warehouse at the end of the street, and making his way between buildings as Beck had instructed, Phineas looked like a man ready for either a physical or an intellectual brawl, the sooner the better.

Alex Liebowitz opened the door for the heavyset Phineas, who stood five ten, dressed in brown corduroy pants, a green cashmere turtleneck sweater, and a long brown fine wool overcoat. Phineas just about filled the width of the doorway. He stepped in and embraced Alex in his usual bear hug.

'Laddie. Trouble afoot for the good guys, ey?'

'Apparently,' said Alex.

'When I drove up Reed to get into the warehouse lot there were a half-dozen coppers milling around back there.'

'Not nearly as many as before. We gotta stay closed down so they don't come busting in here looking for James.'

Phineas took a peek out the front window. The hulk of the burned-out SUV, surrounded by scorched sidewalks and cobblestones was still out front, as well as a single patrol car staking out the entrance to Beck's building.

'That's what I'm here for. Nobody gets in without a proper warrant and plenty of time for us to get organized. God's Christ, you look totally wrecked, boy. When was the last time you slept?'

'You mean like eight hours in a row slept?'

'I mean slept at all.'

Alex waved off the question. 'Can't remember. After today I'll be able to sleep.'

'Good. Good. Where's James?'

'Don't know. But he's due back soon. Certainly before nine-thirty.'

Phineas walked all the way around to the back of the bar. 'Nine-thirty? Why nine-thirty?'

'Markets open at nine-thirty.'

That didn't explain much, but Phineas responded as if it did. 'Ah. I see. I might even get the warrants quashed by then. James says he's already taken care of one witness, and doubts the second will ever show up.'

Phineas began assembling the makings for coffee. While it brewed, he set his mug on the battered old bar and poured in a dollop of Jameson.

'You want some coffee, lad?'

'No thanks.'

'Is it just you?'

'At the moment.'

As if on cue, a knock sounded at the side door. Alex went to answer it. A few moments later, Doctor Brandon Wright appeared in the barroom. Phineas topped off his coffee and waved him in. Behind him came a diminutive woman pulling a wheeled twenty-four-inch suitcase, filled with surgical supplies.

'Good morning, Doctor. I see you followed James's instructions about avoiding the front door.'

'It's not the first time I've taken that route.'

'Coffee?'

'Yes. Thank you.'

The tall, lanky doctor wore jeans, work boots, and a plaid shirt under a fleece-lined Carhartt canvas coat. He carried a large doctor's black bag. Brandon introduced the woman with him.

'Gentlemen, this is Ruth Silverman, my nurse. Ruth, Mr Dunleavy and Mr Liebowitz.'

She nodded.

'How do you do,' said Phineas, politely shaking her hand. Alex raised a hand in her direction.

Phineas asked Brandon, 'When did you speak to James?'

'Yesterday afternoon.'

'I see,' said Phineas.

Brandon asked Alex, 'What happened out there?'

'We were attacked.'

'How many?'

'A lot. Cops came.'

'And our boys?' asked Phineas.

Alex said, 'James had a plan. He can give you the details. I stayed in here.'

Phineas peeked out the window again. 'Well, if they're still looking for James, I'd say he's fallen down pretty low on their list. Looks like they had a lot of other things to take care of last night.'

Just then a loud bang sounded as the kitchen side door opened and hit the wall, accompanied by grunts and voices.

From back in the kitchen, Manny Guzman yelled out, 'Is it clear?'

Alex yelled back. 'All clear.'

Ciro and Manny appeared in the bar, each with one of Joey B's massive arms draped across their shoulders. The big man was clearly in excruciating pain, barely able to walk.

Blood covered Manny's right shoulder and arm.

The left side of Ciro's face was streaked with blood. But the strain of holding up Joey B seemed to be more cause for discomfort than their injuries.

Brandon stepped forward calmly. 'Has he been shot?'

'No,' said Ciro. 'The poor bastard slipped on the ice and went down hard on his ass. He broke something. Can't walk.'

Joey B added, 'Fucking can't even stand. Hurts like hell. Fuck.'

'Should we lay him down?'

Brandon put up both hands, 'No. No. Don't put him on the floor. It'll be too hard to get him up. We have to get him on a table so I can examine him.'

Ciro asked, 'How about the bar?'

Brandon looked at Joey B and at the bar top. 'No, not wide enough.' He looked around and then said, 'Okay, come on. Let's put four of these tables together.'

While Alex and Phineas slid the tables together, Brandon fished around in his medical bag and came out with a syringe and a vial. He filled the syringe, plunged it into Joey B's huge thigh, right through his pants, and emptied the contents into him.

'You won't feel much in a few minutes.' He turned to the others and directed Phineas to take Manny's place. 'Just lay him down on the tables.' He turned to his nurse. 'Ruth, head upstairs. Manny will show you.'

Phineas, Alex, and Ciro maneuvered Joey B onto the tables. The shot already taking effect, Joey B laid his head back and said, 'Jesus, give me some more of that shit, doc.'

'Let me get a little better idea of what happened to you first.'

Ciro asked Alex and Phineas, 'You heard from James and Demarco?'

'No. How'd you get Joey in here?'

'Guys from the market let us borrow a panel truck. We drove it right in the warehouse. I wasn't sure we were going to make it the rest of the way. Manny is stronger than I thought.'

Alex said, 'You okay? You got blood all over your face.'

Ciro peered into the cloudy mirror over the back bar. 'Shit.'

'What happened?'

'I don't know. I think something tore off that SUV out back and it zinged across my face.'

Alex had already wet down half a bar towel and handed it to Ciro, who wiped away the obvious blood and held the dry end against his wounds.

Brandon continued to gently examine Joey B, moving his legs, asking questions.

Ciro asked, 'Many cops around?'

'No. They opened up the streets about an hour ago. I took a walk around. All I saw were Crime Scene people in the back lot. And that one patrol car out front.'

Phincas said, 'Best we get upstairs anyhow. Let's go.'

'What about Joey?'

Brandon had finished his examination. 'He'll be okay. He broke part of his hip, but nothing serious. It's just going to hurt like hell for a while.'

'That's good,' said Beck.

Everybody turned. Beck and Demarco had come in unnoticed. Demarco was still holding him upright. The amount of blood on Beck turned everybody silent.

74

By 9 a.m. the second floor in Beck's building looked like a combination hospital emergency room, computer hacker's headquarters, and law office. With a kitchen.

The dining room table area served as Doctor Wright's emergency room. The wrappers from surgical dressings and suture kits and bloodstained gauze littered the floor around him. The smell of isopropyl alcohol and Betadine mixed with the aroma of ham and eggs.

Phineas Dunleavy had taken over a space near the coffee table seating area, making phone calls to track down the court that had issued the warrants for Beck and Ciro.

Alex Liebowitz sat glued to his computer screens.

From the moment Ciro and Manny appeared with Joey B, Doctor Wright had instituted an efficient triage.

Joey B had been made as comfortable as possible downstairs, covered in blankets and dozing under a large dose of painkiller. Brandon was ninety percent sure that Joey had cracked the ischium, a part of his hip. It was painful, but didn't require surgery. They would get him to a hospital to confirm the diagnosis when the cops cleared out of the neighborhood.

After Joey, he'd come upstairs. His nurse had prepped Manny, and the doctor began treating his bullet wound. His nurse then started prepping Beck.

Manny's wound had given the doctor an open view of

the acromion where a bullet had nicked off a small piece of the bone. There didn't appear to be any fracture that had radiated from the area of impact. Wright already knew it was hopeless to try to get Manny to go for an X-ray. He did not take bullet wounds lightly. He carefully examined, cleaned, disinfected, and sutured everything. When he was done he gave careful instructions.

'Manny, wear that sling I put on you. You'll have to sleep sitting up for a few weeks. Keep the wound clean. Finish the antibiotics. Okay?'

Perched on the edge of the dining table, his legs dangling, Manny nodded.

'Promise to let me know if something looks bad or starts to hurt too much.'

'I will.'

'Or if you start running a fever.'

'I will.'

Brandon looked carefully at Manny Guzman to make sure he wasn't placating him. 'Fine. Don't push it. No fishing with that arm. Six weeks, you should be fine.'

Manny thanked the doctor and walked into the kitchen to continue preparing breakfast for whoever wanted it.

Wright determined that Ciro's wound could wait, and turned his attention to Beck. Beck had been hit by two bullets as he fell to the ground to avoid the shots from Kolenka's bodyguard, both causing fairly superficial wounds. One ran across the side of his left thigh, four inches above his knife wound. The second had slashed across the side of his left arm, just below the shoulder.

Branded injected the wounded areas with enough anesthetics that Beck actually fell asleep during the hour it took to examine, clean, disinfect, and stitch everything. The bullets had torn through clothes, skin, and muscles. They weren't deep, but they had left ragged trails that had to be fixed before they could be sutured shut. As for the long knife wound on his back, it had been open too long to stitch. The doctor used a substance akin to Krazy Glue to hold the skin together, disinfected the area, and expertly bandaged the wounds.

By the time Wright turned to Ciro, he had been working nearly two-and-a-half hours without a break.

Whatever piece of the SUV that hit Ciro had ripped past his left eye and taken a narrow slice out of his eyebrow as it passed across his forehead and temple. Bandon cleaned the wound, pinched it closed, and used butterfly bandages to seal it.

'You'll have a nice line through your eyebrow once this heals.'

'Good. Chicks dig scars.'

Brandon Wright pictured the end result and decided Mr Baldassare's scar would most likely make him look even more intimidating than he already did.

Brandon sat and drank coffee with his surgical nurse while Demarco, who had emerged completely unscathed from his battles, cleaned up the bloody cotton, gauze, used syringe tops, and packaging that littered the floor around the dining room table.

Beck stood next to Wright putting on new clothes that Demarco had brought down when Brandon started working on him.

Wright said nothing, watching Beck gingerly step into fresh jeans and slip on a well-worn flannel shirt.

Wright nodded toward the bloody clothes he had cut off Beck, and his sliced-up bloody shearling coat on the floor and said, 'Do me a favor and burn those clothes in case the cops show up and notice that bullets made those tears.'

'Will do,' said Beck.

Demarco was already stuffing everything into a black construction bag.

'D, can you go through all the pockets before you get rid of that stuff?'

'Sure.'

Beck turned to Brandon. 'I really liked that shearling coat.'

'Be that as it may, you want to hear my lecture on what you should do right now?'

'Not really.'

'I'm giving it to you anyhow. You've suffered significant trauma. Knife wounds and bullet wounds like that are no joke. I just put a couple dozen more stitches into you. There's a ton of shock and trauma to your body. Not to mention blood loss. Not to mention risk of infection. Not to mention all the contusions and hematomas and other assorted damage on you. My point is, you should get into a bed for the next forty-eight hours before you collapse.'

'Right.'

'But you're not going to.'

'I will. But not just yet.'

'Do you realize how idiotic that sounds?'

Beck didn't answer.

'Will you make sure to take the antibiotics I'm leaving for you?'

'Of course.'

Wright started to say something more, but lapsed into silence. He shook his head in frustration.

Beck sat down slowly in the chair opposite Brandon Wright on the other side of the dining table.

'Brandon, you've kept all of us alive, and risked going to jail for it. There's no way I can express my gratitude, except to assure you without any doubt or hesitation that nothing we are doing, nothing I am doing is being done without it being absolutely necessary. We all risked dying tonight. You think I do that casually? Recklessly?'

Brandon Wright raised his hand. 'All right. All right.' The doctor paused. 'Can you tell me one thing?'

'What?'

'How much longer will this go on?'

Beck looked at his watch. 'It's a matter of hours. You have something that can help keep me going?'

'Absolutely not. In your situation there's nothing safe. The last thing you should do is stress yourself with amphetamines. Or unnecessary pain meds. Try coffee. Keep those wounds clean. Sleep. Get out from under this as soon as you can. I don't want to go to your funeral.'

Beck nodded. He didn't press it.

The doctor stood, rolled his neck, flexed his big hands, stretched. He helped Ruth pack up the remaining supplies and instruments, grabbed his Carhartt coat off the back of a chair, and left.

Beck watched the tall man walk across the second floor and disappear down the back stairway without another word, including good-bye.

Beck took a deep breath, exhaled, carefully stood, bent

his arm, lifted his leg, testing the feel of the new sutures, hoping he wouldn't have to do anything to make them open and bleed for the next few days.

This was the endgame. Better get to it. He checked his watch. The market would open in a half hour. Time enough to have the conversation with Manny Guzman that he had to have.

As if on cue, Ricky and Jonas Bolo appeared, coming up the steps with Olivia. They'd probably passed the doctor on the way up.

Good timing, thought Beck. Better she didn't see all the blood and wounds.

Beck wasn't in the mood for small talk. He just nodded at the Bolos and said, 'There's coffee and food in the kitchen.'

To Olivia he asked, 'Did you eat?'

'I will.' She looked at Alex, then back at Beck. 'Anything important happening?'

'Check with Alex.'

Olivia nodded and headed toward the desk and computer monitors. Beck noticed she was beginning to look a little haggard. But as usual with her, it just made her appear attractive in yet another way.

She wore the jeans she'd been wearing, but now instead of the black knit top she wore a striped formfitting shirt. She hadn't tucked in the shirt so it hung outside her jeans.

Seeing her reminded him of the half hour they'd spent in bed together. How long ago was that? Twelve hours? It seemed like twelve days.

Beck followed her over to Alex and as she took a seat next to him he asked, 'You ready, Alex?'

'Ready.'

He said to Olivia, 'We're getting set up for the end. Alex, how many accounts you got set up inside that HSBC Cayman Bank?'

'Fifteen.'

'How long will it take you to move the money around?'

'Only as long as it takes me to type and click. It's all internal. It should happen right away. Seconds.'

'And the wire transfers?'

'Nobody guarantees anything except same business day. But we've got it covered.'

'You do?'

Alex paused. Beck watched him go through it, rehearsing it in his mind. They both knew how complicated their next moves might be.

'Yes.'

'Are we ready with Belize like we planned?'

'Yes.'

'You have the SWIF numbers and all the routing stuff you need?'

This time Alex stopped answering Beck. He gave Beck a look that said he was too tired to answer him. He simply couldn't waste the energy.

Beck nodded, said, 'Don't start the snatch until I tell you, okay?'

And then Beck went to Manny Guzman and said he had to talk to him. They headed for the downstairs kitchen and the most painful conversation of Beck's entire life.

75

Even though Alan Crane had secretly sold his loft, the presence of Markov's mercenaries sleeping on his couches and bed, heating up takeout food in his kitchen, stinking up his bathroom, made him want to set fire to the place.

And now Markov had arrived, looking as bad as Crane had ever seen him. He clearly hadn't changed his clothes in a long time. He stank of a weird smell that Crane was convinced had to do with the drugs he imbibed.

The first thing Markov did when he stepped off the elevator was hand three envelopes, clearly stuffed with cash, to the mercenaries. For a moment, Crane wondered if his murder was included in the payment. He immediately dismissed the thought. This next hour or so was going to be crucial. He had to put everything out of his mind and execute his plan.

Crane smiled. Nothing like the possibility of snagging a hundred million or so to focus the concentration.

Markov dragged a chair from the dining room area over to Crane's computer desk.

Crane cringed as the chair scraped across his precious Calamander wood floor. Still not saying a word, Markov set the chair next to Crane and tried to set up his laptop computer on Crane's desk.

The stench of the man was bad enough, but having him try to crowd into his work space was too much.

'Leonard, please. Don't put that there. I need room.'

'I want to watch.'

'Fine, have your men bring a table over for you. Sit where you can see, but you can't be on my desk. It's too distracting. Come on, the markets are about to open.'

'I want to see my account. How much money is in it?'

Crane clicked and expanded a screen on one of his four monitors that showed Markov's bank deposit account. 'A hundred million and change in the bank. The rest is coming into the brokerage as soon as I close out the last holdings this morning.'

'A hundred!? Where's the fucking rest?'

'In the goddamn brokerage account. For God's sake take it easy. There's a lot more to bring over. I warned you that there would be losses, but I've worked miracles here. Just relax, will you? I have to make these trades. The markets are open now.'

'I want to start moving it.'

'So log on and move it. I don't give a shit. Just leave me alone.'

Markov bent over his laptop. He tried to get online. He couldn't.

He barked, 'What's your Internet password?'

Crane was already clicking and scanning candlestick charts displaying values in one-minute intervals. The charts also showed moving average lines and blossoming Fibonacci radials.

'Aw for fuck's sake, Leonard. Don't you have it on that computer?'

'It's not remembering it. Did you change it? What is it?'

Crane screamed, 'Shit.' He clicked on another file. A

screen opened on one of his monitors. Markov yelled at the mercenaries, 'Get me a fucking table.'

Crane yelled back, 'There's a worktable in the back.'

Markov leaned closer to the screen, expecting to see the passwords, but all that appeared was a small screen asking for a password to unlock the encrypted screen. 'What is the fucking password, Alan?'

'It's in this file. But the file is encrypted. Hold on.'

The tension in the room had ratcheted up to a nearly unbearable level. Harris and Williams hustled to the back of the loft looking for the table. Markov loomed over Crane. Crane had to resist the urge to shove the fat, sweating, stinking man away from him with both hands.

Crane typed in the password that un-encrypted the page that displayed his passwords. It seemed to take for ever. Finally, a screen opened on his monitor. It contained pages of passwords and IDs, all of them with complex series of upper- and lower-case letters, symbols, and numbers.

'Where is it?' demanded Markov.

Crane started scrolling through the pages. 'God fucking dammit, I should be trading, not holding your fucking hand with this shit. There! There it is. And the Cayman passwords are above it. Everything is alphabetical.'

'I have those passwords.'

'Congratulations,' said Crane, as he immediately returned to his mouse and keyboard.

Markov leaned into the screen and started laboriously typing in the access password to Crane's Internet connection on his laptop.

Crane tried to ignore everything. He opened trade

tickets on his platform and started executing trades, routing each one to whatever exchange gave him the best price.

The two mercenaries came in carrying a heavy wooden table, much larger than Markov needed, but they set it up in front of him. It distracted and delayed him, making Markov even more frustrated. He placed the laptop on the table and continued typing in the router access number from Crane's screen.

He entered it.

Nothing.

Markov yelled, 'It's not letting me in.'

Crane didn't even look in his direction. He had calmed himself down, determined now not to deal with Markov. He told him, 'You probably didn't type it in right. It's case sensitive. Do it carefully.'

Markov started muttering Russian curses. He retyped everything. Nothing.

He pulled out a small gun from the voluminous pocket of his sport coat, walked next to Crane, and held the pistol against Crane's temple.

Crane flinched away from the gun. 'What the hell are you doing?'

'I want my money.'

'You have it goddammit.' He pointed to the screen. 'It's in the account. I'm bringing the rest over as we speak. You want to lose millions because you won't let me finish this?'

'Fucking shit. How much is in the account?'

Crane pointed at the screen. 'Including what's left to bring over, one-hundred and seventeen million.'

'What?!'

'And that's better than you deserve. Your losses will be under sixteen percent. Sixteen fucking percent. That's half the thirty-plus percent you should be eating by forcing me to close everything out like this.'

'There was one-hundred forty-eight million.'

'When I'm finished there should be about a hundred-twenty, maybe a bit more if we get lucky. And I'll say it one last time, Leonard, that's more than you fucking deserve, making me close out my trades.'

Markov snarled. 'Why can't I fucking get into the account? Did you change the passwords?'

'No!'

Crane stopped, leaned over to look at Markov's laptop. He opened the control panel and told the computer to search for network connections. A series of connections appeared that were scattered around Crane's building and the neighborhood, but not Crane's.

'For fuck sake, your laptop isn't finding my network. I don't know what's wrong. It's your goddamn computer, not mine. And I'm not fucking rebooting my router now. Just watch my screens. When I'm done, sit down and use my computer to transfer the money wherever the fuck you want. It's stupid to do it while everything is still coming in anyhow. Just relax for chrissake.'

Markov yelled, 'I'm not leaving you the only one in control. I want to transfer a hundred right now.'

Crane had anticipated this. If he could pull off the next move, he could make everything work the way he and Olivia had planned.

'Hold on, hold on. I have to watch these positions. You

want me to stop this and let you use my computer? Are you insane?'

Crane shifted the screens appearing on his four monitors. He consolidated the screen that showed Markov's brokerage account, then brought up another showing the Cayman bank account, placing them next to each other so Markov could see them clearly.

'Here, just watch these, okay? As soon as I'm done, you can move all of it at once. All right?'

Markov sat down, pulled his chair close to Crane, and kept the gun pointed at his head.

'You keep making that number bigger. I see anything happen I don't like, you die.'

'Great. Do whatever the fuck you want.'

Crane felt the tremor in Markov's hand moving the gun barrel pressed against his head.

Crane shut his eyes closed, squeezing them tight, exhaling once, hard, determined to focus.

Fuck! This is going to be close, thought Crane.

76

Manny and Beck had ended up at the same small wooden table in Manny's downstairs kitchen where their first discussion about Olivia had taken place. It seemed like weeks ago, but it had only been four days.

'How bad you banged up, James?'

'It's adding up. How about you?'

Manny pulled his left arm out of the sling the doctor had given him. He tried to lift his elbow above his shoulder. He winced and said, 'It's all right. I got a couple of hours sleep. Ate. You're the one who's been doin' all the running around.' Manny raised his chin toward Beck. 'What'd the doc say?'

'The doc said the cut on my back isn't that deep. Sliced a few of the surface muscles. Says it's going to hurt every time I pick something up for a while.'

'Knives.'

'I fucking hate knife wounds. Shitty, sneaky, dirty. You hardly feel 'em when they hit you, but they can cause a lot of damage.' Beck rotated his shoulder.

Manny nodded. 'And the rest?'

'It's not important now, Manny. We have other hurts to deal with.'

The old gangster shifted in his chair. He wasn't done talking. If he knew what was coming, he didn't give any hint. He wanted to recite for himself his discontents and perhaps delay Beck.

'You know what really got to me?'

'What?' asked Beck.

'The fact that I couldn't kill those guys out there. You know. Few hours back.'

Beck waited, saying nothing.

'No, no . . . ' Manny struggled for a word. 'No *finalidad* to it, you know. Hoping the fire took 'em out. Or the cops. I don't like the idea of them surviving so they can come back at me.'

'If killing them sent you back to prison, what good is it?'

Manny pointed to his head. 'I get that here.' He pointed to his stomach. 'But not here.'

Beck said, 'I understand.'

Manny nodded. 'Okay. Tell me again. You got Kolenka?'

'Devious, double-crossing old bastard, yeah, we got him. We were lucky. He was heading out of town. He won't be sending any more of his people after us.'

Manny nodded. 'You figure it was Kolenka's guys out front here with the gasoline?'

Beck nodded. 'And Markov's Bosnians out back to shoot us down when we tried to escape the fire.'

Beck looked at his watch.

Manny asked, 'What?'

'A couple of things. You know that guy in the cellar?'

'Yeah.'

'He told me the truth about how it was going to go down last night.'

'Good.'

'So before the attack, I let him go.'

Manny nodded. 'If we didn't make it, you didn't want him to die down there.'

'That. And I wanted him to do something for us. We agreed on a price.'

'What'd you have him do?'

'I'll explain later.'

Manny nodded, accepting that Beck didn't have time to tell him the whole plan.

'And you got the head guy in Markov's crew?'

'Right. Stepanovich. Although it might come back at us.'

'How bad?'

'Not bad enough to nail any of us. Maybe bad enough to cause trouble. If we're lucky and the Medical Examiner doesn't look too close, they might believe he cut his neck open on the fence.'

Reciting it all seemed to satisfy Manny Guzman in some inexplicable way. For the moment at least. Beck knew Manny would be sorting it out for a long time.

'You have to be patient for a bit longer, Manny.'

'Okay.'

And now it was time for the final nail. Beck leaned forward and placed his arms on the table. 'So. Manny. Here's the hard part.'

Manny looked at him with his baleful eyes. 'You gonna tell me we can't get Markov?'

'No. I'm gonna tell you forget about Markov for now. That will play out.'

'When?'

'I'm not sure.'

'Meaning what?'

'Meaning, it's got to play out so that we're not fighting off these motherfuckers for the rest of our lives.' Beck paused. 'And so that something else is resolved. Resolved in a way that eliminates any doubts.'

'What doubts are you talking about?'

Beck paused, and then laid it out.

'Olivia has been setting us up from the very beginning.' Beck watched Manny carefully, meeting him eye to eye, not flinching from the truth, making sure Manny heard him.

Beck thought he saw a slight narrowing of Manny's eyes, but nothing more. Beck wondered if maybe he had suspected something all along. Or maybe he was screaming with rage inside his head. Or maybe he was just too stunned to react.

Beck went on. 'I can give you all the proof I've got. But you still might have doubts. You might spin it another way because you love her.'

Manny cleared his throat. Swallowed. Finally, Manny said, 'I can't believe it.'

'I understand.'

Manny shook his head, struggling. 'I can't, I can't . . .'

'Let me explain. She was planning on stealing Markov's money from the very beginning. Markov was right. He was right to pull everything away from Milstein's outfit. Crane and Olivia were after his money all along.'

'Crane?'

'Yes.'

'What about her busted fingers? What about all that shit that he fucked her up at the job and all?'

'It wasn't like she said.'

'How do you know?'

'The medical records.'

'You got her medical records?'

'With Brandon's help. They didn't support the way she said it happened. When I pressed her on it, she admitted she lied. She blamed Crane for it, but she was lying all along.'

For a moment, Manny was trapped between believing Beck and believing Olivia. But he could never believe Beck would lie to him about something like this.

'She was working with Crane?'

'Still is.'

'How do you know?'

'Alex and I have gone over it a half dozen times. Look, I can go over it for you sometime, but there's just too much that we've been able to do. If Olivia and Crane were real enemies, there's no way she'd know so much about his trading. And the odds that our hack would still be working after all this time? Really slim, Manny. Alex is good. They made it very hard. But it should have been impossible.'

Manny looked down and shook his head. At that moment, the criminal in Manny Guzman told him it made sense. He'd been played for a sucker. He'd fallen for the con.

'I can't fucking believe it.'

'I know.'

'Motherfucker.'

Beck didn't respond.

'So what was I for?'

'You, me – we're supposed to take the fall for stealing Markov's money.'

'Fuck.' Manny smirked. 'All those years. All those years she stayed close to me.'

'I can't believe she played you all that time. I can't say when it turned. When she came up with it.'

497

'Then why fucking stay close to me during all those years? I didn't want it. It just made the whole thing worse. It was another thing they could take away from me.'

'Lot of people want to be close to a bad guy, Manny. Hell, a lot of people would want someone like you in their corner.'

Manny pursed his lips. Mulling it over. Shook his head. He looked like he was about to tell himself something, but stopped. Pulled himself back from whatever rage or regret or combination of both was plaguing him.

'I don't know. I still can't believe it.'

'That's where the worst part comes in.'

'What do you mean?'

'I mean the only way you're going to believe it, the only way to eliminate any doubt, you're going to have to have your heart ripped out.' Beck paused. 'Before this day is out, Manny, you're going to have to pay a hell of a price.'

Beck watched Manny stare at him. He knew that Manny Guzman was one of the most implacable men he'd ever known. He knew that the impatience and edginess he'd displayed over the past days stemmed from a deep sense of guilt at having put Beck and the others in such danger. Knowing that, Beck was able to lean forward across the table once more and explain to his friend how his doubt would be expelled, and the debt of guilt would have to be paid.

Manny Guzman simply nodded, more to himself than to Beck. Beck touched the side of his friend's face, and left Manny alone in his small kitchen.

77

The first time Olivia Sanchez sat next to Alex Liebowitz as he worked his computer keyboard and mouse, clicking, typing, opening and closing charts and websites and pages on his monitors, he had been too inhibited to look at her.

But as the hours ticked by, he had loosened up. They had concentrated on the task at hand, but there had been plenty of time to talk while they stared at the data in front of them. Alex shared his knowledge of security systems and firewalls. Olivia explained the complexity of Crane's trading methods, how he had developed the algorithms to program his conditional orders. Oftentimes, she would lean closer to the screen to point something out, closing the physical distance between them. Occasionally, their shoulders had touched. A couple of times, she had actually reached out to rub his back vigorously. Just a few quick strokes to revive or congratulate him.

Alex wasn't naïve enough to think that she actually might be attracted to him. Clearly she was playing him. So what? It still felt good.

He enjoyed the attentions of this incredibly beautiful woman.

Right up until the street fights, the blood, guns, firemen, and police. All of it suddenly blossoming like a virulent disease threatening to overrun them.

Olivia hadn't seen the men shot, maimed, burned, arrested. But Alex had. And he knew that if Olivia Sanchez had helped cause that, even if indirectly, he wanted nothing to do with her. They were back together now, working in their island of cyberspace on the second floor of Beck's loft. Even knowing what he did, on some level Alex enjoyed having Olivia Sanchez next to him again.

Now as the endgame unfolded, Alex took one more sidelong glance at her, and wondered how this was all going to end.

Suddenly, the bulk of James Beck filled the space on Alex's right side.

'Where are we?' he said.

Alex and Olivia began to speak at the same time. Olivia indicated that Alex should answer.

'He's got about five million left to close out. I'd say it's time we pulled the trigger.'

Beck answered immediately. 'No. Not yet. Let him finish.'

'But . . .'

Beck interrupted by holding up his hand. He stared at the screen.

'You sure?' asked Alex. 'You really want to risk losing' – he squinted at the total in the Cayman account – 'a hundred and eleven million to get the last five?'

'Trust me.'

Alex raised a hand and tipped his head in agreement. 'I'm too tired to argue.'

As Alex spoke, the last tranche of holdings were sold. Alex immediately minimized the screen that displayed Crane's trading platform, and expanded the screen that showed the balance in the depository account connected to the Cayman-based brokerage account.

All three of them focused on that screen.

Without taking his eyes off the screen, Alex said, 'Normally, in a US brokerage the trades would clear through in a maximum of two seconds. Offshore like this, it will take a few more seconds for the confirmations to appear.'

Alex pulled up the interaccount transfer screen on his second monitor, knowing that at the other end, the computer system in the Cayman-based brokerage thought it was Crane's computer pulling up the screen.

Alex hadn't bothered to explain to either Beck or Olivia that Crane and Summit had established a relationship with the Cayman brokerage company so that transfers between their brokerage accounts and bank accounts were seamless. He hadn't explained how he had artfully set up the interbank/brokerage accounts and linked them to the independent bank accounts over the past two days, sweating out the possibility that Crane might at any moment discover them.

Every last bit of Alex Liebowitz's waning attention was focused on when to pull the trigger to start the complex maze of interbank transfers from the Crane/Markov brokerage cash account to Alex's hidden bank accounts inside the same Cayman bank used by Summit.

He had prepared five separate transfers, displayed on cascaded screens that nearly filled his third monitor. Each transfer order would whisk money into different pre-established accounts. He had filled in all the amounts on four of the transfer screens. Now he waited for the final amount to begin his transfers.

In an unnoticed blink, the dollar number finally appeared. One moment incomplete and inchoate. The next, final and real. As real as numbers in cyberspace could be. $116,427,179.011.

Each of the four prepopulated screens had an amount of twenty million dollars filled in. Alex mentally calculated the amount of his final transfer and quickly typed it into the fifth transfer screen. $36,427,100.00. He left the $79.11 in the account.

Once he initiated the transfers, Alex would have five or ten minutes of extremely hectic work. He was nearing the end of his endurance, and waiting to start the transfers felt excruciating.

'James, come on, it's all there. What are we waiting for?'

'Hang on. Just a little longer.'

78

The moment Crane finished transferring the final five-plus million dollars, the moment the total amount of cash appeared in Markov's account, he pushed his Pininfarina Aresline desk chair back three feet from his keyboard, raised his hands, and announced, 'Done.'

He stood up and stepped back, putting even more distance between him and his keyboard.

He started yelling and pointing at Markov, an act to distract him. 'Nobody, fucking nobody, nobody but me could have pulled that off. One hundred and sixteen big ones. Done. In the account. All cash. All yours.

'Don't thank me. Just fucking leave me alone. Take over. Go on. I'm out of it.'

Markov nodded and moved to retrieve Crane's chair. He sat down in front of Crane's computer.

Crane walked over behind Markov and said, 'Hang on a second. You should close down the trading platform. And close down the brokerage account. Close all the doors behind you.'

Crane pointed, but made sure to stay away from his keyboard. None of this was necessary, but he wanted to buy more time for Beck.

Markov followed his instructions, until nothing showed on the monitors except for the one account.

Crane left and walked over to the kitchen area. He

opened the refrigerator and pulled out a bottle of Stella Artois. He reached into his freezer and took out a frosted Pilsner glass.

He announced to no one in particular, 'I've been looking forward to this for days.' He poured the beer slowly. The three ex-soldiers watched him from the living room. Crane didn't offer any of them a beer, and didn't intend to. He took a long, slow swallow. When he finished, he yelled out to Markov. 'Leonard.'

Markov answered without looking up from the computer.

'What?'

'After you set up your wire transfer, don't close out the brokerage account. There's going to be money dribbling in there for a few days.'

'Don't bother me.'

But that's exactly what he was doing. Distracting Markov. What the fuck was going on, he wondered. Why was the money still in there?

79

Beck continued to stand behind Alex, his hand on Alex's shoulder, as if to physically hold him back. Alex had given up asking when to initiate the transfers. He was beginning to think Beck had another plan he hadn't told him about.

And then, Olivia spoke up. 'Don't you think that should do it?'

Beck didn't respond. And then, without warning, he patted Alex's shoulder and said, 'Go on. Hit it.'

For a second, Alex did nothing. And then, as if coming out of a trance, he and Olivia began their long rehearsed dance of money manipulation.

Alex began clicking the transfer tabs on each of his five prepopulated screens, first transferring the $36,427,100.00, and then continuing with each block of twenty million. The money began transferring from Markov's bank account into five accounts that were under Markov's name, but controlled by Alex.

Once the first set of transfers was complete, Alex switched computers. He had been working everything through Crane's computer, using his passwords and connection to the Cayman bank. Now that the first of his five bank accounts was funded, he severed all connections to Crane's computer. He and Olivia began waterfalling the money into another set of five accounts, and another set of five after that, varying the amounts to cover their trail.

As soon as the last chunk landed in the second set of five accounts, Olivia got on the phone, made a call through a phone-conference service that Summit Investing used, and started giving instructions to a bank officer to close out the first set of five accounts that they had just filled and emptied. While she talked via a headset, she fed confirming faxes into a fax machine they had already programmed the bank's phone numbers into.

As far as the bank officer knew, Summit was simply doing some housekeeping, closing out empty accounts.

Such maneuvers were not entirely unusual at a Grand Cayman bank. What would have been unusual was for the bank officer to ask what Summit was doing and why. It was entirely none of his business.

As soon as she finished closing out the first five bank accounts, she hung up, called back and got another bank officer on the line, and went through the same procedure for the second five accounts, while Alex was in the process of emptying everything into the fourteenth and fifteenth accounts. This was to make sure no single account ever showed a total that matched the money they had taken from Markov's original account.

She was falling far behind Alex, but neither he nor Beck cared. Alex was confident that the first set of closed accounts would create a good deal of work for anybody trying to find out where the money had gone. Each successive set of closed accounts would only add to the complexity.

Beck's eyes had never left the monitors once Alex and Olivia had started moving the millions. They were now ready for the last move. The final capture of over $116 million.

This last move would take the most time to accomplish. But if they managed it before anybody at the Cayman bank caught up with the money, they were home free.

Well, thought Beck, at least free to finish this goddamn mess once and for all.

80

Markov stared at the final figure on the screen for thirty seconds. The readout that confirmed that over $116 million were in his hands. Or about to be. The money was still in his cash account that Summit had set up for him in their Cayman bank. Markov wanted the money in a personal account, in a different bank, that only he controlled.

Crane stood motionless at his kitchen counter. He could see that the full amount was still in Markov's account. What the fuck was going on? All this time and trouble, all this risk, and Beck still hadn't made his move?

Markov took one more look at the screen, then picked up the computer case he'd placed near the worktable Anastasia's men had moved for him, and set the case down. He had already ordered the wire transfer. Now all he had to do was to confirm it by fax. Inside his computer case was a fax he had already prepared. All he had to do was fill in the final figure. As he wrote the number with his right hand, he picked up his cell phone and speed-dialed the Cayman bank with his left.

He yelled to Crane, who was already opening a second beer in his kitchen area.

'Where's your fax, Alan?'

Crane pointed to a built-in shelf above a row of half-height file cabinets along the wall opposite the kitchen. Amidst a bunch of electronic office equipment on the shelf was a high-speed fax machine set up on the far end.

'Make sure you put the page facedown,' Crane said with a smirk.

Markov was already talking to a bank officer, reciting his name and credentials and answering security questions as he fed the fax into Crane's machine and punched in the bank's fax number.

He told the officer the amount he wanted to wire transfer to a bank in Prague. He waited for the officer to confirm that he had received the fax. And he waited.

Crane stood behind his large kitchen counter watching Markov. He looked over at his computer monitor. He couldn't see the numbers from where he stood, but he could tell from the tone of the phone conversation that if Markov refreshed that screen, the account would show the money had disappeared.

He felt his stomach clench with a combination of fear and excitement. This was it. He would either survive the next few minutes, or he wouldn't.

He watched Markov waiting. He took another swig of his beer as he casually opened a drawer built into the long countertop work area.

He pushed aside the contents of the drawer as if he were looking for something, slid aside the top of a fake bottom section and uncovered a fully loaded 9-mm Beretta.

He heard Markov yell, 'What?' And then shout at whoever was on the other end of the phone, 'The amount is what it says on the fax. One hundred sixteen million, four hundred twenty-seven thousand.' Markov rushed over to the computer screen to read out the rest of the numbers. He leaned down to look at the screen. He moved the cursor and clicked enter. For a moment, he remained absolutely motionless, and then he slowly straightened up.

A calm had suddenly come over him. What was happening, couldn't be happening. He slowly and precisely said to the bank officer at the other end of the phone, 'Who am I speaking to?'

Markov listened.

'All right Mr Beloit.' Markov checked his watch. 'Less than five minutes ago there was precisely one hundred sixteen million, four hundred twenty-seven thousand, one hundred seventy-nine US dollars in that account. I want you to begin tracing where it went. Do not leave the bank until you find it, or until I call you back.'

Markov cut the cell call and turned to Crane. He said very calmly, 'You know, Alan, I was actually going to let you live.'

Alex Liebowitz slapped the enter key for the last time and closed his eyes. The exhaustion crashed down on him. He realized his jaws were so tight that he had to slowly open his mouth wide, close it and open it a few times. He tried to take a deep breath and couldn't. The tension had stiffened and immobilized him. Even if he had wanted to, he knew he wouldn't be able to do anything on his computer for some time.

'That's it,' he said. 'I gotta figure you have at least a half-hour head start, minimum. More likely a couple of hours. How many accounts do you have left to close behind me?'

'Three,' answered Olivia.

'Okay,' said Beck. He grabbed the back of Alex's desk chair and slowly wheeled him away from the computer keyboard. He gently lifted Alex onto his feet and said, 'Go sleep. Nobody else could have done that. It's over.'

Alex mumbled something unintelligible. He had to concentrate on walking to the stairwell leading to the bedrooms on the third floor. He had to actually pause once on the stairwell to get his breath. He turned into the first bedroom, and had just enough energy to remove his shoes before he laid back and more passed out than fell asleep.

Beck waited while Olivia recited instructions and authorization to the bank officer about closing another set of accounts. And for her to call back in and go through the process one more time. When she finally finished and took off the phone headset, he said to her, 'Okay. Time for the last step.'

'Right,' said Olivia.

She took Alex's place at the keyboard.

Beck, Alex, and Olivia had talked over various ways to get the money to a place where only they controlled it. Moving tens of millions of dollars between banks would set off too many alarms, mostly having to do with money laundering.

Olivia had come up with the solution, as Beck figured she would. As of now, all the money was in accounts they controlled, but all those accounts were still connected to Markov and Summit. Everything appeared to have been done from Summit's offices, which was why all the transferring had gone so smoothly. It had all been done inside the HSBC branch Summit used in Cayman.

When they discussed how to get that money out of the Cayman bank, Olivia told Beck that traders running money often set up discrete accounts in order to segregate proceeds from various funds they might be running. She suggested they use one of the offshore banks that Summit already used for such accounts: the Krebs Bank in Belize. Belize was one of the banking centers Summit used for accounts they wanted as far off the radar as possible. It was even more discreet than Cayman banks.

She knew all of Summit's account-opening procedures. And she knew Summit's contact at the Belize bank. He had no idea she no longer worked at Summit, and was happy to hear from her and open a new account. The day before, Olivia set up a holding company called Montana Investments Series XI, an account only she and Beck knew existed.

It could be months before anybody at Summit realized the account existed, if ever. But setting up a hidden Krebs account inside Summit made it easy to wire transfer Markov's money out of Summit's HSBC account.

It also eliminated triggering any alarm bells because although the amounts transferred were in the tens of millions, the money was still technically inside Summit.

Olivia watched the clock as she prepared the wire transfer orders. They knew that the Cayman bank bundled their transfers twice a day: midday and just before bank closing hours at three o'clock. It was only eleven-fifteen. Plenty of time to get the wire transfers in place. But actually they worried it was too much time. They didn't want the wire transfer orders sitting in a pile where someone might find them if Markov tried to get the bank to shut down any wire transfers while he tracked what happened to his money.

In the end, Alex had convinced Beck that hopscotching and waterfalling dozens of different amounts through the fifteen accounts made everything exponentially confusing. And then to transfer out the money to Belize in several different amounts from two different accounts would sufficiently camouflage the move. Olivia convinced Beck that the bank wouldn't jeopardize alienating all the clients who were transferring money that day for the sake of one client.

Finally, they also spaced the time between orders so that their transfers would be mixed in with others.

Olivia finished faxing the last wire transfer order at 11:50 a.m, just under the noon deadline.

The last question was posed by Beck.

'If somebody at Summit suddenly noticed a hundred million plus on their books that wasn't there before, how long would it take them to find the Montana Investments Series XI account?'

Olivia said it would be days or weeks. She knew it would take much less time, but she also knew she was going to mitigate that risk. As soon as she could, she would text the Krebs bank account number, ID, and password to Crane. As soon as he got free of Markov, he would arrange a transfer to their bank in Switzerland, almost certainly before anybody at Summit saw the money.

One more step, thought Olivia. One double cross, and I'm done.

82

'Oh really,' Crane said, pointing his Beretta at Markov. '*You're* going to decide if *I* live.'

Markov turned to Ralph Anastasia, who was sprawled out on Crane's couch. Harris sat at the battered dining room table, hands folded, just waiting. Williams, the South African, stood by the windows looking out onto Hubert Street as if he had nothing to do with any of them.

Anastasia raised a hand and said, 'Our contract with you ended when Mr Crane finished his job. He finished. You paid us. We're done.'

Markov squinted at Crane, looked back at Anastasia. 'How much did he pay you?'

'Quite a bit more than you, Mr Markov.'

'To do what?'

'That's between Mr Crane and us. Like I said, our contract with you has ended.'

Markov looked over at his pistol on the worktable near Crane's computers.

'Don't even think about it, Leonard,' Crane said as he came out from behind his kitchen counter and casually walked to the table. He picked up the revolver and slipped it into his back pocket. Crane then placed his gun on his desk within reach, and sat down.

'Come on, Leonard, you didn't think I was going to

shoot you, did you? But just so you understand that I'm not the source of your fucking problems, how about you take a seat and answer a few questions?'

Crane motioned for Markov to sit at the worktable. Markov complied.

'So, here's how it goes. If you think I had anything to do with taking your money, you're crazy. But let's examine the possibility.

'*I* know I didn't take your fucking money. So let's start there. If I didn't, who did? Well, there aren't a whole lot of choices, are there? At the top of the list is that fucking whore Olivia Sanchez. So first question, did you kill her like you were supposed to?'

Markov glared at Crane.

'I take that as a no. Which means you didn't kill her protector James Beck, either. Did you?'

Markov said nothing.

'What the fuck have you been doing while I was in here busting my ass to save your money? I thought you had an army of assholes led by that maniac Gregor. You fail to do what you're supposed to, and you blame me?'

Markov said nothing.

'What about Kolenka?'

Finally Markov spoke. 'He is dead. And many of his men. And Gregor. And many of his men are dead, or captured by police. It's been all over the news for hours.'

'What? How?'

Markov leaned forward. 'Never mind. I want to know, if you didn't take my money, how did they? You are the one who controls everything. It's your computer. Your brokerage firm. How can they do this?'

'Jeezus Christ, Leonard, I understand your concern for the money, but aren't you worried more about Beck?'

'Never mind Beck. How did they get my money?'

Crane turned to his computer, talking to himself. 'Shit, even with Olivia Sanchez helping him, I don't know. I have to figure this out. You're sure the bank isn't just fucking something up?'

Markov picked up his cell phone to call the Cayman bank again.

Crane started shutting down all his programs. Then he rebooted his computer. He listened carefully to Markov pressing the bank officer. When he paused, Crane asked, 'What is the bank saying?'

'They say it's impossible to transfer out that much money without anybody knowing it. He swears it has to be in the bank. They're tracing it. What the hell is going on?'

'If I knew I'd tell you. Since I haven't been near a phone or a computer or a fax since I gathered everything in your account, clearly I can't tell you what's going on.'

Crane started a scan with his security software programs, but when the program tried to go online to first update, he couldn't connect. 'What the fuck?'

He stood up, walked over to the shelf where his router sat, and rebooted it. Once it cycled through the reboot, he was able to get back online.

'I don't understand this.'

'What? What are you talking about?'

Crane yelled, 'Maybe if I figured it out, it would help the bank.'

Markov yelled back, 'Figure out what?'

Crane started following the fiber-optic cables that connected his modem. He'd play this out. Tell Markov he had to check the transponder connection in the basement. That would give him the evidence that somebody, presumably Beck, had compromised his Internet connection. Which in turn, would give Crane a way to explain how somebody, presumably Beck, had tapped into his computer and taken Markov's money. More important, it would provide him an opportunity to get Olivia's text and start the process that would get Markov's money out of the Belize bank to his and Olivia's account in Switzerland.

He'd sit with Markov long enough to show him the evidence that Beck had his money, send him after Beck, and then get the hell out of town with his newly hired bodyguards making sure nobody stopped him.

In twenty-four hours, he and one of the hottest women he'd ever met would be in Geneva, rich enough to disappear, travel the world, fuck in the best hotels ever built, and indulge whatever desire that might interest them for the rest of their lives.

83

Olivia didn't have to fake being exhausted.

She had concentrated on filling out the last fax that would wire transfer the final block of money from the Cayman bank to the Belize bank. Then she sat back and watched Beck carefully fax the order to the Cayman bank while he talked it through with the Krebs bank vice president in Belize in charge of Summit's affairs. The Krebs VP promised to follow through with HSBC in Cayman.

When he was done, she gave Beck a wan smile and let out a long slow breath of relief. At that moment, they were the only two people who knew the account number and passwords for the Belize bank account. The money was safe.

Beck nodded his acknowledgment.

Olivia felt the attraction that had existed between them like an electric current. She wondered if Beck would survive Markov's next attempt to hunt him down. This time Markov would have even more motivation.

'I'm fried,' she said. 'I've got to lay down. I don't care where. Anywhere is fine.'

'Use my bedroom,' said Beck.

'What are you going to do?'

'Finish up and crash on one of the couches.'

Olivia resisted the urge to invite him upstairs. She nodded and headed for the stairwell.

When she got to Beck's bedroom, she closed the door behind her. Then for added security she went into his bathroom and locked that door. While writing out the last fax, she'd copied the bank account number, customer ID, and access codes of the Belize bank account on a separate piece of paper, which she'd slipped into her back pocket. Now she texted them to Alan Crane's phone.

She had no idea if he had freed himself from Markov and his guards, but he soon would. From then on, it was up to him to get the money out of Belize and into the Swiss bank account they had set up two months prior.

She was too tired to shower. She was down to her last change of clothes anyhow. She tore up her notepaper, flushed it down the toilet, washed her hands and face, and settled onto Beck's bed, fully clothed except for her shoes. She checked her watch. Two minutes after twelve. The plane for Switzerland left at 7:10 p.m. She had plenty of time. Grab a couple of hours sleep. Tell Beck she had to go home. She would catch up with him later. Don't ask about money. Don't ask for a cut. Just ask for her car. Say good-bye to Manny. Thank him as if he'd saved her life. Get her Porsche back and leave.

Her bags were already packed. Shower, change, close down the apartment, store the car as planned, take a limo to JFK and meet Alan.

Her eyes fluttered shut. She felt the exhaustion coming over her. She fought it off, reached for her cell phone. Erase the text message, she told herself. Jeezus, don't screw up now.

She erased the entire string to Crane. Set the phone to

wake her at 2 p.m. Two hours sleep would have to do. She pictured herself resting in a private pod on crisp white sheets with a fresh pillow in the first class section of Swissair. Sleep came almost instantly.

84

Beck was so tired his jaws ached. The local anesthetic on his bullet wounds had worn off and the increasing pain was draining him. But there was no time for sleep.

He thought about taking another bottle of the energy drink, but he didn't think his stomach could take it. For a moment, he thought about closing his eyes for just fifteen minutes. No, no way, he told himself. Have to be awake when Markov calls.

He stood up and went over to the windows facing Conover Street. He pulled the window wide open using just his right arm, but the movement still made his left arm twinge. He stood in the frigid air breathing long, slow deep breaths for a full minute.

He felt better. Awake. Closed the window and began slowly walking around the second floor.

He went through everybody's next role. One by one, he went over it in his mind. All of them would be facing danger, except for him. Now it was Beck's job to make sure this battle would end, that they'd be safe, and that everything they had done was worth it.

His phone rang. Beck checked the ID. Blocked. He took a chance, wanting to gain whatever edge he could.

'Mr Markov.'

There was a pause, then — 'How you know it was me?'

'Who else would it be?'

'You sent Gregor's man Ahmet to my driver with a message to call you.'

'Yes.'

'I assume it's about my money.'

'It is.'

'You have it.'

'I do.'

There was a pause. Crane had been right.

'Now what?'

'Now we meet.'

'Why?'

'Because I say so.'

'So you can kill me, too.'

'If I wanted to kill you, Mr Markov, you'd already be dead.'

Another pause. 'Why do you want to meet me?'

'To finish this.'

'Meaning?'

'Meaning you meet me face-to-face and hear what I have to say.'

'Where?'

'Milstein's office. Be there at two o'clock. Not a minute later. Don't bring any weapons. Don't bring any thugs, or I guarantee, I absolutely promise – I will kill you.'

'I believe you,' said Markov.

Beck drove the Mercury into Manhattan with both front windows open to keep him awake. Parked it in a garage on Fifty-seventh Street just east of Lex. Made his way to the twenty-eighth floor.

The receptionist was expecting him. She directed him to the main conference room.

It was a large room with a conference table big enough for fifteen people. It offered a view of Manhattan facing south. The day was rather mild for February. And overcast. The view limited by mist and fog.

Beck wasn't interested in looking out any windows.

Near the head of the table sat Markov, looking worse than ever. He was covered with a veneer of sweat. His clothes looked like he had been on the run for a couple of days. Beck could smell the man by the time he reached the middle of the room.

Opposite Markov sat Frederick Milstein in his usual business attire of dress shirt, tie, and suit pants. He sat at the edge of his chair, elbows on the conference table, trying to look like he mattered. The chair next to Milstein was filled by the large bulk of Walter Pearce.

Beck took the seat at the head of the table.

He turned to Walter Pearce. 'Are we all set, Walter?'

'I delivered your message, Mr Beck.' Walter looked at his watch. 'At twelve-forty-five as requested.'

He turned to Milstein. 'And you spoke to the bank in Belize, Mr Milstein?'

'Listen, who do you think . . . ?'

Beck raised his voice. 'Be quiet. Walter, did it go as planned?'

'Yes. I gave Mr Milstein the account information; Mr Milstein gave them the order. The man he spoke to seemed to know Mr Milstein. Their conversation was on speakerphone.'

'And Mr Milstein seemed to know the man at the bank.'

'Yes.'

'And Mr Milstein told the Kreb's bank office what, exactly?'

Before Pearce could answer, Milstein said, 'Listen. I want to know the meaning of all this. I don't appreciate taking instructions like this.'

Beck held up a hand. He placed his Browning on the conference room table. 'If you don't want to answer my questions, just shut up. Mr Pearce?'

'He told them that a wire transfer request would be coming in today to transfer out the money in that account.'

'Yes.'

'And that the bank should tell whoever ordered the wire transfer that the money would be sent out end-of-day today for deposit. And that funds would be available at the opening of bank hours Monday morning. But, after they told that to whoever ordered the wire transfer, they should ignore that wire order and lock down the account.'

'That was the conversation?'

'Yes. Apparently, Summit has a good deal of money in that bank, so they agreed.'

'Did you have to put a gun to Mr Milstein's head?'

Pearce smiled and said, 'No. Not really.'

Milstein squirmed in his seat, fighting the urge to say something.

Beck took an envelope out of his back pocket. He slid it across the table to Pearce, who picked up the envelope and slipped it into his suit coat pocket without looking at it.

Beck said, 'So, we're all settled then.'

Pearce nodded. 'Looks that way.'

'I'm sure you have other things to attend to, Mr Pearce.'

'Catching up on my sleep, for starters.'

Pearce looked at both Markov and Milstein for a beat, pushed back his chair, and lumbered out of the conference room. He didn't look back.

As soon as Pearce was gone, Beck said to Milstein. 'Mr Milstein, you can leave now, too.'

That did it. Milstein sat up straight and yelled, 'Who the hell do you think you are? Coming in here giving me orders. Giving Pearce orders. Running an account up here. I should have you arrested.'

Beck had to work hard to contain his fury. He picked up the Browning, racked a bullet into the chamber, and aimed it at Milstein's head. Milstein flinched and put up a hand.

Markov grimaced and pushed back his chair a foot.

Beck spoke quietly, his voice constricted with rage and disgust. This pompous little man had caused him immeasurable trouble, starting with lying to him, setting him up to walk into an ambush at Crane's, sending the cops after him and his men in an attempt to have them killed or sent back to jail. Through clenched teeth he uttered one word: 'Leave.'

The gun paralyzed Milstein. Markov broke in, yelling, 'Get out, Frederick. Now. Get out. Do nothing. Do you understand? Do nothing and wait in your office for me. Now.'

Milstein left.

As soon as they were alone, Beck put back the Browning

on the table and said, 'So, Mr Markov, about your hundred and sixteen million dollars.'

'Yes.'

'Let me explain a few things to you, starting with the fact that I am not a thief.'

85

The alarm on Olivia's iPhone had a gentle ringtone. Gentle, but insistent. It awakened her, but it took nearly thirty seconds of steady chiming to pull her out of the deep sleep she'd fallen into.

She felt around on the bed for the phone and managed to turn it off with her eyes closed. She made sure to sit up and get her feet on the floor so that she wouldn't fall back to sleep.

She forced herself to stand and walk to the bathroom, her gait unsteady.

She rested both hands on the sink basin and let the water run, and rinsed her face with cold water. She felt groggy and numb, but the cold water helped clear her head. She took a deep breath, pushing herself into an alert state.

When she gazed up at the mirror over the bathroom sink, she muttered, 'Shit.'

I'll have time to put myself together when I get home. I'm not leaving New York looking like this.

She gathered her large purse, put on her shoes, and made her way down to the second floor. The entire floor was empty. It felt strange to her. There had been so much commotion, so many men moving around, arriving, leaving, and now nothing.

She really didn't care. Where was Manny? She needed

her car keys. And she had to convince him she was just going home to change and sleep and wait for whatever they wanted her to do.

She went down the back stairs looking for Manny, thinking about how to play it just right. What to say about the money. Something along the lines that she was glad she could help them stick it to Markov. Don't even bring up the topic of how much of it they were going to give her. Let him think she didn't care. That she trusted him and Beck to do the right thing by her. Yes, she'd caused them a huge amount of trouble, but in the end it had paid off.

She found Manny in the small bar kitchen, sitting at his old wooden table. He had a black coffee in front of him, two cubes of brown sugar on the table next to the coffee.

'Cousin Manny.'

'*Novia.* Sit.'

'I'm exhausted. I gotta get home. I gotta change, clean up, get some sleep.'

'Sit,' he repeated.

It was at that moment, the way he said that one word, that Olivia Sanchez knew he knew. Her plan of eight years, all her maneuvering, all her machinations had come down to this moment. It didn't matter. He wasn't going to stop her. Nothing was going to stop her now.

'Do you have my car keys?' she asked as she moved toward the table.

Manny motioned with his head toward a key rack next to the side door. She saw the keys to her Porsche. She took them off the rack, but made note of the fact that he didn't tell her where the car was parked. It can't be too far away, she thought. I'll find it.

She dropped the keys into her purse, as she sat down across from Manny. She left the purse unzipped, resting in her lap.

Manny took a sip of the black coffee. Placing the cup down, warming his hands on the mug, he stared at Olivia, studying her face. His expression gave away very little, but Olivia knew.

'You can't go, Olivia.'

'Why not?'

'James says you lied to me.'

She tried to look surprised. Confused. 'About what?'

'About everything. He says you and Crane were after the money all along.'

'How can he say that?'

Manny answered with a shrug.

'Manny, that's ridiculous. I don't have the money. Crane doesn't have the money. James has it. Where is he? Ask him. He has the money, not me.'

'Doesn't matter. James says you and Crane were after the money.'

'And you believe him?'

'I don't want to believe him,' said Manny.

'Then don't. It's not true.'

'So, when James gets back, you can explain it to him. And to me. Prove to him it's not true. And to me.'

Her hand was in the purse now.

'When is he coming back?'

'Not too long.'

'So you want proof.'

'I want proof.'

'And you're going to make me wait here.'

'Yes. I want to know for sure.'

Before he finished the sentence, Olivia pulled out a snub-nosed thirty-eight revolver and shot Manny Guzman dead center in his chest.

The smoke and flame and roar of the small pistol stunned her. But she pulled the trigger again. And again.

The sound of the gunshots faded. She sat blinking at the gun smoke surrounding her, confused, her heart beating, her ears ringing, unable to comprehend the fact that Manny Guzman sat across the table, unmoved, staring at her.

She had expected the bullets to knock him off his chair. She had expected blood. A cry of pain. But Manny continued to sit across from her, silent, staring at her, unmarked.

And then Olivia Sanchez saw something she never imagined. Manny Guzman was crying. There was little expression on his stolid face, but tears were slowly rolling down his craggy cheeks, dripping off his jaws.

He sniffed and wiped the tears away angrily.

Olivia looked at the smoking gun in her hand. She looked at Manny. What had happened? Why was there no blood?

Then she saw the compact, deadly Charter Arms revolver pointed at her. Manny was still crying when he shot her.

This time, there was blood.

86

Beck told Markov everything that Olivia and Crane had done. Markov listened without interrupting. When Beck finished his careful explanation, he pulled a flash drive out of his shirt pocket and held it up for Markov to see.

'The details of the transfers are on this drive, in case you need further proof.'

'All right,' said Markov. 'Now what?'

'Now I explain to you my fee and my expenses.'

'Your fee.'

'Yes. I intend to get paid for returning your money to you.'

Markov frowned.

Beck continued. 'Here's how it's going to work. At one-fifteen, after Milstein's conversation with the bank, I reset all the IDs and passwords on the account. On this flash drive is also information on how to access an encrypted website. On that website, midday Monday morning, all the information you need to take control of your money will be displayed. Today is Friday. You'll have a nice relaxing weekend, and then on Monday your money will be there for you to do what you want with it.'

'I see. And your fee?'

'Twenty percent. Nonnegotiable.'

'Expenses?'

'Let's call it two hundred thousand.'

Markov continued to stare at Beck. 'You want twenty-three million, four hundred thousand.'

'Twenty-three million, four hundred eighty-five thousand, four hundred, thirty-four. You want the thirty-four bucks, call it twenty-three, four eighty-five, four.'

Markov kept his unwavering gaze at Beck. 'Why don't you just kill me and keep it all?'

'First of all, because I doubt all that money is yours. I got a feeling whatever branch of our government you're running arms for has a good chunk of their money mixed in that account. Maybe it's money they paid for future purchases. Maybe it's operating funds. Who knows? But I'd rather not have to worry about some clandestine wing of the US government coming after me for their money.

'Second, like I said, I'm not a thief. It's not my money. Two people at Summit conspired to steal it. I've already explained how. I got it back for you. So I earned a commission.

'Lastly, I'm going to go on the assumption that when this all started, you would have preferred not to kill me. You could have shot me up at Crane's loft, but you didn't. My take is you fired those shots to keep me from leaving, but not to kill me. Am I right?'

'Yes, as a matter of fact, you are. I wanted to question you. That's why I had Crane taped to his table. To show you what I would do to you.'

'And I'm assuming once I put down those two men of Kolenka's, Kolenka decided I had to go.'

'Yes. And truthfully, I didn't try to change his mind.'

Beck said, 'You couldn't have. So, do we have a deal?'

Markov asked, 'You aren't worried I will try to have you killed?'

'Will you?'

'No. Same reason as you. I don't know who would come after me. You obviously have a lot of men. How else could you wipe out Kolenka and his crew, and Gregor and his men?'

'So, we're agreed. You pay me my commission and costs. I give you ninety-two million and change, which is a hell of a lot more than you have right now. You don't send any more people after me. And I don't kill you right here and now.'

Markov inclined his head toward Beck and gave him a knowing look. 'What does that mean? That you will kill me someplace else, later?'

Beck said, 'No. I won't kill you now, or later.'

Markov smiled, and let out a short laugh. He shook his head, muttering in Russian. He stuck his meaty hand out to Beck and said, 'Take your expenses out of the twenty-three fucking million dollars, and we have a deal.'

Beck didn't hesitate for a second. 'No. You don't really give a shit about two hundred grand. You're just negotiating out of habit. Stop it. There are significant expenses still left to me. I have no doubt that with a stake of over ninety-two million you'll earn back what you're paying me very quickly.'

'What expenses do you have?'

'That's not your business.'

Markov pointed a fat finger at Beck. 'And like you said, this ends it between us. I don't want to look over my shoulder all the time, as they say. And I won't give you any reason to look over yours.'

'This ends our business.'

Beck slid the flash drive across the conference room table. Markov picked it up and held it in front of Beck. 'The balance will be in this account midday Monday?'

'Yes.'

Markov shoved the drive in his coat pocket and sat back. 'Okay. But a question, if you don't mind. What about Crane and the woman?'

'They are not your concern.'

'Meaning?'

Beck said nothing.

'As of now?'

Beck said nothing.

'Expenses, huh?'

Beck tipped his head in agreement.

'All right,' said Markov, 'I'm not negotiating, but I have one last question.'

'What?'

'Why do I have to wait until Monday?'

'Because I need that time for my man to get to the bank in Belize Monday morning. He'll take our commission. We will confirm all is well on Monday, and by twelve noon all the information you need to take control of the account will be posted on the encrypted website.'

'I don't like waiting.'

'Too bad.'

'You don't trust I will pay you your money.'

'I don't have to trust you.'

Markov took a long, slow breath. Scrunched his face. Put his meaty left hand over his eyes and rubbed. He blinked. Looked at Beck and said, 'I underestimated you, Mr Beck.'

'You just didn't know me.'

Beck picked up the Browning, shoved it behind his right hip, stood up, and left Leonard Markov sitting at the conference room table.

Beck walked directly across the street to the Renaissance Hotel where he had reserved a room. He might have preferred the Four Seasons, but there was zero chance he would be going back there. And he wasn't at all sure he could have walked the extra two blocks.

When he got to his room, he closed the blackout drapes, put on the Do Not Disturb sign, stripped down to his underwear, and slowly laid down on the bed, lifting his battered left leg with his sore, stitched and bandaged left arm.

He pulled the covers over himself and adjusted the pillows.

A wave of exhaustion engulfed him. He thought about Manny. He wasn't going to call him. Either his plan with Nydia to persuade Olivia she needed a gun and making sure it was filled with blanks had worked, or it hadn't.

As for everything else, there was nothing more for Beck to do. There was nothing he could do. He had planned the rest carefully. Now it was up to the others. He fell into a deep, dreamless sleep for the next thirteen hours, knowing that by the time he awoke, it would all finally be over.

Epilogue

Demarco's job was complicated, but ultimately quite enjoyable.

The Bolo brothers had one last assignment after returning Olivia to Red Hook. This time they switched their all-purpose van for an even more innocuous Lincoln Town Car, and once more staked out Crane's building. At 4 p.m. a limo appeared, big enough for Crane, his three bodyguards, and all their bags.

Five minutes later, the first of the two mercenaries appeared on Hubert Street. They checked both the limo and the street to make sure there was no sign of trouble.

Ricky and Jonas were parked far enough away at the hydrant of Greenwich Street so they weren't noticed. And even if the Town Car was noticed, so what? Just another car service vehicle waiting for a passenger, most likely from the Smith Barney building.

Once Harris and Williams had checked the street and the limousine, Ralph Anastasia came out with Crane, his gun in his hand. He scanned the street and the surrounding buildings until Crane and the others were in the limo. Only then did he get in the Town Car.

As soon as the limousine left the curb, Ricky and Jonas were on it. They assumed Crane was headed for an airport. There were two likely choices, Newark or JFK. Once the limousine passed Canal Street and didn't go for the

Holland Tunnel, they were ninety percent sure it would be JFK.

Jonas drove. He dropped back nearly out of sight, keeping just close enough to make sure they were heading for the Midtown Tunnel. Once the limo passed the exit to the BQE which would have taken them to LaGuardia, Jonas dropped way back again, now certain they were headed for JFK.

Demarco had been waiting in Olivia's Porsche near the Verrazano Bridge, ready to head for either JFK or Newark when the Bolos called. As soon as he received word from Ricky, he headed for JFK with plenty of time.

As Crane's limo approached the airport, Jonas closed the gap, blending in with all the other Town Cars and Yellow cabs. He followed Crane's limo until it pulled up to the Swissair terminal.

Jonas pulled up to the curb a few cars back of Crane's limo. Ricky got out and followed Anastasia and Crane into the terminal, just like any other passenger. He even had a carry-on piece of luggage.

Jonas pulled away and parked at the far end of the departure area.

Ricky stood in line at the first-class check-in behind Crane. When Crane walked up to Swissair's first class counter, Ricky was close enough to hear the flight number: LX-23 to Geneva.

Crane checked in two large bags and walked away with a carry-on piece of luggage.

Ralph Anastasia accompanied him to the security area, stood in line with Crane, exchanging a few words that looked to Ricky like Crane's final instructions for his bodyguard. While they talked, Ricky phoned Jonas with Crane's flight information.

Crane headed into the security line. Anastasia waited until Crane passed through the body scanner, gathered his belongings, and walked out of sight. Only then did he turn and head for the exit.

Jonas Bolo, parked near the end of the departure area, working on his large-screen smartphone, completing a first-class reservation for Swissair Flight LX-23 at 7:45 p.m. in the name of Antonio Jones.

Conveniently, there were three seats still available in first class.

As Anastasia exited the airport, Ricky Bolo called to him from behind. Anastasia's hand went into the pocket of his silver down jacket. Ricky showed both hands and said, 'Take it easy. I have something for you that might be of help.'

Anastasia raised a hand and said, 'Don't move. Keep your hands where I can see them.'

Ricky held up a piece of paper. 'It's just a bit of information.'

'Say it.'

'You may need to know the location of somebody. Check this website. Where-to-find-the-fat-Russian-dot-com. No spaces.'

Anastasia looked very carefully at Ricky Bolo.

Ricky held out the folded piece of paper. 'It's written on this.'

Anastasia smiled and said, 'No. I got it.'

Ricky turned and walked away. By the time he slid into the passenger seat of the Town Car, Jonas had finished making the reservation on Swissair.

Fifteen minutes later, Demarco pulled Olivia's Porsche up to the departure curb. Ricky jumped out of the Town Car, walked back to the Porsche, and gave Demarco all the information about his flight reservation.

Demarco Jones walked into the Swissair terminal. Ricky jumped into the Porsche and drove out of the airport, followed by Jonas.

When Demarco walked up to the first-class check-in, he looked every bit like a first-class passenger.

He presented his brother's passport to the blond Swissair employee. Using his own was out of the question. She was a nicely coiffed airline professional. Although Demarco's older brother looked quite a bit like him, she barely glanced at the passport. Demarco looked like he'd just stepped out of *Men's Vogue*. His overcoat, a lush brown cashmere, was matched by an extravagantly expensive Borsalino fur felt fedora made of New Zealand red deer. His dark blue suit was Kiton. His gleaming white shirt Charvet, the shoes Allen Edmonds, the tie and pocket square Brioni, both a golden orange with a weave that made the color vary throughout a spectrum of shades.

The Swissair lady couldn't stop smiling at Demarco. When she asked if he had any bags to check, he smiled back and said, 'No.'

She peeked over the counter at his elegant Tumi Woodbridge carry-on garment bag. And smiled again. God, what a beautiful man. What style.

Demarco breezed through security, had his usual drink,

Grand Marnier and decaf coffee in the lounge. He called Elliot to tell him he wouldn't be able to make it upstate this weekend. All he had to say was that something had come up, and he was sorry. The sorry part was enough for Elliot.

By the time Demarco walked into the first-class cabin, the steward asked him if he preferred a window pod. One had become available at the last minute, closer to the front of the cabin.

Demarco settled in next to Alan Crane, in what would have been Olivia's seat, finishing up a text to Beck that read cryptically 'seat empty.' Enough to confirm for Beck when he woke up that Manny had done what he had to do.

Crane, already on his second glass of champagne, seemed a bit distracted, realizing that it was now certain that Olivia Sanchez was not going to make this flight.

By the time the plane landed in Geneva, Switzerland, Demarco had learned Crane's new name, Paul Adler. And the hotel he was staying at: the D'Angleterre.

Demarco arrived at the D'Angleterre well before Crane, since Crane had to wait for his luggage. However, he didn't enter the hotel. He waited across the street, sitting on a bench near the lake, the chill air not affecting him in the least, noticing that next to the hotel was a private branch of HSBC bank. Probably the reason Crane picked the D'Angleterre.

While he waited for Crane to arrive, Demarco booked a junior suite at another hotel, the Beau Rivage, and called for a limo. His limo arrived five minutes after Crane entered the hotel.

Demarco crossed the street, motioned for the driver to roll down his window. He told the driver he was Mr Williams, asked him to take his bag and wait fifteen minutes, he had to take care of something in the bank, which conveniently was open until noon on Saturdays.

He walked into the bank, waited ten minutes for Crane to get to his room. While in the bank, he called the hotel and left word that a document was coming for Mr Adler from the bank. He confirmed the room number. Then he entered the hotel through the service entrance, wearing fine leather gloves and his fedora pulled low to obscure his face from security cameras.

When Demarco arrived on Crane's floor, he lifted a vase full of flowers from a table in the elevator foyer and carried it to Crane's room.

He knocked on the door discreetly, holding the flowers so that they blocked the view through the room's peephole.

When asked who it was, Demarco said, 'Housekeeping.'

Crane must have liked the idea of more flowers for his suite. He opened the door quickly. Demarco punched Crane in the throat at just about the moment Crane recognized Demarco from the plane.

Crane landed on his back hard, clutching his throat, struggling to breathe.

Demarco quickly straddled Crane's head and broke his neck. He stripped him of all valuables: watch, wallet, passport, cash in his pocket.

He grabbed Crane under his armpits and lifted his upper body onto the bed, and then his legs.

Demarco adjusted the body on the luxurious bed into a

more normal position. He picked up the vase which he had set on the carpet and left the room, replacing the vase exactly where it had been on the table in the foyer.

He retraced his steps out the back of the hotel, reentered the bank, went out the front entrance, and slipped into the backseat of his waiting limo. He checked his watch. He'd been in the hotel exactly eleven minutes. Not bad.

Ciro's job was much easier, although he, too, had to dress up a bit. He wore a black wool overcoat, a white silk scarf that covered his neck tattoo, and a wide-brimmed Irish cap pulled low to shadow his face. He had borrowed a dog from his cousin Veronica, an excitable little Yorkshire terrier named Mickey. Not exactly Ciro's type of dog, but Mickey would have to do.

Ciro waited on the quiet path that ran from Seventy-ninth Street past Dog Hill to the boat basin.

Milstein was right on time.

When Milstein saw the large man walking a small dog, heading his way, he hardly gave it a second thought. Ciro looked nothing like the man Milstein had seen briefly in the park four days before. He was just another dog walker.

The stupid dog almost got in Ciro's way. He had the leash in his left hand, the knife in his right, in perfect position as Milstein approached. Then the damn dog veered over to check out Milstein's dog.

Milstein's dog also started to cross in front of him. He yelled, 'goddammit,' and wrenched the leash on the big terrier.

Ciro pulled up on the little dog's leash hard enough so Mickey landed about three feet to the left. The dog emitted a short yelp at the exact moment Ciro buried the knife just below Milstein's sternum, angled straight up toward his heart.

The blade was long, sharp, hardened steel. Ciro plunged it into Milstein with such force that it rose up and severed the pulmonary artery and half the aorta, and lifted Milstein off his feet. Goddammit was the last word Frederick Millstein uttered.

Ciro pulled out the blade. Milstein fell face forward onto the asphalt path.

Ciro looked around. No one in sight. He let go of the dog leash, wiped the blade on Milstein's coat, and pocketed the knife.

He dragged Milstein into the bushes about twenty feet off the path and dumped him well out of sight. He quickly stripped him of everything in his pockets.

Both dogs had stayed where they were on the path, sniffing each other, Mickey jumping around and yipping at the bigger dog.

Ciro picked up both leashes and started to lead both dogs back to Dog Hill. But now his cousin's dog wanted nothing to do with him. Perhaps it had to do with being jerked three feet off his feet.

Ciro picked up the little dog, feeling bad about giving it such a hard tug. Milstein's dog walked along with him as if nothing had happened.

When he got to where Milstein usually let the dog off the leash, he released Tam. The big dog immediately ran off into the dark field.

Ciro kept the small dog cradled in his arm so he wouldn't follow the big dog.

'Sorry about pulling you so hard little guy.'

Mickey looked up at Ciro and licked his gloved hand.

Ciro smiled, and then he realized the little dog was lick-ing Milstein's blood.

Beck had waited until after Olivia's funeral to distribute the cash that Alex Liebowitz had smuggled in with his scuba-diving equipment from Belize.

He'd decided that the bribes he'd paid to Walter Pearce would set the amount. Thirty thousand for setting up the cops, plus twenty for monitoring Milstein's call to the Belize bank. It added up to an even fifty thousand dollars.

He didn't even try to calculate whose efforts might have been worth more than another's. Nydia, the Bolos, Phi-neas, Brandon Wright, Joey B: without any one of them, they would have never survived.

He doubled the amount he gave to Pearce, giving each of them a hundred thousand in cash.

He also paid for Joey B's hospital bills and follow-up care.

He knew Brandon Wright wouldn't accept any money, so he bought him a case of his favorite Irish whiskey, Midleton Very Rare, gave him ten thousand dollars to give to his surgical nurse, and asked Wright to name a charity to which Beck promised to contribute money in the doc-tor's name.

That left Willie Reese and Alex Liebowitz outside the core team. Willie got fifty thousand in cash. Alex got five hundred thousand funneled into his trading account.

After laundering the remaining money through five dummy corporations Alex had set up, paying the corporate taxes to keep clean with the IRS, Beck had enough to give himself, Manny, Ciro, and Demarco three million dollars, leaving a little over four million to keep the house fund they all shared solvent for the foreseeable future.

Given a choice, Demarco and Ciro would have preferred to skip the funeral. Beck had mixed feelings. But out of respect for Manny, they all attended.

Manny had taken care of everything. Beck never asked how he managed to make the funeral arrangements, obtain a death certificate, and cremate the body.

The four of them stood in their best suits in a small chapel at Ferncliff cemetery north of the city. The minister was Hispanic. They listened to the ritual, keeping their thoughts private.

From the chapel they walked a short distance to the mausoleum where the urn containing her ashes was placed into a small crypt.

The day was bright and crisp, the air cold and clean, much like the day when it had all started. As they walked from the mausoleum to their car, Beck thought about Olivia Sanchez. What a terrible, terrible waste. Such a smart, tough, stunning woman. But in the end, so very heartless and reckless, so driven by greed.

Beck resolved to put her out of his thoughts. He would have to concentrate on Manny now.

Tomorrow, thought Beck. After the paper, with my second cup of coffee, I'll sit with Manny. In his kitchen. Across from him at that beat-up old wooden table.

They'd talk over things. He knew, despite whatever grief or hurt or anger Manny felt, he would want to go over everything with him. Again. That was his way.

Confirm that Milstein was dead. And Crane. And Stepanovich. And Kolenka. And all their men either dead, deported, or locked up for a long time.

Beck knew it might take some time to reassure Manny that the last one who had tried to harm them, Markov, was also dead. The mercenaries were sure to destroy the corpse. But he would put the proposition to Manny. Explain his theory that if Crane had paid the ex-Special Forces soldiers to protect him, it stood to reason that he'd paid them to take out Markov.

Crane had to know that when Markov went after Beck and Olivia for his money, one of two things would happen. Beck might kill Markov, and that would be the end of it. Or, Markov would kill Beck. Undoubtedly after torturing him to find out where the money was. At which point, Markov would know that Beck didn't have his money. And that Olivia had disappeared, as had Crane. Which means that Markov would know who really took his money. Therefore, Crane couldn't let Markov live.

Of course, Manny would want to know how they could be sure the mercenaries would succeed. Beck would explain they were very good at such things. And that Markov's protection was based on no one ever knowing where he was. As Ahmet Sukol had explained, Markov never stayed in one place for longer than one night. But Beck had solved that problem. The flash drive he had given Markov with the information about his Belize account also contained a GPS receiver and software that transmitted his location. And Ricky Bolo had confirmed that he gave Ralph Anastasia the URL of a website that would display Markov's location. There was no doubt that Markov would keep the flash drive with him wherever he went until at least noon on Monday. Plenty of time for Anastasia and his team to find him.

As Beck walked the final steps to the gleaming black Mercury Marauder, he hoped knowing all that would give Manny solace. Maybe, he thought. But not enough. Not nearly enough.

Acknowledgments

Sincere thanks to my agent, Alexandra Machinist, who made this happen. Gratitude and respect to Keith Kahla, my editor, a talented and generous man who made this a better story, and to his team at St. Martin's who performed at the highest level on everything from cover to copyediting. And thank you, Hannah Braaten, for watching over everything with great energy and good spirits.

He just wanted a decent book to read ...

Not too much to ask, is it? It was in 1935 when Allen Lane, Managing Director of Bodley Head Publishers, stood on a platform at Exeter railway station looking for something good to read on his journey back to London. His choice was limited to popular magazines and poor-quality paperbacks – the same choice faced every day by the vast majority of readers, few of whom could afford hardbacks. Lane's disappointment and subsequent anger at the range of books generally available led him to found a company – and change the world.

'We believed in the existence in this country of a vast reading public for intelligent books at a low price, and staked everything on it'
Sir Allen Lane, 1902–1970, founder of Penguin Books

The quality paperback had arrived – and not just in bookshops. Lane was adamant that his Penguins should appear in chain stores and tobacconists, and should cost no more than a packet of cigarettes.

Reading habits (and cigarette prices) have changed since 1935, but Penguin still believes in publishing the best books for everybody to enjoy. We still believe that good design costs no more than bad design, and we still believe that quality books published passionately and responsibly make the world a better place.

So wherever you see the little bird – whether it's on a piece of prize-winning literary fiction or a celebrity autobiography, political tour de force or historical masterpiece, a serial-killer thriller, reference book, world classic or a piece of pure escapism – you can bet that it represents the very best that the genre has to offer.

Whatever you like to read – trust Penguin.